3/09/11

THOUGH
Not
DEAD

**Center Point
Large Print**

Also by Dana Stabenow
and available from Center Point Large Print:

Prepared for Rage
Whisper to the Blood

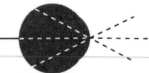

THOUGH
Not
DEAD

DANA STABENOW

CENTER POINT PUBLISHING
THORNDIKE, MAINE

This Center Point Large Print edition
is published in the year 2011 by arrangement with
St. Martin's Press.

Copyright © 2011 by Dana Stabenow.

The text of this Large Print edition is unabridged.
In other aspects, this book may vary
from the original edition.
Printed in the United States of America
on permanent paper.
Set in 16-point Times New Roman type.

ISBN: 978-1-61173-018-0

Library of Congress Cataloging-in-Publication Data

Stabenow, Dana.
  Though not dead : a Kate Shugak novel / Dana Stabenow.
    p. cm.
  ISBN 978-1-61173-018-0 (library binding : alk. paper)
  1. Shugak, Kate (Fictitious character)—Fiction.
  2. Women private investigators—Alaska—Fiction.
  3. Murder—Investigation—Fiction. 4. Alaska—Fiction. 5. Large type books.
  I. Title.
PS3569.T1249T47 2011b
813′.54—dc22

                                                          2010049203

For
Josie and Gerry Ryan,
in gratitude for their custom of taking in strays

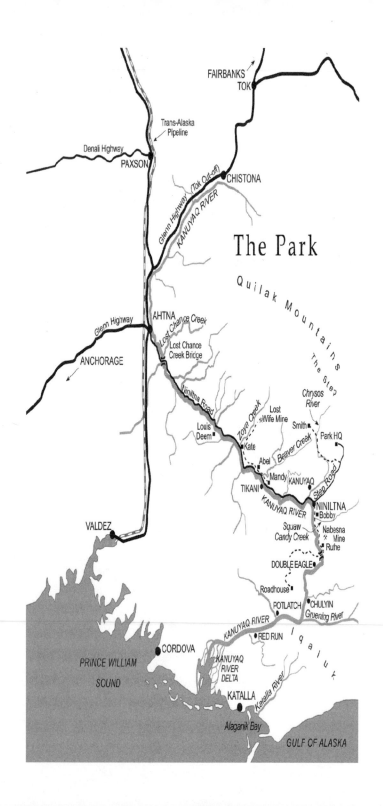

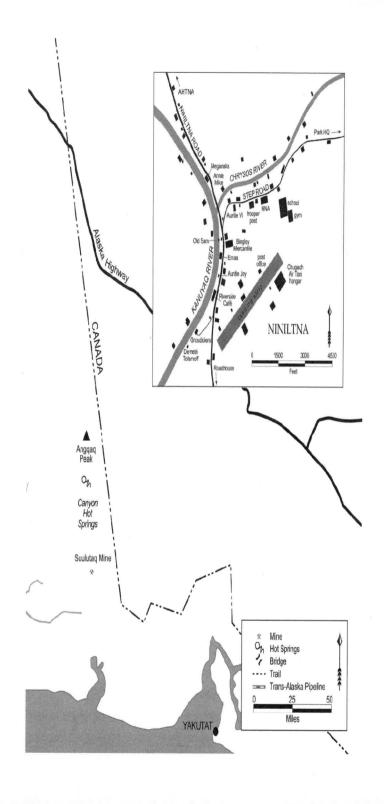

THOUGH
Not
DEAD

1918

Niniltna

The black death didn't get to Alaska until November. When it did, it cut down almost everyone in its path.

The territorial governor imposed a quarantine and restricted travel into the Interior, stationing U.S. Marshals at all ports, trailheads, and river mouths to interdict travel between communities. He issued a special directive urging Alaska Natives to stay at home and avoid public gatherings. Theaters closed, churches canceled services, schools were let out, but because of the inescapably communal nature of traditional life, Natives were infected and died disproportionately. In Brevig Mission, only eight of eighty people survived. In some villages there were no survivors at all. When the influenza pandemic passed late the following spring, those left alive were too weak to hunt for food, and even more died of starvation.

In Niniltna in March 1919, Chief Lev Kookesh and his wife, Alexandra, froze to death because they were too sick to get up and feed the fire in their woodstove. Four miles up the road at the Kanuyaq Mine, mine manager Josiah Greenwood lost his wife and both sons, and one out of four of his workforce.

Some of the uninfected turned to predation and thievery. Harold Halvorsen was beaten to death in a fight over his last bag of flour. Bertha Anelon was assaulted in her own bedroom and died of her injuries two days later, alone in the bed in which she had been attacked. The offices of the Kanuyaq Mine were broken into half a dozen times, the cash box stolen, the glass case housing the Cross of Gold nugget shattered and the nugget gone, the company files rifled and set on fire. Toilets and refrigerators were ripped out of mine workers' homes as residents lay on their beds with no strength to resist. Food, clothes, photographs, personal papers, and jewelry vanished, most never to be recovered by their owners.

Empty homes where entire families had died were stripped and abandoned. Cemeteries overran their boundaries. After seeing their last living family member into the ground, many survivors left for Fairbanks or Anchorage or even Outside. village populations halved by the epidemic were halved again by emigration.

Eventually, inevitably, people rallied. In Niniltna, the memorial potlatch for Chief Lev and his wife was seen by many as a start down the road of recovery from an eight-month-long nightmare of disease and death, a time to mourn the dead, a time for the living to nourish their souls and rebuild their homes and towns. Moving forward was necessary for survival, even if they also understood that life would never be the same for any of them ever again.

Organizing the potlatch fell to Chief Lev's only child, Elizaveta, age seventeen. Her life had nearly been forfeit, too, except that someone had come to their house, a man, a young placer miner, miraculously uninfected, who told her he had been checking house to house for anyone left alive. He found her in her bed, suspecting her parents were dead in the next room but too weak to get up and find out. Now on her feet and like the rest of the survivors, thin and pale and grieving, she was determined to do her best by her tribe, by her parents, and by her chief. The girls from down at the Northern Light still living helped her wash and dress the bodies in their finest clothes. The young placer miner, named Herbert Elmer "Mac" McCullough, kindled a coal fire in the cemetery and used the heat to dig their graves in the still frozen ground.

Some remaining survivors weren't too sick to grumble, starting with the scandal of women no better than they should be helping to lay out tribal elders. Elizaveta had always been a wild child, they told each other, although much of that could be laid at Lev's door. He was the one who'd taught her to hunt and fish and trap in the first place, over the objections of his mother and her sisters and the rest of the elders. Theirs was a conservative and traditional tribe who thought a woman's place was in the home, sewing skins and making babies. Lev had even allowed Elizaveta to spend the previous summer working his gold claim in the Quilak foothills, and with Quinto Dementieff there, too. Chaperoned by her father, it was true, but still.

That summer before the black death had been profitable for everyone. Lev had even opened a bank account in Elizaveta's name. Alexandra was horrified, but Lev was adamant. "She earned it," he told Alexandra, and handed the passbook to his daughter.

Elizaveta was thrilled. She felt a little taller with the passbook in her possession, more substantial somehow. when she went to Kanuyaq to clean house for Angie Greenwood, she looked at the flush toilet she scrubbed out every week in a different way. Suddenly no luxury was unattainable with your own money jingling in your pocket.

All that was changed now, of course. She had used all of her savings to buy gifts for the traditional gift giving at her parents' potlatch, tools, blankets, kitchenware, jewelry, canned food, all of it ordered in bulk from the Sears, Roebuck catalogue. Then there was the cost of shipping it all to Cordova, from where by special dispensation of Mr. Greenwood it was brought in on the Kanuyaq River & Northwestern railroad free of charge. Mr. Greenwood, a kind man, had always been punctilious about maintaining good relations with the people in Kanuyaq, white and Native, amateur and professional, and his own grief did not deter him now. When the day came, her parents' spirits had no cause for shame at what was given to family and friends in their name. No shame either in the hall of the Alaska Native Brotherhood, which she had decorated with pine boughs tied up with green and red ribbons. It gave the long, rectangular room a celebratory, albeit somewhat Christmassy air. Mac had helped her put them up the night before, which was when it had happened, a delicious, delightful interlude of much mutual pleasure. It had been so long since Elizaveta had felt happiness of any kind.

The jewel in the crown of the hall's decorations came when she placed the tribe's icon at the head of the room, on a tall table with a round top, next to the sepia photograph of her parents. She had had the photograph blown up to a large grainy simulacrum of itself by a photographer in Seattle for a fee that had used up the last of her savings. Her father was seated and serious in his regalia, her mother standing behind him in beaded deerskin, one hand resting on Lev's shoulder, an equally serious expression on her face. They looked stiff and very stern, not at all the way Elizaveta remembered them. The frame was made of pine carved with rosettes and trailing vines and gilded with gold paint, a suitable testament to the importance of the people in the photograph.

The icon was a Russian Orthodox triptych, known to the Park as the Sainted Mary. There were three panels, depicting from left to right Mary holding the infant Jesus in a barn, Mary holding the dead Jesus at the foot of the cross, and a resurrected Jesus revealing himself to Mary before a rolled stone. The Sainted Mary was eight inches high, and all three panels together eighteen inches wide. It was made of wood that had been gilded by the original artist's hand. The gilt was now tarnished and flaking. The illustrations were made of pierced and enameled metal with bas-relief figures. The frame was studded with dull colored stones, two missing from their bezels.

It was old, very old, no one could say how old. They knew it had come with the gussuks in their tall ships from across the sea, but no one knew how it had come into the hands of the tribe, although those who counted Tlingits among their ancestors could make a pretty good guess.

It was understood that it was not a personal possession, that the chief only held it in trust for the tribe. The icon had miraculous powers, among them the ability to heal. Most recently Albert Shugak had prayed to the Sainted Mary and had recovered the use of his legs, it was believed until then lost forever in the battle of Verdun. He had married Angelique Halvorsen six months later, and she was now pregnant with their first child, their family one of the few only lightly touched by the black death. The Sainted Mary also held the power to grant wishes. Almira Mike prayed for a son and within the year the Sainted Mary had answered with the birth of William, a happy, moon-faced child. Myron Hansen prayed to the Sainted Mary for a new boat, and his great-uncle in Seattle died and left him a fortune.

Since Chief Lev had had no sons, in whose custody the icon would next be placed was a matter of vital importance to the tribe.

For this and many other reasons, not least that after enduring the horrors of the past year the tribe was in sore need of something to show them that they were in fact still a tribe, with pride and traditions and a history going back ten thousand years, it was imperative that they elect a new chief as soon as possible.

It was in this spirit that they gathered, family from Ketchikan, friends from Sitka, tribal members from Juneau, close kin from Fairbanks and kissing cousins from Circle, and shirttail relatives from Ahtna. They came from all the villages on the river from Tikani to Chulyin, all the villages on the road between Ahtna and Valdez, an astonishing assembly given the decimation of their ranks. Mac McCullough helped Elizaveta distribute the gifts, although many of the guests would not meet his eyes, deeply resenting the intrusion of this round-eyed gussuk into this most important, almost sacred, tribal rite. Instead, they looked at Elizaveta, with reproach. Elizaveta, who despite her parent's death had something of a glow about her.

Well. They all knew what that meant. They accepted their gifts in a spirit of one part entitlement to three parts righteous indignation, gorged themselves on the thin stew made from last year's moose and hunks of bread fresh made from the last of the village's flour, and returned to their tents having taken only the most formal leave of their hostess.

The next morning the Sainted Mary was gone. So was Mac McCullough.

"I don't have it," Elizaveta said, her face white and set, the glow erased from her features. They didn't believe her, and they were not respectful when they searched her house. They threw everything out of the cache and unwrapped the pitifully few packets of moose meat left there to make sure that it was moose meat, they dumped out the nearly empty sacks of rice and beans and sugar and flour, and there was even talk of exhuming the bodies of her parents until some mercifully sane person pointed out that the Sainted Mary had been on display well after Lev and Alexandra were put into their graves.

When at last they were satisfied that Elizaveta truly did not have the icon, suspicion then naturally fell on the missing miner. He was gone. So was the icon. He must have stolen it in the night and made off with it. there could be no other explanation. What else could you expect from someone the other gussuks had nicknamed One-Bucket, allegedly for his ability to pull three hundred dollars' worth of gold out of a creek in one bucket? *Gatcha*, that Elizaveta would shame herself and her tribe so by taking up with such a one.

The tribe fed runners on the last of the potlatch stew and dispatched them to Ahtna, to Cordova, to Fairbanks, and even farther afield with descriptions of the missing man and their missing treasure, seeking news, offering a reward for his apprehension and for the return of the Sainted Mary to her rightful place. Alas for their plans, a spring storm blew in off the Gulf of Alaska the second night after the potlatch and dumped twelve feet of snow from Katalla to Kanuyaq, rendering the roads and trails impassable and any efforts at tracking impossible. Neither One-Bucket nor the icon did they find, and as the days and weeks passed, Elizaveta, shunned by family and neighbors alike, grew even more thin and more pale.

A month after the potlatch came a knock at her door. She was afraid at first to open it. The knock came again, with more force and this time accompanied by a voice she knew. "It's me, Elizaveta. Open up."

It was Quinto Dementieff, a fellow student—and fellow sufferer—at the BIA school in Cordova. They had been friends since childhood, their friendship strengthened by the summer spent together on Lev's gold claim.

She made him coffee, offered him toast from the batch of bread made from the very last bit of flour. There was no butter or jam for the bread, and no sugar or canned milk for his coffee.

He ate and drank without comment, and when he was finished he pushed the mug away and said, "Marry me."

She had been sitting with her head bent over knotted fingers. She looked up at his words, astonished.

"Marry me," he said again. "At least I'll know you'll be eating."

Her eyes filled with tears and she dropped her head again. "I can't."

"Yes, you can."

One hand slid over her belly. "You don't understand, Quinto. I'm—"

"I do understand," he said. He returned her wondering look with a level gaze. "Marry me."

Her hand still on her belly, she looked around the room. "It's not only that, Quinto. I can't stay here. We couldn't stay here. Everyone is so angry, so—"

"We won't stay here," he said. "We'll move to Cordova. Mr. Greenwood says he'll give me a job on the docks."

"You talked to Mr. Greenwood about this?"

"I told him I was going to get married and I needed a job to support my wife and family. He's a good man."

Quinto Dementieff was the son of an Aleut father and a Filipino mother whose parents had been part of the wave of Filipinos who immigrated to Alaska to take all the good jobs in the salmon canneries for a paycheck half the size of what the born-in-the-territory locals would accept. Elizaveta had been an outcast from the morning after the potlatch. Quinto had been an outcast from birth.

He had also been in love with Elizaveta since

they were both ten years old. He reached out to take the hand resting protectively on her belly between his own and kissed it. "Marry me, Eliza. There will be many children. What's one more?"

They were married by the justice of the peace in Ahtna just two days later. The resulting scandal almost eclipsed the loss of the Sainted Mary and kept the tribe's gossips busy for a decade. Of all the people a chief's daughter could have married, and she chose a Filipino! When there were so many good Native boys to choose from! That Eliza girl, so headstrong, so foolish; there was never anything to do with her. First she takes up with a gussuk who robbed the tribe of its most precious possession and then she elopes to Cordova with a Filipino. (Quinto's half-Aleut side was easily ignored.) But it was only to be expected. Look at her father, a good man in most ways, and not a bad chief, but so lacking in wisdom in the raising of his daughter. Alexandra had tried to warn him, oh yes, but had he listened? Stubborn, pigheaded man, no, he had not, and see how it had turned out, Elizaveta married outside the tribe and the Sainted Mary lost to the tribe forever, looted by yet another white man who pretended to be their friend so he could steal everything that wasn't nailed down and sell it Outside to make his fortune.

Elizaveta and Quinto settled in Cordova, two hundred miles away, at that time far enough not to hear all the whispers or endure the glares and the pointed fingers. "Easy to be shunned from a distance," Quinto said cheerfully, and for the first time in months, Elizaveta smiled.

Her pregnancy was not an easy one, and their first and only child, a son, was born the following January.

They named him Samuel Leviticus Dementieff.

One

"HE WAS EIGHTY-NINE," KATE SAID, looking up from a file box.

"Well, we all knew he was older than God," Jim said.

They were at Old Sam's cabin, where Kate was sorting through the old man's belongings. Kate and the aunties had decided that the potlatch would be on the fifteenth of January, which gave them a little over three months to label Old Sam's possessions for the gift giving, and to allow everyone from Alaska and Outside who wanted to attend to make travel arrangements and contact friends and relatives in the Park for a place to unroll their sleeping bags.

It was also the day of the annual shareholder meeting of the Niniltna Native Association. The price of gas being what it was, travel to and from Niniltna was not cheap, no matter if you did it by plane, boat, pickup, four-wheeler, or snowgo. Plus, it cost the same to rent the high school gym for an event that lasted four hours as it did for an event that lasted all day. Kate Shugak was a frugal and practical woman.

There was a file marked "Will" in the back of the box. Kate pulled it out and opened it.

Jim looked at her bent head, and at Mutt, who was leaning up against Kate's side. Whenever

Kate was hurting, Mutt was always as close to her as she could get without actually climbing into her lap. Since Mutt, the half gray wolf half husky who allowed Kate to live with her outweighed Kate by twenty pounds, leaning seemed the better option all around.

Old Sam's cabin was built on a floor plan common to the Park anytime between twenty-five and a hundred years before, a ground floor twenty-five feet square with a sleeping loft reached by a ladder made from two-by-fours. The rungs on the ladder were worn smooth from decades of use. Jim hoped that when he was eighty-nine his knees would be in good enough shape to climb eight feet up a vertical ladder to get to bed.

He looked back at Kate.

If she were waiting for him in that bed, he'd find a way.

The one room downstairs had a counter with an old chipped porcelain farm sink set into it, with shelves built into the wall above and below. The sink came with an old-fashioned swan-necked spout and two spoked faucets. Old Sam had tapped into public water when it had come into Niniltna twenty years before, but the outhouse was still outside. When asked why no indoor toilet, a growled "You don't shit in your own nest" was his invariable reply.

There was an oil stove for cooking and a

woodstove for heat and an old Frigidaire refrigerator that must have been added when they ran the power line out from Ahtna back in the sixties. More built-in shelves covered every inch of the back wall from floor to ceiling beneath the floor of the loft, one section for weapons and ammunition and the rest for books ranging from Zane Grey to a leather-bound, three-volume edition of the log of Captain Cook that made Jim's mouth water just to look at it. A brown vinyl recliner with a dent in the seat the size of Old Sam's skinny ass occupied one corner, next to a pole lamp and a Blazo box standing on one end. The box was covered with mug rings and was filled with a stack of magazines, *National Geographic*, *Alaska* magazine, *Playboy*. There was a workbench next to the door where Old Sam cleaned his guns and did the fine woodworking on projects he'd allowed Park rats to talk him into, wall shelves and cupboards, mostly, with an occasional bed frame or dining table thrown in.

"He revised his will only last month."

Kate was sitting at the chrome-legged dining table in the center of the room, on one of three mismatched chairs. The table had a lazy Susan in the middle of it, filled with salt and pepper shakers, a sugar bowl, a Darigold one-pound butter can with a plastic lid, a bottle of soy sauce. Old Sam liked his sticky rice, a legacy of his half-Filipino father.

27

Had liked. It was still difficult to accept the fact that the old man was dead. It was especially difficult to imagine life in the Park going on without his acid, perspicacious, and occasionally uncomfortably prophetic commentary. Old Sam had been an entire Greek chorus all by himself.

"He had a lot of stuff," Jim said. "Do you want help?" It was Monday morning, and he was past due at work.

She looked up. "Less than two weeks ago."

"What?"

"He revised his will less than two weeks ago."

"Maybe he had a premonition."

She snorted. "There was never anything the least bit fey about Old Sam."

Jim thought of the old man built of bone and sinew, quick, smart, smart-assed. Indomitable, indestructible, and until the day before yesterday, immortal. Kate was right. If anyone had ever lived in the real world, it had been Old Sam Dementieff. Jim was going to miss the hell out of him. "Do you need help here?" he asked again. "I can take a day."

"Thanks, but I got this." She tucked a strand of short dark hair behind an ear, exposing the high, flat cheekbone and the strong throat bisected by the long scar that had faded over the last eight years to a thin white line. With hazel eyes set in skin darkened to bronze by the summer just past and a full seductive mouth set over an obstinate chin, she was a five-foot, one-hundred-and-twenty-pound package of dynamite clad in black sweatshirt, blue jeans, and tennis shoes.

His dynamite. The pronoun came to him without warning, and under its influence he stepped forward to pull the file from her hands. "Come here." He picked her up and sat down again on the chair, setting her on his lap.

She didn't protest. Her head found a place on his shoulder instead, and a moment later he felt the warmth of her tears soak through his shirt.

"Hey," he said, tipping her head up.

She took a shaky breath and tried to smile. "He'd make fun of me if he could see me now."

"Bullshit," Jim said. "He'd be proud you cared enough. Listen, Kate. He went out the way we all wish we could go. He hunted his own moose, packed it home, butchered it out, and threw a feed for everyone he loved. Damn fine feed, too."

Her smile was wobbly. "Yeah, it was."

"And then he turned off the engine and left the shop." Jim's shoulders rose and fell in a slight shrug. "What do you Injuns say? It was a good day to die."

She sniffed and gulped back a laugh that was half sob.

He leaned in, his lips moving across her skin, sipping at the salt tears. Her breath caught, warm on his cheek, and her head turned so her mouth was close to his. He accepted the invitation and their lips met in a long and gentle caress, his hands warm and strong at the back of her neck and on her hip.

It was becoming less frightening to him, this need he found to comfort, to console, to demonstrate an affection that had nothing to do with sex. Although if the nearest bed hadn't belonged to a man not dead forty-eight hours . . . He raised his head and hazel eyes met blue in a long look. "Better?"

She was a little flushed, and the full lips quirked at the corners. "An effective laying on of healing hands."

He grinned and kissed her again, quick and hard. "I'll lay more than that later."

She laughed.

Old Sam would have, too.

The loss of Old Sam Dementieff notwithstanding, Jim drove to the trooper post with a lighter heart. Probably part of that was due to Kate's being as willing to accept his comfort as he was unafraid to give it. They'd been circling each other for so long, wary, suspicious, and let's face it, just plain scared of all the baggage loaded on that slow-moving barge called relationship. You couldn't move a barge on its own, you had to hire a tug. Up until Kate, the women with whom he'd kept company had lasted the length of a ride in a cigarette boat between Miami and Havana.

Sometimes it felt like he'd served more time for Kate than Jacob had for Rachel.

He knew she was still working out the trust issues. Jack Morgan, a government-certified Grade A one-woman man, was a hard act to follow in that respect. It didn't help that despite a visible lack of offspring, Chopper Jim Chopin's *nom d'amour* had once been Father of the Park. Come to think of it, Old Sam had been the one to hang that on him. Right after Misty Lambert had burned the clothes he'd left behind, during the monthly meeting of her book club with all eight members in attendance and more invited over to celebrate the event. At least half of whom he'd slept with at one time or another.

They'd all got a big laugh out of it at the time, both the ritual immolation and Old Sam's nicknaming, but the truth was, Jim Chopin was probably quicker with a condom than he was with his sidearm. Living with Johnny Morgan was as close as he ever wanted to come to being a father. As the only Alaska state trooper in twenty million acres of national Park, he already had eight thousand children requiring primary care.

He pulled up in front of the post, making a mental note to stop in at the high school to suggest to Johnny, man-to-man, that he spend the night in town. Johnny was old enough to recognize the justice of the appeal, and besides, given the way things appeared to be heating up between Johnny and Van, the kid would expect some reciprocity in the not too distant future. Jim had a vivid memory of what sixteen was like. If he couldn't keep his hands off Kate now, at sixteen he would have kept her horizontal for days at a time.

He laughed at himself and got out of the truck. His dispatcher met him at the door, a pink message slip in hand and an expression on her face that wiped his mind free of blithe spirit. "What?" he said, mind racing, sorting through the usual suspects. Howie Katelnikof, Martin Shugak, Wade Roche and what might or might not be going on out at his place, Dulcey Kineen's latest escapade, which he hoped this time did not involve the road grader. "Cindy threatening to shoot Willard again?"

"No, Jim," she said, and right away he knew from the gentleness of her reply that it was going to be bad. "I just got off the satellite phone with Nick."

Nick Luther was head of the Alaska state trooper detachment in Tok, which had been Jim's old post until two years before, when volume of business caused Juneau to open a new trooper post in the Park. He wondered now why he had never wondered before if someone in the state capital had known about the discovery of the world's second largest gold mine in Suulutaq before making that decision.

His mind tended to head off on tangents whenever he wanted to avoid what was coming at him like a steamroller. He took a deep breath. "Go ahead," he said. "Serve it up." When she still hesitated, he said, "Whatever it is, letting it sit won't make it smell any better."

"There's no easy way to say this, Jim," she said. "Your mother called."

His spine stiffened. "Yeah?"

"I'm so sorry. Your father died."

Kate sat on the bed and watched him pack, putting clothes she had never seen him wear into an actual suitcase she'd never seen him use. Out of uniform he wore T-shirts and jeans. Traveling within Alaska he used a pack. The charcoal gray suit looked like something the new and improved Kurt Pletnikof would wear to meet his better-heeled clients in Anchorage. The silver, hard-sided suitcase looked like it had been bought out of the SkyMall catalogue, with which Kate was familiar only because it was in every seat pocket on every Alaska Airlines 737, offering everything from basketballs autographed by Magic Johnson to $900 wine fridges, none of which was much use to anyone about to make a connecting flight to Igiugig. "Gee," she said, "looks just like downtown."

He shot her a quick look, and she wondered if that had come out more intimidated that she had meant it to. "California, here I come," he said.

Try as she might she could not detect any joy in his tone.

They were in his room at Auntie Vi's B and B, or what had been Auntie Vi's B and B before she sold it to the owners of the Suulutaq Mine to be a bunkhouse for mine employees in transit. Auntie Vi was now running it for them. A condition of sale had been that Jim got to keep his room there, which he had had since first moving to the Park to open the post. Mine manager Vern Truax had been more than happy to accommodate a law enforcement presence fifty miles from his mine.

"Right back where you started from," Kate said.

This time he stood up and looked her straight in the eye. "I won't be staying long."

"You don't have any brothers or sisters," she said.

"No."

"And your mother is how old?"

"Seventy-nine."

"Ten years younger than Old Sam."

"Yes."

She thought of how healthy Old Sam had been, right up until he sat down on his dock and died. "Your mom in good shape?"

"Depends on what you mean by 'in good shape.' I'd bet a whole paycheck she looks pretty damn good. She'd sure as hell spend it getting that way." He zipped the suit into a garment bag,

34

something else Kate recognized only from catalogues, and snapped it into the lid of the aluminum suitcase.

"You're, what, forty-two now?"

"Yeah."

"She was thirty-seven when you were born."

He added a couple of white, button-down shirts, neatly folded, to the suitcase. T-shirts, shorts, and socks followed. "I showed up late, when they'd pretty much given up on having kids. Dad was forty-five."

"You never talk about them."

He shrugged. "Not much to say. They were hard of hearing before I was in high school. It was like growing up with grandparents."

Wow, she thought. Didn't that sound affectionate.

When she thought about it later, she wondered if that lack of affection might have been part of what had driven Jim north in the first place.

He pulled a shoebox from beneath the bed and added it to the suitcase. The ditty bag full of toiletries went into a daypack with Craig Johnson's latest Walt Longmire novel and Naomi Novik's *Victory of Eagles*. The books had been waiting for him in the post office when he had cleaned out his mailbox that morning. He hoped two books were enough to get him from Anchorage to Los Angeles, because the rest of his to-read pile was back at Kate's house. He was six four, and there was nothing worse than being shoehorned into last class with nothing to take his mind off the discomfort of having his knees jammed up against the seat in front of him. He'd once been stuck on a flight from Phoenix to Seattle with a Steve Martini book whose perp he'd guessed before they reached cruising altitude. Never again. "Where the hell's my—Oh, here it is," he said, producing a clip-on reading light and tossing it into the daypack with the books. "They've got the seats so close together on the new jets that I can never get the overhead light to shine on anything but the top of the head of the guy sitting in front of me. Especially when he leans his chair back into my lap."

"Jim?"

"What?"

"Why did you come to Alaska?"

He zipped up the daypack. "I read *Coming into the Country* when I was too young to resist."

Always with the smart remark. Fine. "Is anyone coming in to the country to cover for you while you're gone?"

He snapped the suitcase closed and set it on the floor. "Nick will check in with Maggie every morning. Otherwise, I'm relying on you, babe. Oh." He paused to look at her. "Kenny says there's been a rash of break-ins and burglaries in Ahtna over the last month. He says he thinks it's partly due to the economy, people looking for anything they can sell to raise cash. Just FYI, in case it spreads down the river."

"Got it," she said. He felt distant from her somehow, as if he were already in Los Angeles. Land of surf and sand and sun. When he looked at her again she realized she'd said the words out loud.

"I'm not staying there, Kate," he said again. "I work in Alaska. I live in Alaska."

You're in Alaska, he could have said, but didn't.

Instead, he put the daypack on the floor next to the suitcase and took her down to the bed with a soft tackle. Caught off guard, she looked up at him with a startled expression. "Let me just mark my spot," he said, and reached for the buttons on her jeans.

He made George's last flight into Anchorage with sixty seconds to spare. She stood flushed and rumpled at the end of the forty-eight-hundred-foot dirt airstrip, watching the de Havilland single Otter turbo rise into the air, bank right, and head west, its signature whine receding over the horizon.

Mutt gave a soft, plaintive whimper. Kate looked down and said in a stern voice, "We are strong and beautiful women. We can do anything."

And Mutt proved it on the walk back to the red Chevy super cab by catching the hem of Kate's jeans in her teeth and dumping Kate on her ass.

Two

JOHNNY WAS ALREADY HOME FROM school and halfway into his specialty, moose stew. This involved every vegetable in the refrigerator boiled to mush in beef bouillon, which mixture was then strained and thickened with flour sautéed in butter and finished with a dollop of red wine, a deplorable habit he had picked up from Jim. Although Kate, a notorious teetotaler, had been heard to admit out loud that wine added a certain flavor to the broth that was not altogether unpleasant. Into this liquid Johnny dropped chunks of moose fried hot and fast so that they were crusty on the outside and bloody on the inside, a couple of smashed garlic cloves, a generous pinch of dried thyme, onions, and potatoes.

Kate's stomach growled and she realized she hadn't had anything to eat since breakfast. Johnny served up steaming bowls with hunks of the rustic loaf Kate had made the day before, perfect for sopping up what was left in the bottom of the bowl. She ate heartily and felt better for it. Raising her head, she saw Johnny looking at her. "You okay?" he said, his voice tentative.

Her heart turned over at his anxious expression. "Sad. I'll miss him." She'd told Johnny about Jim's father, but she knew without asking that they were talking about Old Sam.

"Me, too," Johnny said with feeling.

Her mouth kicked up a half smile. No time like the present, and moose season was still open in some parts of the Park. "He left you something to remember him by." She nodded at the rifle case standing next to the door.

Johnny's mouth dropped open and stayed that way. "Not . . . not the Winchester?" On the last syllable his voice went up into a high squeak that hadn't been heard since he was twelve.

"Yep." She reached for the file box sitting on the next chair and extracted the list of belongings that had accompanied the will. "He said, 'To Johnny Morgan I leave my Model 70 Winchester, as I find him a boy of more sense than most of my acquaintance and will trust him to save his ammunition for a moose and not his goddamn big toe. Don't try for a head shot—the brain's too small and the skull's too hard. Go for a lung shot every time and you'll be fine. Remember, the best place to shoot a moose is fifty feet from the pickup, and next to a good rifle your best friend is a sharp knife.' "

She had to blink away tears when she was done reading. She'd heard it all before, on fall hunts stretching back decades, Abel and Old Sam instructing her and Ethan and Ethan's brothers. *Those sumbitches will do their damndest to die on you in the most inconvenient place possible, and most of the time the fuckers'll succeed.*

Heart's dry and tough as boot leather but you can eat it right away, along with the liver and the tongue. Get yourself a load of beef suet, grind it up with the scraps for burgers. Small packages are better; if you've got a crowd for dinner you can always thaw out more but you can't thaw out less.

Johnny already had the rifle out of the worn leather case. He looked like someone had just handed him the Hope Diamond. "It's got a serial number below six hundred thousand, doesn't it?"

"Look for yourself," she said, and while he was communing with his new muse she cleared the table and washed the dishes, after which he was still cradling the Winchester like it was his firstborn son. A horrible thought. "Enough," she said. "Put it in the rack and get started on your homework."

"Can't I sight it in?"

She glanced out the windows that formed most of the front wall of the house. "It's too dark. Tomorrow."

"Morning?"

"After school," she said, and added craftily, "You'll want to show it to Van."

On a lesser sixteen-year-old what would have been a pout brightened. Van was the girlfriend. Of course he wanted to show the Winchester off to her. He set it in the gun rack next to the front door with reverent hands, stood back to admire it for a moment, heaved a lovelorn sigh, and fetched his homework from his bedroom.

He sat on one side of the table, working math problems, and she sat on the other, working her way through Old Sam's will as the first, fabulous notes of Ben E. King's "Stand By Me" beat out of the speakers.

Old Sam had kept it simple, leaving everything he owned to Kate outright and attaching a letter disposing of those possessions he wanted to go to specific beneficiaries. It was dated the day after the will, which had been written by one Peter P. Wheeler, an attorney in Ahtna. Kate didn't know him. Two weeks ago had been the end of fishing season and the beginning of hunting season, and she wondered that either of them had had the time.

The letter accompanying the will was in Old Sam's copperplate handwriting. You could always tell an elder by their writing—if they'd gone to school at all they'd had penmanship to rival Laura Ingalls Wilder's beaten into them by a series of teachers intent on beating the Native right out of them, starting with their language. The letter was five pages long, written on what looked like printer paper in black ink by what appeared to be a Bic pen with a medium nib.

The cabin in Niniltna he wanted to go to Phyllis Lestinkof, which came as something of a surprise. Kate sat back. Or did it really? "Girl ain't got a

41

pot to piss in," Old Sam wrote, "let alone a place to lay her head, and those worthless parents of hers ain't going to be no help to her. She needs somewhere to raise that baby. You keep the title, tell her it's hers for as long as she lives in it, year-to-year lease for one dollar a year."

Phyllis Lestinkof was seventeen and pregnant and her parents had kicked her out of the house. The father, a young Suulutaq miner careless of his seed, wanted nothing to do with either Phyllis or his child. Kate had dragooned Old Sam into taking Phyllis on as a deckhand on his fish tender this past summer, along with Petey Jeppsen, another Park rat with his own moderate to heavy personal problems. Phyllis had been raised on her daddy's drifter, and Old Sam wrote, "At least she can tell a humpy from a dog." High praise indeed. Well, well.

Of course this made Kate a landlord, which didn't thrill her, but Old Sam had said it and it must be so, at least for the foreseeable future. He had added, "Kid grows up, Phyllis moves to town, whichever comes first, turn it into a museum. The Samuel Leviticus Dementieff Niniltna Museum of History and Art. Don't that got a fine ring to it, girl?" "Town" meant Anchorage in Parkspeak, and was a place all too many Niniltnans had been moving to—or they had been before the advent of the mine.

Jackie Wilson took over from Ben E. King,

shooby doo wop wopping through his lonely teardrops. Kate looked at Johnny, widely known never to have listened voluntarily to anything recorded before Usher started laying down tracks. The eraser on his pencil tapped out an undeniable rhythm. She looked back at the will.

Old Sam wanted the *Freya* to go to Petey Jeppsen. She had to read it twice before she believed it.

The *Freya* was Old Sam's seventy-five-foot fish tender. It had to be as old as he was, if not older, but he'd put a fresh coat of copper paint on the hull every spring, had renewed the varnish on the trim every winter, and had serviced the engine once a year like the *Freya* was going to sprout wings and require recertification by the FAA. According to Old Sam, who had taken the trouble to seek out her provenance, the *Freya* had started life as a herring tender in Seldovia, owned and operated by Alaska Year Round, which when the herring were fished out had put her up for auction. There followed a varied career hauling passengers and freight between Cordova and Seattle in the 1920s, mostly for the Kanuyaq River & Northern Railroad and Kanuyaq Copper, contracting with the U.S. Navy to provide support to their bases in the Aleutians in the thirties, and a brief but exciting period during World War II when she hosted training missions for Castner's Cutthroats.

Old Sam had bought her in 1950, and continued

hiring her out to whoever had deep enough pockets to haul freight or fish. In later years it had been mostly the latter. You name the species, if there was a market for anything with fins or shells, Old Sam had a positive genius for getting a hold full in time to fetch the highest price per pound.

Kate had long thought the *Freya* was the love of Old Sam's life, that he'd had a stronger romantic attachment to her than even to Mary Balashoff. Which made his handing it off to Petey Jeppsen nothing short of astounding.

She'd sent a note to Mary Balashoff on her set net site in Alaganik by way of Mary's family in Cordova. She still felt guilty for not going down in person. Mary and Old Sam had been an item for as long as Kate could remember.

"I know what you're thinking, girl," Old Sam had written, "and I know what those goddamn women'll say." Kate identified "those goddamn women" as the four aunties without any difficulty. "They'll say I should have left it to somebody with my blood, or at least tribal blood. They'll be all pissed off because Petey's white and his family ain't even been in the Park more than one generation. Well, there ain't nobody with my blood who wanted her enough to work summers on her. I thought about leavin' her to Martin—"

Kate's own blood ran cold.

"—hoping maybe owning something of value

might jump-start him out of the general worthlessness he's adopted since grade school, but realistically you just know he'd sell her to the first person with enough cash to rent him a lifetime stool at the Cordova House. And if he couldn't sell her he'd let her sink at the dock. I'm going to be too busy to haunt anybody who mistreats her and you got other fish to fry. So let Petey have her. At least this summer he learned to tell her bow from her stern, and he might just treat her right. That's about all I can make sure of from here."

She could almost hear the old man cackle.

He'd added a postscript. "Make sure to fetch the compass off the bridge before you hand the *Freya* over to Petey. You learned to steer on that compass, and I want you to have her. Petey can get one of those goddamn GPS things."

Old Sam's compass. Kate put down the will and stared off into space. Well did she remember standing at the big wooden wheel on the *Freya*'s bridge, turning it one spoke at a time and waiting for the bow to answer as she watched the floating dial of the compass slowly revolve beneath the glass. The antique brass compass was set on gimbals in a square teak box. No speck of tarnish was ever allowed to mar the brass, and the wood gleamed with polish, the special care of the skinny, cranky Captain Bligh standing at her shoulder. No one else was allowed to touch it.

Jackie Wilson segued to Ray Charles, drowning in his own tears. Tears seemed to be the order of the evening. Kate blinked her eyes clear again. She'd have to go into town tomorrow and find Petey to give him the good news. Last she'd heard he was renting a room from Iris Meganack, as Iris's daughter Laurel had moved in with Matt Grosdidier. Matt's brothers, Mark, Luke, and Peter, were said to be overjoyed, as well they should have been because Laurel was one hell of a cook. Iris was known to be tight with a buck and Kate had no doubt she was alleviating her displeasure at Laurel's moving in with someone without benefit of clergy by charging Petey rent on the order of summer rates at the Kanuyaq River Princess Lodge in Ahtna. At the very least he could now move on board the *Freya* and save himself some money. Since the *Freya* was docked in Cordova, it would also move him out of range of his parents, another good thing.

Kate knew a huge feeling of relief, and it didn't have anything to do with the potential for improvement in Petey's lifestyle. Thinking of the jumbled mess of wooden pallets and coiled lines and spare engine parts and tools that was her last view of the *Freya*'s fo'c'sle, her courage had almost failed her. Old Sam was a true Alaskan, he never threw anything away, he just tossed it in the fo'c'sle. He'd been doing so for sixty years, and Kate had not been looking forward to inventorying and disposing of the contents. Now she didn't have to.

More good news followed. "You get the books, girl," Old Sam had written. "Keep the ones you want and farm the rest of them out to the library." The school library served as the community library and was chronically short of both books and funds to buy books, although they had approached Vern Truax about the Suulutaq Mine's becoming a Friend of the Library. Since Global Harvest seemed to have given Truax a blank check for local sponsorships designed to smooth the mine's way with Park rats, the latest of which featured a ThinkPad for every student in Niniltna Public School and a satellite dish on the roof to connect them all to the Internet, Kate thought the library had a pretty good shot at an affirmative response.

"You been eying that log of Captain Cook's pretty near since you learned how to read," Old Sam wrote. "I figure it's the one thing guarantees you won't miss me all that awful goddamn much."

She laughed and sniffled.

"You okay?" Johnny said.

She blew her nose on a paper towel. "Just Old Sam being Old Sam."

Reassured, he went back to his math, and she returned to the will. She was taking her time, savoring each paragraph, each sentence. It was her final communication from Old Sam and she wanted to make it last as long as possible.

He'd owned a couple of pieces of property she hadn't known about, a lot in Ahtna that she thought might be on First Street, another in Niniltna adjacent to the lot his cabin stood on that appeared to take in most of the riverfront between his house and Harvey and Iris Meganack's, and a third identified only by latitude and longitude. At a rough guess, after a quick consult with the map of the Park on the wall in the living room, this last was in the Quilaks, this side of Canada somewhere between Park Headquarters and the Suulutaq Mine, which took in a lot of territory. Probably a mining claim Old Sam had staked back in the day when every second Park rat and a whole bunch of Outside boomers were claiming every loose rock that didn't manage to get out of the way first.

She looked at the lat and long again. The dimensions looked pretty substantial. She was fuzzy on the rules of claim staking but she had a vague recollection that mining claims were limited in size by law. The Park's chief ranger, Dan O'Brian, would know. She'd head up to the Step tomorrow. The map on his wall was a lot bigger, too, and had better topographical detail than hers did.

As to whether there was enough gold or whatever ore was there to pull out of the ground, economically speaking, was anybody's guess. Odds were always against, but Old Sam hadn't acquired that property for no reason. Too bad Mac Devlin wasn't still around. While he'd never been one of her favorite people, he'd had a good nose for the viability of a gold claim. Just never one of his own.

She looked at the clock. Nine thirty. Jim was taking the redeye to Los Angeles, departing at 1:00 A.M. Three-hour layover in Seattle. If you were flying Alaska Airlines and you wanted to go to hell you had to fly through Seattle to get there. He was scheduled to arrive in Long Beach at ten thirty tomorrow morning, Pacific time. Thirteen hours from now, less one for the time zone change. Around two thousand air miles. Three thousand six hundred miles if you were driving.

Wilson Pickett weighed in on the midnight hour.

Johnny looked up and caught her staring at the clock. "If we had cell phones in the Park you could call him," he said.

She jumped, startled. His grin was sly.

"Smart-ass," she said.

He snickered. "That would be me."

She looked at the gangly sixteen-, no, seventeen-year-old with the almost ugly mug and the carefully groomed thatch of hair streaked with remnants of the summer sun. His father had been a giant teddy bear of a man with a deep, rumbling voice, eyes as bright and blue as his son's, a jaw as firm. Almost his last living act had been to entrust his son to Kate's care. Four years later, she didn't know who she loved more, the man then or the boy now. "Want some cocoa?"

"Sure. Long as I get some of those no-bake cookies to go along with it."

"Chocolate, more chocolate, and peanut butter, may God forgive me," she said, and got to her feet.

While she was waiting for the milk to heat on the stove she went out on the deck. It was cold enough to see her breath, clear enough to follow Merak and Dubhe to the North Star almost directly overhead, no mosquitoes and as of yet no snow. A perfect September evening. The sun set farther to the south every night after less time in the sky every day, but in compensation the stars were back, the Pleiades fleeing across the sky as Orion climbed up over the jagged bulk of the Quilaks in hot pursuit. Ever wilt thou love and they be fair. Johnny would be getting out his telescope when the homework was done.

Far overhead a light moved steadily from north to south. A jet? A satellite, more likely. How many did the state have now, three? She hadn't kept track, and for all she knew by now it was probably twice that. All those cell phones.

She sighed. As chair of the board of directors of the Niniltna Native Association, she had already instructed Annie Mike, the Association secretary, to begin talks with the two major cell phone companies in Alaska, as well as to put out feelers to any other telecommunications companies who might be interested. If nothing else, maybe Kate would be able to score an iPhone out of the process.

But before long, perhaps even before winter set in, one of them could be building the first of their galvanized steel Tinkertoy towers, in a string that would follow the Kanuyaq River from Ahtna to Chulyin, and from there overland to the Suulutaq Mine, where the world's second largest deposit of gold had been discovered two years before. When they were done, Annie assured Kate, cell phone coverage would cover at minimum half of the twenty million acres of the Park, leaving only the remotest areas out of reach. In exchange for sponsoring their requests for leases on the likeliest locations in the best areas to locate their towers, the companies were even willing to discuss the possibility of constructing towers and providing coverage to the more outremer Park rats. They wanted the business, they'd left the NNA board in no doubt about that. And Ranger Dan had no intention of Park HQ being left in a no-service area, so whoever their cell phone provider wound up being would also be running towers up to the Step.

Kate wondered what the elders had thought when the discovery of copper at Kanuyaq in 1900 had caused the first telephone line to be strung in the Park, although it hadn't been a Park yet and wouldn't be for another seventy years. The telephone lines had not survived the closing of the mine. Now, a century later, twenty-four-seven communication was about to come back with a vengeance. She'd done a little after-hours Googling on one of those donated computers at Niniltna Public School at the start of the school year. Typically, mobile communications service providers paid anywhere from a thousand to three thousand a month to lease tower space, for five-year terms that customarily included an option for extending the lease in five-year increments up to twenty-five years. The price paid generally increased in direct proportion to how long the landowner was willing to lease the land for. If Tikani looked like a good prospect for a tower, for example, Vidar Johansen, its last living resident (or last living resident who wasn't in jail), could pull down as much as a hundred and seventy-five large.

Money like that hadn't been seen in the Park in a long, long time, the Suulutaq Mine notwithstanding, and Kate could only imagine the stampede when the news got out.

She hated talking on the telephone. She just wasn't one of those people who had an answer when it rang and someone said, "Hey, how ya doing?" She wanted to see the face of the person she was talking to, watch as their expression changed, take in the lift of an eyebrow or the sideways glance that told her what they were really saying. In Kate's experience, and after five and half years working sex crimes as an investigator for the Anchorage DA and another—god, was it really?—almost ten years now working as a private investigator out of the Park, the difference was vast. Words could mean anything, anything at all. Faces, now, faces told a different story, often as you were sitting there listening to their mouths say something else entirely.

Still. The brat had a point. If they'd had cell phone service in the Park right now, Jim could have called her from the airport. The airport in Anchorage. The airport in Seattle. The airport in Long Beach.

Every day he was gone.

A shooting star painted a fading streak across the night sky. She looked north to see if the lights were out, but it was too early in the evening. A cold nose touched her hand and she looked down to see that Mutt had followed her outside.

"Yeah, yeah," she said, "I know. In the immortal words of Billie Holiday, what lonely hours the evening shadows bring, when your lover has gone."

Mutt stared at her with wise yellow eyes.

"Oh, shut up," Kate said, and went back inside to make cocoa.

Three

JOHNNY DROVE HIS OWN PICKUP TO school the next morning, Kate and Mutt following behind an hour later. She paused at the Riverside Café long enough for one of Laurel Meganack's first-rate americanos and a giant two-pump French vanilla nonfat latte, Dan's favorite, extra hot so there was a chance it'd still be lukewarm by the time it got to the Step. Lucky she wasn't staying for breakfast, as every table and booth and counter was jammed with raucous, unshaven Suulutaq miners. Every Park rat with a four-wheeler was renting it out by the hour to any miner who came along, and the miners had lost no time in tearing a track into the muskeg between the Suulutaq and Niniltna, after which they had very quickly found their way to Bernie's Roadhouse. When it snowed, the Park rats would probably switch out rentals from four-wheelers to snowmobiles, at equally extortionate rates.

When she stepped outside again, Luke Grosdidier was just pulling up on a four-wheeler with a trailer attached. The trailer had two newly fabricated metal bench seats bolted inside it and three people Kate didn't even know sitting on them. They climbed out, counted money into Luke's hand, and vanished inside the café.

Kate looked at Luke. He grinned. "Niniltna

Taxi, at your service. Sorry, gotta go, got another fare." He fired up the engine, made a U-turn, and roared off.

Kate headed up to the Step in a gloomy frame of mind. There, the double-wide trailers and modular buildings that formed Park Headquarters huddled together on a long, narrow plateau against the nearly vertical wall that was the western face of one of the more intransigent of the Quilak Mountains. A dirt strip ran a couple of thousand feet before disappearing into the tall grass and the encroaching alders, which were turning an autumnal gold. An unfamiliar helicopter was parked to one side, bright shiny new. Kate instantly began to think of ways to finagle a ride out of the Parks Service. George Perry, a fixed-wing man all the way, would disapprove, but what he didn't know wouldn't hurt him. Jim had left the helicopter that had given rise to his other nickname, Chopper Jim, in Tok when he'd made the move into the Park.

Dan was in his office, filling out forms. "If we can't do it in heptaplicate, the federal government don't do it at all," he said. He tossed the paperwork aside, gave Mutt an affectionate cuff when she trotted forward for the attention that was her due, and leaned back in his chair, linking his hands behind his head. "How the hell are you, Shugak?"

A burly man with bright blue eyes in a red face

beneath reddish orange hair cut in a flattop, Dan O'Brian had joined the Parks Service fresh out of college. He had served time at various parks across the nation before arriving in Alaska and in the Park, where he had thus far resisted every subsequent effort at transfer, promotion, or retirement. A confirmed bachelor, a raging heterosexual whose record for seduction was second only to Chopper Jim's, Dan was a man of such highly developed interpersonal skills that he was the only ranger in the entire state of Alaska who had never been shot at, even while evicting squatters off Park lands, arresting bear poachers, and enforcing fishing regulations. "Ranger Dan isn't an asshole," Old Sam had once famously opined from the bar of the Roadhouse, "his job is."

Even this fleeting memory of the quintessential Alaskan old fart was enough to give her pause. "Fine," she said, recovering. "I'm fine."

He rocked a little, looking at her, saying nothing.

"Yeah, okay, I've been better," she said. "Did you know he was eighty-nine?"

"That all? I'd have figured a hundred and three, easy."

She had to smile. "New helo out there, I see."

He nodded. "AStar B3. The Lama burned too much fuel. This one's got more power, more payload, and a hundred-forty-knot cruising speed with a full load."

"Do you even know what any of that means?"

He laughed. "No. But it sounds good."

"Why didn't you ever learn to fly, Dan?"

He shrugged. "I never have a problem scoring a ride wherever I want to go." He grinned. "It's good to be king. How about you?"

She reflected. "Have you ever noticed how when somebody gets their pilot's license, they stop being whatever else they were the second before? Like if someone asks them what they do, from that moment on they say, 'Oh, I'm a pilot. And, you know, a nuclear physicist.' "

"What, Kate Shugak afraid she's going to lose her identity at five thousand feet?"

"I don't know. Maybe I'm just scared of heights."

He laughed again. "Yeah, right."

"Who'd you get checked out on it?"

"The new helo? Nobody, yet, but one of George's new hires has an instructor's rating. When things slow down this winter at the mine, I'll send Ernie down to Niniltna to get qualified. What can I do for you today, Kate?"

"I'm Old Sam's executor. He's got a piece of property listed in his will only by lat and long. Near as I can figure from the map I've got at home, it's somewhere between here and Yakutat."

"That covers a few miles," he said.

"You're telling me."

He got up and went to the map of the Park that,

when pulled down, covered the better part of an entire wall of his office. It was mostly green in color, indicating twenty million acres' worth of federal lands in the stewardship of the National Park Service. Niniltna, Ahtna, and Cordova, along with the few larger villages, were red specks within the green. Blue parcels indicated Native lands granted by ANCSA and ANILCA, most of them choice lots on or near the Kanuyaq River, the main highway for Park rats in the summer after it thawed and in the winter after it froze, not so much in the spring and the fall.

Yellow dots, widely scattered and minuscule in size by comparison to everything else, indicated the 9.8 percent of the Park that was privately owned. Most of the dots had been homesteads, granted under the Homestead Act of 1862, signed into law by Abraham Lincoln himself, granting an applicant freehold title to a maximum of one hundred sixty acres, subject to said applicant's improving the land while living on it for five years. Those still in possession in 1972 ("It's amazing how many people just walked away from that much sweat equity in that much land," Dan said) had had their parcels grandfathered in as the Park was created around them. Those who had missed the boat in 1972 jumped on the ANILCA bandwagon in 1979. Today many homesteads were still owned by descendents of the people who had built the first cabins on them. Kate was one of them, and, like her, most of them were friends of Chief Ranger Dan O'Brian's.

Which didn't stop him from growling like an angry grizzly every time his eye caught sight of a yellow dot on his map. On principle, Dan hated the idea of privately owned property in the middle of a national park, and in particular his Park. In reality, he got along well enough with most of the owners to remain a lead-free zone.

There were a very few widely scattered brown areas on the map, too, indicating areas of natural resources in which the Parks Department had with a show of great reluctance granted various exploration companies permission to look for natural resources—timber, copper, coal, and oil.

And gold. Kate discovered that she and Dan were both looking at the bull's-eye he had drawn around the valley that contained the Suulutaq Mine. He saw her looking, and made a great show of tracing the lines of latitude and longitude she had given him to the intersection on the map. He stared at his forefinger for a moment, brow creased. "That can't be right."

"What?" Kate said.

"Wait a minute." He went to his desk and picked up a small rectangular device. He gave her a shamefaced grin. "GPS."

She was exasperated. "Why didn't you just use that in the first place?"

He squirmed. "I keep forgetting I have it. What were those numbers again?"

She read them out. He tapped them in and then waited for the result. Mutt, who'd thought they were about to leave, decided all the effort of getting to her feet shouldn't be wasted and departed for the kitchen in hopes of gustatory largesse.

"What?" Kate said, when Dan stood staring at the tiny screen.

He raised his eyes. "I don't believe it."

"Believe what?"

He walked across the room and after a brief moment put his forefinger on the map. Kate leaned in and squinted.

Just above his blunt-cut fingernail was the black circle and attached squiggle that indicated Canyon Hot Springs. It was not colored yellow as private property, it was shaded green as being part of the acreage apportioned to the Park.

"You're kidding me," Kate said.

"Nope." With a nearly grim intensity, Dan abandoned the GPS and headed for the door, Kate at his heels. He hoofed it down the hall to another room, this one filled with filing cabinets. "The records are being transferred into digital databases but it's labor-intensive and it takes a hell of a lot of time," he said over his shoulder. "We're transferring the newest records first, because they're always going to be the ones most

60

requested, so the older ones we have to look up by hand for now." He pulled down an ancient volume.

"What's that?"

"A cross-reference of anyone who has ever staked a claim or applied for an allotment anywhere in the Park." He opened it. The pages, some of which were bound into the volume and some of which had been added later, were lined and dated and filled with writing in many different hands. "Jesus, there are a lot of people in the Park whose last names begin with D." He ran his finger down one column, then another. "Dementieff, Dementieff." He turned the page. Halfway down the column he stopped. "Samuel— Leviticus?" He looked at Kate.

"That was his middle name." Dan remained incredulous, and Kate said, "It was in his will and everything."

"Jesus," Dan said again, "the things some people name their kids. You'd think they wanted them to get beat up in kindergarten. Okay, Samuel Leviticus Dementieff, a single man, applied for"—his voice changed, acquiring an edge—"a hundred and sixty fucking acres of unimproved land in March of 1938." There was a corresponding file number, and after ten minutes of yanking open various file drawers, swearing, and a paper cut that left a trail of bloody fingerprints from 1935 to 1939, they had the file open on the table and were standing side by side, staring down at it.

There were three documents, all handwritten in that spiked longhand with the sky-reaching *P*'s that dated its creator as having learned to write English in America sometime before Leon Czolgosz shot President McKinley. Each document was clearly marked "Copy" with a black stamp. The first was the application itself, in two paragraphs, dated March 30, 1938. The paper was yellowed with age and the ink had bled and faded but the words were perfectly legible.

"'I, Samuel Leviticus Dementieff,'" Kate read out loud, "'of the city of Cordova, Alaska Territory, do hereby apply to enter under the provisions of the Homestead Act of 1862 the one hundred sixty acres in the Quilak Mountain foothills located approximately eighty-five miles east of the village of Niniltna. . . .'" There followed latitude and longitude of the four corners of the property, with a note made thirty-six years later of the property tax number given the parcel by what was then the state of Alaska.

"How did he get a surveyor out there?" Dan said. "He'd have had to import one from Fairbanks, or even Anchorage. Must have cost him a bundle."

Kate shook her head. "You're forgetting the Kanuyaq Mine."

Dan frowned. "It was closed by then, wasn't it?"

"It closed that year, but until then they would have needed their own surveyor on staff. With the right encouragement, he probably wasn't averse to doing a little moonlighting on the side."

"I hope he charged Old Sam a chunk of change. Jesus, think of the bushwhacking it would have taken to get back there then, not to mention humping the theodolite and the tripod in. And a tent, and food, and a gun. Hell, I'll bet you couldn't get a GPS to work back there today."

The second paragraph began, "Land office at City of Ahtna, Alaska Territory." This time Dan read it out loud. " 'I, Frederick Cyril McQueen, Register of the Land Office, do hereby certify that the above application is for surveyed lands which the applicant is legally eligible to enter under the Homestead Act of 1862'—Abraham fucking Lincoln—'and that there is no prior valid adverse right to the same.' "

"Title search should be so easy nowadays," Kate said. "Or so cheap. Not to mention which, I think you might have gotten Lincoln's middle name wrong." Dan rolled a fulminating eye in her direction and she added hastily, "Just a guess."

They turned back to the file. The second document was a printed form titled "Proof Required Under the 1862 Homestead Act," the blanks filled in by the same hand than the application. " 'We, Peter Everard Heiman' "—

"Hey," Kate said, "must be Pete Heiman's dad."

"Or his grandfather, more like. 'We, Peter Everard Heiman and Chester Arthur Wheeler, do solemnly swear that we have known Samuel Leviticus Dementieff for over five years last past; that he is the head of a family . . .'" Dan looked at Kate. "I never heard Old Sam was married."

"Me, either," Kate said.

"'. . . that he is the head of a family'—okay, wife and number of children left blank—'and is a citizen of the United States, and that is an inhabitant of,' yeah, yeah, we know the numbers, 'and that no other person resided on the said land entitled to the right of Homestead or Pre-Emption.'"

"I love the idea that anyone could pre-empt the federal government's ownership of land."

"You would. 'That the said Samuel Leviticus Dementieff entered upon and made settlement on said land March 31, 1938, and has built a house thereon.'"

A description of the house followed. Kate stared at it, trying to reconcile "part log, part frame, two doors, two windows, shingle roof" with the near ruins she remembered from the previous winter, when she and Mutt had apprehended three Kanuyaq River highwaymen at Canyon Hot Springs. "I never knew Canyon Hot Springs belonged to Old Sam. And nobody said, not the aunties, Emaa, Old Sam himself—no one. Why the hell not?"

64

Dan kept reading. "'. . . and has lived in said house and made it his exclusive home from March 30, 1938, to the present day.'" He looked up. "No way, Kate, did these guys go all that way, with no road—hell, no trail—through all that brush and muck to check that Old Sam had built his house."

But the witnesses had signed the document of proof, with flourishes, as did Frederick Cyril McQueen, Register. "Present day" for the second document was October 3, 1945.

"When he got home from the war," Kate said.

"Which war? World War Two?"

Kate nodded. "He was in the Aleutians. One of Castner's Cutthroats."

"Wow." In spite of himself, Dan was impressed. "I bet he could tell some stories."

"I bet he could have, but he never did. What's next?"

The third document was Old Sam's certificate and patent, signed the same day as his Proof of Improvements. This, too, was a printed form. "'Now, therefore, let it be known, that on presentation of this Certificate to the Commissioner of the General Land Office, the said Samuel Leviticus Dementieff shall be entitled to a Patent for the Tract of Land above described.'"

It was signed, again, by Frederick Cyril McQueen, Register.

Kate and Dan stood staring down at the three documents until a low "Woof" made them both look up. Mutt was standing in the doorway, head cocked, a quizzical eyebrow raised.

Kate looked at Dan. "May I have copies of these?"

Dan hesitated a little before answering, an unreadable expression on his face. "He should have had the originals," he said at last.

"I haven't found them," Kate said. "At least not yet." Her brows drew together. "That is odd. You'd think he would have kept them in the file box with his will and the rest of his papers." She shook her head. "They're probably tucked into a book on one of his shelves. So, may I have copies for the meantime, until I find them?"

He hesitated a little longer before he said, "Sure." As if making up his mind, he scooped the documents back into the file. "Sure you can have copies. But they won't be official documents, you understand. There could be problems if they were all you had to establish title."

She looked at him, a little puzzled. "Let's hope I find the originals, then. What's the problem, Dan?"

He took a deep breath and let it out slowly. "May I make a suggestion?"

"Who's ever been able to stop you?" she said, even more puzzled at this unaccustomed deference. Dan O'Brian was notoriously loud and up-front by nature, it was one of the reasons he got on so well with the Park rats.

It seemed to her he chose his words with care, as if he were tiptoeing over a minefield expecting one of them to explode whether he stepped on it or not. "You might like to consider the possibility of deeding Canyon Hot Springs over to the Park Service."

Her eyes widened. It might even be fair to say they nearly popped out of her head.

"We have the ability to look after it," Dan said. "Maybe even develop it as a remote, hike-in-only campsite."

Kate's laugh was deep and spontaneous, and then she realized he was serious and the smile vanished from her face. She squared her shoulders and pushed out her jaw. "Old Sam left it to me," she said. "Why would I give it to you? The Parks Service has made a career out of sequestering millions of acres of public land that is public only insofar as people can afford to get to it. At least if I keep hold of the springs I can say they're open for everyone to use."

His mouth pulled up at one corner. "Yeah, and how much do you think the shareholders of the Niniltna Native Association are going to like that idea?"

"What the hell are you talking about?"

"I heard Auntie Joy wants to start charging people for berry picking on Native lands in the Park."

"Canyon Hot Springs belongs to me, not the NNA."

Dan looked down at the file in his hand and didn't say anything.

She remembered that Canyon Hot Springs was colored in in green on the map in his office. "Dan? Would you have even told me about the homestead Old Sam filed on Canyon Hot Springs if he hadn't mentioned it in his will?"

Dan didn't answer.

She looked around the room, at the file cabinets lining the walls. "How many so-called abandoned claims have you got in these files, Dan? Have you even tried to find the claimants' heirs? Or do you just ignore them in hopes people will forget about them?"

Again, he didn't answer.

She grabbed his arm. "Dan? Does title revert to the government if the land remains unoccupied?"

He pulled free of her grasp. "I'll make you those copies," he said, and vanished down the hall.

Kate left the Step in a state of considerable disquiet.

It wasn't like she had to have title to Canyon Hot Springs. It wasn't like she spent a lot of time there. It was an overnight trip in winter, and in summer the thick brush made it nearly impassable to anyone without a machete and the determination of Genghis Khan. The unmapped rocky outcrops and sudden spurs of the Quilaks provided their own effective camouflage, too. Kate had gotten lost two or three times on the way there last year.

The hot springs sat in a narrow canyon where the majority of the real estate was essentially vertical. There was no airstrip and there never would be because there was no conceivable place to put one. She doubted there was enough room to land Dan's new helicopter there. Probably couldn't squeeze in a parachute, for that matter. The brush was too thick to bring in a four-wheeler in summer. No, certain access was only by snow machine or by piton, pickaxe, and rappelling rope.

Two thirds of the Park was taken up by an undulating topography that gradually descended westward from the foothills of the Quilaks, punctuated by glaciers, glacial moraines, rivers, creeks and streams, a butte here and there, and a few freestanding mountains. The other third was given over to the Quilaks themselves in the east and the Chugach Mountains on the southwest coast. The Quilaks and the Chugachs were separated by the Kanuyaq River, which wound sinuously through the Park from above Ahtna to Prince William Sound. The Trans-Alaska Pipeline marked the Park's western boundary, as did the Glenn Highway, which along with the Kanuyaq River provided relatively easy access to the adjacent land.

The eastern boundary was marked by the Canadian border, on the other side of which were more mountains and gorges and glaciers, all as impassable as the ones on the Alaska side and as overrun with wildlife, much of it bigger than you were and all of it hungry.

There was no easy way into the Canyon Hot Springs, and getting out could be as problematic as getting in. Why the hell had Old Sam chosen the most remote, the most difficult to access hundred and sixty acres in the whole Park and possibly all of Alaska to homestead?

She had never thought of Old Sam as an unsociable guy per se, but then she had yet to be born when he'd staked his claim, so she couldn't attest to the man he'd been then.

But she knew people who could.

Four

AUNTIE JOY LIVED IN ANOTHER OF those ubiquitous log cabins with a floor plan that appeared to have been the only design option for anything built in the Park up to the Good Friday Earthquake of 1964. Kate's grandmother's original cabin, Old Sam's cabin, Kate's parents' cabin—they were all one large room on the main floor with a sleeping loft above. Auntie Joy's cabin was on the riverbank in Niniltna, about equidistant between Emaa's and Auntie Edna's, only a little farther to Auntie Vi's, an easy walk for a mug up and a good gossip in either direction.

The square windows set into the log walls were hung with ruffles and lace, and as usual when Auntie Joy threw open the door with her trademark beam of a smile and pulled Kate inside, in stepping over the threshold Kate felt immediately transformed into a claustrophobic elephant in a stained-glass factory. "Mutt," she said, "stay," and pointed to the patch of grass next to the door before the gates of mercy closed behind her.

Inside, every vertical surface was covered with framed photos dating back to the century before last, from sepia prints in gilt frames to black-and-white photos with scalloped edges to Polaroids whose color was fading to a complete set of senior pictures of this year's graduating class. Every horizontal surface was covered first by a tablecloth or a scarf or a handkerchief or sometimes all three. The next layer involved lace of some kind, usually tatted by Auntie Joy's own fair hands. The third and ever-changing final layer was decorative, ivory carvings of seals and bears and loons, glass animals that held votive candles, woven baskets from the size of a thimble to big enough to cradle a baby. Old glass bottles elbowed for room with Aladdin oil lamps, including a brass one that looked like it was still warm from Aladdin's hands, and a dozen different tea sets.

There were a great many horizontal surfaces,

Auntie Joy never having met a piece of furniture she didn't like, the older the better, and the room was crowded with chairs and end tables and a dining set that perched uneasily on delicate carved legs on a faded but scrupulously clean linoleum floor. Kate had never been to the sleeping loft but she would have bet large that Auntie Joy had managed to squeeze a tulle-draped canopy in under the roof.

There was also an overwhelming preponderance of pink, pink ruffles, pink lace, pink doilies, an afghan knitted in different shades of pink, a quilt assembled from squares that ran from pink plaids to pink polka dots. Kate wondered if Auntie Joy had ever read Christina Rossetti.

There must have been a cookstove in the clutter somewhere because Auntie Joy said, "You sit now, Katya. I make tea."

She gave Kate a slight push, and Kate almost stumbled over a pair of porcelain dogs guarding a high, round, spindle-legged table covered with china figurines dressed like characters out of the Angelique novels. She caught her balance, sucked in her gut and edged between the dogs and a bright red La-Z-Boy recliner. It was by far the newest thing under this roof and Kate more or less fell into it.

Auntie Joy bustled, if one could be allowed to bustle in that jam-packed little room without breaking anything, and shortly Kate had tea in a cup and saucer adorned with a dainty tracery of leaves and vines and pink roses that she hoped wouldn't break in her hands, and a matching plate of cookies baked to a crisp brown glory that melted in the mouth. "I want the recipe for these, Auntie," she said indistinctly.

Auntie Joy beamed. "Before you go, I write." She settled herself into an elegant openwork chair carved from some dark wood and inlaid with mother-of-pearl, picked up her tatting, and let her fingers busy themselves with an intricate pattern while she fixed Kate with an expectant gaze.

Time for business. Kate put the saucer down on the only available square inch of empty space on the top of a wooden spool draped in some pink velveteen fabric, then drained the cup and set it down even more carefully on the saucer. Then she watched it for a moment to make sure everything else on the tabletop wasn't going to shove it over the edge. Satisfied, she turned to Auntie Joy. "I'm—Old Sam named me executor of his will."

It was as if someone had flipped a switch. The tatting shuttle slowed, the beam dimmed and then went out entirely, and for the first time in a long time Auntie Joy looked her age. "He say he do that," she said, in a voice devoid of emotion.

The way life had drained from Auntie Joy's voice from one sentence to the next was unexpected and startling. "When?" Kate said. "When did he tell you?"

Auntie Joy made a vague gesture. "Back a ways. He tell us all." Kate divined that Auntie Joy meant Old Sam had told all four aunties about his will. "Long time gone."

"Well, it would have been nice if someone had told me," Kate said. "Maybe given me some advance notice."

Auntie Joy gave Kate a very auntly look, and Kate was instantly ashamed of herself for whining. "Sorry, Auntie. But it is a little overwhelming, the amount of property he had." She noticed a slight stiffening in the chair opposite. "For one thing, I didn't know Uncle had proved up on a homestead claim on Canyon Hot Springs."

To her further surprise, Auntie Joy, already gray around the edges, turned ashen. "He do that, yes," she said, almost whispering. "Long time gone, he do that." She raised her head. "He leave it to you?"

Kate nodded. "He left me the whole kit and caboodle outright, with a letter telling me how he wanted everything distributed." She thought of telling Auntie Joy about Old Sam's Niniltna cabin and the *Freya*, and then she thought better of it. Incrementalization in this case could be dangerous, especially to her. If all four aunties were going to explode with outrage over the disposition of Old Sam's worldly possessions, better she give them the news in a body. Detonate it in a single blast in a safe place somewhere, away from women and children.

Then she thought about telling Auntie Joy about Dan O'Brian's offer to incorporate the hot springs into the Park. Again, she thought better of it. The love-hate relationship between the Park rats and the Parks Service was such an insubstantial little tightrope, capable of dissolving underfoot and dumping the high-wire walker on his or her ass at the slightest misstep. Park rats reveled in a subsistence lifestyle that was in great part due to the management skills of Chief Ranger Dan O'Brian and his pitifully small staff of tree-hugging bunny lovers. If a grizzly walked through someone's yard, his presence could very well be attributed to Dan's taking down yet another poacher hunting bears for their bladders, which ounce for ounce were the highest-selling commodity on the Asian black market. If you got your moose that year, most likely it was because Dan had been so vigilant in policing the moose population that dishonest big game guides had moved their illegal trophy hunting operations up to the Gates of the Arctic or over to the Wood-Tikchik State Park.

Like every other Park rat, Kate owed a great deal of the quality of her life to Ranger Dan and his gang. Unlike too many other Park rats, she knew it. She didn't want to start a war between the Park rats and the Parks Service if she could possibly help it. Besides, it was Auntie Joy's reaction that interested Kate most at present.

She waited, saying nothing, and finally, in a soft, insubstantial voice, Auntie Joy said, "He say what to do with hot springs?"

Kate shook her head. "No, Auntie. He told me what to do with a lot of his other stuff, but not that."

The plump little woman with the faded, wrinkled face looked down at the tatting in her lap.

"Auntie?" Kate said, leaning forward, a hand outstretched. "What is it? What's wrong?"

Auntie Joy looked up, and the tears had filled her eyes and were slipping down her cheeks. Her smile was shaky. "Nothing, Katya. Ay, who knew we miss that cranky old man so much?"

And with a finality that would not be gainsaid, she changed the subject to Laurel Meganack and Matt Grosdidier, and Auntie Edna's ballooning restaurant business, and the prospects for the Kanuyaq Kings basketball teams in this year's forthcoming season. That little point guard on the women's team, Anushka Tuktoyuktuk's daughter—had Kate ever seen anyone go up after her own rebound like that? Gatcha, but that girl ferocious like a wolverine. If she don't foul out, the women's team never have to worry over turnovers like last year, didn't Kate agree?

If anything, Kate was even more upset when she left Auntie Joy's than she had been when she'd left the Step.

It wasn't that she didn't expect Old Sam to be

76

missed. She missed him herself. She always would. He'd had an innate ability to cut through the crap in a way she admired and tried hard to emulate. That she had a bullshit detector at all was very much due to Old Sam, and her association with him had only fine-tuned it. It was one of her most useful tools, both on the job in Anchorage and today in her profession as private investigator. Nobody could lie to Old Sam, and that included Kate. He'd peeled her like an onion last spring, dissecting the reasons behind her general dissatisfaction at being stuck in the whirlpool between the Scylla of the Suulutaq Mine and the Charybdis of the board of directors of the Niniltna Native Association. Everybody wanted a piece of her. She had felt like the barbarians were at the gates and she was holding those gates against them all alone, with no surety that she—or the Association, or the Park, for that matter—would be able to outlast the siege.

Old Sam hadn't waved a magic wand and cured all her ills that spring day, but in a few words and with one surprising quotation, he had illuminated her problem, given her insight, and made her feel better. She didn't know anyone else who could do that.

Maybe Jim.

But Jim was in California.

She shoved her instinctive and knee-jerk resentment back down beneath the surface of her psyche and drove to one of six matching houses sitting on six matching lots. They were downriver from town, about halfway to Squaw Candy Creek and the turnoff to Bobby and Dinah's. The little housing development was five years old, financed with HUD funds administered by the Niniltna Native Association. Bush Alaska was always low on housing, and this little development had been Kate's Emaa's last hurrah before she died, half a dozen brand-new homes brought upriver in modules via barge and assembled by Park rats grateful for paying jobs they didn't have to go to Anchorage to find. Two bedrooms, one bathroom, with earth stoves for heat, propane for cooking, and running water from a communal well and wired for electricity to the Ahtna power line. These were the *ne plus ultra* in Park accommodation, all modern conveniences laid on and with minimal monthly mortgage payments at a negligible interest rate. Now that Kate thought about it, they might have been the first new houses built in Niniltna since Harvey and Auntie Vi built theirs twenty years before, when they got their ANCSA land allotments.

She pulled her pickup in next to a battered Ford Ranger that looked as if it had more miles on it than the space shuttle, killed the engine, and got out, followed by Mutt. The door opened and Virginia Anahonak stuck her head out. "Hi, Kate. Heard you pull up."

"Hi, Virginia. Heard you were renting a room to Phyllis Lestinkof."

"You heard right."

"She here?"

"She's here. Did you want to talk to her?"

"Please."

"Come on, I'll pour you a cup of coffee."

"That's okay," Kate said. "I'll wait out here."

Virginia's eyebrows worked a little overtime at that but she went back inside. Kate wanted to give the news to Phyllis first, without anyone listening in. She didn't know how thin the walls were in these little houses, but Virginia had a well-deserved reputation as the Niniltna town crier.

The door opened and Phyllis came out, looking a little puzzled. "You wanted to see me, Kate?"

Phyllis looked thinner than she had the last time Kate had seen her, in the Riverside Café last May, pleading for help from the father of her child. She wasn't much taller than Kate, with short dark hair, dark eyes, and smooth brown skin. She wore a loose-fitting T-shirt over jeans with the top button undone. She was eighteen years younger than Kate and a distant relative by way of, if Kate remembered correctly, Auntie Balasha. The Lestinkofs were originally from Tatitlek and relative newcomers to the Park, the family having moved here after the destruction of the original village during the tidal wave that followed the

1964 earthquake. The Lestinkofs had lost so much family that Mrs. Lestinkof, Phyllis's grandmother, could not bear the thought of relocating with the rest of the village to a new site on the mainland. Phyllis's father married into the Park, one of the Anahonak sisters, which made Virginia her aunt. It made Ulanie Anahonak her aunt, too, the difference being that Ulanie was a churchy type with definite opinions on children born out of wedlock to godless and amoral mothers. Virginia's moral stance was far more relaxed.

Virginia peered at them through the living room curtains. "Walk with me," Kate said.

Phyllis fell in next to her. Mutt took point, trotting ahead to sniff at various clumps of grass and tree roots, choosing a select few to anoint along the way.

"You deckhanded for Old Sam on the *Freya* this summer," Kate said.

"Yes," Phyllis said.

"He thought you did a pretty good job."

They reached the river road and turned left, Kate walking slowly with her hands in the pockets of her jacket. It wasn't really cold yet but it wasn't warm anymore, either. The river moved past on their right, and the Quilaks bulked large on their left. A trio of ravens nagged at an eagle flying low across the river, prospecting for a late silver to take home to the nest.

"He said that?" Phyllis said.

"He wrote me a letter," Kate said. "You know, to read after he died. He said so in that."

"Oh." They walked a couple more steps. "Is that what you wanted to tell me?"

They were far enough away from the house now. Kate stopped. "No. I've got some good news, or I hope you'll think it is. Old Sam left me his cabin on the river, but he wanted you to live there when he was gone."

Phyllis stopped dead in her tracks. "What?"

Kate had to repeat herself, and then say it a third time before Phyllis believed her. She started to cry. "Please tell me this isn't a joke. Please, please tell me you aren't kidding."

"I'm not joking," Kate said. "I own the cabin, but Old Sam told me to let you live there as long as you wanted to. With the baby coming, he knew you needed a place, and he knew your parents' house wasn't an option."

Phyllis was so overcome she had to sit down on a driftwood log. Kate sat next to her. "That old man," Phyllis said over and over again, hugging herself and rocking back and forth. "That old man." She wiped her nose on the back of her hand and looked at Kate. "Virginia's been really nice, but she doesn't have room for me and her own kids, too, especially after the baby comes. Do you mean it, Kate? This really isn't a joke?"

Kate looked at the round, anxious face swollen

with tears. "It really isn't, Phyllis. Old Sam's cabin is yours to live in. Old Sam said to charge you rent."

"Oh. Rent. Yeah." Phyllis bit her lip. "How much?"

"A buck a year."

Phyllis stared at her, dazed, and Kate let the grin she'd been holding back spread over her face. "Yes, I actually said that, a dollar a year, every year. What say we let the rental period begin the first of October?"

"I guess," Phyllis said, still dazed. "Sure. I—I don't have anything, like dishes or sheets, but it doesn't matter; I'll manage. I saved all the money I earned on the *Freya* and I can hitch a ride to the Salvation Army thrift store in Ahtna and—"

"You don't have to," Kate said. "I'll leave all of Old Sam's dishes and linens and household stuff in the cabin. Yeah, yeah, I know, and you're welcome. Give me a day or two to pack up his books and guns and a few other personal things. Phyllis, listen to me now." This said as Phyllis departed this realm for another altogether, one with her own roof over her own and her baby's heads. "There's a dozen cords of firewood; you can use that. You have to pay for your own electricity, and if anything breaks, you fix it. Okay?"

"Okay," Phyllis said. "Okay, Kate." She stood

up, a different person than the one who had sat down ten minutes before. "I'm going to go tell Virginia. She'll probably be as happy about it as I am."

Kate noticed that Phyllis didn't call Virginia auntie.

She wondered if that was yet another thing that was changing, from one generation to the next, in the maelstrom of other changes that had engulfed the Park when gold in commercial quantities was discovered fifty miles away.

Five

THE RED PICKUP STOPPED IN THE driveway leading to Old Sam's cabin, which included a sod roof and a wooden walkway to a floating dock. The dock had a woven alder bench on it. Kate still had a hard time looking at the bench without seeing Old Sam slumped there, before a serene, slow-moving river, beneath a dark sky scored with stars.

She set her teeth and walked out to the end of the dock anyway. Clouds had rolled in overnight, according to the weather report the thin end of a frontal wedge that would probably bring with it the first fall storm. She sniffed. Next to her, Mutt raised her nose and sniffed, too. The breeze was not quite sharp and smelled moist. It was too cold for rain, not yet cold enough for snow, but there would be precipitation of some kind within the week.

Across the river the deciduous trees had yet to drop their leaves, and so formed a billowing golden glory that followed the water's edge and even on this overcast day turned the usually gray surface of the river a dull yellow. Behind them the occasional tall sentinel spruce etched a lonely outline against the sky. They were few and far between following the past decade's onslaught by the insatiable spruce bark beetle. The docks attached to the dwellings on the opposite shore tugged at the water flowing past, carving furrows and ripples into its surface.

She heard the sound of an airplane, identifying the high-pitched whine as Chugach Air Taxi's single Otter turbo well before she looked up to track its path overhead. She waved, and George waggled his wings in reply. The plane disappeared behind the trees lining the airstrip in back of town. The same plane that had taken Jim away the night before was now returning with a load of Suulutaq Mine workers for Tuesday shift change. The Suulutaq changed out their hourly employees ten to twelve a day, five days a week. The salaried employees changed out less often. One of them was Vern Truax, the mine superintendent. Kate wondered how much longer he was going to remain superintendent, since two of his employees had recently been found to have committed industrial espionage and a third had tried to cover it up with murder. She imagined he was at this very moment doing some pretty fancy tap dancing in front of Global Harvest's board of directors, and if his own libido had not contributed to his problems in the first place she could almost have found it in her heart to feel sorry for him. But for a guy who allowed himself to be led around by his dick, he was very smart, and very experienced in pulling minerals out of the ground.

Only four days had passed since the murderer had been apprehended.

To Kate it felt like a year.

She went back up the dock and let herself into the cabin.

With Phyllis in mind, she climbed the ladder to the loft and peered over the edge. A queen-sized bed, big enough for Old Sam if he slept from corner to corner, took up most of the floor space. There was a lamp on a Blazo box next to the head of the bed, and beneath the eave on the opposite wall more Blazo boxes were stacked on their sides, open ends facing the room, clothes sorted and folded inside them. She smiled. Old Sam had arranged the boxes in an attractive pattern by alternating which side they stood on, wide or narrow, and had painted them the same soft cream color as the rest of the loft. There were no windows in the loft and only four in the whole cabin, and the light-colored paint gave the area an inviting look, a place where sleep would be peaceful and deep.

Kate climbed down the ladder and looked at the back wall. Here Old Sam had spared no effort in a construction that must have taken more than one winter to complete. These shelves had been handmade from hand-fallen and hand-finished birch planks, and made with love and attention, too, the nails countersunk and filled, the edges and corners sanded into smooth, blemish-free curves. The shelves were staggered in size but never more than three feet in length, designed not to sink beneath the weight of what was on them, and the wood glowed from a continual application of hand-rubbed wax. It must have been the undertaking of several days every winter to empty out each shelf, wax it, polish it, and return everything to its proper place.

Every single shelf was filled, too, but not to overcrowding. You got the feeling looking at them that there would always be room for another can of Campbell's tomato soup, or another box of .458 Winchester Magnum cartridges, and always, always room for another book.

Kate had been pacing herself because she hadn't wanted to go for the books first thing, hadn't wanted to reveal even to herself how shamefully eager she was to get her hands on the contents of Old Sam's library. She looked at the recliner and imagined him sitting in it, footrest up, feet hanging over the end, a sardonic glint in his eyes. *Stop fiddle farting around and get on with it, girl.*

She got on with it.

He hadn't been a collector; every one of his books was for reading. She thought she might have acquired her habit of marginalia from him, so she was expecting the underlined passages, the scribbles in pen and pencil, the dog-eared pages, the occasional yellow highlighting. Truth to tell, it only made the books more precious in her eyes. His voice spoke out to her from those notes and scribbles, from beyond the grave they had laid him in on Sunday, a rush job before the ground froze so they wouldn't have to put him in cold storage for the winter and bury him the next spring.

His interests were fairly narrow but within those confines pretty catholic. He liked Western fiction, so there was a lot of Zane Grey and Louis L'Amour and Rex Beach and Steward Edward White and Owen Wister and Jack Schaefer. There was even Wallace Stegner. "Eew," she said. "Uncle. How could you."

He was a hunter who liked to read about other hunters, so there was a lot of Robert Ruark, Peter Capstick, and inevitably, and here Kate stifled a groan, Ernest Hemingway. She pulled down the Capstick edition of Teddy Roosevelt's *African Game Trails* and let the book fall open where it would, reading

After reaching Suez the ordinary tourist type of passenger ceased to be predominant; in his place were Italian officers going out to a desolate coast town on the edge of Somaliland; missionaries, German, English, and American; Portuguese civil officials; traders of different nationalities; and planters and military and civil officers bound to German and British East Africa. The English included planters, magistrates, forest officers, army officers on leave from India, and other army officers going out to take command of black native levys in out-of-the-way regions where the English flag stands for all that makes life worth living.

She laughed out loud at the last line, and replaced the time machine back on the shelf. Her hand lingered, though. She harbored a warm feeling in her heart for Teddy and his big stick. He had after all been the proximate cause of the creation of the National Park Service and of Yellowstone, its first park. He was one of the reasons there was any wild land left in the United States. Considering the robber barons he'd been raised with, that was no mean achievement.

What the hell. She took the book down again and searched further. Teddy Roosevelt had taken his son Kermit on safari in Africa in 1909, three weeks almost to the day after leaving office, and only eleven years before Old Sam had been born. Old Sam had seemed very much a man of the present, but it was impossible to deny the age you were born into. Women hadn't been able to vote the year Old Sam was born. Orville Wright was still alive. A generation of women never married because a generation of men had been killed on the fields of Verdun, Ypres, and the Somme.

She looked up, puzzled. Why had Old Sam never married? His long association with Mary Balashoff declared his heterosexuality, so the obvious answer to many a crusty old bachelorhood was out. It wasn't as if there weren't women of his own generation around, and he would have been a superb provider. Any woman worth the name within fifty miles would have inveigled him down the aisle. Hell, one of the aunties for that matter. Three of them were much-married, and from what Kate had managed to glean from the rarely dropped reminiscence, they'd always had a weather eye out for a good-looking man. Auntie Joy was the only one who hadn't remarried after her first husband had died. You would think . . .

Kate froze in place, one arm in the act of replacing the book on the shelf. "Holy shit."

Ay, who knew we miss that cranky old man so much?

Auntie Joy. Auntie Joy and Old Sam. Auntie Joy and Old Sam?

Had Old Sam staked his homestead in Canyon Hot Springs to build a home for himself and his bride?

But if Auntie Joy's grief was that of a lover, what had happened? Why had they not married?

A memory flashed into her mind, of deviled eggs, always a dozen, always served on Auntie Joy's prized Alexandrine rose platter, always with exactly the right amount of mustard in the yolk mix, always with the finest dusting of paprika, always beautifully arranged on a lush bed of dark green lettuce. She had brought the same thing every time, to every single one of Old Sam's summer's end barbecues, for as long as Kate could remember. There was never any doubt about their reception, either, Old Sam invariably fell on the eggs as if he hadn't eaten in a month.

Maybe those deviled eggs had been less substance than symbol.

She thought of all the things Old Sam had done for all four of the aunties. Hunted for their caches, filled their woodpiles, tuned up their vehicles, built on and plumbed their bathrooms. He was always available to patch a leaky roof or install a new light fixture. If memory served, Auntie Joy had always been first in the line.

Maybe service to the four aunties was a blind for service to one particular auntie.

She had not heard before now so much as a word about a possible relationship between Auntie Joy and Old Sam, but she knew from bitter experience that that meant nothing. That generation, as near as dammit Victorian in character and as personified by Emaa and the aunties and Old Sam, never told the children anything about each other's personal lives if they could help it.

There was a whine from the door. She turned to see Mutt poking an inquisitive head in the door Kate had left open for light. "Nothing," Kate said. "Go find yourself some lunch."

Mutt disappeared. Kate looked back at the shelves. All the books and tools and other personal belongings—and the ammunition—all of it would have to be packed and stored at her homestead before she could let Phyllis and her baby move in here. The food, the dishes and flatware, the towels and linens, those would stay. It had been a nice thing to do for Phyllis, and she was sure Old Sam would have approved, but it also made that much less for her to pack up.

She fetched the flattened cardboard boxes she'd had stored in a corner of her garage against future need (no Park rat would ever dream of throwing away anything as useful as a cardboard box) and began. The ammunition and gun paraphernalia fit into one box, along with a collection of black-and-white photographs going as far back as the 1940s. She taped the box shut and wrote "Guns and ammo and photos" on the top in firm black Marks-A-Lot. It was a start.

She reassembled two boxes this time, one for books she wanted to keep, another for the ones she would give to the library. There were five bookshelves with five shelves each. The books were a mixture of hardcovers and trade paperbacks.

The first book, at the left of the first shelf, proved not to be a book at all but a spiral-bound notebook of lined pages used by schoolchildren before computers. Kate thumbed through the pages, which were filled with Old Sam's handwriting. It was a collection of quotations, listed alphabetically by author. There was poetry, songs with all of their stanzas painstakingly copied down, and observant acerbity from many names she recognized and some she didn't. "The dog barking at you from behind his master's fence acts for a motive indistinguishable from that of his master when the fence was built." Robert Ardrey. Who the hell was Robert Ardrey? ". . . the human instinct to kill immediately any creature of a species not his own." Kate recognized the name this time, Elspeth Huxley, author of a couple of those white-British-colonial-in-Africa memoirs, and as she recalled, two of the best of a very over-written genre. Kate's copies had burned along with her cabin two, almost three years ago. Had Old Sam given her those books? She couldn't remember.

"I am aware of what every single unwed person

knows—that the world is always a little out of focus when there is no one who gives the final total damn about whether you live or die." John D. MacDonald, and Kate would bet spoken in the voice of Travis McGee. A most uncomfortable passage altogether, given her speculations about Old Sam and Auntie Joy. And of course none at all about her and Jim.

One entry brought her to a full stop. "All change is of itself an evil, which ought not to be hazarded but for evident advantage." Samuel Johnson.

Old Sam had quoted that very passage to her last spring, standing in the clearing where they had shortly thereafter been charged by a very pissed-off grizzly bear.

She blinked several times, and looked down at the notebook. No leaving that behind, or donating it to the school library.

She put the notebook in her box.

The second book was *The Voyagers: Being Legends and Romances of Atlantic Discovery*, by Padraic Colum, published in 1925 with illustrations by Wilfred Jones. The book fell open naturally to "The Children of Eric the Red," surmounted by a drawing of a ship that looked more like something in Sir Francis Drake's command.

The job took the rest of the day, not only because every third or fourth book tempted Kate to dip into it but also because every five minutes some Park rat would drop by. Many of them, after offering condolences, would wonder in a casual voice what Kate was going to do with this set of socket wrenches or that fifty-pound bag of flour, and oh by the way, had Old Sam said anything about the *Freya* and who might be running it next year, because they were going to need a good tender man down on the Alaganik next summer, and you couldn't trust Ringo Rogers not to run the *Reckless* aground on the flats again and a whole period's catch along with her. To all these inquiries and many more Kate replied with civil thanks and a vague "Don't know yet." It satisfied no one, but when she made it clear that was all the answer they were getting they would at least go away.

The drive-bys began to lessen as the light leached from the sky. Mutt had yet to return, so the hunting must have been either good or fun. Most of the books were in boxes when Kate came to an oversize ledger, bound in leather, with gilt lettering on the spine that had flaked so badly it was unreadable. She opened it and found it to be a sort of daily diary, written by hand in a penmanship strongly reminiscent of the writing on the homestead documents she and Dan had looked at that morning.

She switched on the floor lamp next to the recliner and held the open ledger beneath it, frowning over the spiky writing in the fading ink.

Paycheck arrived, only three months late this time. In the A.C. Company we trust, and in the pay packet finally, finally a check for $12,000.00 to build the courthouse. Mr. McQueen has very kindly found two adjoining lots abandoned on Copper Way, a good location in the very center of the town, if town this may be called. Two tracts of public land, each forty by one hundred feet, one for the courthouse, the other for the jail. I believe Mr. McQueen harbors designs on the position of Register, which he may have with my very good will and heartiest recommendation if he continues in this helpful fashion.

Mr. McQueen. Mr. Frederick Cyril McQueen, perhaps? Kate flipped back and forth, looking for a date or a signature. She found both. The journal belonged to one U.S. Judge Albert Arthur Anglebrandt, a triple-barreled name if there ever was one. Below it was written the date, July 10, 1937, City of Ahtna, Alaska Territory.

Kate looked up. Well. Well?

Well, first of all, why Ahtna? Why not Niniltna? Ahtna had started life as a roadhouse, back when there was little more than a mule trail linking Interior Alaska with the coast. The populations of Kanuyaq, the mining town, and Niniltna, the good-time town four miles down the road, added together would have had a hundred times the population of Ahtna at that time. She looked at the date again.

And that would be why. The mine was about to go out of business, pulling the railroad ties up behind it as it retreated to Cordova and took ship for Outside. Kanuyaq and Niniltna were fifty miles off the main north-south route. Ahtna, on the other hand, was right on the road, roughly midway between Fairbanks and Valdez. Anchorage at that time was still barely a step up from the tent city it had begun as. In a territory the size of Alaska, with a population so widely scattered, travel time would be a big factor—it still was—and Ahtna would seem the most obvious choice for a sitting court.

If Mr. McQueen was in fact the same Frederick Cyril McQueen who had signed Old Sam's homestead application and the other two documents as well, Kate could understand why Old Sam would want the ledger. But where had the old fart acquired it? Although as a one-time officer of the court she should probably be asking herself why the ledger wasn't in an hermetically sealed storeroom in Juneau somewhere, part of the record of law and the history of the state of Alaska.

She opened the book again and found a list of amounts preceded by dollar signs, which upon further study revealed themselves to be licensing fees for the various businesses in operation in Ahtna, more of them than she would have thought. Federal funds were conspicuous by their absence. If the locals wanted law, they could pay for it. A bank, two stores, three saloons, a draper, a dry goods store, a garage, and two hotels were all assessed quarterly fees in sums that appeared to be commensurate with the amount of income their business generated. There was a Mrs. Beatrice Beaton's Boardinghouse, another triple-barreled name a little too euphonious to be true. By the size of the license fee, Kate thought Mrs. Beaton might perhaps be renting her beds by the hour, and not empty, either.

She was charmed. It was the picture of an entire community on one page, and so rapt was she in this snapshot of what was essentially a frontier town that she hadn't felt the cold stealing into the room through the open door. The brush of rip-stop nylon on the door frame, the scuff of Vibram rubber soles on the wood floor, these registered, but too late, and for once her famous reflexes failed her.

She raised her head and looked toward the door, and as she did so the sixteen-inch piece of firewood coming around in a two-handed swing smacked her square on the side of the head.

She didn't even remember falling down.

Six

THE PLANE LANDED FIFTEEN MINUTES ahead of schedule and they had to wait for a gate at the John Wayne Airport, which bore no resemblance in size or traffic to the one-horse terminal Jim remembered. When the seat belt light went off he got to his feet, relieved that his legs still worked. He followed the signs to baggage claim, waited fifteen minutes for his suitcase to be the last bag on the carousel before the "Last Bag" sandwich board came out, and climbed in a cab to give the driver the address of the house where he had grown up.

Palm trees—he remembered the palm trees. The strip malls were new, and the sky looked less blue than it used to. He looked at the umber hills against the horizon, puny compared to the Quilaks. Which ones were they? The San Gabriels? The Santa Monicas? For the life of him he couldn't remember.

He didn't remember this much traffic, either, a cacophony of cars, every tenth one a convertible, every eleventh one a Hummer. They inched along, getting caught at three successive lights. A drive that should have taken twenty minutes was going to take twice that long. Where the hell were all these people going? At this hour of the morning, why weren't they at work? A siren sounded somewhere behind them, and cars bad-temperedly wedged themselves to either side of the road so a cruiser with lights and siren going full out could edge past and drive down an exit.

An image of the dirt roads of the Park flashed through his mind, the wide, gray Kanuyaq running beside them, the great, ferocious peaks of the Quilaks elbowing their way over the eastern horizon, backed by the hot pinks and nugget golds of a rising sun. He thought of the peace, the clear, almost pure silence, that came with that view. He had never used the siren on his rig. He couldn't remember the last time a Park rat had used his horn. There was no road rage because even if you were mad at someone who cut you off—and where on a Park road was there enough room to cut someone off?—you knew him and he knew you and you weren't going to flip off someone who would be buying you a beer at the Roadhouse that evening.

He repressed a strong urge to tell the driver to turn around and take him back to the airport.

Something wailed out of the radio that reminded Jim of the last practice session of the belly dancers at Bernie's. The driver was watching him in the rearview mirror. "Where you from?" he said.

"Alaska," Jim said.

"Wow, no kidding, Alaska? How cold is it up there now?"

"Not very."

"Is it true that it's dark up there all the time?"

"Half true."

"What's that sexy governor of yours up to these days?"

"She quit."

The driver gave up.

When they finally got to it, the neighborhood hadn't changed much. Tall, canopied trees turned the wide, leisurely streets a dappled green. The sidewalks were edged with manicured grass. No house was so small it didn't need a staff of two or more to run. There had been some rehabs, a neo-Greek temple here, an ersatz Tuscan villa there, but when the cab pulled into the driveway the old home was still true to the fake Mexican roots of the developer who had built it, with its stucco walls, tiled roof, and thick cloak of magenta bougainvillea drooping over the heavy Spanish doors.

He paid the cabbie, hefted his suitcase and his daypack, and walked to the door, where he hesitated for a full minute before pushing the doorbell. The days when he'd just walked in were long gone.

The heavy wooden door opened. "Hi, Mom," he said.

"James." He was offered a cool cheek to kiss. "Please come in."

He stepped into the tiled hallway.

"Maria," his mother said, "this is my son, James. Please take his bags to the guest bedroom and then bring us some lemonade on the terrace."

"*Si, señora.*" The Latina almost curtsied and hurried away with the bags.

"This way, James."

He followed her through the house and out a back door to a sunlit terrace paved with broad flagstones, in between which had been planted some bright green moss with tiny white flowers. There was more bougainvillea and a variety of leafy trees and flowering shrubs arranged artfully around a winding path of more flagstones, right up to the eight-foot stone wall that restrained the yard from spilling out into the street. It looked very beautiful. Compared to the Park, it also looked very domesticated.

He looked at his mother. An upright five foot nine, a carefully maintained one hundred fifteen pounds, she had always epitomized the Duchess of Windsor's dictum that one could never be too rich or too thin. Any renegade drooping or sagging was covered in raw cream-colored silk tailored to fit those slender arms and those long legs, and her feet were clad in brown leather sandals consisting mainly of a few thin straps that even to his uneducated eye shrieked designer prices. Her hair was the same white blond it had always been, although now it brushed her shoulders in a disciplined pageboy, the wings curving gently beneath the square jaw that was so obviously his own. Her makeup was subtle, and her rings, watch, and earrings delicately and expensively made. Her fingernails, filed to perfect ovals, were coated in a discreet clear polish, and no shred of cuticle dared to rear its ugly head. The wrinkles at the corners of her eyes and mouth were very faint, and the skin of her neck was smooth and firm. She'd had some work done, but then she lived in the work capital of the world. It was probably the law in LA that you had to have work done. She was seventy-nine. She didn't look a day over sixty.

"You look great, Mom," he said, because one of them had to say something.

She looked at his T-shirt and jeans, her gaze lingering on his scuffed boots. "Thank you," she said.

"I have a suit in my bag," he said.

She raised beautifully shaped eyebrows. "I would hope so."

He had to unclench his jaw to ask his next question. "When is the funeral?"

"The day after tomorrow. There will be a memorial for everyone at the church, and then a graveside service for family."

"There's only you and me."

"Followed by a reception at the club."

The club. Of course.

Maria brought the lemonade in a frosty pitcher and two tall glasses.

"That will be all, Maria, thank you," his mother said. Maria genuflected herself off the terrace. His mother poured.

"Monday, Mr. Abernathy will come here for the reading of the will."

He thought of the four long days between the funeral and the reading of the will. "Why? We both know what's in it."

She ignored him. It was one of her best things.

"Tell me about Dad," he said.

She took a deep breath and let it out very slowly and deliberately. Whatever he thought of her, he had never doubted that she loved his father. "A year ago," she said, "he began to lose strength in his hands. He started dropping things. I wanted him to go see his doctor. He wouldn't hear of it, said it was nothing, that it would pass."

He watched her face in profile, the mouth unsmiling, even stern. "Then he began to tire halfway through our evening walk. So I made the appointment and I drove him there. They did all the usual tests. Nothing checked all of their little boxes. Dr. Mortimer said if he had to make a bad guess that it would be amyotrophic lateral sclerosis."

"Lou Gehrig's disease."

"Yes."

"Last year?" he said.

She turned to look at him and answered his real question. "He forbid me to tell you. You may believe that or not as you choose, but it's true."

She paused, as if she were debating whether to say what came next. In the end, her own ironclad sense of propriety won out. "I don't think he could bear the thought of you seeing him like that." She faced forward again, duty done. "He was reasonably active until, well, until last week, really, capable of walking, if slowly. Talking. Breathing." She swallowed, her first and only sign of distress. "And then I think he just . . . stopped. He developed a staph infection, though he had no open wound near the infection and he hadn't been near a hospital or even the doctor's office for two weeks before that. I almost think it was deliberate, although I couldn't tell you how. They tried antibiotics, but the infection wouldn't respond to them, and his organs began to shut down. Things progressed very rapidly after that. He went into the hospital on Friday night. He died Sunday afternoon. I was with him."

Jim saw that his hand was clenched on the table. He forced it to relax. "I wish I could have been here to say good-bye."

"Had I known he was dying, I would have called you sooner."

It was as close as he'd ever get to an apology.

"He told me to tell you," she said, "right before . . ." She stopped.

"Tell me what?"

It was hard for her to get the words out, and it showed. "He wanted you to know he was proud of you." Her mouth twisted for a moment only, before being smoothed back to its usual firm line.

He would take what he could get. "Thank you for telling me." He got to his feet and walked to the edge of the terrace so she wouldn't see the tears in his eyes.

A well-mannered car purred past on the other side of the wall. A door somewhere opened and closed again with no unseemly haste or force. The leaves rustled in the breeze. Some fortunate bird that had found its way from the smog-choked environs outside into this comparative paradise gave song. The setting sun cast longer and ever more illusive rays across the mossy stones of the path.

"How long did the swimming pool last after I left?" he said.

"Three weeks," she said, and he turned to see a tight smile on her face.

Maria came out again. "Dinner is ready, *señora*."

The interruption didn't matter. They understood each other perfectly.

They always had.

Seven

THE SEA AROUND HER WAS THICK AND black and bottomless. It felt like she would never reach the surface. When she did, after a long and painful swim that stretched her muscles and strained her lungs, the waves slapped at her face, rough, urgent, sandpapering her skin. She moaned.

She heard a siren. She moaned again.

The slapping of the waves increased. So did the volume of the siren. "Stop," she said, "please stop."

She opened her eyes, or tried to. One was swollen shut, the other almost so, and the lids were gummed with some sticky substance, the subject of determined removal by Mutt's tongue.

Mutt was standing with her forepaws on either side of Kate's head and her rear paws on either side of Kate's hips, engaged in a vigorous cleaning of Kate's face. In between licks she would raise her head and growl at the door, a rumbling, menacing sound designed to terrorize anything standing outside of it, up to and including an F-15.

The decibel level of the siren moderated and became the fearful whine Mutt alternated with the ferocious growl.

Kate put up an arm to try to fend her off. " 'S okay, girl," she said, or that was what she had meant to say. Her mouth felt as if it were full of sawdust. "Mutt," she said, "knock it off."

Mutt kept licking and whining and growling and snapping her excellent and very pointed set of teeth.

A stray thought occurred to Kate. At least with

the licking, her face would be clean of all the blood.

Blood. What blood? And why blood?

She thought about this for a while, but someone kept shouting at her. That was annoying. "Shut up," she said, and then couldn't remember if she'd only thought the words.

She heard her name. "Kate?"

"Uh," she said. She was pretty sure she'd said that.

"Kate, can you call her off?"

"Uh," she said.

"Kate, work with us now. You have to stand her down. She won't let us in the cabin."

"Uh," she said.

"Kate, come on, wake up." The familiar voice put some English on his tone. "Kate. Snap out of it, dammit."

Mutt's growl that time had to have registered on the seismometer at the Alaska Volcano Observatory. Matt Grosdidier swore later that the door of Old Sam's cabin reverberated beneath his hand.

"Mutt," Kate said, and this time managed to raise a reassuring hand to Mutt's head. " 'S okay, girl. I'm all right."

Her hand missed Mutt's head by six inches. Mutt whined at Kate and growled at the door.

Kate tried to raise her hand again, and connected this time with Mutt's neck. She

107

knotted her fist in Mutt's thick gray mane and gave her a shake that was feeble at best. "Mutt." She tried to sit up and couldn't, only partly because Mutt wouldn't move. Kate made a tremendous effort and achieved near coherent speech. "Mutt, babe, you need to relax. I'm still here."

Mutt wouldn't be moved, so Kate got her other arm up around Mutt's neck and used her to pull herself to a sitting position. After about a year, she got there. It took another year to shove Mutt to one side, so that Kate was between her and the door. Moving one hundred and forty pounds of half wolf half husky was never an easy proposition, and when the one-hundred-and-forty-pound half wolf half husky was ready, willing, and eager to take out someone, anyone, for the damage done to her human, the problem increased exponentially. Kate cajoled, cursed, and shoved, and finally managed it, although Mutt wouldn't move more than six inches away and remained on stiff legs, hackles raised, that low, menacing growl continuing to rumble from her throat.

Kate, exhausted, leaned against her, one arm still hooked loosely around Mutt's neck, and worked on mustering enough energy to get to her feet. If that was ever going to be possible again. Her head hurt so bad it might be dangerous to increase its altitude even by five feet. Maybe she should just lay down again. She couldn't remember why she'd wanted to get up in the first place.

Movement near the door caught the corner of her eye. At the expense of pain that shot all the way down her spine, followed by a wave of nausea, she turned her head and saw Matt Grosdidier poking a nervous nose inside the cabin. "Kate?" he said in a tentative voice.

Oh yeah. That was why. "It's okay," she said. "It's safe to come in now."

A tentative footstep sounded on the floor. Mutt gave a sharp warning bark right over Kate's head, baring her teeth at Matt.

One giant step backward and he was once again on the correct side of the door. There was some nervous whispering. There seemed to be a lot of other people behind Matt but she couldn't see their faces in the dark.

When had the sun gone down? The last she remembered it was full daylight.

"Kate?" Matt said.

"Mutt," Kate said tiredly. "Enough. Sit."

There was a long pause when nobody moved. Kate opened the one eye still working and glared at Mutt. "Sit," she said again, this time with enough force to be felt.

Yellow eyes narrowed, but Mutt sat. She took her time, and no one was fooled into thinking she had relaxed her guard.

Kate, making another tremendous effort, resulting in another throb of pain and another wave of nausea, turned her head again to see Matt just inside the door, the daypack with the red cross on it in his hand. Behind him she could see the faces of Mark, Luke, and Peter Grosdidier and Harvey Meganack. There might have been others. She closed her eyes again.

"Kate, stay with me. If you pass out again, she'll probably go berserk. Again."

Kate opened her eyes every morning, no reason she couldn't do it now. Was there? She hoisted her eyelids into their original upright and locked position. "Okay."

Matt advanced. Mutt's growl increased in volume. "Mutt, you know me. It's Matt. You know I'm not going to hurt her." His foot slipped on something and he lost his balance and swore. Mutt amped it up. "Come on, girl, stand down. It's okay. I'm going to help Kate, and then you can have her back, I promise."

And then Matt was kneeling next to Kate, and to his credit he didn't flinch when Mutt thrust her muzzle at him, that growl sawing back and forth like a hacksaw through rusty iron. He'd opened the daypack before he came into the cabin so he wouldn't have to fumble around with the zipper, and the alcohol swabs were ready to hand.

"You did a great job of cleaning her up, Mutt, good girl, nice girl, please don't rip my face off, girl, nice girl, I'm just doing a little cleanup work here, good girl." Mutt backed off a fraction of an inch and without changing his tone Matt said, "Jesus, Kate, what the hell happened?"

"I don't know," she said. The smell of alcohol stung her nostrils and she flinched at Matt's touch. "Somebody hit me."

"No shit," Matt said. "You've got a lump on your head the size of a cantaloupe. You're gonna have shiners that glow in the dark."

Kate groaned. Mutt growled and snapped. A testament to his nerves, again Matt managed not to jerk back. "Mutt, you are one pissed-off dog. I get that. But I didn't hit Kate, and I'm trying to help her, so just give me a little room to work here, okay?"

He checked Kate's pupils and made her squeeze his hands and move her feet. He put a C-collar around her neck. "Will she let us put you on a stretcher?"

"I don't need a stretcher. Help me up."

"Kate—"

"Help. Me. Up."

Matt shook his head and muttered something uncomplimentary under his breath. He got an arm around her waist and heaved her to her feet. The room whirled around her as if she were on a merry-go-round and she almost threw up.

"Take deep breaths," Matt said.

She took deep breaths. The whirling subsided a

little, and Matt assisted her into Old Sam's recliner. He looked about him immediately for a receptacle of some kind, found a plastic bucket that had once contained paint stripper, and set it next to her. The fumes nearly finished her off and Matt hastily replaced the bucket with an old Tupperware container Old Sam had been using for spare nuts and bolts and screws. It didn't look big enough to him, so he swapped it out for an ancient coal scuttle Old Sam had used for his woodstove tools.

Seeing Kate in a more or less vertical position seemed to reassure Mutt, and her hackles lowered. She leaned so hard into Kate's knee she pushed her into the opposite armrest. "It's okay, girl, really," Kate said, although she wasn't quite sure if she meant it. She blinked, and for the first time since she'd regained consciousness, the rest of the cabin came into focus. "What the hell?"

Now she understood why Matt had tripped. The cabin was completely trashed. All the books she had so carefully packed away were out of their boxes and tumbled across the floor. All the books remaining on the bookshelves, any item left on every shelf and both tables, was on the floor, too. Canned goods had rolled beneath the dining table. Boxes of ammunition had burst open where they landed; bright brass cartridges shone from all four corners. Pots and pans and plates and knives and forks and spoons looked as if they had been thrown over a shoulder and left to fall where they might. Nuts and bolts and nails and screwdrivers rolled underfoot. There were clothes everywhere, too, jeans and bib overalls and plaid shirts and moth-eaten T-shirts and Jockey shorts, so whoever had trashed the main floor must also have climbed the ladder to the loft.

"Can you remember what happened?" Matt said.

Kate tried to think. "I was packing up his books. I hadn't closed the door. I think . . . somebody hit me."

"No shit," Matt said again. "With this." He hefted a piece of firewood. "See the blood? Betting that's yours." He looked at Mutt. "And you were where?"

Mutt dropped her head and gave a soft whine unlike any of the others she had given that night. There was what appeared to be a tuft of rabbit hair hanging from a corner of her mouth.

"Did you see who did it?" Matt said.

Kate started to shake her head and thought better of it. "No. I heard a sound, a footstep, something. And then somebody lowered the boom." The room started to go around again, and Kate shut her eyes.

"Okay." Matt stood up. "You're not driving home tonight. No, you're not," he said. "You're spending the night in our clinic, under observation. Since she'd probably rip my arm off if I tried to shut her out, your werewolf is welcome to stay with you."

Any resistance drained out of her. "Okay," she said. "Need to lock the door."

"There isn't a lock."

"Then Mutt and I stay here," Kate said.

"Kate—"

"Look at this cabin," she said. It wasn't easy to get the words out, but it was necessary. "Old Sam's not dead three days and somebody trashes his place. Why? What were they looking for? And does it look to you like they found it?"

"Kate."

She looked up to see Harvey Meganack standing in the doorway, although he wasn't coming any farther in. "I've got a spare hasp and a padlock," he said. "I'll go get it and put it on the door. I won't give anyone the keys except you. Okay?"

"What are you doing here?" she said.

"Harvey's the one who found you," Matt said. "He came and got us."

She looked at Harvey. In spite of her blurred vision and throbbing pain and recurring nausea, there was still room for the old antagonism to raise its ugly head, and mistrust and suspicion along with it. "How did you know somebody had jumped me?"

"Are you kidding me?" Matt said. "You could have heard Mutt from Anchorage. Harvey just got here first, is all."

The next morning the swelling had gone down, to be replaced by the promised shiners. The Grosdidier brothers stood around her in an awed circle. "She looks like Joan Collins on Oscar night," Peter said.

"Scorpius on *Farscape*," Luke said.

"I was thinking a panda," Mark said.

Mutt stared up at her with solemn yellow eyes. At least Kate's dog still recognized her.

Matt handed Kate a mirror. The brothers weren't exaggerating. "How long?" she said.

They communed with one another for a moment. "Ten days," Matt said. "Two weeks at most."

"Great." She put the mirror aside with a sigh.

"Pair of sunglasses will cover up most of that," Mark said.

"Yeah," Kate said. "Can I go now?"

"Sure. No evidence of concussion. Your hard head wins again. You're good to go."

"You want me to tell Nick Luther?" This from Maggie Montgomery, Jim's dispatcher and the closest thing left in the Park to a trooper after Jim went Outside.

Kate shrugged, relieved after the fact to have felt no pain in the act. There was a localized ache in her forehead, and her shoulder was sore from where she had fallen, but that was all. "You can tell him, but there's no suspect and no reason for him to fly down here. Tell him I said I was fine, and I don't have a clue who did it or why."

Maggie looked doubtful, but she said, "Okay."

"Could you give me a ride to Old Sam's?" Kate didn't want to walk through the village with these beauties, mostly because she didn't want to have to explain what had happened two hundred times. She had a thought, and looked at her trauma team. "You didn't tell the aunties, did you? Tell me you didn't tell the aunties." Johnny had already been to the clinic and gone to school that morning. Once assured of her well-being, he had seemed more inclined to laugh over her shiners than worry about the attack. Men. The aunties would be a different story.

The brothers exchanged a look. "Well, we didn't tell them," Matt said.

Kate was able to finish that sentence on her own. She stood up. "But they'll know soon enough. Get me out of here, Maggie."

Maggie dropped Kate and Mutt at Old Sam's cabin after a detour to Harvey's to pick up the key to the sturdy padlock that now secured the door. The mess inside looked even worse than what Kate remembered in her admittedly less than functional state the night before.

Most of the boxes had survived, and those that hadn't could be repaired with duct tape. Sighing, she got to work.

By late that afternoon, all of Old Sam's books were in boxes in the back of Kate's pickup, and everything else had been restored to its proper place. Operations had been hampered somewhat by Mutt's insistence on remaining no less than twelve inches from Kate at any given time. She had actually growled at Kate when Kate tried to shut the outhouse door on her.

Kate stood in the center of the room, hands on her hips, and addressed the ceiling. "What the hell happened here last night?"

Why had she been attacked? She wasn't familiar enough with Old Sam's belongings to say with confidence that nothing was missing, but there was enough of value left to preclude the motive as simple robbery, some opportunist hearing of Old Sam's death and coming to clear out what he could. None of the ammunition had been stolen, all the cans from the case of Campbell's cream of mushroom soup were still present and accounted for—even the loose bills and coins in the Darigold butter can were still inside, the plastic lid still on, though the butter can had been tossed to the floor. If the object of the attack had been burglary, she would have instantly suspected that weasel Howie Katelnikof, but even Howie was smart enough to wait until

Kate was gone. What on earth was the purpose in smacking her upside the head at that particular—

She stood very still. And then she went out to the pickup and opened up every single one of the boxes of books to check every single title.

Judge Albert Arthur Anglebrandt's daily journal was missing.

Eight

SHE WENT TO THE SCHOOL TO TELL Johnny he was spending the night at Annie Mike's in town, stopped at Annie's to tell her she'd have an extra kid for the night, and drove home, where she unloaded the boxes into the shop and for the first time in living memory padlocked the shop door. She debated leaving Mutt to guard the premises, but Mutt divined this intention via some heretofore unsuspected lupine telepathy and refused categorically to get out of the pickup. Kate swore at her, went into the house to pack some necessaries into her daypack, and spent ten blasphemous minutes searching in vain for her cell phone only to have it drop from the driver's-side visor halfway to Ahtna after they bumped through a particularly obnoxious pothole. She spent at least part of the journey casting anxious glances at the gray sky. If it snowed before she made it home, her pickup would remain in Ahtna until the snow had been packed down by enough snow-machine and four-wheeler traffic to sustain the drive. Which could be December, depending on how thick the snow fell, and how fast.

At least it held off as far as the Lost Chance Creek bridge, an ex–railroad trestle seven hundred feet long and three hundred feet high and a bitch to navigate in low visibility. This milestone safely negotiated, Kate stepped on the gas and achieved pavement in record time. She drove straight to the courthouse, a massive, curving two-story building on the edge of the river, with a striking metal sculpture of Raven stealing the sun, the moon, and the stars spread across the front doors. The door opened as she came up the steps, Ben Gunn holding it open for Roberta Singh.

"Your Honor," Kate said, pausing. She exchanged a nod with Ben.

"Kate, how nice to see you." Judge Singh looked like a cross between a ballerina and a princess out of the Arabian nights, tall, slim, sloe-eyed, her black hair pulled back from a broad forehead and knotted at the nape of her neck. She had such immense dignity that she seemed always to be attired in her robes, although today she was in fact dressed with her usual panache in a smart tweed coat with a fur collar, high-heeled boots, and black leather gloves. Kate always felt like the ugly stepsister in Judge Singh's presence, but then so did every other woman in the Park. Sartorial misery loves company.

"I was so sorry to hear about Old Sam," Judge Singh said.

"Me, too," Kate said. "But thanks."

"We shall not look upon his like again," Judge Singh said.

Kate smiled. "No. We shall not."

Singh nodded at the courthouse. "You're here to begin settling his affairs?"

"Yes, I'm his heir. I'm hoping Jane Silver can help me straighten it all out."

"I'm sure she can. Well, if there's anything I can do . . ."

A smile, a handshake, and Judge Singh swept down the steps, the reporter pattering behind. "Judge, I just need to know if—"

"Mr. Gunn, you know very well I may not discuss—"

Whatever it was Judge Singh couldn't say on the record was cut off by the closing of the door.

Not by so much as the raising of an eyebrow had the judge remarked on Kate's shiners. A class act, the judge.

The local lands office was tucked into a corner of the first floor and consisted of a single, very small room containing a desk with a bank of gray filing cabinets crammed behind it.

At the desk sat Jane Silver, who looked like she ought to be hunched over a steaming cauldron chanting in chorus with the other two weird sisters. A large head lowered between humped shoulders, scalp shining pink through thin flyaway gray hair cut short in no perceptible style, a nose that could have been used to hook halibut, long, yellow teeth—she even had warts. Her faded polyester plaid two-piece suit was missing a button and her orthopedic shoes squeaked even while she was sitting down.

She looked up when the door opened and fixed Kate with a piercing stare. "Kate Shugak," she said, in a mellow soprano voice that sounded nothing at all like the cackle it should have been. "That is you, isn't it?"

"Yeah, it's me," Kate said, stepping inside, followed by her four-footed shadow.

"What the hell happened to you?"

Kate had been asking that same question just the night before. "Somebody walloped me with a piece of firewood."

Jane inspected her. "Well, they were sincere about it, I'll give them that."

Kate grinned. "Keep the women and children off the streets when they see me coming, for sure."

Mutt went around the counter to rest her chin on the top of Jane's desk. "No mistaking who you are," Jane told her, and fished around in a bottom drawer, producing a pepperoni stick. She stripped it of shrink-wrap and held it out. Mutt took it delicately between her teeth and it vanished in two bites. She retired to the door, the office being so small and its occupant so decrepit (and so willing to pay homage to Mutt's Muttness) that she could be reasonably certain no one was going to bash her human over the head again, at least not in here. She kept one yellow eye peeled for anyone coming down the hall with fell intent, though, and frightened Bobby Singh's law clerk into dropping a document box on the floor, where it burst open with a splat and scattered files from there to the back door. Mutt, watching with no more than casual interest, sent the clerk scuttling upstairs for the public defender, a musher in his off time who might be expected to have the sangfroid to face down an indoor wolf.

Jane Silver was older than god and had been the lands clerk for the Park since before Kate was born. She was a tough old bird with a sharp tongue and an encyclopedic memory, and held the record at the Alaska State Fair for the most blue ribbons won in a row for jam making. Her specialty was rhubarb butter, just the memory of which made Kate's tongue prickle and her mouth fill with anticipatory saliva.

"I was sorry to hear about Old Sam," Jane said.

"Thanks," Kate said, "me, too." Had it really only been five days? "Me, too," she said again, and cleared her throat to speak in a stronger voice. "He's why I'm here. I'm the executor of his will, as well as his main beneficiary."

"I had an idea. What's up?"

122

Kate pulled out the will. "Turns out the old fart had some property nobody knew about."

"The Canyon Hot Springs homestead?"

Kate picked up her jaw and put it back into working position. "Well, yeah, now that you mention it. Nobody knew he'd staked a homestead up there."

Jane reeled off the numbers and Kate looked down at the paper she held to see that Jane had them down pat. "Jesus, Jane, is there a tax ID or a property ID in the Park that you haven't memorized?"

"No," Jane said, like it was the simple truth, which it probably was. She typed something into the keyboard sitting in front of her and watched the monitor. Something beeped and the reflected light from the monitor changed on her face. She got to her feet, shoes creaking, and went to a filing cabinet, opened a drawer, and extracted a file. "Hmm, yes," she said. "Nothing unusual here. Homestead requirements met and applicant's eligibility sworn to by reputable members of the community."

"He was underage," Kate said, "and he wasn't married. He wasn't a father, either."

Jane gave a dismissive wave with a hand that more nearly resembled a claw, a similarity enhanced by the long, bloodred nails that tipped each finger. Kate wondered how Jane could type. "The government was in a hurry to get as much land settled as fast as possible, so there was a lot of winking at that particular requirement. The only thing they really stuck at was if you had borne arms against the United States. Sam had a strong back and a reputation for paying his bills." Jane paused, her ugly face unreadable. "It was assumed he'd marry eventually. Most everyone did back then."

"You remember all that?" Kate said.

Jane looked up and grinned in an alarming display of long yellow teeth. "Hard to believe, I know, but yes, I am that old."

"You lived in Ahtna then?"

Jane nodded, eyes back on the file. "I came to town with Mrs. Beaton."

Again, Kate had difficulty in getting her jaw back in place. "Mrs. Beatrice Beaton? Of Mrs. Beaton's Boardinghouse?"

Jane gave her a sharp look. "Yes. How do you know that name?"

"I, ah, I saw it in an old ledger Old Sam had. Written by the first judge in Ahtna."

"That would be Albie Anglebrandt." It wasn't quite a question.

Albie? Kate nodded. "He had a list of all the license fees each business paid to the government. Mrs. Beaton's Boardinghouse was one of the businesses listed there." She fixed her eyes on a map of the Park tacked to the wall behind Jane's desk and said, "I would guess a boardinghouse would require a lot of hired help. Cooks and waitresses and maids and suchlike."

If she hadn't been watching for it out of the corner of her eye she wouldn't have seen that infinitesimal relaxation in the muscles around Jane's mouth. However curious Kate was—and however titillating might be the answers to any questions she might ask—she decided on the spot that this was no time to enquire into what, besides room and board, Mrs. Beatrice Beaton had been selling in Ahtna back in the day. Kate couldn't help seeing Jane Silver with new eyes, though. Jane Silver, lady of the evening? Of course she would have looked a lot different all those years ago. And there had been even fewer women in Bush Alaska then than there were now, so the customers would have been a lot less picky. She remembered pictures she'd seen of some of the women on the infamous Fairbanks Line. A younger Jane would not have been out of place. For that matter, neither would an older Jane.

"Is there any question about the title Old Sam held to the hot springs property?"

Jane shook her head. "Nope."

"Are you sure?" At Jane's look Kate said, "The reason I ask is because homesteaders were supposed to prove up in five years and he took eight. Dan O'Brian at Park headquarters? He showed me copies of the original paperwork. The

125

application was taken out in 1937. It wasn't granted until 1945."

Jane's eyes narrowed. "There were a lot of rules forgiven an Alaskan homesteader between December 1941 and August 1945. Especially when he came back a war hero."

She said it in such a way that Kate found herself rushing to assure Jane that she had actually heard of World War II. "And I know he was one of the Cutthroats. It's just, I think, well, I got the feeling that Dan felt that there might be something wrong with the title, given the, um, irregularities."

Jane snorted. "Irregularities! I'll give that fish hawk irregularities right up his rule-ridden, land-thieving keister if he doesn't watch out. There was nothing irregular in Sam going off to fight for his country. And there was nothing irregular in his government holding his coat while he did."

"I couldn't agree more," Kate said.

"Quite a war they fought out there," Jane said. "He ever talk to you about it?"

Kate shook her head. "He'd change the subject any time the war came up."

Jane gave a thoughtful nod. "Most vets, the healthy ones, put it behind them and move on. Sam was one of those."

Kate noticed the omission of the honorific, and began to wonder just how well Jane had known Old Sam. Jane saw the expression on Kate's face and said with a shrug that Kate saw as unconvincing, "I'd run into him at the Lodge every now and then. One thing I remember he mentioned about that time. Did you know he met Dashiell Hammett?"

Kate knew she was being diverted, but the bait was too good to resist. "You're kidding! Really?"

"Yeah, he was in the army and stationed on Adak. Sam—Old Sam said he ran the army newspaper there."

"Geez." Kate digested this in silence for a moment. She'd never read one of Hammett's books, but like everyone else she'd seen *The Maltese Falcon.* " 'I don't mind a reasonable amount of trouble,' " she said.

Jane grinned. "Okay, I'll play," she said. " 'You always think you know what you're doing, but you're too slick for your own good. Someday you're going to find it out.' "

This fell a little flatter than it should have. After an uneasy moment, Kate said, "Um, one other thing, Jane. I don't seem to be able to find the original documents relating to the hot springs homestead. Is that going to be a problem?"

Jane stood there, fully occupied with looking inscrutable. Moments passed before she stirred and said in a brusque tone, "You're the heir, didn't you say? You going to be paying the taxes?"

"For now, yes."

"Okay, then, fill out this form. We can start the

process of getting the title changed over to your name."

"How long will it take?"

Jane gave her a look. "Overnight."

"Right," Kate said. "Forgive me. Forgot who I was talking to for a minute. Good thing I'm overnighting in Ahtna."

"Come back in the morning, I'll have it for you then. We can get the tax records changed over to your name, too."

"Thanks, Jane." Kate lingered at the door.

"What?" Jane said. "I'm working here."

Kate would never find a better source about that place and time. "Judge Anglebrandt kept a daily journal."

The expression on Jane's face didn't change, but there was an immediate change in the air temperature. "How would you know about that?"

"Old Sam had it, or one of them, and from what little I saw, the first one. I was reading it when whoever it was clunked me over the head."

"Really." Jane brooded over her desk, and it was probably Kate's imagination that her expression took on a tragic cast, as if Jane was mourning something that had happened long ago and far away, but not too long ago or far away to be forgotten.

"Do you know if Judge Anglebrandt keep that journal the whole time he was here?"

"Yes." That came out way too definite and Jane knew it. "So far as I know."

The damage was done, but Kate wasn't going to brace Jane on any possible relationship with Judge Anglebrandt, at least not yet. "Was the diary all business? It seemed like it from the little I read."

"So far as I know it was a log of the court's business," Jane said.

"What I don't understand is how Old Sam wound up with it," Kate said. "Isn't it part of the official record?"

"Not necessarily. There was a clerk of the court who kept that." Jane hesitated. Kate waited for her to make up her mind to trust Kate with whatever it was. "Tell you what," Jane said. "Come back tomorrow morning, pick up your title, get your tax records in order. I might have something else to show you then."

"What?" Kate said.

Jane grinned. "Youth today, it's gratification in five minutes or they're gone. I have to find something, and it'll take a while. Come back tomorrow morning."

Kate heaved a martyred sigh, mostly for effect. "Elders today, it's driving the youth crazy in four minutes or their life isn't worth living."

They both laughed, and Kate collected Mutt and went looking for a place to lay her head for the night.

Nine

SHE WENT TO THE AHTNA LODGE FOR A room and Tony took one look at her and signed her in with a voice trembling with repressed amusement. Stan, Tony's partner in the lodge as well as in life, didn't even try to hold back his bellow of laughter when she walked into the dining room. "Jesus, Shugak," he said, choking, "just tell me the other guy looks worse."

"I never even saw him," she said.

"Yeah, well, when you do," he said. "The usual?"

He seated her at a table next to the window and five minutes later she had a fresh papaya sitting in front of her, halved and seeded. Standing next to her table, Stan squeezed the juice from half a lime over it.

Kate looked at her plate with disfavor. "I didn't order this."

"Papaya has an enzyme that helps the body absorb the blood, good for your shiners," Stan said. "Pineapple does, too, but I don't have any fresh pineapple in the kitchen. Eat up. You're getting one for breakfast, too. Oh, and here."

Kate took the capsule automatically. "What's this?"

"Vitamin C supplement. It'll help, too."

Kate didn't take vitamins, but under Stan's

watchful eye she washed this one down with a swallow of water and then dutifully if unenthusiastically ate all her papaya. She was rewarded with one of his justly famous steak sandwiches, and one of those same steaks for Mutt, raw and chopped fine with an egg and seasoned just as she liked it with salt and extra pepper. "You," Kate informed her, "are spoiled beyond belief."

Mutt, lapping up her steak tartare with the air of one who knows what is her due, gave her a look that said "You should talk."

Tony slid into the seat opposite. "I stuck up a note at reception so I could come keep you company while you eat. Listen, Kate, Stan and I both want to say how sorry we were to hear about Old Sam."

Kate swallowed a mouthful that was suddenly too large. "Thanks," she said. "I appreciate it."

"He used to call us the Fairy Barn," Tony said.

Kate was surprised into a laugh. "You're kidding."

Tony grinned. "No. Only to me and Stan, never in front of anyone else. Just trying to stir the shit."

"He was good at that."

"He'd close down the bar and hang out with us, and Mary Balashoff when they were here together on one of their weekends."

"What did you talk about?"

Tony laughed. "What didn't we. Nothing was

131

off-limits. Old Sam had an opinion about everything—politics, religion. And don't get him started on Alaska history. Hell, he lived through most of it. He knew a lot about Captain Cook, too. When he got on that hobbyhorse it could get really interesting. Sometimes it was like listening to Scheherazade, it'd be three, four o'clock before we'd break up. Did you know Cook was raised by Quakers?"

Kate shook her head.

"Me, either. And Old Sam said Cook was born in a pigsty, too. I'd always figured him for, I don't know, one of those bastard sons of a crown prince whose legitimate son was a no-goodnik, and they had to give the illegitimate but more able kid a job that would get him out of the country."

Kate paused. "Either you have an active fantasy life or you read too much Frances Hodgson Burnett when you were a kid."

Tony gave a modest shrug. "Why not both?"

Kate sopped up the last remaining dribble of juice on her plate with the last sliver of bread and savored it for a moment. "Old Sam had a copy of Cook's log. Three volumes, one for each voyage."

"Wow. I'd like to see that."

"He left me his books." Kate gave her plate a significant look. "Play your cards right and I'll let you look at them next time you're in the Park."

"Yeah, but would you let me borrow them to read?"

She grinned. "Limited, supervised visitation rights."

She pushed her plate away and sat back in her chair. The river moved past the window. It was lower and slower than it had been even a week ago. Every day closer to winter the temperature dropped even more, and it got colder faster at the higher altitudes, where the year-round snow and the glaciers were. Melt off was over and freeze up was on its way.

She turned to look at the dining room, less than half full. The snow marched down the sides of the mountains, and the tourists emptied out of the state.

"He loved you." When she looked at him, he said, "Oh, God, no, he'd never say so in so many words, but it was obvious in the way he spoke of you. He took such pride in you."

"He talked about me?" Kate took another look around the room, at the bar along one end, the door to the kitchen at the other, the tables and chairs spaced evenly between. It was odd to think of Old Sam perched on one of the stools there, surrounded by a dumbstruck audience as he held forth on her manifest virtues.

"Who doesn't?" Tony said. "He was in here a little over two weeks ago. I guess, yes, that would have been the last time I saw him."

Which would have been when Old Sam had revised his will, Kate thought. "What did he talk about that night?"

Tony's brows drew together. "Some about the fishing season." He smiled. "Some about the two new deckhands you wished on him. And . . ."

"What?"

"Well." Tony spread his hands. "World War Two."

"Really?" Kate was startled.

"Yeah."

"Well, he was in it, in the Aleutians."

"So he said. I hadn't known that before." Tony grimaced. "And now I have to go buy the book about Castner's Cutthroats."

Kate's smile was wry. "Yeah. Talking to Old Sam did tend to have that effect. Nothing like meeting someone who lived through it to make you want to read up on it."

Tony stood up and reached for Kate's plate. "Dessert?"

"What you got?"

Tony's grin was evil in the way of someone who was about to serve you three thousand calories in three bites. "It's chocolate."

"Sold."

He laughed and turned, and then turned back. "Oh, hey, one more thing we talked about that evening."

"What?"

Tony came back and rested the dishes on the table. He was smiling. "He spun us this tale about Dashiell Hammett. Said they were both stationed on Adak for part of the war."

Jane had told her the same thing an hour before, and only then did Kate remember the complete works of Dashiell Hammett on Old Sam's shelves, the only crime fiction represented thereon. So that was why. "He never told me he met Hammett."

She was trying not to sound aggrieved and she didn't think succeeding very well, but Tony, caught up in the story, didn't pick up on it. "Yeah. Funny. He said Hammett wrote him after the war, too. Oh yeah, and he said that Hammett was writing a book."

"Not all that surprising," Kate said. "Kinda what he did."

Tony laughed. "Sounded that way when Old Sam told it, too. He had us right up until the time the manuscript went missing, and then he cussed us out when we started laughing. He was a spellbinder." He picked up the dishes again. "And a helluva good guy. I'm sure going to miss him."

"We all will," Kate said, laughter draining out of her.

Tony touched her shoulder briefly with his free hand, and vanished through the swinging door into the kitchen.

135

Kate looked at her cell phone, which had been charging in her room since before dinner. Alaska was only an hour off California. Jim's cell number was number one on her speed dial. Come to think of it, it was the only number on her speed dial.

She hesitated, and didn't know why.

The phone vibrated in her hand. She jumped and dropped it. It fell on the bed and bounced out of reach and she scrambled after it, catching it just before it went off the other side onto the floor.

The number on the screen was Jim's cell. She fumbled to answer and pressed the wrong button and disconnected the call. "Damn it!" While she was trying to figure out how to call him back the phone vibrated again. This time she took her time, located the button with the green phone on it and pressed it. "Hello?"

There was a brief silence and for a moment she thought she'd disconnected him again. "Kate?"

"Yeah, it's me."

"I didn't expect you to pick up."

"Why'd you call then?"

She could hear the smile in his voice. "I was going to leave you a message that you'd get the next time you went to town. Something that would have embarrassed you to listen to in company."

She laughed, a husky sound. "Sorry I answered then."

" 'S okay. Next time. Where are you?"

"Had to make a run into Ahtna. I'm staying the night."

"Business?"

Kate looked up to see her reflection in the mirror over the dresser. The shiners had achieved an almost fluorescent hue, a sort of neon plum. "The snow's holding off so I figured I'd come into town to check with Old Sam's attorney. How are you?"

A sigh. "Fine."

"And your mom?"

She could almost hear the muscles in his jaw tighten. "She's fine, too."

A brief silence. "Talk to me," she said, her voice as soft as the scar on her throat would allow.

"They figure it was ALS."

She winced. "Lou Gehrig's disease."

"Yeah."

"You said he was a pretty active guy."

"Yeah. Well, for someone who lived in LA. He didn't have an aerobics instructor or anything, but he went a couple of rounds of golf every weekend, and he played tennis. He taught me to swim and to surf. His board's still in the garage, so I'm guessing he kept it up."

She was silent for a moment. "You should take his board out."

"What?"

"Take his board out. Go surfing. Remember him that way."

They listened to each other breathe for a few moments. The wonder was, it did not feel awkward to either one of them. "Is there a service?"

Another sigh. "The funeral's two days from now. There'll be a memorial in their church, a graveside service, and a reception following at the club. Monday will be the reading of the will."

Kate didn't let herself say the first thing that came into her mind, which was, *You're going to be there another five days?* Instead she said, "It sounds like the prologue to a country house murder in an Agatha Christie novel."

He laughed, and sounded surprised that he could. "That's exactly what it's like. All very structured and well-mannered. Butter wouldn't melt in our mouths."

"What is it with you and your mom?"

For moment she thought he wouldn't tell her. "I don't know," he said at last. "Chemistry, maybe? And different ideas about what I wanted to do with my life, oh yeah. My best friend when I was eight was Enrique, the gardener's son, so she fired the gardener. I walked away from the prep school she put me in after a month. I wouldn't study art or literature, I insisted on sociology and the law, and then I wouldn't go to law school, because what else was I going to do with a BA in criminal justice. She was all for me going to work for Dad's firm and making partner before I was thirty-five." She heard a joint pop as he stretched. "And then of course I refused to marry any of her friends' daughters. When I brought Sylvia home to meet them—not one of my better moves—I thought the air in the house was going to freeze solid."

"Uh-huh," Kate said. "Who was Sylvia?"

A telling silence, while he thought about whether he should tell her who Sylvia was.

"It doesn't matter," she said, "It's none of my business, before my time. I didn't mean to pry, I was just—"

"Sylvia Hernandez," he said briskly, giving the *r* its proper roll, "was the daughter of the LA county sheriff with whom I had my first ride along when I was making up my mind to be a cop. Jesus invited me to dinner at his house, where I met his eldest child, Sylvia. We dated for about a year."

"A year," Kate said, proud her voice didn't squeak. In the Park, until her, Chopper Jim Chopin's legendary string of girlfriends had considered themselves lucky if they'd lasted a month each. "Sounds serious."

He told her the truth and she was grateful. "I don't know how serious it was, but then I was accepted into the Alaska state trooper academy in Sitka." A ghost of a laugh. "A Hispanic daughter-in-law or her son a cop. I don't know to this day which my mother considered the greater evil."

Kate wondered what his mother's reaction would be to his current girlfriend. "She may be my best friend," Kate said. "One way or the other, you came to Alaska."

The smile again. "I was always coming to Alaska, Kate. You were just the bonus."

It didn't occur to Kate until later that one of the reasons she might have decided on her trip to Ahtna was that her cell phone worked there.

Kate slept later than usual the following morning, and got to the dining room just as Stan was about to come roust her out so he could clean the griddle between breakfast and lunch. She got her papaya, sweetened with bacon waffles and homemade maple syrup that came steaming to the table in its own gravy boat. The coffee was excellent, a dark roast that would have peeled the enamel from her teeth if it had been allowed to brew one second longer, and there was cream in the pitcher, not half-and-half. Kate cleaned her plate, ignoring the sideways glances of the only other people in the room, a couple whose off-the-REI-rack outfits screamed tourist. Kate had never seen so many zippers on one article of clothing before in her entire life. They couldn't decide what was more interesting, Kate's shiners or Mutt sitting at her side. When she got up to leave they exchanged a glance and the man cleared his throat and said, a little nervously, "Excuse me?"

"Yes?"

"Is that, uh, a wolf?"

"Only half," Kate said.

Mutt, bored, lifted her lip at him and he spilled his coffee all over the table. It seemed like a pretty good exit line so they took it.

She and Mutt made their farewells to Tony and Stan and climbed into the pickup. It was nippy inside and out. She started the engine and turned on the heater for the first time that year and cranked it up to high. She wasn't worried about gas consumption. Ahtna's prices were cheaper than anything she could get in Niniltna, even in barrels she brought in herself, and she wanted to be running on empty by the time she hit the gas station on her way out of town.

She pulled the Ahtna phone book from beneath the seat. Pete Wheeler answered his own phone. She introduced herself and he gave her directions to his office, telling her any time before noon was okay but after that he was going hunting.

Kate disconnected and craned her neck to give the sky a long, hard look. It was still gray and it still smelled like snow, but so far it was holding it in. She went to Costco and loaded up the back of the pickup with dry and canned goods and tarped it. As an afterthought to Stan's black eye prescription, she bought a fresh pineapple, which perfumed the air of the cab on the drive to the courthouse.

Jane Silver wasn't in her office. Kate backtracked to the front desk and asked for her, only to be told Jane hadn't come in that morning.

"Did she call in sick?"

The clerk shook her head. "She just didn't show up."

Kate knew a sudden, undefined chill. "Where does she live?"

The house on Quartz Street was sided with old wooden clapboards recently painted baby blue with white trim. The gray asbestos shingles looked new, too. Compared to the houses on either side, Jane's house was small, from the outside maybe a thousand square feet, with most of the lot given over to Jane's garden habit. Every square inch of dirt inside the chain-link fence that surrounded the yard was divided into square plots separated by neat, narrow paths. The raspberries were pruned to single canes, the rhubarb was cut back to the ground, the strawberries were headed and weeded, and everything was heaped high with mulch. Some kind of climbing vine covered the links of the fence, with no single identifying leaf remaining behind.

Kate looked at the house. The curtains were drawn. Jane's elderly blue Pinto sat in rusty dignity in the narrow driveway to the right of the house, about halfway up the drive. Something looked odd and she walked over to see that the driver's-side door was not fully latched. She ducked down and looked in the window to find that the dome light was still on. A beat-up black leather purse sat in the passenger seat.

Alarm bells went off in Kate's mind. The Pinto hadn't been sitting there all night with the door open or the battery would have run down. She looked at Mutt and saw her on tiptoe, nose sniffing the air, ears pricked. Mutt looked up at Kate and let out something between a growl and a whine. "Yeah," Kate said. "I know."

Kate walked up the steps and knocked on the door. "Jane? Jane, it's Kate Shugak. You there?"

There was movement inside but no answer.

"Jane?" Kate said. She put her hand on the doorknob.

Mutt barked once, a sharp, unmistakable warning.

There was a faint cry from behind the door, followed by thudding footsteps going away very fast. Mutt's ears went back and she snarled. Kate turned the knob and shoved her shoulder against the door. It was unlocked, and she stumbled into the room and nearly fell.

Jane Silver was lying on the floor of her living room, surrounded by books pulled from shelves against the wall. It was a scene so reminiscent of Kate's own awakening in Old Sam's cabin two days before that she was stunned into immobility, but for no more than a second. "Jane," she said, dropping down next to the old woman. "Jane, it's Kate Shugak. Can you hear me?"

Jane moaned. She had a fast-contusing bruise on her left cheek and a cut on her temple above it that had bled a bright red cascade down her face and into her hair. Beneath her head a red pool was spreading across the floor.

"Jane, stay with me now. I'm going to call an ambulance, we'll get you to the hospital." She fumbled in a pocket for her cell phone.

She heard a door at the back of the house crash open and more rapid footsteps coming from the backyard. She looked toward the sound, looked back down at Jane, and then looked at Mutt, who was quivering next to her, hind legs gathered in readiness, only waiting for the word.

She didn't get it.

Jane moaned, a faint, distressed sound, and Kate looked down to see the bright eyes fixed on her face. Jane's mouth opened and she tried to say something. Kate leaned down, one hand still excavating pockets in search of her damn phone, finding her pickup keys, a couple of peppermints, a quarter, lint, but still no fucking phone. "Stay with me, Jane. I'm calling for help right now."

Jane raised her hand, reaching for something, and Kate caught it in her own. There was the feeblest of tugs. "Jane, let me call someone." She shrugged out of her jacket and laid it over Jane's torso, tucking it under her chin. She stripped off

144

her T-shirt and held it against the cut on Jane's head. The white of the fabric turned pink and then red at shocking speed.

Mutt whined. That feeble tug on her hand was repeated, and Jane tried again to say something. "Can you tell me who did this, Jane?" Kate leaned down, eyes on Jane's face. "Just a name, one name, Jane, and I swear Mutt and I will find the son of a bitch who did this to you and I promise you he'll look a lot worse than you do when we're done with him."

Impossible, but Jane's mouth quirked at the corners, as if she were trying to smile. The tug again, so weak this time Kate barely felt it, but feel it she did. This time she put her ear right next to Jane's mouth. "All right, tell me, Jane, and then we'll get you an ambulance and get you to the hospital."

A word floated out on a breath of air.

"What?" Kate was trying to look for Jane's home phone without moving.

Jane's chest rose and fell. On the exhale she managed a few words, only one of which Kate could truly understand. "Paper?" Kate said. "What kind of paper?"

Jane's face twisted with effort. It was a horrible sight.

"All right, Jane," Kate said. "I heard you, I got it. Take it easy. I'm going to get you some help." She spotted Jane's phone on the floor next to an overturned end table. Keeping her T-shirt pressed against Jane's wound, she scrabbled crabwise over Jane's body and the scattered books to snatch up the phone with her free hand and dial 911. The dispatcher was blessedly matter-of-fact and efficient and it wasn't five minutes before Kate heard the wail of the siren.

But in that time Jane Silver had breathed her last.

Kenny Hazen's Blazer pulled up behind Kate's pickup. Big and beefy, he had a dark beard that wouldn't go away no matter how many times a day he shaved. He wore a khaki uniform shirt with a badge fastened over the pocket, faded jeans, and hiking boots that looked like they'd just come over the Chilkoot Pass.

He came up the sidewalk with deliberate tread. "Kate."

"Kenny." She was sitting on the top step. Mutt was pressed close to her side and she'd put her jacket back on and zipped it up to the throat, but she was still shivering.

He inspected her face for a moment. "I thought we didn't have raccoons in Alaska," he said. "My mistake."

"I really have heard them all," she said.

"What happened?"

She glanced over her shoulder at Jane's house. "As unlikely as it sounds, pretty much what

146

happened here this morning. Only I was luckier."

He seemed to sigh, and went past her and through the door. Kate remained where she was, her hand knotted in Mutt's mane, but she couldn't stop her imagination from following him.

The door opened into the living room, which encompassed the front half of the house. The bedroom was in the left-hand corner, the kitchen in the right-hand corner, and the bathroom in between. There was a pass-through between the kitchen and the living room, with a tiny dining table and two straight-backed chairs on either side of it. A second door led from the kitchen to a tiny porch and into the back garden, a heavily planted square like the front garden, surrounded by a continuation of the same chain-link fence. When Kenny looked, he'd see the same fresh set of footprints Kate had seen, big feet in heavy-soled boots in a running stride headed for the back fence.

There were three sets of freestanding shelves between the windows and against the back wall of the living room, filled with old books and old photographs in tarnished silver gilt frames and a row of dusty china dolls with their hair in Gibson Girl pompadours dressed in long skirts and leg-o'-mutton sleeves. There was an easy chair, fake brown leather on a steel frame, with a matching footstool, both looking worn and comfortable. A floor lamp with a tray table had been knocked over, and half the books on the shelves were on the floor.

Kate looked down and realized she was still carrying the handset of Jane's phone. The knees of her jeans were soaked with Jane's blood.

Kenny came back out on the porch and pulled the door closed behind him. He joined Kate and Mutt on the top step. "Well, shit," he said.

"There's blood on the corner of the shelf closest to the door," Kate said.

"I saw that."

"Her car is unlocked and the keys are in it," Kate said. "The driver's-side door isn't closed all the way. And her purse is in the passenger seat."

This wouldn't have been unusual in the Park, but Ahtna was on a major highway between Fairbanks and Anchorage. Ahtnaners kept their vehicles locked at home and at work.

They meditated in unison on the little garden that Jane had cared for with so much love and diligence. "You think she forgot something," Kenny said, "remembered it on her way to work, turned around to come get it, and surprised a burglar in the act?"

Kate nodded.

"Why are you here?" Kenny said.

The air was getting colder, not warmer with the increase in daylight. Kate shivered again. She pointed at her eyes. "I was packing up Old Sam's cabin. Somebody coldcocked me with a piece of firewood while I was reading a journal written back in 1938 by the first judge in Ahtna."

"Judge Anglebrandt?"

"You've heard of him?"

"Oh yeah." He jerked his head toward the house. "Jane volunteered at the library, led a monthly book club. I go sometimes. Once she picked a book called *The Irish R.M.* She said it was the story of Anglebrandt's first years in Alaska. Stranger in a strange land. Pretty funny."

"Jane led a discussion group at the library?"

His eyebrows raised. "Yes."

"Who else came?"

He shrugged. "Anybody who wanted to. Anyone who read for fun. The same people never come every time. Just if you were interested in the book she picked for that month. Sometimes there'd be tourists in town overnight and they'd come whether they'd read the book or not. Why?"

"I just—," Kate said, and sighed. "I didn't know. It appears I didn't know a hell of a lot about Jane Silver. Anyway. When I woke up at Old Sam's, the journal was gone."

"What was in it?"

Kate hugged her arms. "A diary of the judge's activities his first year in Ahtna."

"So you came to Ahtna to . . . what?"

"Jane Silver has—had—been the recorder for property transactions in the Park since before I was born. There's no one in state government, in

149

Ahtna anyway, with more time served. She knows—knew—where all the bodies are buried. I thought she might know what was in the judge's journal. Why someone would be willing to commit assault in the first degree to get their hands on it. Why Old Sam had it in his library."

"And?"

"She knew something." Kate's head drooped and she sighed again. "But she didn't say anything. She put the change of title paperwork through on the property Old Sam left me, and then told me to come back this morning."

"Why?"

"She said she might have something else for me to look at."

"Helpful."

"Yeah. I went to the office. She wasn't there, and she hadn't called in sick. Scared me, somehow. Figured I should check on her. Got here in time to hear whoever it was beat feet out the back door." Kate looked up at him. "This doesn't have to be related. Jim told me you've had a rash of break-ins and burglaries. But if this wasn't that, if anything I said or did—"

"Stop right there," Kenny said. "You didn't attack her. Don't blame yourself."

But she did.

Ten

PETE WHEELER'S OFFICE WAS TUCKED into the corner of a strip mall around the corner from the courthouse. It was one room and it contained one desk, one computer, and one phone, plus a continuous and contiguous series of white cardboard document boxes pushed against the walls, in two places stacked all the way to the ceiling. On the wall behind the desk was a series of framed diplomas. Bachelor of arts in justice from the University of Alaska Anchorage College of Health and Social Welfare. Master of arts in history from the University of Washington. Juris Doctor from the University of Oregon School of Law. On another wall were some framed prints, including an old Alaska Airlines poster with a grizzled sourdough bent over a mountain stream, a gold pan in his hands.

On the adjacent wall were three maps of Alaska, same size, same scale, side by side, hung in chronological order. The first was of Russian America, dated 1864, three years before it was purchased by the United States. The second was of the Territory of Alaska, dated 1915. The third was a combined topographical-political map, recent enough to get Nanwalek's name right. Above the maps were two gold pans, old ones, rusty with use, hung on either side of a crossed shovel and pickaxe, also showing evidence of being more than just decorative.

Wheeler looked up from stuffing papers into a beat-up briefcase. His eyes traveled from Kate to Mutt and then back to Kate. "Kate Shugak?"

"Yes." She stepped forward. "Sorry, I got delayed."

"Pete Wheeler. You just caught me."

He was young, balding, and pouter pigeon plump, with a round face and ears that stuck out from his head at ninety-degree angles. There was something attractive in the twinkle in his eye. "Appreciate your time," Kate said. "You wrote a will for Samuel Leviticus Dementieff of Niniltna last month."

"Yes."

It was still hard to say the words. It was doubly hard given the scene she had left on Quartz Street that morning. "He died on Saturday."

"I know, I heard," he said, closing the briefcase and setting it on the floor next to his desk. "I've heard about you, too, and"—he looked at Mutt—"she pretty much confirms your identity, but to observe the formalities, may I see some picture ID?"

She pulled out her wallet, extracted her driver's license, and passed it over. He looked from it to her face and back, and returned it. "Thank you." He eyed the blood stains on her knees, but when she didn't say anything he sat down, folding his hands on the belly that strained the buttons of his blue button-down shirt, and regarded her with a professionally sympathetic eye. "He told me you'd be here."

"I beg your pardon?"

He waved her to a chair. "When he came in to sign his will, what was that, two, three weeks ago? He said when he kicked off—his words, Ms. Shugak—to expect you on my doorstep shortly thereafter."

Kate sat down, Mutt taking up station on her left. "He didn't—did he say he felt like he was about to die?"

"Guy was nearly ninety, and even a damn well preserved ninety is still ninety," Wheeler said.

There was a little arrangement of rocks in a miniature gold pan on Wheeler's desk. Kate focused her attention on them so she wouldn't have to see the understanding in his eyes. "He never said—he never talked about it. Dying."

"I only met him three times, Ms. Shugak, but he struck me as someone who lived very much in the now."

They weren't rocks. They were gold nuggets, ranging in size from a pencil eraser to a quarter. "True."

She looked up to see Wheeler smiling at her, revealing a charming pair of deep dimples. "Like I said, I only met him three times, but it's pretty easy to see a man like that would have hated being ill."

"He could have been a quadriplegic and you couldn't have forced him through the doors of a hospital," Kate said. "He hated hospitals even more than he hated doctors."

"I got that impression when I suggested he sign a DNR. He was very, ah, colorful and pretty adamant about not falling into the hands of the medical profession, whatever his condition." Wheeler glanced at the clock on the wall. "So you found his copy of the will."

"I did."

"He left a note for you."

"I know, I've got it, although it's more like a letter. Five pages telling me what to do with his stuff."

He shook his head. "Not that one. The one he told me to give you when you came in."

"What note?" Kate said. To be fair, it was barely past noon and it had already been a very long day.

He reached into a drawer and pulled out a nine-by-twelve manila envelope. There was a notary seal and signature over the flap. "To Pete Wheeler, shyster, Ahtna," Old Sam had written across the front. "After I die, when Kate Shugak, my executor and chief beneficiary, comes to your office, give her this. Samuel Leviticus Dementieff," followed by the same date on his will.

It was signed by Old Sam, all right, but it was the notary's signature that made her feel as if the room were beginning to revolve around her. "Jane Silver notarized this?"

"Yeah. Old Sam had her stop by my office that day. She witnessed the will, too."

Kate pulled out her copy of the will and for the first time looked at the last page. There it was, the same name in the same hand next to the same seal. She said the first thing that came into her head. "Didn't those used to be embossed?"

"Now they're peel-and-stick. Or ink stamps."

Kate looked down at the envelope. Was this the paper Jane had meant? But if so, why hadn't she said "letter"? And why alert Kate to it when she knew it would be put in Kate's hands? She looked up. "Do you know what it says?"

He shook his head. "He wrote it himself, he sealed it himself, and then he handed it over to Jane so she could seal it in front of both of us. Your eyes only, he said." He looked at the clock again, and got to his feet.

She rose with him, and on impulse said, "The homestead he left me?"

"Yeah?" he said, shrugging into his jacket.

"The Parks Service might think it's theirs."

His eyebrows went up. "They'd be wrong about that. I cleared the title before your uncle signed the will."

"You did?"

"Of course," he said, a little stiffly.

"Did he show you the original documents?"

155

"Of course."

"Do you still have them?" His eyebrows drew together, and she said, "Because I can't find them. He kept everything else in a file box"—she hoped—"but not those."

"Really," he said. "How very odd."

"I talked to Jane Silver yesterday, and she arranged for the names to be changed on the title deed and in the tax records, and she said there shouldn't be any problem, but if the Parks Service wants to argue about it . . ."

He grinned. "Am I available? Sure. They won't, though. Their lawyers don't like spending money on cases they can't win."

Kate thought of Dan's set expression and wasn't so sure.

Wheeler looked at the clock again and came out from behind his desk. "Sorry, Ms. Shugak, but if I don't leave now I'm going to be late, and I really don't want to be late today."

The door to his office opened and the reason why stepped inside. Wheeler's face lit up. "Babe. You didn't have to walk over."

"I spend all my time sitting. I can use the exercise."

They didn't embrace but they might as well have for all the heavy lifting the vibe was doing.

Sabine Rafferty was one of the new pilots George Perry had hired to cope with all the extra work the Suulutaq Mine had brought into the

Park. She was a little older than Kate, with streaked brown hair and artfully applied makeup. She wore a brown bomber jacket lined with sheepskin over a cream-colored turtleneck and a pair of jeans. It should have been jodhpurs to complete the Amelia Earhart ensemble. Her figure was excellent and her clothes fit as if they'd been tailored to the purpose. "Sabine," Kate said.

"Hello, Kate," Sabine said all eyes for Wheeler.

Just for the hell of it Kate said, "So, you're going hunting?"

"Hmm? Hunting? Oh. Yeah, I spotted a smallish herd wandering around Blowout Creek on my way back from Anchorage yesterday. Ready?" she said to Wheeler.

"Oh yeah," he said wholeheartedly. "Ms. Shugak? If you have any questions, don't hesitate to ask, but right now I hear a caribou calling my name."

Kate thought he was hearing a little more than that but she and Mutt took the door held open as a hint.

Back in the pickup, she watched Rafferty and Wheeler move quickly down the street and around the corner, heading for the Ahtna airport. Or his house, whichever came first. She looked at the sky. Still low, still thick, still a dark gray, still holding back on the snow, but she could almost feel the kiss of the first flake of a four-foot drift on her cheek. She didn't think Sabine would be going anywhere in the air for a while. But then she didn't think it was what either she or Wheeler had had in mind.

The *Ahtna Adit* had been publishing weekly since 1910, when it was started by George Washington Gunn, a stampeder who had come north in 1898 and stayed. He married locally and had a son, John Adams Gunn, who had also stayed, married locally, and had his own son, Benjamin Franklin Gunn.

The newspaper had begun life as a broadsheet, mostly merchant ads that paid for stories about goings-on in the Park and the territory that would have had its owner up for libel in the local courts, if there had been any local courts around at the time. Grandfather, father, and son had succeeded to the concurrently held posts of publisher, editor, and chief correspondent over the years, until five years before Benjamin Franklin Gunn had yielded to the blandishments of a communications conglomerate from California that made a hobby out of snapping up local Alaska newspapers and radio and television stations. Now they were all run out of a single building in Anchorage with a sales manager to market ad space and a small pool of reporters to generate copy, so that the same story ran the same week on the front page of the *Ahtna Adit* as on the *Bering Beat* and the

Newenham Seiner. The only consistently local news and the first item anyone turned to was Cops and Courts, a compilation of local arrest reports from state and local police and a list of arraignments, trials, and judgments from the clerk of the Ahtna court.

The good news was that Ben had been able to pay off his mortgage and send his own son, Alexander Hamilton Gunn, to college. His new overlords had kept him on at a decent salary in the rare event that anything of statewide interest happened in the Park so he could cover it for the news bureau back in town. Either lucky or foresighted for them, because the Suulutaq Mine certainly qualified as a story of statewide and possibly even global interest, and he'd been in and out of Niniltna on a monthly basis ever since Global Harvest had announced their discovery.

The *Adit*'s local office was in another strip mall on another street corner about a mile down the road. Kate parked next to a large white pickup with the chassis jacked up over snow tires large enough to rumble over a decent sized butte without pausing for breath, and went in. There was a counter between the door and a couple of desks and rows of rickety shelving holding up stacks of yellowing issues. Ben sat at one of the desks, typing at a keyboard, staring into a monitor with a bad-tempered expression. As she closed the door behind her he said "Shit!" with great feeling. He put his finger on the delete key and held it down.

"Want me to go back out and come in again?" she said.

He looked up. "Oh, hi, Kate." He let up on the delete key.

"Work not going well?"

He looked back at the monitor and made a disgusted sound. "Writing copy and writing fiction are two very different things, I'm finding out."

Kate thought of all the things she could have said to a journalist about what appeared in his newspaper. Instead she said, "Fiction?"

He looked a little embarrassed. "Yeah, well, I'm trying my hand at a novel."

"You're kidding." Again she refrained from the obvious comment. "What about?"

"Based on my grandfather's life. You know. Klondike stampeder to frontier journalist to delegate to the state constitutional convention. Sort of a look at that fifty years of Alaska history through one person's lifetime."

"Sounds interesting."

"Not the way I'm writing it," he said, glaring at the monitor again.

She looked at the books stacked on the desk, some open, some closed, all of them festooned with yellow sticky notes. "Research?"

He gave a gloomy nod. "I swear to god, I don't

think anyone's ever come to Alaska without writing a book about it. Hell, I think half of them come with that intention." He nudged one stack of books, which teetered alarmingly. "Granddad kept a journal, too, but at least he had the sense not to publish it."

"Maybe you should just write his biography."

He shook his head. "Nobody'd believe the truth. The Wild West had nothing on the Frozen North, Kate, believe me. Soapy Smith was an amateur compared to some of the crooks that operated around here, taking the miners for everything they could get. Christ, if even a fraction of Granddad's stories are true, half the gold they took out of Alaska during those years was stolen before it ever got to the assayer's office. And a lot of the time people had been murdered for it."

"Make for a fun read, I would think," she said, and wished Old Sam had kept a journal. The letter Wheeler had given her, which she had yet to open, felt heavy in the inside breast pocket of her jacket.

"It is that. When you can read it. Granddad had the world's worst penmanship." He grinned at her. "What can I do for you, Kate? Oh." He sat up and looked at her, eyebrows raised. "Come to give me that interview I keep asking you for? The Niniltna Native Association Chief Speaks?"

"I'm not the chief," Kate said.

"Near as," he said. "Well?"

"No." Kate looked down at her hands, which

had folded themselves on the counter. "Can you help me write an obituary?"

His grin faded. "Old Sam?"

"Yes."

He got up and held open the swinging half door at the end of the counter. "Have a seat."

She settled into a chair next to his desk. She talked, he typed. It took a full hour because Kate kept remembering more stuff, and when they were done he sent it to print and sat back in his chair. "Had one hell of a life," he said. "I didn't know he was Chief Lev's grandson. That's back a ways." He counted on his fingers, and whistled. "Damn, going on a century now."

"You know about Chief Lev?"

"Granddad knew him. There was some stuff about the chief and his tribe early in the journals. A lot of crap went down during and after the Spanish flu epidemic. Lev and his wife both died in it." He frowned. "There was something about the potlatch—"

"Your grandfather wrote about the Natives in this area?" Ben nodded. "I wouldn't mind reading that myself."

"Sure, anytime. Like I said, though, you sort of have to decipher it as you go along."

"Sounds like something to do on a dark winter night."

"Yeah, with a hundred-fifty-watt bulb and a magnifying glass." He leaned forward to pull Old

Sam's obituary out of the printer tray. "I'm guessing you want copies."

"A thousand," she said. At his look she said, "Potlatch in January. All the people who come will want their own copies so they can tell me everything I got wrong."

He laughed. "Mail them to Niniltna when they're done?"

"Yeah."

"You want it in the paper, too?"

She nodded.

"Hate to have to tell you this, but we charge to print obituaries nowadays."

"I figured. How much?" When he told her she only blanched and dug out the fistful of cash she'd gotten from the bank when she hit town yesterday afternoon.

"You want to run it statewide?"

She hesitated. The *Ahtna Adit* was a local paper. Old Sam had been very much a local guy. So far as she knew, the farthest he'd ever been from home was the Aleutians in World War II. Still, he'd been well known statewide in the Native community. He'd taken over Emaa's seat on the board, serving in the capacity of resident old fart without fear or favor. He had leavened more than one board meeting with an acid commentary that had flayed the skin off any board member unwise enough to float a plan Old Sam considered to be either too expensive to implement or just plain silly on the face of it. She smiled at the memory, and winced a little, too, because she had not been exempt.

Old Sam had been the Greek chorus of the NNA board. Who could fill those shoes?

She sat up with a jolt. Oh god, no.

She saw by Ben's expression that she'd said the words out loud. "Sorry. Thinking about something else." His journalist's nose gave an inquisitive twitch, and she said, "How much to run his obituary statewide, in all of your newspapers, one time?"

More money exchanged hands. Ben busied himself logging on so he could distribute Old Sam's obituary to the other newspapers via e-mail, while she sat and thought with increasing dread about who would take Old Sam's place on the board. How could she have forgotten the empty seat he'd left behind until this moment?

The waters the NNA board sailed could get pretty choppy, especially with Ulanie Anahonak ready to fire the first shot in a Park culture war on one side, and Harvey Meganack on the other ready to sign off on anything anybody wanted to dig up or cut down or fish out in the Park. Old Sam had been her sheet anchor on the board, ready to cut the argument from beneath the feet of whichever board member he considered to be behaving foolishly, selfishly, or greedily. The perfect mixture of sarcasm and common sense, along with the rock-ribbed fearlessness to say what he thought when he thought it, added to the already considerable gravitas of having more time served in the Park than anyone else around the table.

Old Sam had sat on her left hand. Auntie Joy sat on her right. In neither word nor deed had either ever betrayed a prior relationship other than that of cousins. He'd cut Auntie Joy no slack over her motion to charge for berry picking on Native lands in the Park at the last board meeting, either. There had certainly been nothing of the lover or even ex-lover about him that day.

Come to that, how close cousins were they? First cousins, or third cousins once removed? It might have something to do with why their relationship, if a relationship there had been, had gone south. "When did your grandfather die?" she said.

He looked up from the keyboard, surprised. "Granddad? Ah, October 1945. He made it through the war. He waited until Dad got home from the Aleutians. He died two days later, I think it was."

October 1945. The same month Old Sam's homestead claim had been affirmed. Kate couldn't see what the connection might be, if any. A lot of veterans coming home at the same time. "Your dad was in the Aleutians?"

Ben nodded. "Castner's Cutthroats. Same as

Old Sam. You know the kind Castner was looking for. The Aleutians in wartime weren't for sissies." He shuddered. "Ever read up on the Battle of Attu? Two weeks of some of the bloodiest fighting of the whole war, including Europe and the South Pacific. When you look at the casualty rate as a percentage of troops involved, the Battle of Attu rates second only to Iwo Jima. And that's just the Americans. When it was over, there were only twenty-eight Japanese taken prisoner, none of them officers. Six hundred Japanese troops committed suicide at once by exploding their own grenades against their chests."

"Old Sam never talked about it."

"Neither did Dad. I learned most of what I know about their war the way we all did."

Kate gave a rueful nod. "Garfield's *The Thousand-Mile War*. Who ran the paper while your dad was gone?"

"Mom and Granddad. Mom would write any stories that came in the door and Granddad ran the press. Never missed an issue. Even if it was mostly rip-and-read." He saw Kate's look and elaborated. "Cut and paste from the wires, like the Associated Press and Reuters. But hell, Granddad said all anybody wanted to read back then was war news, and that's about all there was on the wires."

On impulse Kate said, "Did your father ever talk about meeting Dashiell Hammett in the Aleutians?"

"Dashiell Hammett?"

Ben raised an eyebrow, and Kate supposed it was something of a stretch for a segue. "The guy who wrote *The Maltese Falcon*."

"I know who wrote *The Maltese Falcon*, Kate. He also wrote *The Thin Man*."

"Yeah, well—"

"Also *Red Harvest*, *The Dain Curse*, *The Glass Key*—"

"Yeah, okay, Ben—"

"And a bunch of short stories about the Continental Op under various titles, my favorite of which is 'The Creeping Siamese.' His CO in the Aleutians was a big fan and made him the editor of the camp newspaper. The *Adakian* was said to be the best written and the best edited newspaper in the army."

Kate waited a moment before saying, "Are you done?"

"Not even." He was still a little miffed. "Why do you ask if Dad met Hammett?"

"Jane Silver was telling me yesterday that Old Sam met him." And Tony at the Ahtna Lodge, and who knew who else before she was done winding up Old Sam's affairs.

Ben frowned. "Old Sam met Hammett, did he?"

"That's what Jane said. When they were both in the Aleutians." She paused. "Did your dad say anything about meeting him?"

167

He shook his head. "Not a peep. I'll have to rod on over to the courthouse, interview Jane myself."

"Jane Silver is dead," she said.

He stared at her. "You're kidding me."

"No. She died at her house this morning." The blood on the knees of her jeans had dried to a mud-brown.

"I . . . I didn't know," he said, and Kate thought she saw his eyes tear up. But then he cleared his throat and straightened his shoulders. "No surprise, I guess. She was six hundred years old. I guess I'd better work up another obit."

Kate opened her mouth, and closed it again. Kenny Hazen would not thank her for spreading his business around town.

But he had seen. "What aren't you telling me, Kate?"

She stood up. "Thanks for your help with the obituary. It reads a lot better than if I'd written it."

"Kate?"

She opened the door and without turning around, "It's Chief Hazen's business now, Ben. Talk to him."

Mutt got to her feet and shook herself vigorously. She looked at Kate as if to say, Can we just go home now?

At least they were once again safely across the Lost Chance Creek bridge before the snow hit. When it did hit, it hit fast and it hit hard. One minute there was a low-hanging, dour gray sky, the next a nearly impenetrable curtain of giant fat white flakes so thick Kate had a hard time seeing the fluorescent road markers, which in her opinion were spaced too far apart on the side of the road. She slowed down, way down, picking her way from one marker to the next at twenty miles an hour. Another vehicle passed them, with the speed of its passage pulling up a cloud of snow behind it so thick that Kate had to slam on the brakes because for a few minutes she saw nothing but white. The engine stalled and the pickup bucked and skidded, the back end coming around a little until the freight in the back reminded the rear wheels it was there and stopped the slide. Mutt lost her purchase on her seat and did a kind of scrambling slam against the dash, letting out a very un-Mutt-like squeal. She righted herself and gave Kate a reproachful look.

"Sorry, girl," Kate said. She took a deep breath and let it out, and managed to unclamp her hands from the painful grip they had on the steering wheel. "What idiot passes in a whiteout?"

Mutt growled.

"With any luck we'll find them in a ditch and you can teach them some manners." The engine came back to life at a single turn of the key and Kate started down the road again, one marker at a time, as slowly as possible without stalling out. The pineapple tucked behind her seat gave off a tropical scent, incongruous in the present circumstances. The windows were starting to fog up, so she cranked the fan to high, and hit the on button on the CD player, which held the CD Johnny had most recently burned for her. Jimmy Buffett advised her to take another road to a higher place. Or was it hiding place? Either would have been preferable in her present circumstances. Still, she was on her way home, always a good thing, and she raised her voice in a rough-edged sing-along.

Mutt put up with it, and with John Hiatt belting out "Child of the Wild Blue Yonder," but when Tommy Tucker showed up in high-heeled sneakers she couldn't stand it. Her head came up and she started to howl along.

Kate started laughing and couldn't stop, and they crept along, laughing and howling and blaring music down the road through the blizzard, one marker at a time. Each marker was seventy-eight inches high, made of white recycled plastic pressed into a single slender curve, the top twelve inches coated with super-high-intensity retroreflective sheeting, a blindingly bright yellow in color. Their official name was Standard Traffic Delineator. Kate knew this because at her instigation the Niniltna Native Association had bought them and, further, had hired this year's senior class of Niniltna High School to install them on the Niniltna-Ahtna road in late August.

Never had money been better spent. She whiled away a few miles by imagining the letter she would write to the state Department of Transportation. Just because the state didn't maintain this road didn't mean people didn't drive on it.

Even when they shouldn't.

Michelle Branch, "Sweet Misery." Kate could relate, although "stay with me a little while" was a little too close to the target, especially when she was going home to a house that didn't contain Jim Chopin.

"So what?" she said out loud, irritated. If she had dared she would have used the skip button, but she was too scared to take her eyes off the road. Or the markers, because her headlights illuminated about three feet into a swirling cloud of white and that was it. The yellow tops of the markers were all she could see. She was amazed she could see that much. The pickup lurched a little. Great, now the wind was picking up, which meant the snow would begin to drift. She looked at the odometer. Another twenty-five miles to go. Crap.

The windshield wipers beat back and forth in time to the music. Marc Cohn, "Walking in Memphis." She'd never been to Memphis. She'd only ever been to Quantico, Virginia, for the FBI course, and Arizona and New Mexico on that vacation with Jack. Alaska was big enough. So various, so beautiful, so new. Who said that? Matthew Arnold, right. Typical dreary Brit. She'd take Robert Frost any day. Cranky as he could be, the old bastard still had a sense of humor. "At present I'd rather be living in Vermont, too," she said out loud.

Next to her Mutt stirred but made no reply. She was as tense as Kate, strung like bow, staring through the windshield as if by sheer force of will she could see through the whiteout to clear road on the other side.

"If anybody can do it, you can, girl," Kate said.

Almost in response to her remark the snow eased for one fleeting moment to reveal two enormous cottonwoods on either side of the road, with immense ridged trunks and limbs like lightning bolts, before the snow closed in again.

The Two Towers, a mile up from Deadman's Curve, a bitch of a curve where the road from Ahtna met and married the old railroad grade that ran from Kanuyaq to Cordova. She slowed down to a crawl.

John Hiatt again. "Drive South." She was trying. Southeast, anyway. And she was with the one she loved. "Right?" she said to Mutt.

It wasn't like she could be mad at Jim for leaving. His father had died. Of course he had to go. Although from the phone call it didn't sound as if he was enjoying himself. His mother must be a serious piece of work. Still, he had one, living.

Maybe she'd mellow while he was there. Maybe she'd invite Sylvia Hernandez over for dinner.

Easy, Barenaked Ladies. "I've been burned before . . ."

"No kidding," Kate said.

But Jack had never burned her. Not once.

Neither had Jim.

Not yet.

She kept waiting for him to, watching, knowing it was just a matter of time. The man was a dog, had been one long before she'd come along, would be one again when he moved on.

Thing was, he showed no signs of moving on. Unless you counted getting on a plane for California.

"God damn it," she said out loud, spacing out the words with deliberation. "I've got other things to worry about than Jim Chopin. Who clobbered me? Who stole the judge's journal? What was in it they wanted? Did Jane Silver surprise a random burglar in the act and he knocked her over on his way out the door? Or did she die because of what she wanted to show me? Something she had about Old Sam, and the same person who walloped me walloped her?"

Bo Diddley. "Up your house and gone again."

She checked the odometer. Deadman's Curve coming up. She slowed down to ten miles an hour. The markers moved to the left. She followed them carefully.

Mutt sat up and barked, once, sharply.

"What?" Kate said.

Headlights, suddenly, right in front of them.

"What the—Get out of the way!"

The headlights were exactly at the height of her eyes, and they were so bright she could feel her eyeballs blister. She flinched and realized she couldn't look away because the headlights were on the same side of the road. She laid on the horn and the brakes simultaneously.

The headlights kept coming. The brakes locked up and the back end of the pickup started coming around. It was an older model, no anti-lock brakes, and she turned into the skid and pumped them.

The headlights kept coming. In the very few seconds she had left to think about it, she tried frantically to remember what was on which side of the road. A ditch? A meadow? A steep slope ending in a creek? Trees? Boulders?

The headlights kept coming, and in the end she yanked the steering wheel to the left and hit the gas, hoping to pull the ass end of the pickup around, try for a controlled skid that would swing the pickup onto the other side of the road facing in the opposite direction, anything to get out of the way of the oncoming vehicle.

She almost did it. The Chevy's bed swung hard right, pivoting around the weight of the engine in front, so that they were facing back the way they had come.

That helped, too, when the other vehicle hit them going at what later estimates put at thirty miles an hour. It didn't sound fast after the fact.

It felt like it, though, and it was more than enough to jolt the right front tire off the road, where the ditch caught it and flipped the pickup.

The last thing she remembered was reaching for the ignition and turning it off.

They landed upside down and the lights went out.

May 1943

Long before Pearl Harbor, even longer before the Japanese invasion of the Aleutians, General Simon Bolivar Buckner Jr. sent out the call for men schooled in the Alaskan Bush and skilled in survival to form a combat platoon to do reconnaissance and find landing zones for amphibious assaults on Japanese emplacements in the Aleutians. They were hunters and trappers, miners and engineers, doctors and anthropologists, whites, Aleuts, Eskimos, Indians. They were lightly armed with their own choice of weapon, and Colonel Castner went easy on the military discipline, which included saluting and shaving.

Sam Dementieff signed up as soon as the unit was formed. He was twenty-one years old, a keen eye with a rifle, a steady hand with a knife, and a seemingly inexhaustible store of energy. He took everything Castner threw at them in training, accepted all the inevitable ragging and practical jokes from his older and more experienced brethren, Quicksilver, Aleut Pete, and Haystack, and came back for more. In the fullness of time and in recognition of his talent and abilities he was awarded his own nickname, Old Sam, in recognition of his relative youth.

It didn't have to make sense. This was war.

On May 11, 1943, he was one of those hung by his heels over the side of a landing craft so he could help feel the way ashore through dense fog and perilous shoals to land on Beach Red, the first day of the Battle of Attu.

The Japanese had the heights, and they'd had plenty of time to dig in. The Americans got lost in the fog and stuck in the mud and developed frostbite from the cold temperatures. It took twenty-four hours for their first meal to arrive, and all the while the enemy troops pounded at them with artillery fire. Five hundred forty-nine Americans and 2,351 Japanese lost their lives in nineteen days.

Sam was among those who stayed on for the mop-up that followed, flushing Japanese soldiers out of the hills. One of them nearly shot him, would have if his buddy Mac the Knife hadn't spotted the sniper and tackled Old Sam to the ground. The bullet missed him and hit Mac in the hip. Tore him up pretty good, and Old Sam toted Mac out of the hills on his back and got him on a destroyer bound for Adak and the 179th Station Hospital.

A month later Sam finagled a ride on a C-47 to Adak to see how Mac was getting on, and found his bed in the ward surrounded by a bevy of nurses dressed in olive drab. His leg was in a cast and elevated but it didn't seem to be slowing him down much.

Mac looked up from his bed and saw Sam in the doorway. "Hey, buddy! Ladies, meet my partner, Old Sam."

"Old Sam?" one of the nurses said with a skeptical look. Sam had been unable to grow the trademark Scout beard.

Mac grinned. "Skinny bastard's old enough to know better but too young to die."

He held out a hand and the nurses scattered when Sam came forward and took the hand and a seat next to Mac's bed. "Guess I don't have to ask how you're doing."

Mac laughed. "Aw hell, boy, I'm fine. They're going to let me up pretty soon so I can start learning how to walk again. They say when I'm mobile enough they'll ship me to a vet hospital Outside, put the expert mechanics to work on me. You?"

"Looks like some of us will be riding out the rest of the war right here," Sam said. "You coming back after?"

"Who else'd have me?" Mac laughed, and then coughed.

Sam didn't like the look of him. Mac had lost a lot of weight, and there was an unhealthy flush to his cheeks. "Did you do anything in particular in civilian life?" Sam took care to be as nonspecific as possible. It wasn't good manners to ask an Alaskan about his past, and in spite of the instant rapport the two men had felt when they met in boot, it still made Sam a little nervous to ask the direct question.

But Mac was good-natured about it, shrugging a shoulder. "Fishing, hunting, a little prospecting. Did some longshoring in Juneau and Kodiak. Did some lumberjacking in Ketchikan. Why?"

Sam leaned his hands on his knees and met Mac's eyes. "Haven't heard you mention a lot in the way of family, or a home. You need a place to go when this is over, I got one."

Mac raised his eyebrows. He was a tall man, almost as tall as Sam, with lighter hair, blue eyes, and a killer smile that explained the nurse contingent. He'd been very cagey about his age around the other Scouts, but he was one of those people upon whom the years sat lightly, and he could have been anywhere from thirty to fifty, although Sam did notice that recent events had deepened the lines in his face. "Where is this place?"

"North and east of Cordova, on the Kanuyaq River. Little town called Niniltna. It's about four miles from the Kanuyaq Copper Mine."

There was a moment of silence. Sam dropped his eyes. He didn't want to see the gratitude, if gratitude there was.

Mac stirred, and Sam looked up to see that Mac had linked his hands behind his head and was staring at the ceiling. "Thought I'd heard the Kanuyaq closed down."

"It did. But there's plenty to eat walking around on four feet, and a man can stake a homestead in five years, as much as a hundred and sixty acres. Look." Sam dug out his wallet. "I've got pictures."

Mac accepted the wallet and flipped through the black-and-white pictures in silence. He came to one of a couple, the woman a Native, the man also a Native, with something added to the mix. He looked at it for a long time, his expression unreadable. "Your parents?" he said at last.

Sam nodded. "They live in Cordova. I'll be claiming a homestead east of Niniltna." He smiled to himself. "I've already filed on the spot. Here." He took his wallet and flipped to another picture. It was a girl, another Native, plump and round-cheeked, dark of hair and eye. She ducked her head, as if she was shy, and looked at the camera from the corners of her eyes, but her beaming smile was impossible to hide.

"Your girl?"

Sam nodded. "We're going to get married when the war's over." He looked down at the photo, and then, aware of Mac's eye on him, closed the wallet and stuck it back in his pants. "When it's over," he said, "write to me care of general delivery in Ahtna. I'll meet you there, get you started off right. There's a pretty decent living to be made there if a man isn't afraid to work."

"Sounds good," Mac said.

Sam was about to extend his hand to seal the deal when a gaunt soldier walked up to stand on the other side of the bed.

"Sergeant Hammett, as I live and breathe, you're back again," Mac said. "You're as bad as the nurses, you just can't stay away from me."

"What can I say, Mac, you're one of the best bullshitters on the base. I'm just naturally drawn to you."

Hammett was as tall as the both of them, with hair cut close on the sides and a sprouting mess of white turkey feathers on top. Heavy pouches beneath the eyes and a thick white mustache provided the only stopping places in a long face with cavernous cheekbones. He wore round glasses perched on a thin blade of a nose, and carried a notebook.

"Pop, this is Old Sam Dementieff, my buddy. Sam, this is the editor of the camp newspaper, so be careful what you say around him."

Hammett looked at Sam and raised an eyebrow. "Old Sam?"

"It's just a nickname," Sam said, a little testily.

Hammett looked at him a little longer, and then turned to look at Mac a little longer than that. "You brothers?"

"Not hardly." Sam was looking at Mac when he said it. Mac was looking at Hammett, and his eyes carried a clear warning.

After a moment Hammett said, "Had a few more questions I wanted to ask for my piece on the mop-up."

Mac rolled his eyes, but Sam could feel his relief. He got to his feet. "I gotta get going; I got a pilot talked into a ride back to my unit. You know flyboys and how they don't like to be kept waiting. Mac."

Mac took Sam's hand in a painful grip. "Sam."

"Thanks, Mac," Sam said. He looked at the leg encased in plaster, suspended with ropes and weights and pulleys. "Thanks a lot."

Mac shrugged. "You saved my ass on that friggin' mountain a couple of times, way I remember it. Call it even."

He let Sam's hand go, finally. Sam walked down the ward and paused for a look back, and saw Hammett and Mac both watching him. He raised his hand in half wave, half salute, and left.

Sam got back to his unit in time to board a ship bound for the navy base on Kodiak Island. He spent the rest of the war there, the tedium of camp life broken by occasional reconnaissance missions to the outer islands, but the Japanese had left before the invasion of Kiska and they didn't come back. The Lend-Lease route for hop-scotching war materiel across Alaska to Russia was safe.

Six months after the Battle of Attu Sam got word that Joyce had married Davy Moonin. He'd known of her parents' opposition to himself, but it was still a very heavy blow. For the next year he did his duty in a robotic funk, until the end of 1944, when he heard that Davy had died and that Joyce was now a young widow. He began to be very anxious for the war to be over.

The bomb fell on Hiroshima in August 1945 and the war in the Pacific was over. He was demobbed in September and he went straight home, by boat to Valdez, by thumb and on foot to Ahtna.

He'd been writing to Mac once a month, although the writing did not come easily to him. Mac's replies were infrequent and seldom more than a few sentences scribbled on the back of a postcard.

Mac wasn't in Ahtna when he got there, but he hadn't really expected him to be.

There was a package waiting for him at the post office. The return address was in an unfamiliar hand. He opened it up and found

184

another box, securely taped, along with Sam's last four letters to Mac.

The accompanying note read, "Private McCullough died of tuberculosis just before being shipped stateside. He asked me to forward this to you when you got in touch."

It was signed Sgt. D. Hammett.

Eleven

HER FIRST REALIZATION WAS THAT SHE was upside down. Her second was that she was cold. Very cold.

She blinked, recognized the cab of the pickup. She was hanging from the seat belt, and her first instinct was to fumble with the catch to open it. "No," she said out loud, "don't do that."

The sound of her own voice reassured her. Something was still working.

She looked at the dashboard. The engine was off. That was a good thing. She sniffed the air. No gasoline smell. Good again. She squeezed her hands, moved her feet, stretched her spine as much as she was able. The rest of her seemed to be working, too. The good news kept on coming. Although she had a sore spot on the back of her head, where she presumed her skull had come into brief, violent contact with the back window. "My week for running my head into firewood and car windows," she said.

Although this was good news, too, in a backassward kind of way. Hitting the back of her head this time meant she shouldn't get another set of shiners. Maybe.

She listened. There was nothing to hear but the wind. The windshield, cracked but still intact, was buried in snow. The driver's-side window was, another miracle, also still intact. She turned her head to look right.

The passenger window was gone. So was Mutt. Not a good thing.

She braced one hand against the roof of the cab, released the seat belt with the other, and dropped down in a sort of controlled tumble. Her knee knocked against something prickly, and she felt around until she found it. The pineapple.

She noticed that her hands felt almost numb with cold. Now that she thought about it, her feet weren't much warmer. Also not a good thing. She reached up to fumble with both hands behind the seat for her emergency kit, which included a flat white metal box twelve by eighteen inches, and her parka. She eeled into her parka and opened the latches on the box.

Taped to the inside of the top was a book light. She clipped the light to one of the visors and turned it on.

She found the hand warmers and stuffed one each into the mittens in the parka's right hand pocket. She put her back to the open window and removed her boots to stick toe warmers to the bottoms of her socks. She pulled the boots back on, zipped up her parka, and pulled on the mittens. Blessed warmth began to seep into her extremities.

She was aware enough to realize she was light-headed, and that there had to be more aches and pains that would begin to register the moment she stopped moving. She knew enough to stay with the truck, but some reconnaissance was a must. Even if she could have gotten one of the doors open she wouldn't have dared for fear she wouldn't be able to get it closed again. Snow was already drifting in through the broken window. She squeezed through it, parka and all, and stood up to get a snootful of snow courtesy of the wind that was blowing fiercely and horizontally over the ground.

She circled the pickup, right hand maintaining contact with the truck bed, leaning into the wind, the snow stinging her face. It was wheels up; no possibility of righting it without a come-along. The tarp over the supplies in the back was bellied out into the snow, but so far as she could tell her knots had held on the lines tying it down. There was a Swiss Army knife with a can opener on it in the parka's left pocket, another one in the glove compartment, a third in the emergency kit. She wouldn't starve.

She pulled off a glove and laid a hand on the engine. It was cold, which meant she'd been out for a while. Maybe not, in this wind. She didn't have a watch, and with the engine off so was the clock on the truck's dash. She tried to remember when sunrise was this time of year. Seven? Seven thirty?

"Mutt? Mutt!" She circled the truck again,

calling. "Mutt! Come here, girl!" There was no response. Two steps away and she couldn't see the book light through the cab windows. Three steps away and she couldn't see the truck. She didn't dare go any farther than that.

She wriggled back inside the cab and took further inventory. There was a moth-eaten olive drab army blanket she hadn't remembered putting there beneath the seat, and there was a roll of duct tape in the emergency kit. She took the blanket and the tape outside and rigged a cover for the broken window. She crawled back inside and invented a whole new language for popping the bench seat loose so she wouldn't have to sit on the metal roof all night.

It did come loose, finally, in a shower of candy wrappers and loose screws and bits of gravel she'd tracked into the cab. She beat it clean, pulled the sleeping bag that was the last item of her emergency kit free of its stuff bag, unzipped it, tossed in a couple of the hand warmers, and crawled inside, boots, gloves, parka, and all. It hadn't been out of the stuff bag in years and it smelled pretty musty, but so far as she could tell the only livestock in it was her.

She wasn't hungry but she forced herself to eat one of the power bars in the emergency kit, and washed it down with some water. The water was starting to get a little slushy inside its plastic bottle so she put it inside the sleeping bag with her.

She didn't know how long the book light's battery would last and she didn't know how long the storm was going to last, either, so she turned the light off. She checked the blanket. The weight of snow drifting outside was pushing it into the open space left by the broken window but it was big enough that it should hold.

She pulled the hood of the parka over her head and zipped up the sleeping bag as far as it would go and lay there and listened to the wind howl and the trees creak ominously in the gale. She cursed herself for leaving Ahtna when it should have been obvious to any near idiot that a storm was about to hit. When images of Mutt hurt and helpless out there somewhere in that maelstrom threatened to take over, she forced herself to think of something else.

She wondered what the temperature was in LA.

The memorial at the church had been everything that was dignified and restrained. The graveside service was brief and decorous. Afterward, Jim and his mother were driven in a black stretch limousine to the reception at the club, where the driver, appropriately subdued, deposited them at the front door, where another appropriately subdued functionary whisked them inside.

The room was large, with a wall of windows overlooking the first hole of the golf course in the foreground and the Pacific Ocean in the background. The bar had a line in front of it and one wall was taken up by a banquet table laden with food. Jim stood at the door, watching his mother move slowly across the room, black-silk-clad spine straight, perfectly coiffed head erect, shaking hands, accepting condolences, offering a cool cheek for those brave enough to offer her affection. If you could call it that.

She looked like a one-woman fashion plate right out of the AARP magazine, chic, elegant, and fashionable. To be fair, everyone in attendance was similarly attired, the women in subdued colors with discreet necklines, the men in suits with silk ties in muted patterns, everything fitting in a way you just knew was personally tailored and designed on the most recent dicta from *Vogue* and *GQ*.

He snorted beneath his breath. The only fashion season Jim recognized was when Kate switched from jeans in summer to lined jeans in winter. Mostly all he cared about were the buttons, a fashion statement he'd always liked better than zippers. Zippers were over so fast. With buttons you could take your time.

He stopped looking at clothes and looked at faces instead. It took a while to find them in the crowd, but there were a few people who looked familiar in a twenty-years-ago sort of way. Before approaching them he decided he required some liquid courage and got in line at the bar. The conversations he overheard were exactly what he expected.

"It's such a shame. He wasn't that old." This from a Methuselah who looked a hundred if he was a day.

"I didn't even know he was ill. Did you?" His companion, a woman who had given up on her figure, was heaping her plate high with shrimp.

"Beverly would never have told anyone anything *about any*thing. She's pretty reserved."

"Is that what you'd call it?" A woman his mother's age who was even thinner and better put together sounded like a cat and looked as if she'd meant to. "I've always thought of her as an iceberg, myself."

"A fine-looking woman," said the man standing next to her. "He owned the building his law firm occupies, did you say? Even in this market, that'll fetch a nice chunk of change."

"She won't need it, his broker told a friend of my sister's that James left behind a very healthy portfolio."

"Really." Jim could almost hear the calculator clicking between Methuselah's ears. "Haven't I heard something about a son?"

Jim and his mother had been early to the church and Jim, quailing at the thought of being polite to that many people and more than a little upset by all the stories about his father he'd never heard being told by people he'd never met, had delayed walking out until almost everyone was gone. His mother had not introduced him to anyone, and few people who'd seen him knew him for who he was. It was a blessing in keeping himself below the radar.

Not so much standing in line for a beer.

They had it on tap, a nice crisp lager, and just looking at it in its tall, frosty glass made him feel a little better. From the corner of his eye he could see his mother looking his way, an unmistakable command in her eye. He took himself off to the terrace.

The breeze was warm and balmy and only faintly tainted by the layer of car exhaust hanging heavily over the greater Los Angeles area. You never smelled car exhaust in the Park unless you'd duct-taped yourself to the rear bumper of somebody's Ford F-150.

He wondered what the temperature was in Niniltna.

"Hey."

He turned. It took him a minute, not because he didn't recognize her but because he couldn't believe she was there. "Sylvia?"

She smiled. "Here come the Mounties, somebody hide."

"Sylvia," he said, and it was the most natural thing in the world to step forward and sweep her up into a bear hug.

She emerged from it laughing and a little

flushed. "Long time no see, Chopin. How the hell are you?"

He inspected her from the top of her head to the tips of her toes. She was five seven and a hundred and thirty-five pounds that was mostly muscle, clad today in a short black dress with a scoop neck and three-quarter-length sleeves. She wore modest gold hoops and a thin gold chain with a cross on it, and her heels weren't so high she couldn't run in them if she had to. She was tanned, there were laugh lines at the corners of her bright brown eyes, and her hair was an artfully tousled cap of rich dark brown streaked with highlights that looked natural. But then everyone in LA had great hair. Great hair and great teeth. There was probably a law for that, too. "Looking good, Hernandez."

"Backatcha, Chopin." Her smile faded. "I'm sorry about your dad."

"Yeah." He let her go. "Me, too." He looked through the glass door and saw an older man dressed in a hand-tailored three-piece suit—one of his father's partners? Henderson? Harrigan? Haverman, that was it—take one of his mother's hands in both of his and bend over it in what was nearly a bow. Jim looked back at Sylvia. "She didn't even tell me he was sick."

She grimaced but she didn't say anything. Sylvia Hernandez knew everything she needed to know about Beverly Chopin. "How are you otherwise?" She smiled again. "How's life up in the frozen north?"

"Good," he said. "Better than, even."

"Still with the troopers?"

"Yeah. Sergeant now, with my own post."

She raised an eyebrow. "On the fast track?"

He shuddered. "No way, no how. They keep trying to promote me. I keep resisting."

"Tell me about the post."

He described Niniltna and the Park, cutting himself short when he became aware of the unconscious longing in his voice. "How about you?"

"Like father, like daughter. County sheriff. Detective division."

He raised an eyebrow. "Homicide?"

She shook her head. "Major crimes."

"Impressive."

"Well, I don't fly to work in my own airplane," she said.

He grinned. "How's your dad?"

"Good. Retired. Him and Mom moved up to Shasta. Took a woodworking class and now everybody gets whatnot shelves for Christmas."

He laughed. "I bet they're good shelves."

"Yeah, well." Sylvia's smile was sly. "Okay, I'll ask first. You married?"

"No." For a moment he hesitated, thinking of how to describe his relationship with Kate. Hell, he couldn't even describe Kate out of her Alaska context, nobody'd believe it, especially no one in sunny, ultra-civilized southern California. "There is someone, though. And you?"

"Was."

"Ah. It was his fault, of course. Is he still living?"

She laughed. "So far as I know. He moved away. Most of the men in my life do."

"Yeah, well." His smile matched her own in slyness. "You could do a better job of picking 'em."

She punched his arm with her free hand, hard enough to be felt.

"Police brutality," he said.

"James."

They turned to see his mother standing in the doorway. Jim tried not to look as guilty as he felt at laughing out loud at his own father's memorial reception. And then he got pissed off that his mother would dare to condemn his behavior anywhere, at any time. His jaw set, and he met her glacial stare for glacial stare.

Beverly was first to look away. "I'm glad you could come, Sylvia. My husband always spoke fondly of you."

That was the first Jim had heard of it.

"Thank you for inviting me, Mrs. Chopin," Sylvia said.

Beverly had invited Sylvia to the reception? Jim felt the earth move beneath his feet, and it wasn't the San Andreas fault.

His mother looked at him. "There are some people who would like to renew their acquaintance with you, James."

Jim downed the rest of his beer. "Later?" he said to Sylvia.

She toasted him with her wine. "Later."

Twelve

THE SNOW STARTED IN NINILTNA JUST as school let out.

"You could stay the night again," Van said. "You know Annie won't mind." A slight, slender girl with glossy brown hair, creamy skin, and wide-set brown eyes, she stood next to him just outside the main door of the school, her face upturned to catch the first flakes on her cheeks.

Who could not have kissed her in that moment? So he did, to a chorus of jeers and cheers from everyone in seventh through twelfth grades erupting out of the doors behind them. He raised his head and grinned down at her. "I know she wouldn't, but Kate will be back from Ahtna by now. I want to make sure she's okay. But I'll give you a ride home." The privacy of the cab of his pickup, even for a brief time, was an alluring prospect.

They started to walk toward it. "Is she pretty shook up over Old Sam?"

"I think so." A gust of wind enveloped them in

a swirl of snow. "He's about the last Park rat of his generation, if you don't count the aunties, and they were pretty close."

"How were they related, exactly?"

"I think he was her great-uncle, or maybe her great-great-uncle."

Van worked this out. "He was her grandmother's uncle?"

"Or maybe her grandmother's brother? I don't know, I never asked. Annie probably knows."

"Annie won't tell." He looked at her and she said, "Haven't you ever noticed? None of the aunties will talk about family in front of the children. Even their own."

He hunched his shoulders against another gust of wind. "Doesn't matter how or if they were related by blood. Her father died when she was pretty young. I think Old Sam kind of stepped into the role. He sounded like her dad every time he yelled at her, that's for sure."

They climbed into his pickup and spent the next fifteen minutes in an exchange of mutual admiration, before Van pulled back and said, "Okay, that's enough for now."

His heart was pounding in his ears and he was breathing as fast as she was, but he let her move to the other side of the seat. It took him a minute to remember where the ignition was. He turned the key and looked at her before putting the engine in gear. "No pressure, Van. When you're ready."

She nodded, her hair falling forward to hide her expression.

And sure as hell not in the front seat of his pickup, he thought, and spent the too-short drive to Annie Mike's wondering where.

He got home to find the house dark. The snow was piling up fast, and he parked the pickup between the old outhouse and the shop, where he knew from experience there was at least some shelter from drifting. He checked to make sure the snow shovel was next to the door, kicked the snow from his boots, and went inside.

Mindful of the cost of fuel, instead of turning up the thermostat he started a fire in the fireplace, although he veered immediately from the path of rectitude afterward, assembling the ingredients for an enormous sandwich, piling the very small portion of the plate that remained high with potato chips, putting *Transporter 3* on the television, and cranking the volume on the remote as far up as it would go. An empty house was not to be wasted.

He woke up when the credits were rolling to peer out the door at the foot of snow that had accumulated on the deck and the stairs. Kate, whose weather sense he knew to be pretty acute, was most likely sitting out the storm in Ahtna. "Probably eating one of Stan's steak sandwiches right now," he said to the storm, and had to close the door hastily before any more snow blew inside the house.

If Kate had been home, she would have nagged him to do his homework and he would have bitched and moaned and whined and complained before allowing himself to be forced to the books. He didn't feel like it would be fair to take advantage of her absence, so he settled down at the dining room table with a martyred sigh he was sorry no one was there to hear. Could have been worse, could have been civics. It was history, American history from 1900 to the present day, with the new teacher, Mr. Tyler, who was kinda cool. He wasn't much taller than Kate and he wasn't much older than his students, and he crackled with energy in the classroom. Every class period was a performance. Nobody ever dozed off in one of Mr. Tyler's classes.

His list of required reading was interesting, too. It was mostly novels, one a week, and some of them really old novels, too, like *The Great Gatsby*, *All the King's Men*, *The Heart Is a Lonely Hunter*, *Native Son*. Right now they were reading *The Magnificent Ambersons*, although there was a rumor that somebody had made a movie out of it, albeit in black-and-white, which Jessica Totemoff was said to have put on her Netflix queue.

They were supposed to write a one-page report on every book, identifying things that happened in the book with events that had happened in real life. There was a timeline of events in their lone textbook. Mr. Tyler had already been discovered to be a stickler for spelling and grammar—at the beginning of the semester he'd threatened to fail anyone who screwed up *lay* and *lie*—so Johnny found Kate's copy of *The Elements of Style* on the shelves in the living room and set to work.

An hour later he had a paper that wasn't too bad. The book hadn't been that hard to take, either—surprising since it was almost older than Niniltna. He looked at the copyright page of his paperback edition. Nineteen eighteen. Two years older than Old Sam. He wondered if Old Sam had read the book. Would have been interesting to have asked him what he'd thought of it.

He put the book down and thought about that tough, stringy old man who had hounded him from bow to stern of the *Freya* his first summer on board. Pitching fish, swabbing decks, scrubbing pots—Old Sam kept him moving every moment he wasn't actually asleep, and he rolled him out of his bunk pretty early every morning. He'd never dared complain.

He smiled. The first time Old Sam had let him take delivery on his own was one of the proudest moments of his life. He could remember the details of his first boat as if he'd caught the bow line yesterday, Hank Carlson on the *Annie C.*, eleven kings and a hundred seventeen reds with an average weight of seven-point-nine pounds.

He looked at the Model 70 in the gun rack. There was another proud moment. Old Sam wouldn't have left his pride and joy to Johnny if he hadn't thought Johnny could and would take care of it. Then and there, he made a vow to himself that he would never use it without cleaning it immediately afterward. And that he would do his best to shoot straight and clean, to wait for the shot, never to be in so much of a hurry that he would shame himself or his weapon by not taking the time to zero in on the heart or the lung.

Johnny was going to miss the hell out of the old man, and at the same time he was excited at the thought of getting his first moose with his new classic rifle. He thought Old Sam would have understood.

He looked at the clock. It was half past ten, and he stood up, stretching and yawning.

At that precise moment the door opened, spilling a drift of snow onto the floor and Mutt into the room with it.

"Mutt!" he said. "Where's Kate?" He went to the door and peered out. "Kate? Kate!" He grabbed the flashlight next to the door and shined it around the clearing. He couldn't see anything so he postholed through the snow to the edge of the deck. "Kate!"

Still nothing—no pickup looming against the

drifts, no headlights gleaming through the dark and the blowing snow. He went back inside. "Mutt, where's Kate?"

Mutt whined, and for the first time he noticed the shape she was in. Her feet were clumps of ice and she looked tired. In his life, in her life, he'd never seen Mutt look tired. He got a towel and got down on his knees to clean her feet. When he was done she went to the door, looking over her shoulder at him, yellow eyes wide and urgent.

"Kate's in trouble?" Johnny said.

Mutt whined louder at the sound of Kate's name.

"Shit," Johnny said, and stood where he was, towel dangling from one hand.

Kate must have gone off the road in the pickup somewhere between here and Ahtna. She must have been hurt or Mutt would never have taken off, to come here, to get help.

Mutt would lead him back to Kate.

He looked at Mutt, her yellow eyes wide and anxious, her whining devolving into an impatient and demanding yip. He looked out the windows. Through the driving snow he could see the railing at the edge of the deck, barely. "We can't go out in this, girl; we'll just get lost ourselves," he said. "We have to wait till morning, see if the storm blows out by then."

Something in the tone of his voice told her they weren't going anywhere just yet and she didn't like it. Her lips peeled back from her teeth and she growled at him.

He reacted as instinctively as she had. "Knock that crap off," he said, raising his voice.

To the surprise of both, she did.

He went down on his knee and put his arm around Mutt's neck. "We'll leave at first light, Mutt," he said, hoping she would hear from his tone that they would be doing something as soon as it was safe to. "We'll take the snowgo and the trailer. You'll take me right to her, I know."

He half coaxed, half bullied her over to the crumpled quilt in front of the fireplace, and built up the fire that he had meant to let die down. He found some moose in the freezer and nuked it and chopped it up and fed it to her, along with a large bowl of water, which she virtually inhaled. She had barely enough energy after that to paw the quilt into an acceptable heap, go around three times in a circle, and flop down. Sixty seconds later she was snoring.

Johnny forced himself to his own bed, knowing the chance of finding Kate was a lot less if he wasn't rested. On the way to his room he paused to look at the thermometer fastened outside the window. Twenty-seven degrees. He remembered the winter survival kit Kate had insisted he carry in his pickup—food, bottled water, a parka, a sleeping bag, a knife—and knew she had one just as well-equipped with her. So long as she was conscious enough to make use of it.

His night was restless, and Mutt shouldered through his door to whine in his face at first light. The wind had stopped and the snow had eased off. The sky wasn't clear but it didn't look anywhere near as dark and threatening as it had the day before. The temperature was down a degree.

Mutt was whining, nosing at the small of his back, trying to drag him to the door first by the hem and then by the seat of his sweats. Although he wanted to be on the road as badly as she did, he refused to let her rush him. He ate a large breakfast, made another one for Mutt, made some instant soup and put it in a thermos, donned bibs, parka and Sorels, got the snowgo out of the garage and checked the gas and oil, hitched up the trailer, checked that the emergency kit for the snowgo had all the necessary items, stowed a spare can of gas on the trailer. He lashed and tarped everything down and then went for the Model 70, which he loaded. He snicked on the safety and stowed it in the scabbard on the snowgo.

He frowned at the rig, at all the supplies he'd packed into it. He had to be thinking for both him and Kate. Was he missing anything? That one vital piece of equipment that could mean the difference between life and death? They had serviced the snowgos together the previous week;

he had to trust that they'd done the job well enough to get him where he needed to go and back again.

"All right, girl," he said, and climbed on the seat. The engine started at a touch, Mutt leapt up behind him, her nose over his shoulder, and they set out down the trail. Once on the road he followed the fluorescent yellow road markers, keeping his speed at forty miles an hour, knowing Mutt would hurl herself headlong from the seat as soon as they were near Kate and not wanting to be going too fast when she did so. He would far rather Kate be hurt herself than have to answer to her for getting Mutt hurt finding her.

There was no other traffic and no sign that there had been any. In spite of his worry and the urgency of the situation he was almost enjoying himself—a capable, fully equipped man on a rescue mission, alone in the middle of a wilderness with only himself to rely on. He could almost hear the *William Tell Overture* playing in the background.

He slowed down for Deadman's Curve, twenty-four miles from the homestead, a lethal-looking turn even when its edgy grade was softened by snow.

Mutt barked once, sharply, right next to his face.

He winced and took his thumb off the gas. "Okay." He slowed down almost to a stop, but Mutt had dropped off long before then and was loping out ahead of him, her enormous feet skimming the surface of the snow. He followed her, around the curve and then off the road through a thicket of alders that showered him with more snow as he pushed through. There he found a snow-covered mound. Mutt was pawing at it with urgent whines.

The snow had done such an effective job of camouflage that he did not at once recognize an upside-down pickup truck. "Jesus fucking Christ," he said, and his hands went slack and the snowgo stopped with an abruptness that nearly pitched him over the windshield. She'd flipped her truck. There were a couple of horrible, dragging seconds when all the ways she could have been hurt, unconscious, incapable of securing herself against the storm, flashed through his mind. She could have died of exposure while he was asleep in his bed.

Then, before he could vault from the snowgo and join Mutt in her efforts at excavation, the snow heaved. For one heart-stopping moment he wondered if his eyes had deceived him, if this wasn't her truck, if Mutt had led him instead to a bear den. In the next, a parka-clad Kate had crawled from behind what looked like a snow-encrusted army blanket, to be immediately knocked on her back. She landed soft in the new-fallen snow and Mutt planted both feet on her chest and laved her with an enthusiastic tongue.

Kate was laughing, trying to hold her off. "I'm okay, girl. I'm all right. Mutt! Knock it off!"

She got to her feet, sinking to her knees, and pushed the hood of her parka back from her head, a smile on a face that looked unsurpassingly beautiful to him, in spite of the twin shiners that had now faded from royal purple to a bilious green. "Heard you coming," she said. "What took you so long?"

He killed the engine, which gave him a second to gulp back unmanly tears. Until this moment he hadn't realized how frightened he'd been. "Yeah, well, you know. Didn't want you to think I was worried or anything." He assessed her fitness with a critical gaze, and saw the blood on the knees of her jeans. Unlike Gunn, he recognized it for what it was. "Jesus, Kate, what's that? Are you hurt?"

Her smile faded. "Not my blood. I got another lump on my head is all. I was out for a while. When I woke up Mutt was gone. I crawled out to look for her but it was snowing so hard I couldn't see my hand in front of my face, so I figured I'd better stick with the truck and hope she'd gone for help." She looked down at Mutt, whose tongue was lolling out of the side of her mouth in a big doggy grin, whose tail was wagging hard enough to stir up a small flurry from the snow in back of her. "Yeah, yeah, I owe you. Again." She dropped to one knee to give Mutt a rough hug. "My girl. Sunshine on a cloudy day."

"You banged your head?" he said. "Are you seeing double or anything?"

"It's sore, but I think I'm okay. I even slept some."

"I brought hot soup." An out-of-context aroma reached his nostrils. His brows came together and he sniffed the air. "What's that smell?"

She laughed again into Mutt's gray fur, and looked up at him.

"Pineapple."

"Pineapple," he said.

"Yeah," she said, "Stan says it cures black eyes."

He stared at her.

"Papaya, too," she said.

"Okay," Johnny said. "What the hell happened in Ahtna?"

"Later," she said. "Let's clean up what we can here while we've still got daylight." She looked at the southern horizon, an ominous and encroaching dark. "And while the weather's on our side. There's more storm coming."

Thirteen

JOHNNY TOOK KATE BACK TO GET HER own snowgo and a jack and the two of them spent what was left of the daylight ferrying the supplies from the back of the pickup to the homestead. The last trailer full was safely under cover by nightfall. Kate and Johnny and Mutt trooped up the stairs and into the house. Kate kept going straight up to her room, shedding boots, parka, and clothes as she went. "You're up for dinner. I'm taking a bath."

"Be happy to cook," he yelled after her. "Thanks for asking."

Content, he shed his own outer gear, hung it and hers where it wouldn't drip melting snow all over the floor, and set to work on fried Spam and eggs and hash browns and toast. "Pineapple," he said to himself. "Huh." Maybe they'd have it for dessert.

Water gurgled in the pipes as he built a fire in the fireplace, and he was putting laden plates on the table when she came downstairs again, flushed and damp, attired in navy blue sweats with the UAF nanook across the chest and blue and gold stripes running down legs that ended in feet encased in thick wool socks.

"I love you," she said, and fell to.

He sent her to the couch afterward, a mug of hot, sweet cocoa in hand, while he cleared the table and did the dishes. Then he joined her in the living room. "Okay. What the hell happened?"

"I got run off the road."

He looked stern, a neat trick on a seventeen-year-old face. His height had long since outstripped his weight, making him a gangling six-footer, all knuckles and knees and bony shoulders. His brown hair was as thick as his father's had been and much more carefully tended. His blue eyes were wide and clear and a little older than they should have been, in an iron-jawed, eagle-beaked face full of irregular features that worked together to form a heartbreaking reminder of his parentage.

He'd lost his father too young, had been abandoned by a mother who had conceived him in the first place primarily as a lever against his father, and had survived a hitchhike from Arizona to Alaska at the age of twelve that still frightened the living hell out of Kate every time she thought about it. Particularly when she remembered who had followed him home.

But he was safe now, and he was here, and his experiences had matured him in a way his years had yet to do. He was intelligent and courageous, with a sense of the ridiculous that on occasion out-distanced her own, and a practical view of life worthy of a man twice his age.

Johnny was a gift, the last gift his father had given her before he died, but it wasn't the only reason to treasure him, or even the most important one. Johnny was himself the gift, more precious even than Jack's act in giving him to her. That had not always been true. She wasn't a mommy, as she had once told Jack. But Johnny had grown from an obligation, a responsibility, a debt of honor to be paid in full, to an essential part of her life. She would resist most strenuously any attempt to remove him from her sphere of influence.

Fortunately, his mother was no longer a problem. Kate smiled at her cocoa. She looked up to see him watching her from the other end of the couch, one quizzical eyebrow raised. "What the hell happened?" he said again.

A clear, fresh eye on current events would be most useful. The truth, the whole truth, and nothing but the truth, then. "I got run off the road."

"So you said. Did you see who did it?"

She shook her head. "The storm had reached whiteout conditions and it happened so fast."

He leaned forward, intent. "What happened, exactly?"

"We were coming up on Deadman's Curve, where you found me." Her hand dropped for a brief moment on Mutt's head. "I saw the Towers and I knew the curve was coming up. I don't think I was doing twenty, maybe not even fifteen. Probably what saved us. All of a sudden, there were oncoming headlights on my side of the road. Yes, my headlights were on, and I laid on the horn, but they kept coming. And they were coming fast."

"No way to recognize the vehicle?"

She shook her head again. "It was big, at least a full-size pickup. It was pushing a lot of snow in front of it. If I had to guess, I'd say it was a dark color. Blue, maybe black." She thought about it, and added, "And something tells me a newer model. The shape of the cab, maybe. But I can't be sure about either. The snow was just too thick."

"Okay, you don't know who it was," he said. "Who do you think it was?"

"I don't know," she said, her mouth pulling into such a grim line it made him nervous. "Any more than I know who it was who walloped me upside the head at Old Sam's cabin. Let me run it down out loud, okay? All of it, even the stuff you know."

He was sitting on the floor, his legs stretched out, feet just touching Mutt's back. The fire crackled. He drained his mug and said, "Okay, go."

"Old Sam dies." Kate spoke for twenty minutes, keeping the story chronological and her opinions to a minimum.

Once Johnny said, "I been thinking how I shouldn't have taken that job at the mine. That I should have gone ahead and deckhanded for him like usual."

"You think I haven't?" she said. "That's six, eight more weeks I didn't have with him, and I can never get them back. But you know he'd tear a strip off us both for saying so, so let it go." She paused, and added, "Try to, anyway."

Another time he said, "Why? They must have

214

clobbered you because they wanted the journal and they could see you through the open door, standing there, reading it. So why trash the cabin? What else were they looking for?"

She stared at him for a moment. "You are not just another pretty face," she said.

His smile was smug.

"I would have gotten there."

His smile got smugger.

When she spoke of Jane, his forehead wrinkled. "Really old ugly woman, short, looked like a spawned-out humpy?"

She had to laugh. "That's her. She was in fact at least as old as Old Sam, if not older, and I'm pretty sure she knew where even more of the bodies are buried in the Park than Old Sam, Emaa, and the aunties put together. She was in a position to follow the money." She paused. "I think she might also have been a good-time girl at the Ahtna fancy house, which would surely have put her on the receiving end of all the best stories."

His jaw dropped. "Fishface was a hooker?"

She gave him a reproving look. "You malign some of the founding mothers of the state of Alaska with your slander, sir." She grinned. "Including one of my own ancestors."

Later, he said, "Did you send Mutt after him? The guy you heard running out the back of Jane's house?"

"No." That came out with more force than she had meant it to. She saw his look, and moderated her tone. "No, I didn't. Jane . . . Jane was dying. I didn't have time for anything but talking to her and trying to find my goddamn cell phone so I could call 911."

He opened his mouth, looked at Mutt snoozing on her quilt, and changed whatever he had been about to say to "What did she mean? When she said 'paper'?"

"I don't know. She was the lands officer for the Park. I'm guessing a title, a deed, some kind of document that had something to do with Old Sam. She knew him. I'm starting to think she knew him pretty well."

"Did you find it? The paper?"

"She had a wall full of books, too, most of it Alaskana. We got there before all of them had been tossed on the floor."

"Just like at Old Sam's."

"Yes."

"Any old journals?"

"Yes."

"Any written by this judge, this—"

"Judge Albert Arthur Anglebrandt."

He looked slightly stunned for a moment, and then rallied. "Any written by him?"

"No." And then she said, "Oh. Oh for dumb."

"What?"

"I just remembered." She got up and crossed to

where he'd hung her jacket. "I can't believe I forgot."

"What?"

From the inside pocket she produced a creased manila envelope. "The lawyer gave me this. Said Old Sam gave it to him when he updated his will a couple of weeks ago. Said to give it to me when I came in."

"You didn't open it right away? What, are you nuts?"

"Whatever it was I knew it wouldn't help me beat the snow home. Figured I'd wait." The envelope lay in her hands.

"Well?" Johnny gave an impatient wriggle. "Go on, open it."

She turned the envelope in her hands. "I thought the letter he wrote with his will was the last time I'd hear from him." She looked up with a rueful smile. "As usual, the old fart surprised me. Turns out this the last thing he'll ever say to me. I guess the truth is I wanted to wait as long as possible before I read it."

"You've been assaulted twice in three days," he said, with elaborate sarcasm. "You could have been killed both times. Not to mention Mutt."

Mutt heard her name and raised her head to give a concurring yip.

"Whatever it is," Johnny said, "he didn't want to say it to you until he died." To make sure she understood, he added, "He didn't want you to know it until after he was dead. It has to be important, Kate. Open it!"

She acknowledged his point with a faint sigh, and slid her finger beneath the flap of the manila envelope. Inside was a single sheet of paper with three words in handwriting that matched that on the outside of the envelope.

Find my father.

That was all. Old Sam hadn't even bothered to sign it.

She stood there staring at it until Johnny said, "What? What! What'd he say?"

She handed him the letter and went to sit down on the couch. "Damned if I know."

He read it, frowning, and then he read it again. He looked up and said, "Who was his father?"

"His name was Quinto Dementieff."

"What kind of a name is Quinto?"

"Filipino. His grandmother was from the Philippines. A bunch of them came over to work cheap in the salmon canneries around the turn of the last century, and some of them stuck."

"What happened to him? To Quinto?"

"I'm trying to remember. He worked in Cordova, if I remember right. Long shoring? On the Blue Canoes? I'd have to ask. One of the aunties will know."

"What's the mystery about him?"

She looked at him. "I don't have a clue. So far as I know Old Sam's parents were pretty ordinary people. They lived in Cordova. I think Old Sam was born in Cordova."

"Yeah, okay, so Old Sam's father is dead, right?"

"Of course."

"Explain to me how you're supposed to find somebody who's dead?"

She looked back at Old Sam's letter. Still said the same thing. *Find my father.* "I don't know. Maybe I'm supposed to find his grave?" She remembered another grave hundreds of miles north, and the carved round of wood that had answered questions she'd had about her own family. Was this something similar?

He took the letter from her hand and read it again. It hadn't changed since the last time he looked at it, so he handed it back. "I don't get it."

"Neither do I."

"Why does he want us to find his father?"

"I don't know."

"Why'd he have to be so cryptic?"

Johnny was starting to sound a little annoyed. That was okay because Kate was starting to feel a little annoyed. "I don't know."

She got up and found Old Sam's file box and looked through it again. "No birth certificates here for either one of his parents, but that's not surprising. There were hardly any doctors in Alaska back then. Oh."

"What?"

She extracted a piece of paper, thick and yellowing, inscribed with fancy lettering. "It's their marriage certificate."

He looked over her should. "April 1919." He saw her frown. "What now?"

"There was a rumor . . ." Her voice trailed off as she stared into the distance. Mutt, who had followed her from the couch to the coatrack and back again, rested her chin on Kate's knee.

He waited until he couldn't wait any longer. "A rumor? What kind of rumor? About who?"

"That maybe Quinto wasn't Old Sam's father."

Johnny blinked. "Wow. Really?" He thought about it. "Back then that would be kind of a big deal, wouldn't it?"

She shook her head. "You have no idea, and you don't even know why. Quinto was half Filipino, back when non-Natives were flooding into the Territory. A lot of them were adventurers, boomers, mostly men with an eye for the main chance, looking to grab up anything anybody didn't move out of reach first."

"So—who was Old Sam's mom?"

"Elizaveta Kookesh." Kate leaned back against the couch and closed her eyes briefly. "That was probably what pissed off people most. She was a chief's daughter." She thought back to the conversation with Ben in the *Ahtna Adit* office, and thought again how much she'd like to read his father's journals.

"Wow." Johnny, as white as you get without bleach but from extensive and intensive propinquity fully alive to the hierarchy of Alaska Native life, was properly impressed. "So it'd be twice as bad for her to marry outside the tribe."

"It would."

"How bad?"

"Not tar and feathers bad," she said. She paused. "I don't think. But they could have made things pretty uncomfortable for her." She snapped her fingers and pointed at him. "That's why Old Sam was born in Cordova. He's even got a birth certificate." She dove back into the file box and emerged with it in hand. "See?"

He looked at it. "I see." He pointed. "See what I mean?"

"He was born in September," she said.

"And they were married in April."

"Doesn't prove anything," she said. "Lots of couples jump the gun, even back then."

"Still, pretty obvious she had to get married," he said. "Mr. Tyler's making us read a bunch of old books for American history. Being a bastard was a big deal back then."

"Say 'illegitimate' instead," Kate said.

"Why?"

" 'Bastard' is harsh. It's turned into a swear word."

"I've heard you call people bastards."

"I prefer son of a bitch."

"Whatever. The point is Elizaveta might not have cared if the guy she married was the father of her baby or not."

She looked at Old Sam's birth certificate. The father's name stood out in bold black ink. Quinto Sergei Dementieff. "I wonder if he knew."

"Old Sam or Quinto?"

"Quinto. Old Sam must have known, at least that he'd been conceived out of wedlock. He had the certificates, and he could read as well as we can."

"Did Old Sam have any brothers or sisters?"

Kate shook her head.

"So his father got a son out of the deal. He might not have cared." Johnny shrugged. "I mean, Old Sam didn't act like he had a chip on his shoulder, like he'd been raised by a stepfather who hated his guts. He ever mention his father to you?"

"A few times."

"Who's the guy in the rumor?"

"What? Oh." Kate shook her head. "I only ever heard a nickname. I walked into Auntie Vi's one day and all the aunties were sitting around the table. They didn't hear me at the door and they were talking about Old Sam. I heard them mention Chief Lev's daughter and some guy. They used a nickname. Kick the Bucket?" She shook her head. "Doesn't sound right, but it was something like that."

"You could ask them."

She snorted. "Yeah, I could. If they'd tell me is another story."

"I thought they told you everything."

"Oh, they tell me everything, all right," Kate said. "They tell me how to run the Association, they tell me to sort out this screwed-up adolescent and that messed-up family, they tell me to move into Niniltna—"

"What?"

"—they tell me I should get a Native boyfriend—"

"What!"

"—but they're mum on the family history. I think there's a lot that wouldn't stand up to close scrutiny." She paused, thinking again of the Dawson Darling. "Well, that they think wouldn't. Old scandals aren't old to the elders; to them they happened just the day before." She thought about the expression on Auntie Joy's face the last time Kate had been in Niniltna. "Or maybe even that morning." She wasn't going to tell Johnny about Old Sam and Auntie Joy, not yet. For one thing, she didn't know the story, not for sure. For another thing, it wasn't her story, and one of its characters was still living.

"What are you going to do next?"

She yawned suddenly. "Go to bed."

He caught her yawn and returned it with interest. "What time is it?"

"Time to go to bed." She put the certificates back in the file box, Mutt padding behind her. Kate would not be sleeping alone tonight, no matter where Jim was.

"Hey," Johnny said, "have you heard from Jim?"

"Yeah. I talked to him on the phone from Ahtna, I guess night before last?"

"He okay?"

"As okay as you can be when you've just lost your father." *And it sounds like you have the mother from hell.*

"You just lost yours," he said. "How are you?"

She met his eyes, and they were both horrified when tears welled up in hers. She blinked furiously and had to try twice before she could say anything in a recognizable voice. "I miss him. I always will."

"Me, too," he said.

She gave a lopsided smile. "I know." She started up the stairs. "I'm wrecked. Time for bed."

"Yeah," he said, a huge yawn breaking across his face. "Hey, Kate?"

She looked over her shoulder at him. "What?"

"You know you're going to have to give me a note excusing my absence from school today."

She grinned. "I believe I can do that."

She looked tired, but her shiners had faded from

neon to pastel, and her grin was still recognizable as a bona fide Kate Shugak grin, wide and joyous and evil, ready, willing, and able to take a bite out of the absurdities of life.

A lot like Old Sam's grin, in fact.

It was an oddly comforting realization to take to bed with him.

After all, Old Sam had been well nigh indestructible for most of his time on earth.

Fourteen

IT SNOWED ANOTHER FOOT OVERNIGHT. They put Johnny's pickup in the garage and ran their snowgos into town the next morning, waving when they split at the Y, Johnny to go to school, Kate to run down to Demetri Totemoff's place. Demetri had a come-along on his pickup, and if Kate was lucky he would already have changed from his summer tires to his Wile E. Coyote tires.

His Wile E. Coyote tires, so named by Kate the first time she'd seen them, raised the body of Demetri's pickup a good four feet off the ground. He left them low on air, and combined with a V-8 300-horsepower engine they could accomplish most of the heavy lifting that was necessary during a Park winter.

Like traveling sixty miles over three feet of new snow without getting stuck, and pulling her pickup right side up without putting on the parking break.

His wife, Auntie Edna's eldest daughter, also Edna, answered the door. When she saw who it was the expression on her face only enhanced her resemblance to her mother. Kate wondered if Demetri ever looked at Auntie Edna and saw what was coming his way in twenty years. Kate liked him, so she hoped not.

She gave Edna a pleasant smile. "Hi, Edna. Is Demetri home?"

Edna hesitated just long enough to be rude.

Mutt, standing next to Kate, lifted her lip.

Edna's expression didn't change but she fell back a step and gestured Kate inside out of the cold. "I'll get him."

She did not, Kate noticed, offer anyone on two legs or four feet food or beverage, but Demetri appeared a moment later in his stocking feet, a burly, big-chested man of medium height. He was in his mid-fifties, with dark Aleut eyes and dark Aleut hair and high flat Aleut cheekbones clad in Aleut skin, which like Kate's still held a golden cast from the previous summer's work. In his case this was guiding Outside hunters and fishers to wall mounts. His luxury lodge in the Quilaks was a single-destination resort for big spenders from as far away as Germany and Japan. They flew into Anchorage in their private jets and were whisked directly from there to the lodge via floatplane. In years past Kate had done some work for him, acting as an assistant guide, mostly as insurance so none of his clients would shoot themselves in the foot or set a Vibrax spinner in a friend's eye.

She hadn't done any guiding in four years, she thought. Not since Jack's death.

There was a wary look in Demetri's eyes that would puzzle her later, but she didn't have time to worry about it now. She explained and the wary look vanished. "Sure, no problem, put the tundra tires on last week," he said, and raised his voice as he grabbed for the parka hanging next to the door and stepped into his Sorels. "Edna, I'm going to help Kate get her pickup out of a ditch. Be back in a couple of hours."

It took more like four, but Demetri's truck lived up to its reputation. Kate's pickup was flipped right side up about as fast as it had turned turtle, if with less velocity, and the come-along had it on the snow-covered roadbed shortly thereafter. Demetri helped Kate replace the seat.

She grinned at him. "Here's the acid test." She climbed in, brushed off the ice that had collected on the keys, which were still in the ignition, and turned.

The engine ground a couple of times and then it caught. Kate whooped and thumped the crumpled roof. Demetri stepped back, and Mutt made a neat leap through the broken window, landing on the army blanket Kate had tossed inside.

"Let me put the tow rope on you now," he said. "Easier on me if you get stuck on the way."

She didn't get stuck until the turnoff to her house, and the Wile E. Coyote tires make quick work of that. Once in the clearing Demetri helped get the truck into the garage next to Johnny's. There they'd stay until the snow was packed down on the road, and if this was one of those winters where there was so much of it the snow never did pack down, the trucks would stay in the garage until breakup.

"Man," Demetri said, staring at the once jaunty red pickup, now with a smashed-in roof on top of all the other injuries Kate had inflicted over the years. "That's just pitiful."

"It runs," Kate said cheerfully, and closed the garage doors. "Coffee?"

Again that oddly wary look flashed in his eyes, and again was gone before she could put a name to it. "Sure."

Mutt had disappeared into the undergrowth, probably making a beeline for the Arctic hare pantry across the creek. Demetri followed Kate up the steps and into the house. She put the kettle on. "Sandwich?"

"Sure."

She pulled out a jar of ground cooked moose meat, mixed it with chopped onion and sweet pickle and mayonnaise, and served it on bread with a thick wedge of lettuce. The result was some four inches high. They were done the same time as the coffee and she carried it all to the dining table. For a while there was silence as they ate and drank, and when they were full they both sat back and looked at the world with new eyes. Food is a great leveler.

"Good bread," he said. "Edna can't make bread."

"Why?"

"It won't rise."

"She kill the yeast? I've heard that happens sometimes."

"I guess. We eat store-bought." He shuddered, and looked around the room. "Place is looking good."

She followed his gaze with satisfaction. "It is."

He looked at her. "You finally forgive us for giving it to you?"

She was surprised into a laugh. "I guess I have. It was just that—"

He interrupted her. "I know what it was. You're more used to being on the giving end than on the receiving."

She shrugged. "Yeah. Well."

His voice grew a little acerbic. "Yeah, well, sometimes accepting the gift in the spirit in which it was originally given is as important as giving yourself. Sometimes maybe more."

They both shifted uncomfortably at this display of sentiment. "Why, Demetri," she said, "I didn't know you cared."

He grunted something unintelligible, and changed the subject. "Heard something about you and Jim hauling somebody out of the Suulutaq in chains?"

"They weren't in chains," Kate said, annoyed, and when he grinned she knew that she'd been had. She caught him up on the latest criminal doings, although it felt as if everything she talked about had happened a year ago. The looming shadow of Old Sam's death and the subsequent events had eclipsed everything in the recent past.

Demetri nodded, taking it all in. "Anybody going to lose their job over it?"

"That, thank god, is not my call. The best thing I can say about it is it turned into a job I can bill the state for. I want Suulutaq's corporate and employee problems to stay their problems."

He frowned down into his mug.

"What?" she said.

He looked up. "Their problems are going to be our problems whether we want them to be or not."

There was a brief silence. "I know," she said at last. "What can we do, Demetri? We can't undiscover the gold. Anything that is selling on the open market for—What is it this month? Eleven hundred an ounce?—someone is always going to be wanting to pull that out of the ground and sell it to somebody else. That's pretty much the history of Alaska: we pull stuff out. We pull it out of the ground and we pull it out of the water, and we sell it to the highest bidder. And I'll tell you what else," she added. "There is no point in demonizing these people; they legally obtained those leases. We keep bad-mouthing them and they're going to start feeling like they don't owe us any favors."

"You think we should just bend over?"

She was taken aback by what sounded very much like contempt in his tone. "No," she said as mildly as she could. "I do not think that at all. This is our backyard, and we have the right, hell, the responsibility, to control access to it and activity in it. We owe at least that much to our kids." She gave him an assessing look. "You've been pretty reticent about the Suulutaq Mine so far, Demetri. Do I understand you to say that you're against it?"

He sat back and looked at the ceiling for inspiration. "Can we be simply for it or against it at this stage?" He looked back at her. "Are you going to take a stand one way or the other? Is the chair of the board of directors of the Niniltna Native Association going to come out for it, or against it? Fight it, or go along?"

"Jesus, Demetri, you're starting to sound like George W. Bush. I'm either with you or against you, is that what you're telling me?"

"That's not what I meant," he said, but he didn't sound very convincing.

"How about none of the above?" she said, but

he wasn't in the mood for humor, either. "I don't like either of those options," she said. "Fighting Suulutaq strikes me as pissing into the wind. In the end they'll dig that damn hole and start producing the gold and we end up wet and smelling bad. Going along means Global Harvest gets to do whatever they want, which makes me or anyone who thinks about it for more than five minutes nervous as hell. There has to be some kind of middle ground."

"That hole is going to be a mile deep and two miles wide," he said. "Square in the middle of the Park. A lot of people won't ever be able to find middle ground with that."

"You're sounding like one of them," she said bluntly. "Are you?"

He shrugged and went back to studying the ceiling. "It's something to think about."

She thought about his lodge, set on a pristine lake in the southern end of the Quilak Mountains. On a very clear day his guests could see all the way to Prince William Sound.

And then she thought of Old Sam, born into a Park with a fully operational copper mine. "It's not like this hasn't happened before," she said. "Our grandparents worked at the Kanuyaq Copper Mine. They survived. The Park survived. And that was back when no one was watching, when Carnegie and Mellon and Rockefeller had it all their own way, laughable wages, no unions, no employee benefits, a company store. This time, all the lights are on, everyone's watching, and Global Harvest knows it. They're working on an environmental impact statement, which will take two years and cost millions of dollars. They've funded a grant program for just about anyone in the Park who wants to apply to work at the mine and needs to go to school to learn the necessary skills. They just donated a satellite dish and a computer for every kid in the school. So far, they've demonstrated pretty good faith."

He was silent for a moment before he spoke again. "They say they'll be in operation here for twenty years or more."

"And that's not a good thing, either? Good-paying jobs for the kids so they don't have to move to Anchorage or Outside?"

He sighed and let his arms unknot themselves. "Ah, hell, Kate. You're probably right. Control as much as we can, and make sure the mine pays its own way. Not a whole lot else we can do."

It had been too quick a turnaround, but she let it go for the moment. Besides, there were other things on her mind. "Demetri," she said, "aren't you descended from Chief Lev somehow?"

"Chief Lev Kookesh?" He looked surprised, but was willing to let her change the subject. "Sure, he was a great-great-uncle." He thought. "Maybe a triple great. Why?"

"Did you know Old Sam was his grandson?"

"Hell, I don't know. I guess so. Maybe." He frowned. "Wasn't there some scandal about Chief Lev? Or no. Maybe his kid?"

"Old Sam's mom?"

"Yeah. Chief Lev and his wife died in the flu epidemic at the end of World War I. His daughter hosted their potlatch, and a tribal artifact went missing."

Kate blinked. "A tribal artifact?"

"Well, part of the tribal history, anyway. A Russian icon. You know, those saint's pictures the Russian Orthodox have in their churches?"

"I didn't know we ever had a Russian Orthodox church in Niniltna. I didn't know we ever had a church of any kind in Niniltna." She thought. "Except for the Pentecostal yurt."

Demetri stood up and shrugged into his parka. "With a name like Kookesh, his people had to be from Southeast. Maybe they brought it up from Klukwan or Huna or somewhere. Anyway, the story is, there was this Russian icon, and it was supposed to have healing properties."

"You mean like Our Lady of Lourdes? Are you kidding me?"

"No. Chief Lev would bring it out whenever there was a potlatch or a gathering. People who were sick or blind or lame or had something else wrong with them would come from all over to pray to be healed. And it, you know, would heal them."

"Right."

"Hey, don't shoot the messenger. I'm just telling the story the way I heard it."

"Wait a minute," Kate said. "If it was a family thing, should somebody still have it? You, or maybe, I don't know, Old Sam?"

"That's just it. At Chief Lev's potlatch, it was stolen. Vanished overnight. A lot of people said Chief Lev's daughter stole it and hid it because she figured they'd take it from her."

"Why?"

"Because she was a woman and she couldn't be chief."

She wouldn't have been able to be, then. Kate suffered a moment of nostalgia for the good old days. "So did she? Steal it?"

"The story says not. There was something about some stampeder who came into the Park and charmed it out of her."

Kate stiffened. "He have a name?"

"Oh, geez, now you're asking. Something about a bucket? Kick the Bucket? Bucket of Blood?" He shrugged. "I don't know. Why don't you ask Ruthe?"

"Ruthe Bauman?"

"Yeah."

"Why would she know what his name was?"

He looked at her as if she were an idiot. "Didn't you know? Dan O'Brian hired her to write a piece on the history of the Park for the Parks Service website. Old Sam spent a lot of time with her lately, telling her stuff." He paused. "You better be careful how you go there. The aunties are all pissed off that a white woman's writing it."

"They're pissed at Ruthe?" Kate's voice went up high enough to bring Mutt up on her feet.

"No, at Dan." Demetri stamped his feet into his boots and paused, a hand on the door, and said in a casual tone, "Not that I mean to rush things, but who do you want to name to replace Old Sam on the board?"

"No one can replace him," Kate said flatly. "We can fill his seat, and that's about all we can do."

Demetri wasn't going to let it go. "Okay, then, to fill his seat?"

He was right, she told herself. The sooner it was done, the better, to get the new board member up to speed on Association issues and shareholder politics. "I was thinking we ought to pull in someone from Anchorage. One of the share-holders who live outside the Park. Bring a different perspective to the board."

"Who?"

"I don't know," Kate lied. "A discussion for around the table next month, maybe?"

"Maybe. Might be a good idea if we had some names to put forward by then, though. Then we could just vote on it and whoever it is would be worked in by the shareholder's meeting in January."

"Be thinking, then."

He nodded. "You, too."

"And Demetri? Thanks."

He waved her off, and she stood there as the door closed behind him, as his footsteps receded down the stairs, as the engine of his truck turned over, and wondered if she had been reading Demetri Totemoff wrong all these years.

Kick the Bucket? Bucket of Blood?

Fifteen

RUTHE BAUMAN OPENED THE DOOR and said, "You look exactly like a green-spectacled eider."

"I really, really have heard them all," Kate said. "Although, now that I think of it, no, I hadn't heard that one. But now I have, so you're done. I need to talk to you about Old Sam."

"Come on in." Ruthe stepped back and opened the door wide. Galadrial was stretched out in front of the woodstove. She hissed at Mutt without moving. Mutt growled back without showing her teeth. Honor served, Mutt curled up in front of the stove on the opposite corner from Gal and stuck her nose under her tail, and cat and dog ignored each other from that moment on.

"I'll get some coffee while you shuck out," Ruthe said, and bustled over to the kitchen.

Ruthe Bauman was in her late seventies and still

237

thin and spry, with clear brown eyes and an untidy head of hair that was a very attractive white gold. There were wrinkles at the corners of her eyes and her lean cheeks were lined, but like Old Sam she seemed ageless. Barring illness or injury, longevity was something the Park seemed to confer on residents who stuck around. When her time came Ruthe would probably go out the same way Old Sam did, just sit down and not get up again.

She had first come to Alaska with her friend Dina Willner, both of them ex-WASPs who couldn't find jobs in aviation Outside after World War II and so came looking for them in Alaska. They had joined forces with and then bought out a big-game guide in Fairbanks, and in the fifties started Camp Teddy, one of the very first resorts that catered to eco-tourists, on eighty acres twenty-five miles south of Niniltna. Ruthe was the Park's self-styled conservationist. She kept independent population counts of the various species of wildlife that challenged all Dan O'Brian's counts of those same species, and she wasn't shy about saying so when her counts came in lower than his. When Dan okayed a moose hunt on Nugget Creek, he'd by god better have checked with Ruthe first, because she could and would challenge him on whether the moose population of Nugget Creek would stand up to the harvest.

"How are you doing?" Ruthe said, setting mugs,

a stack of sliced homemade bread, and a Darigold one-pound butter can on the table. For a change, the butter can was actually full of butter, instead of foam earplugs or leftover nails. Or spare cash.

"I'm okay," Kate said. "I already miss the hell out of the son of a bitch."

Ruthe smiled, a reminiscent gleam in her eye. "Me, too."

"Wait a minute," Kate said. "I thought Old Sam and Mary Balashoff—"

Ruthe waved a hand. "Don't worry. Old news. Very old news, back when Dina and I first came into the country. Sam brought up a lot of the construction material we used to build Camp Teddy on the *Freya*. We . . . got acquainted."

Jesus, Kate thought, is there anyone in the Park you haven't slept with? Ruthe and Jim had been a brief and relatively unknown item back when he first came into the country. Kate could not forbear a glance at the floor of this very cabin, that had supported, barely, what had followed her own discovery of that interesting fact. Now Old Sam, too?

Ruthe read Kate's thought with no difficulty, and chuckled. "Hard to believe a couple of old codgers like us could be—"

Kate held up a hand. "Stop right there. I'm begging you."

At that Ruthe laughed outright. "Don't worry, Kate, I'm just ragging on you. Old Sam and I were friends, good friends. I'll miss him, too." But she paused. "Is there a time you can foresee when you won't want to sleep with Jim?"

It might have been Kate's overactive imagination, but Ruthe seemed to cast a significant glance at the floor of her cabin as she spoke. She couldn't know. Oh god, please, she couldn't possibly know.

And then Ruthe's words wormed their way into her consciousness. She thought of the night just past, when she had woken in the wee hours to reach for the man who wasn't there, his side of the bed cold and lonely. "It's a moot point," she said out loud. "Everybody knows what Jim's like. He won't be around when it becomes a question."

Ruthe cast her an amused glance. "Sure, he won't."

"He's in California right now," Kate said, with perhaps a little more force than she was aware of.

"Why?"

"His father died."

"Oh well," Ruthe said, sitting down across from Kate and picking up a spoon to stir sugar into her coffee. "The man has abandoned you for no good reason. Throw him out, by all means."

"I didn't mean that," Kate said.

Ruthe's glance was cool. "Didn't you?"

Nettled, Kate said, "You know, Ruthe, I didn't come here to talk about my love life."

Ruthe raised her eyebrows. " 'Love' life, is it?"

"Ruthe!"

The older woman burst out laughing. "Sorry, Kate, it was irresistible. What's up?"

"It's about Old Sam."

"So you said." Ruthe's gaze sharpened. "What about him?"

"Demetri told me—"

"Demetri?"

"Demetri Totemoff, yeah." There was a note in Ruthe's tone that Kate couldn't identify. "What about Demetri?"

Ruthe made a dismissive gesture. "Later. What did he say?"

"He said Dan O'Brian had commissioned you to write an article on the history of the Park for the Parks Service."

Ruthe nodded. "True, for their website. Everything's on a website nowadays. Mostly it's a timeline, who came here when. Sort of an exercise in global perspective, you know: Spanish flu kills fifty million people worldwide March 1918 to June 1920, kills thirteen thousand people in Alaska November 1918 to June 1919, Chief Lev Kookesh and wife Alexandra die in Spanish flu pandemic in Niniltna in 1919."

"Context," Kate said, sidetracked for a moment. Ruthe nodded.

"But I'll have to go online to see it."

"You will," Ruthe said.

Kate sighed. "Okay. Demetri said you might

know something about Chief Lev, and Chief Lev's daughter, and Chief Lev's grandson, who to my surprise turns out to be Old Sam."

"You didn't know?"

Kate shook her head. "He never told me. In all the time I knew him, I don't think he ever talked about his grandparents. For that matter, he didn't talk about his parents much."

"Ah."

"Does that 'ah' have something to do with the possibility that Quinto Dementieff was not Old Sam's natural father?"

Ruthe's gaze sharpened. "You know that?"

"I don't know it, per se," Kate said. "I heard the aunties talking about it once, sort of, and Demetri says there was a rumor going around that Elizaveta, Old Sam's mother, was friendly with a stampeder before she married Quinto."

Ruthe nodded, and seemed to make up her mind. She began with a caveat. "I don't know anything for sure, you understand."

"Yeah, but you just said that you and Old Sam were buds."

Ruthe grinned. "Were we ever," she said, and laughed again when Kate made a cross of her fingers and held it up between them. "I made a remark once about his height, which as you know wasn't your Alaska Native's average height, and he said his father was six two."

Old Sam had been a tall man. Why had Kate

242

never made the connection? "Quinto Dementieff was half Filipino and half Aleut," she said. "Doubtful if he was much over five feet."

"Filipinos not being known for their tallness, either." Ruthe watched Kate, waiting. Waiting for what?

"Do you know the stampeder's name?" Kate said. "Demetri said it was something weird like Bucket of Blood."

Ruthe smiled approvingly, as if Kate had just said something very smart. "One-Bucket," she said. "One-Bucket McCullough."

Many of the stampeders who came north in the Klondike Gold Rush had colorful nicknames, usually with an equally colorful story attached to it. "Why One-Bucket?"

"I was interested, too, so I did a little research in the newspapers back then."

"The *Ahtna Adit*?"

"That was one of them," Ruthe said, nodding. "He's mentioned in passing in a couple of books written by stampeders, too."

Kate remembered Ben's remark that every stampeder who stepped foot in the Klondike wrote a book about it.

"It seems," Ruth said, "that One-Bucket McCullough was famous in certain circles for his ability to stake a claim on the richest section of any creek, pull one bucket of nuggets out, and sell the claim to the first guy who asked."

Kate thought about it. "Sounds too good to be true. What's the catch?"

"Well," Ruthe said, "from the accounts of the miners who bought his claims, which never paid out in a manner you might expect of a claim previously productive of a full bucket of nuggets in one day, there was some speculation as to whether he sold the same bucket of nuggets more than once."

"Oh." Kate started laughing, and Ruthe joined in. "And that was Old Sam's father?"

Ruthe shrugged. "Might have been. Old Sam never came right out and said so. Why this interest?"

"Old Sam left me this note." Kate pulled it out and handed it over.

Ruthe read it. "Hmm. Not particularly self-explanatory, is it."

"No," Kate said with feeling. "It isn't."

Ruthe gave her a speculative glance. "Anything to do with you getting attacked in Old Sam's house?"

"I don't know. I was packing up his books, and I'd gotten sidetracked by a judge's journal, the first judge in Ahtna before World War Two. The next thing I know I'm trying not to throw up in Matt Grosdidier's lap. And you haven't heard the latest." She told Ruthe about her eventful trip to Ahtna, and the even more eventful return.

"Jane Silver's dead?" Ruthe said.

Kate nodded. "You knew her?"

"Who didn't. She had a front-row seat to the last seventy years of Alaska history. I tried to use her as a source for the timeline but she just wouldn't play."

Kate cleared her throat delicately. "There may have been a reason she didn't want anyone looking too closely into her history."

Ruthe made a rude noise. "I know all about Beatrice Beaton's Boardinghouse," she said.

"Oh," Kate said. "Well. Not as big a secret as Jane had hoped, then."

"And you say she's dead?"

Kate nodded. "Day before yesterday."

"How?"

Kate sighed. "It looks like she surprised a burglar. They shoved her and she fell and hit her head."

"A burglar, huh?"

"Yeah. Her place was ransacked, or in the process of being ransacked. I heard him heading out the back door when we were coming in the front."

Ruthe looked at Mutt, snoozing peacefully in front of the wood stove. "Mutt with you?"

"Yeah."

"You didn't send her after him?"

"No."

Ruthe raised an eyebrow. "Time was you wouldn't have hesitated."

Kate looked at Mutt, too. Time was she hadn't seen Mutt near death from intercepting a bullet that had been meant for Kate.

Mutt's eyes snapped open and she raised her head to meet Kate's stare full on.

Kate was the first one to look away. "There have been a lot of break-ins in Ahtna lately," she said. "It could be that simple. Or . . ."

"Or what?"

Kate shrugged. "Working Mrs. Beaton's side of the street does put one in the way of hearing the real story behind all the gossip. Best snitch any cop can have is a working girl."

"You think she knew something to do with Old Sam? And that that was what got her killed?"

"It could be that complicated." Kate drained her mug and got to her feet. "Johnny's pretty sure it is."

Ruthe grinned. "And how is my boy?"

Unbeknownst to her, Kate's expression was one of love and pride. "Damn near perfect."

Ruthe nodded as if it was only to be expected. "You're very lucky," she said.

"I know," Kate said.

At Old Sam's the snow was drifted three feet high against the door and there was a set of fresh tracks circumnavigating the cabin. It looked as if the person had stopped to peer into every window. Kate squatted for a closer look. "Small," Kate said to Mutt, who was peering over her shoulder. "An older child or a younger woman. I'm betting Phyllis. Maybe she'll come back while we're here."

Mutt made a noise that could have been agreement, but when Kate unlocked the padlock Mutt stationed herself squarely in front of the door, and she did not relax her vigilance until they left. Mutt had a long memory, and she was not about to suffer the indignity of leaving her human undefended from attack a second time.

She'd already taken care of the books. As promised, Kate left towels and bedding, dishes and food. She packed Old Sam's clothes and personal belongings, listing the contents on the outside of each box in black Marks-A-Lot. By the end of the day she was heartily sick of the whole operation—Who knew the old man would have had so much stuff in him? Although she was sure Mike Doogan would have called it gear—and had begun to toss boxes of ammunition in the same box with frayed Jockey underwear and Christmas ornaments. Where the hell had Old Sam come by those?

Phyllis, if it had been her, didn't come back. On the way home Kate dropped off Old Sam's clothes with Auntie Balasha, who ran a sort of thrift shop out of her garage. When Johnny got home from school that afternoon he found Kate unloading the last of the boxes from the snowgo trailer. He gave her a hand and they closed up the garage against a wind-driven snowfall that promised to have a lot more on the ground by morning.

Kate busied herself with dinner as Johnny leaned on the counter and kibitzed. The pork chops were in the oven and Kate was using the last of a bunch of very sad apples from the fruit bin in the refrigerator for applesauce by the time she was done catching him up on the day's activities. "We were just talking about the Spanish flu in history today," he said. "Mr. Tyler says it was proportionally really bad in Alaska, partly because of the communal lifestyle of Alaska Natives."

Kate nodded, turning on the rice cooker. "It's estimated that half the Native population died. The elders called it the Black Death. They still do."

"Wow." Johnny was impressed. "Reminds me of that stuff in the Middle Ages."

"The bubonic plague."

"Yeah. Only this wasn't rats."

"No." She turned on the rice cooker and leaned on the sink. "Think about it, Johnny. Every second person you know, dead. Me, Jim, you, Van, the aunties, Ruthe, Annie. Count them off."

Johnny looked stricken. "I hadn't thought of it like that."

"It was exactly like that. And the people who got it who didn't die were too weak and debilitated to fight off the vultures, and the people who didn't get the flu had enough on their hands caring for the survivors to be paying attention."

"So you think this One-Bucket McCullough seduced Old Sam's mom and stole this icon thing?"

"That's what it sounds like to me."

"And then his mom married Quinto Dementieff." He thought about that for a while. "Do you think Quinto knew?"

"If he didn't know before, he would have known when Old Sam started growing up looking like he does. Did."

"I hope he didn't . . ." Johnny's voice trailed off.

"Yeah. Me, too."

"Do you think Old Sam knew?"

"Yes." Kate folded a dish towel and hung it over the handle on the oven door. "Maybe not until later, but he knew. It's the only way to explain his note."

"So you think he wanted you to find this One-Bucket McCullough?"

"Yeah."

"Why?"

Kate's laugh sounded more like a sob. "Beats the hell out of me." She paused. "But one thing about Old Sam."

"What?"

"He wasn't interested in information that didn't have a practical purpose. Whatever this crazy road is he's sending me down . . ."

"There's something important at the end of that road."

"I think so. Christ, I hope so."

She started loading plates, and nothing interfered with dinner, not even Old Sam's edicts from beyond the grave. But afterward Johnny said, "So. What are you going to do next?"

"I've been thinking about that." It was Kate's turn to lean on the counter and kibitz while Johnny did the dishes. It was black and dark on the other side of the windows and the house creaked in what sounded like gale-force winds. "If this blows itself out by morning, I think I'm going to take the snowgo up to Canyon Hot Springs."

"Why?"

Kate gave a half laugh. "I wish I had a good answer for that." She moved her shoulders, as if trying to shake off a persistent fly. "I've got a feeling I'm supposed to. I didn't know he owned it until he left it to me in his will. Now there's this business about who his father was or wasn't, and the—I can't believe I'm saying this—the missing treasure."

"The icon."

"Yeah."

"Mr. Tyler's been telling us about the Russian Revolution, and the massacre of the czar and his family. Did you know the Russian Orthodox Church made them saints?"

250

"Yeah?"

"Yeah, and he showed us pictures of icons with their pictures on them. All kinds of gold and jewels. Is this icon like that?"

"I don't know," Kate said slowly. "I never saw it. No member of my generation has." Maybe *treasure* wasn't too overblown a word after all.

"Would the aunties know?"

"They might. All four of them were contemporaries of Old Sam. More or less." She thought of Auntie Joy. She didn't want to add to Auntie Joy's pain, but she knew the reaction she'd get trying to ask questions of the other three. Auntie Edna would scowl and refuse to answer on general principle, Auntie Vi would scold and refuse to answer on the grounds that Kate was poking her nose into elder business ("You not there yet, Katya!"), and Auntie Balasha would smile and offer her fresh cookies and give Mutt some moose jerky and get her grandson Willard to service Kate's truck and give Kate half a dozen jars of her justly famous smoked salmon to take home, all the while never answering anything to the purpose. Auntie Balasha was the most approachable of all the aunties, and without question the most inaccessible.

"You could ask them."

"I could," she said. Another gust of wind hit the house. "But not tonight." She pointed at the table, and at his daypack sitting on one of the chairs. "Homework for you."

"What are you going to do?"

She gestured at the boxes stacked in the living room. "Get Old Sam's books up on the shelves."

He grumbled less than usual over the homework, which led her to think better of Mr. Tyler than she already did. One good teacher made all the difference.

They worked away at their respective jobs for the next couple of hours to the sound of Jimmy Buffett. It wasn't even October, so she wasn't ready to shoot six holes in her freezer. Come to think of it she wasn't ever ready to do that.

After the frenzied activity of an Alaskan summer—quick catch the fish, quick clean the fish, quick smoke and can the fish, quick pick the berries, quick make the jam, quick weed the garden and chop the wood and fix the roof and paint the shed and get your moose and fill the cache and make that last Anchorage run for new glasses and get your teeth cleaned and buy school clothes and supplies—you were just plain exhausted, worn-out, ready to crawl into a hole and sleep the winter away.

Winter in the Park, everything slowed down. You had enough time for the first time in months, enough time to sleep in, read a book, spend days experimenting with a new bread recipe until you got it right. You had time to snowshoe over to

Mandy's or spend an evening at the Roadhouse or a couple of days at Bobby and Dinah's getting to know your goddaughter again.

So it was dark, so it was cold—so what? Kate never sentimentalized her life, but when you lived a subsistence lifestyle, if Alaskan summers were a time for nonstop work, then Alaskan winters were a time for nonstop leisure, at least comparatively.

Unless of course your surrogate father died on you, the son of a bitch, and seemed to have deliberately left a mystery to unravel that stretched back to before the moment of his conception.

She shelved a biography of Captain Cook by Alistair MacLean with unnecessary force.

Tomorrow she was going to go back into town and talk to Auntie Joy about Old Sam, and Elizaveta Kookesh, and Chief Lev, and find out who the hell One-Bucket McCullough was.

And then she was going to go up to Canyon Hot Springs to find whatever the hell Old Sam had left her to find.

Sixteen

A FOOT OF SNOW HAD FALLEN OVER-night, and the day dawned with a high overcast that promised more snow but not right this minute. Her most recent experience in survival very much on her mind, she packed enough food and supplies and extra fuel for a small army into the trailer and hitched it to the snowgo before heading out.

On the way to Auntie Joy's she detoured by Virginia Anahonak's to see Phyllis, who confirmed that she'd waded through the snow to the cabin the day before. Phyllis was overjoyed to hear that she could move in that very moment. "There's wood enough to last the winter," Kate said. "It's yours to use. I checked the oil drums; they're about half full. There is flour and salt and sugar and butter and some canned goods, and sheets and towels."

Phyllis started to cry again. "I spent last night packing." She then shocked and embarrassed Kate by throwing her arms around her and kissing her, as Virginia watched from her open door, all eyes and ears.

"Uh, yeah," Kate said, extricating herself from Phyllis's embrace. "I'm heading out to the hot springs, I'd better get going so I don't lose the light before I get there."

"I can never thank you enough," Phyllis said, sobbing.

"Don't thank me, Old Sam did it. You need a ride?"

Phyllis wiped her eyes on her sleeve and gulped. "You've got a full trailer. Virginia will take me over, she wants to see the place anyway."

Of course she did. Phyllis bolted back inside the

house, presumably to grab her stuff, and Kate started the engine and got out of there.

She was an only child who'd been orphaned young and raised by two old men and one old woman, none of whom was comfortable with either emotion or gratitude. It showed.

Auntie Joy's usual beaming smile was absent when she opened the door to Kate that morning.

"Hi, Auntie," Kate said brightly. "Where's your shovel? I'll dig you out while you make me coffee, and if you've got any of those great cookies left I wouldn't turn them down."

Thus serving her elder's needs as well as serving her elder notice that she was there for however long it took to get the story. In half an hour she had cleared the path between Niniltna's main street and Auntie Joy's front door. She leaned the shovel against the cabin wall, kicked the snow from her boots, and went inside. Mutt, who had provided an honor guard for the ungainfully employed, sat down square in the middle of the doorstep with an intimidating thump that was audible inside.

The round mahogany dining table was set with the full rosebud tea service this time, creamer, sugar bowl with the delicate lid, cups and saucers and dessert plates on a lace tablecloth. She'd even gotten out the rose flatware, which Kate remembered from back in the day when Auntie

Joy still hoped the child Kate would succumb to the lure of ruffles and dolls and tea parties.

Yes, Auntie Joy had her own defenses. For one thing, Kate was immediately sidetracked into trying to remember how many of the fragile little cups the child Kate had broken before Auntie Joy finally put them up out of her reach.

It was odd, but however many cups Kate broke, there was always a full set the next time she appeared.

"Sit," Auntie Joy said.

It was an order, not an invitation. Kate sat. Tea was poured, milk was added, sugar was offered, cookies were placed on dessert plates. Polite conversation ensued while the proprieties of Park hospitality were observed. Early snow this year. More on the way. Auntie Vi was wearing herself out changing the beds so often in her B and B, she was thinking of hiring help, perhaps a high school girl. Did Kate think Vanessa would be interested? The kids sure liked those new computers, and the things they found. Little Anuska Moonin had found a website—Auntie Joy was very proud of her mastery of this new word—a website that had tatting patterns by the hundreds. She had printed some out and brought them to her auntie. Such a thoughtful girl. Auntie Balasha had taken her grandson Willard to Anchorage for his annual checkup. Auntie Edna was still doing a roaring business in Filipino take-out from the back door of her house. Katya Clark was in preschool, and the principal had had to physically stop her father from wheeling his chair into the classroom to take up a permanent position along the back wall. He was armed, if the principal, a veteran himself, was not mistaken, with a 7.62-mm Tokarev automatic pistol that weighed over two pounds fully loaded, on the off chance any terrorists infiltrated the school during nap time.

Kate ate and drank and waited until Auntie Joy ran out of words. The silence that followed yawned between them, uneasy and fraught with portent. Kate put her cup down on its saucer with the exaggerated care she employed with all of Auntie Joy's china, and said, "Auntie, there are things I must know so I can carry out Old Sam's wishes."

Auntie Joy put down her own cup with equal care and a certain finality. "All right, Katya," she said. "I tell you, then."

Kate had had her arguments prepared and ready to trot out, and she was caught flat-footed by this unexpectedly capitulation. "Why now?"

Auntie Joy shrugged. "I think about it after you leave other day." She looked at Kate, the love and pride shining in her eyes like a beacon. Kate, as uncomfortable with love and pride as she was with gratitude, tried not to squirm in her chair. "You the one, Katya. You carry it all forward for everyone. I think at first too heavy for you, too much the weight on your shoulders. And what matter now, so many years gone by?"

Kate waited.

"But it matter to Old Sam," Auntie Joy said. "Oh yes." Her eyes filled with tears, and she said in a low voice, "To him it matter too much."

"What mattered, Auntie? What mattered so much to Old Sam?"

Auntie Joy blinked away tears, and began to testify in a soft voice. Listening to her, Kate could feel the years roll away, to that fallow period following gold rushes and copper rushes and the First World War, when Alaska was only a territory, forgotten by most, with a population of less than sixty thousand people. There was nothing like regular air service. The roads were unpaved, unmaintained, and unnavigable most of the time. You ordered your groceries for the year from Seattle and had them shipped up by Alaska Steam, which offloaded them in Valdez or Cordova, and you either packed them into the Park yourself or hired P and H to do so at extortionate prices.

"P and H?" Kate said.

"Heiman Transportation, after."

Moose and caribou and salmon were the staples, Auntie Joy said, everybody hunted and everybody shared. More and more Outsiders came into the country, Filipinos to work in the canneries, Americans to mine for gold, Scandinavians on

258

whaling ships. Inevitably, some married local girls and stayed.

The Natives in the Park were much more conservative and insular when she was a girl, Auntie Joy said, and the elders were alert to the danger of their children marrying outside the tribe. It wasn't forbidden, exactly, but it might as well have been because those who did so were never regarded as full tribal members again. Many moved away altogether, to Fairbanks and Anchorage and even Outside. It took the loss of many children to their families and another generation to relax those taboos.

"Too late for us," Auntie Joy said.

"You and Old Sam?"

Auntie Joy nodded, her face set in sad lines. "Then some parents send childrens to BIA school in Cordova. My parents send me there. Old Sam parents live in Cordova. He go to school there, too."

Auntie Joy's eyes shone with a tender light unlike Kate had ever seen before. "He look at me. I look at him. We know."

The simplicity and truth of the words took Kate's breath away. The two women sat in a silence that grew in length and sorrow. "What happened?" Kate said at last.

"Then war comes." Auntie Joy looked down at the table and said in a voice dropped to a whisper, "Sam join up."

"And you?"

"I marry my parents' choice."

Kate waited.

"Davy Moonin. He one of them come from the Aleutians in the war. Viola's cousins. They lose everything in that war, homes, villages, all. A lot of work after to settle them down. Many parents marry local girls to newcomers. For one thing, our men gone. For another, good way to make Aleutian Aleuts at home. Davy . . . Davy, he work hard, respectful of elders. Fisherman, so exempted from army service. My parents think a good man for me."

The remembered pain in Auntie Joy's expression was obvious for anyone to read. Kate, caught between pity and rage, didn't know what to say.

Auntie Joy read Kate's face without difficulty. "Not all his fault, Katya. He not my choice. He know. Make him angry. Resentful. He . . . unhappy. And there are no children. My fault again, he think." She closed her eyes briefly. "I think so, too."

"It's always a choice to raise your hand against someone else, Auntie," Kate said, her jaw tight, and stopped herself when Auntie Joy looked away. "Is that why you went back to Shugak after he died?"

Auntie Joy was silent.

Kate took a deep breath and let it out. "And Uncle?"

The soft light came back to Auntie Joy's eyes. "After war, he come home to the Park."

"And you?"

"And me."

Kate tried to remember how long Auntie Joy had been widowed. "Were you—free, then?"

"Free." Auntie Joy's laugh was without humor. "What a word, Katya. In 1944 Davy delivering fish to tender, fall between boats, is crush. I am widow then, yes, but not free." She took a deep breath and let it out in a long sigh. "No. Not free."

"Old Sam still wanted to marry you?"

Auntie Joy nodded.

Kate, unable to keep the incredulity out of her voice, said, "And you refused him? Again?"

The light in Auntie Joy's eyes dimmed. "First my parents. They don't like his father."

Which father? Kate almost said.

"His father half Filipino. His grandmother all Filipino. Back then, my parents want me to marry Native only. No gussuk, no Japs, they said. To them all Asian men Japs. The war make them hate Japs. My brother die on Tarawa. No gussuks for their daughter. No Japs for their daughter. Only Native." Her mouth twisted.

"You couldn't—"

Auntie Joy's eyes met Kate's. "No. Not like now, childrens go their own way. Good thing," she said, smacking her hand down on the table. All the china jumped. So did Kate. There was a muted "Woof" from the other side of the door, too.

"So Old Sam wanted to marry you, and you wanted to marry him, but your parents forbid it."

Auntie Joy's shoulders slumped. "Yes. Before the war, after the war. All the same, yes."

"He homesteaded the hot springs for you, didn't he?"

Auntie Joy rallied at this. "He homestead the hot springs because his mother say so."

"But . . . why?" Kate said. "Why on earth did she want him to stake his claim so far back in the mountains? There's like five hundred square feet of horizontal land in the whole hundred and sixty acres, and either you bushwhack in on foot in the summer or snowgo in winter, or you don't get there at all." Did they even have snow machines back then? "How did she expect him to survive?"

Auntie Joy spread her hands. "He say only that his mother say he must homestead there."

Kate's eyes narrowed. "What's up there besides the hot springs, Auntie Joy?"

"He don't tell me, Katya," Auntie Joy said, in a manner that brooked no contradiction.

This time Kate almost believed her.

"Something else," Auntie Joy said, in a voice so low Kate had to strain to hear the words. "One time, I have baby in the belly. Davy . . . our baby comes too soon." Auntie Joy's voice was the barest thread of sound. "After, no children for me."

Kate worked it out and was too shocked to be tactful. "Davy beat you into a miscarriage, you couldn't have children afterward, Davy died, and when Old Sam came home you wouldn't marry him this time because you were barren?"

Auntie Joy avoided her gaze. "Every man deserve his chance at children, Katya."

"I'm raising a kid I didn't give birth to right now, Auntie. God." She shook her head. "And Uncle never married, and so far as I know never had children with anyone else. All this time you spent apart, and for what?" She saw the look of misery on Auntie Joy's face and stopped herself before she went any farther. There was no point in telling Auntie Joy that all her life choices had been wrong. "What did Old Sam do then?"

"Angry." Auntie Joy sighed. "Very angry. He bring story home about his father, he say no reason no more why we don't marry, times different anyway, he don't care about kids. When I still say no, he—" Her voice broke and it took her a moment to recover it. "He go away angry." Her mouth twisted. "I don't see him again until 1956."

Over ten years. And then Kate said, "Wait, what? What story, Auntie? And which father?"

Auntie Joy's head came up with a snap. "You know about Old Sam's father?"

"I know my whole life I thought his father was Quinto Dementieff, and I know now there is a good chance it was some guy named One-Bucket McCullough. Are you saying Old Sam wrote it down?" Kate sat up straight in her chair. "Auntie," she said, barely breathing the words, "do you still have it?"

Auntie Joy rose to her feet and went to a chestnut armoire polished to a blinding gleam, hulking in one corner of the cabin. It was surmounted by what Kate thought was called a cornice, which overhung the armoire by a good six inches on three sides. She wondered where Auntie Joy had gotten it. She wondered how she had gotten it to Niniltna from wherever Outside she'd bought it, because nothing like that was for sale anywhere this side of Seattle.

She wondered how Auntie Joy had gotten it through the door.

Auntie Joy opened the doors and felt around inside. There was a click, and a hidden drawer popped out of the bottom.

"Hey," Kate said, and got up for a closer look.

For a moment both women forgot the painful topic under discussion in a mutual admiration of the cunning little drawer that fit invisibly into the base of the armoire. Auntie Joy closed the drawer again and showed Kate the latch that released it. "That is really clever," Kate said, closing the drawer and opening it again. She stood back and looked at the armoire. "You'd never know it was there if you didn't compare the outside dimensions to the inside ones, and maybe not even then." She even got down on her knees to examine the foot of the armoire at close range. "Man, it fits together so well, even close up you can't tell the drawer from the base. Whoever did this knew what he was doing and then some."

She pulled herself together. The air seemed suddenly thick with secrets—Park secrets, tribal secrets, family secrets. Secrets in the frickin' furniture.

She sat back and stared at the foot of the armoire. She knew a sudden impulse to leave the drawer shut and turn away.

In the nine days since Old Sam had died, it was as if someone had focussed the lens through which she viewed the history of her family in the Park. Things, people, events that had seemed to her clear, fixed, and immutable were now blurred and less substantial. It was unnerving to lose that kind of solidity, that kind of permanence at your back. Somehow she knew that she was never again going to be able to look over her shoulder without fearing that the view had changed from the last time she had seen it.

She felt unsettled, and apprehensive. She looked up at Auntie Joy, who stood with her hands folded in front of her, waiting.

Up to you if you want to know or not. Auntie Joy might have spoken the words out loud. Kate wiped suddenly sweaty palms down her jeans and reached inside the armoire to feel for the latch. The drawer popped open again.

They both stared down at the contents, a tattered, nine-by-twelve box tied up with string. "Is that it?"

Auntie Joy nodded.

"May I take it and read it?"

"No." At Kate's expression Auntie Joy said, "Read here. Samuel give that story to me."

"He threw it at you, you said."

"He leave it with me," Auntie Joy said again. "He never ask for it back." She hesitated, looking half defiant, half fearful, and all stubborn. "You read it here." She reached for the box and gave it to Kate with both hands and part of a bow, as if she were handing over the keys to the kingdom to the heir apparent, which maybe she was. "You understand when you read it."

"Understand what?" Kate said.

Auntie Joy pointed at the recliner. There was no gainsaying that finger, and it wasn't like Kate was going to wrest the box from Auntie Joy's hands and depart the premises. She wasted a moment or two hoping that the new storm louring on the southern horizon would hold off another day, and subsided into the chair with equal parts resignation and anticipation.

The string was kitchen string, the box the thinnest of gray cardboard, the pages loose and numbered top right, fifty-three in total. The paper was onionskin, aged and translucent and fragile, and the text had been typed on a manual typewriter with the *e* and the *i* out of alignment and the *q*, the *d*, the *o*, and the *p* filled in. It was double-spaced, with one-inch margins, and it had been edited by hand.

The story began without title or preamble, on the first page, halfway down.

Halfway through the manuscript she raised her eyes to see Auntie Joy watching her. "Jesus Christ, Auntie."

Auntie Joy, that prim and proper woman of faith and goodness, didn't so much as wince at Kate taking the Lord's name in vain. "Read more," she said.

1945

Niniltna

Sam slammed out of Joy's cabin in a rage that kept him going all the way to Ahtna. There he went straight to Bea's, ordered his own bottle of the good stuff at a prohibitive price he ignored, and towed January Jane upstairs. JJ, so called because of her ability to warm up a man even in the depths of January, had cause to complain of his roughness. As angry as he was, Old Sam would never hurt a woman. Besides, he'd read between the lines, he knew what kind of a marriage Joyce had had with Davy Moonin, and part of his rage was at that dead man. No need to take it out on JJ, though, and he apologized and finished his business at a more considerate pace.

"What had you so wound up, anyway?" JJ said, reaching over the bed to where he'd dropped the bottle.

Under the influence of whiskey and sympathy, Sam told her more than he might have otherwise.

"So first she wouldn't marry you because her parents said you weren't good enough, and now she won't marry you because she can't have kids?" JJ said.

"That's about it," Sam said, getting angry all over again.

JJ soothed him with an adroit caress. She was a professional, adept at turning anger to the purpose for which she was paid. After another interlude they lay together long into the night, talking. He told JJ how Mac McCullough had saved his life in the clean-up operation on Attu, about the dim suspicion that had been born next to Mac's deathbed on Adak, about meeting Dashiell Hammett, about the news of Mac's death that had come to him with the story of Mac's life.

She listened because she was paid to listen, and she filed it all away.

The next day, without regret, he left most of what remained in his wallet in Bea's rapacious palm, nodded a greeting to Albie Anglebrandt who was on his way in, and hitched a ride up the Glenn Highway to Tok. There he hitched another ride down the Alaska Highway with a couple of guys from Wallace, Idaho, driving a Lincoln Zephyr. The Alcan, shoved through in one hell of a hurry three years before to provide support for the war effort, was pretty much in the same condition the U.S. Army had left it. Most of it was in Canada, who weren't that interested in maintaining it. Much of the trip was spent digging the Lincoln Zephyr out of the mud, but twenty days later they made Spokane, where they parted company.

Old Sam hitched across Washington state to Seattle, where he bunked in at the local Salvation Army, always good for a meal and a bed, until he found a room in a boardinghouse that was reasonably clean. The following week he got a job in Ballard working for a marine contractor who was happy to find someone who knew a bow from a stern and who put him to work tearing down PT boats for conversion to commercial fishing. Two and a half weeks and a considerable bump in salary later, he was supervising the night shift.

But the job was only to pay his way, to pay for food and clothing and a roof over his head, and build a stake for the trip home. No, his purpose in Seattle was personal.

He was determined to track down the curio dealer to whom Mac had sold the icon at dockside just before the Pinkerton agent had picked him up. If Mac hadn't lied to Hammett, if Hammett hadn't just made it up out of whole cloth, if Old Sam had in fact sold the icon to a dealer on the Seattle docks, it was a safe bet it was to someone in business in Seattle. Someone in business twenty-five years before, true, but he had to start somewhere. Every afternoon before he went to work and every weekend was spent tracking down every antiques dealer, junkyard, thrift shop, and curio store in the Yellow Pages, from Seattle north to dingy Lake City and south to boomtown Kent. He was bitten by a Doberman pinscher in a junkyard, escaped barely virtu intacta from a woman twice his age who was selling chipped tea sets on tatted doilies in a dusty one-room shop on First Avenue that looked sadder than she did, and learned a great deal more than he wished to about Hull Pottery piggy banks, first of all that they even existed.

It was a hopeless task and he knew it, but he was determined to exhaust every possibility. Somewhere at the back of his mind lingered the hope that if he returned to Niniltna bearing the icon, proving his worth to the tribe, Joyce would be his reward. By then, perhaps enough time would have passed that Joyce would have gotten over her marriage, and maybe, too, by then she would miss him as much as he missed her. He could give a good damn about having kids, it was Joyce he wanted. It had always been Joyce.

Trudging through this odyssey, he was still trying to assimilate the story of his own unknown history, set down in stark black-and-white in unsparing prose devoid of judgment or sentimentality. Not to mention through a third-

272

party filter. Oh yes, Hammett had made a good story of it, in part, Sam had to admit, because it was a good story. He wondered what Joyce had done with the manuscript, if she'd kept it or burned it, but it didn't matter. He didn't need to see it ever again. The words on the pages were burned on the inside of his eyelids.

Herbert Elmer McCullough, also known variously as Mac, One-Bucket, and Scotty, had been a liar, a cheat, a confidence man, and a thief. He'd been born in Vancouver, British Columbia, to Scots immigrants who booted him out of the house when he was caught seducing the upstairs maid, so add conscienceless Casanova to the list of his lifetime achievements. He'd come north during the Klondike Gold Rush, and according to him—and at this stage Samuel Leviticus Dementieff (bar sinister McCullough) was not in a credulous mood—had made a good living out of salting and selling gold claims.

He'd migrated from the Klondike into Alaska and arrived in Niniltna in company with the Spanish flu. It would have been entirely in character, Old Sam thought, for Mac to have brought the flu bug in with him.

Mac had gone up into the mountains to stake a claim and perform his usual alchemical magic before putting the claim up for sale. When he'd come down to announce his "strike," half the town and most of the mine workers out at Kanuyaq were already ill.

He himself was one of the lucky few who appeared to be immune, and from then on it was easy pickings. All he had to do was wait until a household was struck down and volunteer to help find food or fetch wood, play the good Samaritan only doing his bit. It was literally a license to steal. He was free to walk in and out of their homes and businesses at will and collect whatever caught his fancy. He stuck to smaller, more portable items, as he was not a man to weigh himself down with either possessions or people. Jewelry, loose cash, gold pokes, some of the smaller ivory carvings—if it could fit into his pocket he put it there. Let's face it, most of the people he stole from, as sick and incapable as they were, would have considered it fair exchange for the food and firewood he left behind.

He shuttled back and forth between the town and the mine, and his pack grew ever heavier. And then Mac had heard that the Niniltna chief and his wife and daughter had caught the influenza in their turn, and he figured that a tribal chief ought to have something worth liberating. He went inside, where he found the house freezing cold, the chief and his wife dead in their bed, and their daughter, Elizaveta, nearly dead in hers.

Mac had known many women in his life, and not beginning with the upstairs maid, either. Elizaveta was in that moment he first laid eyes on her gaunt and sallow, with hollow eyes and phlegmy breath, so it wasn't as if she had overwhelmed him with her pulchritude. And she could barely speak, so it wasn't as if she had charmed him with witty repartee.

But he looked at her, and he knew.

Well, Sam thought, he was like his father in that respect, at least.

Every moment he spent chopping wood for the house, every second he stayed in Niniltna to scrounge food for Elizaveta, every hour spent helping her lay out her parents and clean the meetinghouse was one moment closer to the discovery of his thefts.

Or to the Pinkertons catching up with him. They'd been on Mac's trail ever since that incident with the bank in San Francisco, and although he hadn't gone into the details with Hammett he'd made it clear he was one step ahead of them when he shipped out on that northbound steamer. They or someone like them had been sniffing around Dawson City, which was when he'd nipped over the border. He was a Canadian citizen who'd committed his crimes on U.S. soil—well, most of them, but he didn't go into detail there, either—and both nations were out for his blood.

Sam wondered if Mac had changed his name, if perhaps he had been born under something other than McCullough. Not that Sam had any intention of hunting up long-lost relatives in British Columbia who it didn't sound like would be happy to acknowledge a son of his father's get anyway.

Mac knew it was madness to stay one more day in Niniltna, one more hour. And yet stay he did, nursing Elizaveta and helping her with the aftermath of the epidemic and her parent's deaths. The inevitable happened. When she told him she was in the family way he panicked.

But he didn't run. No, he did not run.

At least not at first. So far as he knew this was his only child, and while he had always considered himself immune to romantic notions like love and marriage, Elizaveta was special to him in a way no woman had ever been before. He had to provide for them both somehow.

How does a thief solve his problems?

He does what he does best. He steals.

So Mac stole the Cross of Gold Nugget, which he had not bothered with before because it was so damn big, twenty pounds and six ounces of pure gold. The morning after the potlatch he slipped out of town and up into the mountains, where he had discovered a difficult but traversable pass into Canada when he'd staked his gold claim. So far as he knew it was unknown to anyone save himself. He had regarded it as a back door, in the event that Niniltna and Kanuyaq grew too hot to hold him and for whatever reason the road to Ahtna was not an option.

Mac had always had a fondness for back doors, and owed his minimal amount of jail time to date to including one in all of his various schemes.

So he stole the Cross of Gold, planning to hock it in Canada and bring the money back to Elizaveta and the child. On the way out the door, he picked up the Sainted Mary, the tribal icon on display at the big wake. It was there and so was he, and he'd need some walking-around money when he got to Canada.

What does a thief do best? He steals.

The weather had had other ideas, though. A late spring storm lasting three days filled the pass with twenty feet of snow. He'd nearly frozen to death, and came stumbling back down on numb feet to make the shelter of his claim cabin in the nick of time. Tiny, ramshackle, it warmed up only when enough snow drifted against the walls to keep the wind from whistling through. He holed up there to thaw out, and the storm lasted long enough for him to think the situation through and make some plans.

He stayed at the claim until the weather

cleared. He hid the Cross of Gold (he hadn't told Hammett where) and then snuck back down to Niniltna to see Elizaveta.

Where he found that she had left Niniltna with Quinto Dementieff two days before.

Poor bastard, Sam might have thought, if he'd been in a more forgiving mood. As it was, he thought if Mac had really meant to come back he would at least have left Elizaveta a note saying so.

It had hit Mac pretty hard at first, but after he thought it over he decided Elizaveta had made the right decision. He wasn't the type to settle down, and if she was going to raise their child in anything like civilized surroundings, she needed a man who could. He'd met Quinto at the potlatch, and he had seemed to be a good man. He would treat Elizaveta and the baby right.

But Mac was still determined to do right by them himself, and to Mac, that meant money. He was carrying quite a haul in his pack, and the price would be better Outside. By far and away the majority of the stampeders never hit it big, and most of them spent their last dime on the ticket south. When they debarked in Seattle or Portland or San Francisco they were ready to sell off whatever they had left for money to get the rest of the way home, and there were always people on the docks, waiting for them with a wad of cash.

He avoided Niniltna (whose residents had to have noticed by now that certain items were missing), and by various furtive ways he hied himself to Seward to take the first boat that spring. He'd sold everything in his pack to the first man on the Seattle docks who'd had enough cash money, and according to Hammett's story he was just about to buy a ticket back north on the proceeds when the law clapped him on the shoulder.

Right, Sam thought.

Mac was extradited to California, where he was tried and convicted of bank robbery, grand theft, and involuntary manslaughter, which last was what got him the bulk of his sentence. He said he hadn't done it. Old Sam believed that about as much as he believed the rest of the story.

From San Quentin Mac had a letter smuggled out and sent to Elizaveta in Cordova. In it he told her to keep his mining claim, to restake it or homestead it if need be.

This Sam did believe, because his mother was the one who had insisted that he claim his homestead there, in nosebleed country, where the rock was so solid a spud would have to sprout wings to grow in place. Sam, at first incredulous, had demanded to know why there, of all the godforsaken places. Elizaveta wouldn't tell him, afraid, Sam realized now, of his reaction to the news of his true parentage. Quinto Dementieff had been a good man and a good father who never by word or deed hinted that Sam wasn't his son by blood. He'd died in a dockside accident while Sam was in the Aleutians. Sam had loved him very much and had grieved his loss.

In the story, Mac didn't say if he told Elizaveta about the Cross of Gold. He also didn't say if Mac told her where he had hidden it on the claim. Gold nuts never gave up a claim, or a find.

Or, evidently, a stolen object.

When Mac was released in 1941, he did in fact come north once more, intending, so the manuscript read, to sell the Cross of Gold and give the money to Elizaveta. But then the Japanese invaded the Aleutians and the army was looking for men wise in the ways of the Alaskan backwoods, hardy men skilled in survival. Mac, for what Sam was certain was only the second time in his life, was spurred to an act of altruism and volunteered for the Alaska Scouts. He very carefully didn't tell them about the case of tuberculosis he'd picked up in San Quentin because he'd completely recovered and was fit as a fiddle.

Sam remembered Mac laying in that hospital bed in Adak, his cheeks flushed and his hollow cough, and the terse message accompanying the manuscript, informing him of Mac's death. He hadn't even lived to get off Adak.

Not completely recovered. No.

In spite of himself, as he walked the streets and alleys and neighborhoods of Seattle, braving the separate gauntlets of junk shop and junkyard, Old Sam wondered if Mac had recognized him in boot. Had he intentionally befriended the man he recognized as his son? Who had Mac saved from that Jap sniper that day, Old Sam, his buddy, or his son Sam?

You brothers? Even Hammett had seen the resemblance.

But Mac hadn't said. And now Old Sam would never know.

Seventeen

IT'S ALMOST DICKENSIAN," KATE SAID, looking up from the last page. "I mean, what are the odds, Auntie? That Old Sam would wind up fighting alongside the man who was his real father? And that his father would save his life?"

"That!" Out came the forefinger again. "That the worse thing!"

"What?" Kate said, feeling skewered.

Auntie Joy waved agitated hands. "That Samuel find out Quinto not his father. Why his real father tell him this story? Samuel never know elsewise."

"Don't you think it's better to know than not know, Auntie?"

"No!" Auntie Joy became if anything even more upset. "Blood makes no father. Love, care, being there"—again Auntie Joy thumped the table hard enough to make the china jump, and this time there was a concerned whine from the other side of the door—"that make a parent. This man!" She made a scornful gesture at the manuscript sitting in Kate's lap. "This man only—this man only a— a—" She couldn't think of anything opprobrious enough to say.

"This man was only a sperm donor?" Kate said.

"Yes!" Thump. China teeth chattered. "Exactly right. Sperm donor. He donate sperm— unwanted!—and then he run. Pah!" It wasn't a word with enough force to describe the extent of her contempt. "Quinto worth ten of that useless man."

Kate wasn't so sure. Elizaveta Kookesh had married Quinto Dementieff less than a month after Mac McCullough had disappeared. If Mac had come back to find Elizaveta not only gone but married and gone, why wouldn't he leave?

And he had saved Old Sam's life on Attu. For that alone Kate could forgive him much.

Auntie Joy's level of indignation could have much more to do with the depth of her feeling for Sam than it did her contempt for his father.

And possibly the theft of the icon. Auntie Joy was very much a daughter of her tribe. "What about this icon, Auntie?"

Auntie Joy's indignation abated a little, to be replaced by something that looked like reverence. "The Sainted Mary. Yes."

Kate had heard some of this from Demetri but she wanted Auntie Joy's unadulterated perspective. Demetri was two generations removed from the icon, Auntie Joy only one. "The Sainted Mary?"

"My parents call it that. A holy thing, Katya." This punctuated by an empathetic nod. "A holy thing. I never see, of course," she said apologetically, like it was her fault. "But a holy thing for sure, touched by God's grace. You sick, you pray, you healed."

Kate thought that the original Latin might have been a little corrupted there but she didn't say so. "It had healing properties?"

"Oh yes," Auntie Joy said. "My mother say Aloysius Peterson blind until he kneel to pray before the Sainted Mary. She give him his sight back. A miracle." Kate didn't think her expression changed but Auntie Joy said again, with more force this time, "A miracle, Katya."

Kate, less interested in alleged miracles than in tracking the chain of custody, said, "Who kept the Sainted Mary?"

"Chief keep. Always with the chief the Sainted Mary stay. When he home, she with him. When he fish, she with him. When he travel, she with him. His responsibility always."

"So anybody who owned the Sainted Mary was the de facto chief of the tribe."

Auntie Joy looked shocked. "Not owned, Katya. The Sainted Mary never owned. Chief part mother, part father, part tribe." She gave Kate a meaningful glance.

Present company excepted, Kate thought. If nominated I will not run, if elected I will not serve. Except she had. "The chief was voted in?" she said. "And then he got the Sainted Mary?"

Auntie Joy looked dissatisfied with this description, but she nodded. "Sainted Mary part of chief job since the Sainted Mary comes to the people."

"When was that, exactly?"

Auntie Joy was impatient was such pedantry. "Not matter, Katya. My mother say Raven bring her over the sea to her true home. I say God does. He see our need, He provide like always."

"Got it," Kate said. "And then Old Sam's father stole it."

"Yes." Auntie Joy gave a solemn nod. "Very bad for chief's daughter, Elizaveta."

"So bad she'd marry a man maybe more to get out of town than to give her baby a name?" Really, Kate thought as the last phrase came out of her mouth, the middle ages are never very far away from any of us.

Auntie Joy shook her head. "No, Katya. My mother say Quinto love Elizaveta always. Before, after One-Bucket." She paused. "My father say Quinto a fool."

There speaks the man who sold you into marital slavery, Kate thought. I'll consider the source. She leafed through the manuscript again, pausing to read a paragraph here and there. It was a sober, linear recitation of a man's life—simple, straightforward, with no pretensions to literary style or grace. There might even be a hint of someone taking dictation. Maybe that's why it wasn't signed. Still, the juxtaposition of Old Sam and the man who invented noir was impossible to ignore. "Auntie, I'm no expert, but this could be an original, previously unknown manuscript by a very famous American writer. You probably don't know him, but—"

Auntie Joy's eyes flashed. "I not stupid, Katya," she said sharply. "I go to school. I can read."

"You've read Dashiell Hammett?" Kate said, too surprised for tact. She'd thought Auntie Joy's primary recreational reading consisted of the Bible and *True Romance* magazines.

"No," Auntie Joy said, still defiant. "But I watch Humphrey Bogart."

Kate laughed, and after a moment, Auntie Joy relaxed and laughed, too.

"Okay, Auntie. I'm sorry if I sounded patronizing. I didn't mean to."

Auntie Joy, gracious in victory, said, "So who this Hammett is?"

"He invented the hard-boiled detective in mysteries," Kate said, remembering Ben Gunn's near adoration of the writer. "And you're right, he is best known for *The Maltese Falcon*."

Auntie Joy loved the old movies. On the shelves above the secret drawer in the armoire were a television, a DVD player, and a movie library, most of it films in black-and-white. Ekaterina, Kate's grandmother and Auntie Joy's cousin, had held an after-school open house for all the grade-schoolers in Niniltna, featuring fry bread right out of the pan, Nestlé's cocoa made with evaporated milk, and stories about the Trickster. Since her death, Auntie Joy had stepped in as the default after-school special, although Kate heard that it was now tea with milk, shortbread, and Fred Astaire and Ginger Rogers dancing to *Swing Time* on the television. She was willing to bet it was just as well-attended, though. Auntie Joy had a fatal attraction for anyone under the age of twelve. And for most over it.

Auntie Joy raised her eyebrows. "And Hammett in the Aleutians in the war."

"He was, Auntie." Without thinking Kate added, "Jane Silver told me Old Sam told her that he met Hammett during the war."

Auntie Joy stiffened. "That woman."

"Oh," Kate said. "Ah. Um. You knew about her. And, uh, him. Them."

"I say to you already, I not stupid," Auntie Joy said in an acid tone. "Of course I know. Everyone know unmarried men go to Beatrice in Niniltna, and married men, too. When Northern Light close down in Ahtna, nowhere else for them to go for that."

"The Dawson Darling's place," Kate said.

Auntie Joy nodded. "Where Meganack house is now."

"Really." Kate smiled. She loved the idea of Iris Meganack's rigidly rectitudinal ass sitting on the foundation of a house of ill repute. She wondered if Iris knew.

And if not, how and when she might be

informed of such an interesting piece of Niniltna history.

Kate gave herself a mental shake. "Jane Silver is dead, Auntie."

"What?"

"She was killed Thursday in her own home. Chief Hazen says it looks like she forgot something on her way to work, went home to get it, and surprised a burglar in the act."

Auntie Joy was motionless for a moment, staring into space.

"Auntie?"

Auntie Joy came out of her trance and fixed Kate with a beady stare. "You think this burglar maybe have something to do with Old Sam?"

So much for keeping Kenny's suspicions quiet. "Yes, Auntie. I do."

"Maybe with people who attack you, too?"

"Yes, Auntie. I do." Kate tidied the manuscript, tucked it into its box, and replaced it in the secret drawer. The drawer vanished into the base of the armoire without a trace. "Apart from the priceless value it has as a piece of tribal history, I'm thinking that manuscript might be commercially valuable, Auntie. You want to take very good care of it. Keep it in the drawer. Don't tell anyone else it's here."

"Valuable?" Auntie Joy paled, and she looked at Kate, eyes suddenly fierce. "You be careful out there, Katya."

"I always am, Auntie."

Auntie Joy gave Kate's shiners a pointed glance.

"They snuck up on me," Kate said.

Auntie Joy looked at the door.

"Mutt was off feeding her face."

Auntie Joy's raised eyebrow said it all.

On impulse, when Kate left Auntie Joy's she went up to the school, where Mr. Tyler was happy to let her use one of the computers, and to root around in his bottom drawer for a piece of beef jerky for Mutt, which of course made her his slave for life. The feeling appeared to be mutual. Mutt vamping the male half of the Park with her usual abandon was almost comforting. At least there was one thing that didn't change.

At the computer Kate got online. After she'd read Mac's story in Auntie Joy's house this afternoon, she thought she now knew why she'd been attacked in Old Sam's cabin.

She had been standing there reading what was obviously an old book. The slip case for it had been laying on the seat of Old Sam's recliner, visible in a clear line of sight from the door. To someone looking in from outside, it could have looked like a box of a size to contain an icon.

According to his own confession, One-Bucket McCullough had stolen the icon.

She immediately cautioned herself. The

manuscript was undated and unattributed. There was no return address on the box. Old Sam hadn't left any message saying who had written it or who had sent it to him.

But One-Bucket was a known con man, according to Ruthe Bauman. According to Auntie Joy, he and the icon had disappeared at the same time. And he had confessed to it in the manuscript.

The last paragraph had read, "Pop's writing this down for me and he'll see that it gets to you. I picked up the consumption when I was on the inside and the docs tell me I haven't got much time. Tell your mother I'm sorry, son."

It might even be a dying declaration.

How would someone find out about Mac's thievery, sans access to the manuscript?

That was even easier. Pillow talk between Old Sam and Jane Silver. At that time and since, Jane's experience of the world of Ahtna and the Park would have been large and varied. She called Judge Anglebrandt "Albie," for crissake.

Old Sam must have told her the story. She could have told anyone and everyone.

If Mac had stolen the icon, and if it became known that Old Sam was Mac's son, and then Old Sam died . . .

The icon had pretty much fallen off the radar. Kate's generation of Park rats had gone secular in a big way. Ekaterina had enthralled the after-school youngsters with all kinds of stories, and Kate thought she might even remember one about a lost treasure, but she'd been so young she'd thought it meant a chest full of pieces of eight. She certainly didn't remember any stories about a holy tribal relic with a direct line to God and the power to heal.

It was odd, that. She would have thought a scandal that had changed so many lives would have lasted at least three generations. Although to be fair, the Park had suffered a great deal of incident in the interim. The Kanuyaq mine closing. War. The influx of Aleuts displaced from the Aleutians resettling in the Park, and the consequent friction between them and the tribes already living there, whether they were related or not. The oil boom, the discoveries on the Kenai Peninsula and in Prudhoe Bay that changed every Alaskan's life. Statehood. The Alaska Native Claims Settlement Act, the Alaska National Interest Lands Conservation Act, the consequences of which were still being worked out between the tribes and the courts. A string of Republican representatives in Washington who had channeled federal funds into the state like they were holding a fire hose.

When you lined it up like that, it was a wonder anyone had a moment to spare for an item venerated with superstitious awe by a small and insular group of people almost a century before.

The old customs and traditions had been left behind. Hell, who even went to fish camp anymore? The aunties, yeah, but nobody under fifty. Commercial fishing for pay rather than subsistence fishing for survival was the order of the day. Ekaterina was the last elder who had spoken English as a second language, and her Native dialect had been altered by the move from the Aleutians to the Park. The BIA schools and the Molly Hootch law had finished off Native dialects all over the state, and various native cultures along with them.

Jack Morgan had still been alive the last time Kate danced when it hadn't been at a potlatch to honor the dead.

There was more than one motive here, Kate thought. If there was someone out there who was watching this happen, who deplored the loss of culture and tradition, someone who was trying to think of a way to stop it or even just slow it down, if they had heard of the existence of an icon revered in a collective ethnic memory that wasn't quite extinguished, what would they do to recover it?

She thought of Jane Silver, dying on the floor of her house five days before.

Maybe that question should be, what wouldn't they do?

That hole is going to be a mile deep and two miles wide square in the middle of the Park,

Demetri had said. *A lot of people won't ever be able to find middle ground with that.*

And Demetri was a descendent of Chief Lev, a man many believed was the last of the great chiefs. The last known guardian of the Sainted Mary.

Kate thought how ironic it was that a Russian Orthodox icon had come to be a tribal icon, a gussuk's creation subverted to the service of an Alaskan Native tribe.

She Googled Russian icons, and the result rocked her back in her chair.

A Russian icon made in 1894 that had been in the private possession of the last Russian czar had recently sold at auction for $854,000.

That many decimal places was a powerful motivator.

So, someone was looking for the icon, either for its own cultural value to the tribe or for its monetary value on the open marketplace.

Or both.

One-Bucket McCullough had told his story, say to Dashiell Hammett because why not, who had written it down and sent it to Old Sam. Old Sam had told Jane, and whoever was now looking for the icon had learned about it from Jane or from someone Jane had told.

True, Jane Silver had never struck Kate as the confiding type, but she supposed everyone had a weak spot.

The fact that they had waited for Old Sam to die to come after the icon argued that they knew him, or at least knew of him. No one in their right mind who did would ever have tried to steal from him when he was alive.

Which meant there was a good chance she knew them, too.

Kate frowned down at her crossed arms.

But why would they think that Old Sam had the icon? The story clearly said that Mac had sold it off to someone on the docks, but only three people, four if you counted Hammett, had ever read it.

Someone in Seattle.

Had Old Sam gone to Seattle in pursuit of the icon? He'd suffered through a pretty traumatic week in Niniltna, finding out his father wasn't who he'd thought he was, which experience had been capped off by being rejected yet again by the love of his life. He would not have been a happy man in the days following, and unhappy men were prone to rash and often unwise action.

Kate's brows drew together. Would Old Sam have wondered what would happen if he found the icon and brought it home? Would he think the tribe would forgive him his Filipino blood? Or, now, his white blood?

Perhaps more important, would he think that Auntie Joy's parents might decide he was a fit person for her to marry after all?

If he had gone after the icon, he hadn't told Auntie Joy about it. And if he'd found it, he hadn't told her that, either.

Kate called up the computer's menu and found that someone had downloaded Skype. She created an account and called Jim's cell phone.

Voice mail. Shit. "Hey," she said brightly. "It's me. I'm in Niniltna overnight and I'll be sleeping in your room at Auntie Vi's. I just wanted you to know I'll be tossing the room, pulling up floorboards and lifting ceiling panels, looking for all those love letters you wrote to your other girlfriends. I'm thinking I could get a good price for them on eBay."

By not so much as a raised eyebrow did Mr. Tyler, grading papers at his desk, betray that he had overhead one word.

Auntie Vi was happy to let Kate sleep in Jim's room at the B and B. Kate parked the snowgo out front and checked in with Annie Mike before Auntie Vi served her a hearty meal of smoked moose hocks and beans, along with a litany of complaints about how hard she was working. "You could quit," Kate said, and was roundly snubbed for daring to suggest anything so sensible.

In Jim's room, she undressed and got between the sheets naked. Two-hundred-count percale against her bare skin wasn't much of a substitute, but at least it was percale that had touched his skin, too.

Mutt lay down in front of the door, and spent the night listening to Kate toss and turn.

Mr. Abernathy looked so much like a Hollywood version of the old family attorney that Jim wondered if it was an impression he deliberately cultivated. His three-piece suit was tweedy and bagged a little at the elbows and knees; his bow tie was bright red and flamboyant enough that it gave the impression it would squirt you if you got too close. He wore round, black-rimmed glasses behind which gray eyes could be imagined to twinkle, and his white hair was a positive pompadour in the style of Lyle Lovett. There was the merest hint of a drawl when he spoke, as if he'd come west from South Carolina long enough ago to be forgiven secession but not too long ago to have forgotten his roots.

"I don't see the need for this," Jim said. "There is no legal requirement for reading a will. Besides, both my mother and I have copies. We already know what's in it."

"James," his mother said, radiating an austere reproof.

Abernathy twinkled at him from behind his black rims. Jim had a suspicion the lenses were plain glass. "It was your father's wish that the will be read in your and your mother's presence, Sergeant Chopin."

From the corner of his eye Jim could see the

moue of distaste cross his mother's face. General, admiral, attorney general, those were titles she could have lived with. Sergeant? Much too far below the salt. "Call me Jim," he said. She didn't like that, either, a deplorable lack of formality, yet another characteristic of the great unwashed.

Abernathy inclined his head without taking advantage of the invitation. "There being no further objection, let us proceed."

He cleared his throat, rattled his papers, and got to it. He was a pretty good reader, Jim thought, only half listening, lending life to the spare, dry language that summed up the material reward of his father's life and works. There were no surprises, not at first. His mother got the house and its contents outright. The firm's building was to be sold to the surviving partners at fair market value. The rest of the real property was to be sold on the open market—his father had even named the realtor to be employed—and the proceeds were to be divided equally between Jim and his mother following the settlement of any outstanding debt. Jim's share was left to him outright, with no conditions. His mother's share was left half to her outright and half in trust, the income from the latter going to her during her lifetime and reverting to Jim following her death.

Most of the real estate was within an hour's drive of the chair he was sitting in. His father had always had a kick-the-tire philosophy when it came to investing. Even in the current economy the proceeds would realize a huge chunk of change. Jim would never have to work again, if he didn't want to.

There were a few small bequests to longtime associates and employees. An original edition of *Blackstone's Commentaries on the Laws of England* to a friend at the office. His set of TaylorMade clubs to his golfing partner. Lump sums to Maria and the manager of the club and to half a dozen charities. Jim was surprised and touched when he heard that the largest amount went to the Los Angeles Police Foundation. "When did he do that?"

"James revised his will six months ago," Abernathy said. "There were two alterations. That was the first."

Jim looked at his mother. "My copy must have been lost in the mail."

Her mouth tightened.

Jim looked back at the attorney. "What was the second?"

Abernathy adjusted his glasses. "To my only child, James, in addition to his share of the estate as specified above, I also bequeath my mahogany writing box and all of its contents outright." The lawyer picked up a box sitting at his elbow and stood to hand it to Jim. "He left this in my custody at the time he revised his will."

It was twenty inches long, nine inches wide, and

six inches deep, and a hymn to the woodworker's art. The joints were dovetailed and reinforced with brass strips and brass screws that had been ground down to be even with the brass strips. There was a brass handle at each end and a brass lock on the front. The wood was like satin to the touch, the brass smooth and cool. It looked as well-loved as it looked well-used, and it had sat on his father's desk in his office at the firm for as long as Jim could remember.

He swallowed hard and looked at Abernathy. "What's in it?"

Abernathy, as well-trained as he was, could not forbear a glance at Jim's mother. Jim looked at her, too, and then both of them looked away from the expression of suppressed rage they saw there.

"I was most specifically enjoined by my client not to inventory the contents," Abernathy said primly. He pulled an envelope from the pocket inside his jacket and handed it to Jim. "Here is the key."

Jim's name was written on the envelope in his father's hand, a little shakier than the last time he'd seen it. The small brass key had fallen into one corner. The flap of the envelope was securely sealed. The key was all that was inside. "Thank you," he said, his voice barely above a whisper.

"Is that all, Mr. Abernathy?" his mother said.

Mr. Abernathy tided his papers. "Yes, Mrs. Chopin, I believe that concludes our business for today. I will put James's instructions in hand at once, and I will of course keep you apprised of my progress."

"Thank you." The two of them rose to their feet and Beverly showed Mr. Abernathy to the door.

Jim sat where he was, fighting back unexpected tears.

The happiest times he had spent with his father had been those all too few late afternoons after school in his father's office. He'd had to be quiet or he would be sent home, his father had said, and being sent home to his mother was sufficient threat to achieve practical invisibility. Tucked into an enormous Windsor chair, he sometimes lost himself in a book, sometimes drank in the language of the law as clients and colleagues and employees came and went and his father dispensed his wisdom to them all.

Or what had seemed like wisdom to the little boy in the corner. He looked down at the box in his lap. It was old, over two hundred years old. His father had told him that it had been carried by a family member who fought in the Revolutionary War, and George Washington and the rest of those old long-haired guys in their pedal pushers had never seemed so interesting to an eight-year-old. Some days, when the last client had gone, the elder Chopin would call the boy to him. They would bend their heads, one white, one blond, over the writing box as his father demonstrated the adjustable brass prop that held up the reading stand, the removable wooden stop that kept the paper or the book from sliding down, the ink-stained blotter, the original cut-glass inkwells with their brass tops, the storage compartment, the secret drawers.

For Jim, that writing box was filled with more mystery and more romance than any treasure chest buried by Blackbeard. It was a portal to another era. He'd grown up surrounded by screens—television screens, video game screens, computer screens—and the idea of putting ink in a pen and then using that pen to write on a thick sheet of cream-colored paper was almost exotic. The secret drawers didn't hurt.

Neither did the time spent with his father.

Beverly never came to the office.

Eighteen

SHE SET OFF AT FIRST LIGHT, TAKING the road south out of Niniltna and then cutting east cross-country well before Squaw Candy Creek. The last thing she needed was Bobby Clark demanding an explanation of her shiners. Or Dinah Clark deciding they needed to be filmed for posterity.

It had snowed another foot during the night. It was hard going in places where its own weight had yet to pack it down. Still, there was enough to make it an enjoyable ride, especially since yesterday's dull overcast was broken today by the occasional errant beam of sunlight.

At noon they stopped for lunch at the entrance of what she prayed was the right canyon. Mutt went foraging while Kate lit a Sterno one-burner and made some instant chicken soup. She used it to wash down a sandwich made in Auntie Vi's kitchen that morning, thick slabs of homemade bread, slices of roast moose alternating with slices of tomato, cream cheese, lettuce, mustard, and mayonnaise. The stuff cross-country snow machine treks were made of.

The snowgo was perched at the top of a rise that wind and avalanche kept clear of trees, and the view extended for miles. The Quilaks loomed at her back, magnificent and menacing. From here, the Kanuyaq River was a gray ribbon twisting between distant, snow-covered banks. In another month or two, it would be frozen solid beneath Park rats in pickups and on snowgos and four-wheelers, going to school, going to the store, going over the river and through the woods to grandmother's house. A few intrepid tourists had even been known to travel it on skis.

In summer the river was succor and sustenance, the birthplace and the harvest place of the salmon that fed them all. In winter it was transportation.

It was beautiful in any season.

She turned to look in the other direction. If the

river was the heart of the Park, the Quilaks were its backbone, a ragged set of vertebrae trending in a great eastward arc, turning when they hit the Canadian border and from there running south, stopping just short of the Gulf of Alaska.

From where Kate sat, rocky spurs rose high on one side and higher on the other, with the intimidating bulk of the Quilaks taking up most of the eastern sky. They were not shrinking violets, the Quilaks, not some soft, rounded little knolls short enough to spit over masquerading in a mountain costume for Halloween. The year Kate had spent at Quantico, she'd made several weekend expeditions with classmates into what passed for wilderness east of the Mississippi, and the first time someone had pointed and said, "Look, there's Mount Jefferson," Kate had said in genuine confusion, "Where?" It had taken her a while to get used to the idea that you could call something a mountain that was only eight hundred feet tall.

The Quilaks were individually anywhere between five and sixteen thousand feet high, with Angqaq Peak at nineteen thousand and change the highest of them all.

The mountain, Angqaq was a brutal wedge sharp enough to tear open the sky. Its nearly vertical peak dared climbers from all over the world to a duel that ended either in death or in the knocking back of a Middle Finger at Bernie's Roadhouse.

There were previously triumphant climbers who post–Middle Finger might have wished to have left their carcasses in a crevasse on Big Bump instead. The next mountain over, similar in shape, stood ready to take on whatever climbing fool might imagine two thousand feet less in height would be easier to summit. Climbers nicknamed it and Angqaq "Mother and Child," not infrequently shortening that to "Mother," and occasionally with feeling lengthening it again to "you mother."

Big Bump dominated the skyline with a swagger and a sneer, but its cohorts were nothing to sneeze at, either, and taken together the Quilaks did not give way easily to the incursions of man. They were easier to drive around. On a clear day you could admire them at a safe distance from the Beaver Creek border crossing, which was as close as most people ever got. The range formed a very effective border, as the stampeders on the Klondike trail had learned in the winter of 1898–1899.

It wasn't the great statue laying broken in the desert that inspired awe and despair, Kate thought, it was this eternal, unchanging bulwark thrown up by four billion years of tectonic shifts that squelched any sense of self-importance.

"You don't scare me," she said out loud.

Mutt, trotting up that instant with a ptarmigan feather caught in her teeth, gave her an odd look, and she laughed.

Whistling past the graveyard.

She packed up and they moved on.

The last time she'd traveled to the hot springs, a little over a year ago, she had lost the way three times before finding the correct dogleg that hid the entrance to the narrow little canyon. This time, she took it more slowly, paying attention. It looked like they were the first to visit this year. The only tracks she saw were the tiny prints of shrews and voles, the larger, leaping prints of the arctic hare, and the occasional disappearance of said tracks with the imprint of wing tips on either side as an explanation.

They came to a small saddle of rock. If you had never been there before, unless you looked closely you would never see that the saddle stopped short of the opposite wall, leaving a passage open to the narrow canyon on the other side. She slowed down even more, and Mutt hopped off and trotted ahead. Kate followed, with care.

They emerged from the passageway into a tapered vee of irregular stone walls, which met almost perpendicularly in an inclined floor that rose gradually from the saddle to what appeared to be a dead end. Next stop, sky.

The hot springs seeped out of the floor of the canyon, a series of seven interconnected pools that steamed gently in the cold air. The sides of the canyon were carpeted with spruce trees, a dark healthy green. The heat from the springs had created a microclimate for this lush little oasis, and the dogleg entrance and the steep walls had thus far protected the trees from the voracious appetite of the spruce bark beetles that had decimated the forests across the North American continent.

The tumbledown log cabin at the top of the springs still had a roof and walls—just. She pulled up in front of the door and killed the engine. Mutt came loping around the corner of the cabin, her tongue hanging out of the side of her mouth, and followed Kate through the door that hung cattywampus from its hinges.

Inside was a mess, courtesy of the cabin's last occupants, not to mention decades of Park rats packing in and not packing out again like they were supposed to. Someone had replaced the original cast-iron woodstove with a crude but functional stove made from an oil drum, and Kate had seen a stack of firewood outside the door.

She cleaned the cabin by the simple expedient of propping open the door and pitching all the trash outside, building a burn pile a safe distance away from the cabin. Place could use a burn barrel. She made a broom out of a couple of spruce boughs bound together and swept the floor, which proved to be made of wood planks that creaked protestingly beneath her feet, but held. A screwdriver and some new screws from the tool kit on her snowgo lessened the draft between the door and the jamb.

The outhouse in back had fallen over the last time Kate had been there, not entirely at her instigation. It was still lying on its side. Kate held her breath and used the number two shovel she'd brought to knock down the pile of shit that had accumulated in the hole over the past sixty years. A bucket of lime had been inside the outhouse when it went over and there was enough left for a thick layer. A makeshift rope and pulley rigged to the nearest tree got the outhouse back on its feet, and she shifted it one corner at a time until it was recentered over the hole. Snow piled up around the sides would give it some insulation and help keep it steady, at least for a while. A roll of toilet paper placed in a coffee can with a plastic lid, and it was back in business. No flies this time of year, either.

She unpacked the rest of the supplies from the trailer and carried everything inside. She went back out to tarp snowgo and trailer both against the possibility of more snow, although if she stood still and looked straight up at what little sky the sides of the canyon allowed she could see a few faint stars beginning to appear. The mouth of the canyon faced south, so it wasn't completely devoid of sunlight, but during the winter the high rock walls ensured that the day would be brief indeed.

She went back into the cabin, lit the Coleman lantern she had brought with her, and surveyed the scene. Someone had done a good job on the drum stove because the room was palpably warmer. The ventilated walls were a vivid memory of her last trip out to the hot springs, and she had brought more tarps because of it. She shed her parka and got to work with a hammer and tacks, covering most of three walls with two bright blue tarps and one dark green tarp. It made for a colorful interior and reduced the drafts to where the stove could go to work in earnest.

There was a whine and a scratch at the door. Kate opened the door and Mutt padded inside. "I'm guessing you've already had your supper," Kate said, and indeed there was a trace of blood and fur on the iron gray muzzle. "I don't suppose you'd care to share?"

Mutt looked shifty.

"Yeah, I didn't think so, greedy guts."

Kate got out a small cast-iron Dutch oven and lid and put it on top of the drum stove. A little oil, some sliced garlic quick fried and removed before it burned, and she added slices of a small caribou roast, the last of last year's harvest. She might have to combine a neighborly visit to the Suulutaq Mine with a hunting trip up the Gruening River, which supported a healthy little herd of caribou. Or it had before Howie Katelnikof had orchestrated his hunt of wholesale proportions the previous winter. Kate would check with Ruthe before the season opened.

The meat had a nice crisp crust and a pink interior when she took it out of the pan, into which she now put a sliced onion and waited for it to turn translucent before draining a can of green beans. Stirred together, the leftover oil, the browned onion, and the green beans made Kate's favorite vegetable dish, and it was even almost healthy, too.

Well. It was green.

She ate with a hearty appetite—there was nothing like working outside in the winter to make you hungry—and washed up with snowmelt. She melted more snow for cocoa and sat on the snowgo seat she had removed from the chassis and brought inside. She leaned against the dark green tarp tacked to the back wall, and looked around the cabin.

It was old enough to have been built by a young Samuel Leviticus Dementieff, and now that she was looking for them she could see the bones of the original floor plan, which was very like that of Old Sam's cabin and Auntie Joy's cabin. And the cabin Kate's father had brought her mother home to, where Kate had been born and in which she had lived most of her life, until some asshole under the mistaken impression that Kate was inside had burned it down.

It was roughly the same size as the others. She

remembered the description on Old Sam's document of proof. *Part log, part frame, two doors, two windows, shingle roof.* The walls were log, still neatly fitting together although virtually every log had bowed after years of drying and there wasn't the vestige of a chink left to fill any of the resulting gaps. The roof was intact, Kate suspected in part because it was sod over planks, like the one on Old Sam's cabin in Niniltna. The two windows, one on either side of the door, faced the hot springs and the mouth of the canyon, although both had been broken out long since and subsequently boarded up. The second door, leading out back to the outhouse, had also been boarded up long ago, and was now covered by one of the tarps.

She got to her feet and picked up the lantern, casting the light up. Yes, there were the posts halfway up the wall that would have supported the sleeping loft across the back half of the cabin. Very likely the loft had been taken down and used for firewood by those too lazy to go chop their own. Upon closer examination, the floorboards looked hand planed. As old and infirm as they were, they reminded her of the floorboards of Old Sam's cabin in Niniltna.

She thought of all the tools he had in his shop, including the old plane with the sharp blade set into the wooden body. As a little girl she had watched, fascinated, as Old Sam's large-knuckled

311

hands had run the plane back and forth and the wood came up in long, almost translucent curls.

All the varnish had been worn off the plane by the time she had seen Old Sam using it. She wondered if he had bought it new or if it was one of the tools he had inherited from Quinto Dementieff. If Quinto had had tools, and if he had left them to Old Sam.

Old Sam had never talked much about his father, and now Kate knew why.

It had been a long day, and a longer week. Her body ached suddenly with all the remembered bumps and bruises she had sustained during the past seven days, from the bang on the head to the rollover to the not inconsiderable succession of mental and emotional shocks she had sustained with each new revelation of Old Sam's life. She had barely enough energy to pull her sleeping bag from its stuff sack and unroll it next to Mutt, sprawled in post-hunt splendor in front of the stove. She put some more wood on the fire, extinguished the lamp, and shucked out of her clothes. The flannel lining of the bag was warm by the time she slid inside. She snuggled down and was asleep in seconds.

The howls woke her hours later. Next to her Mutt was on her feet. Kate sat up, feeling unusually thickheaded. "What is it, girl?"

Then she heard the howls again. She tugged on

jeans and boots, grabbed parka and rifle, and opened the door.

The full moon had risen, flooding the canyon with light, the new snow reflecting it back double strength. In a small notch halfway up the canyon wall, figures outlined in the moonlight as if someone was training a spotlight on them, stood three wolves.

As if they had only been waiting for the door to open, the middle one paced forward, put his muzzle up to the sky, and let loose with a long, ululating howl that frightened the living hell out of everything on two and four feet within earshot.

Just outside the door of the cabin Mutt sat down, wrapped her tail around her feet, and waited in composed silence, head cocked a little to one side. When the big wolf was done, he dropped his head and trotted back to his pack mates.

Mutt rose to her feet and sashayed—it was the only word descriptive enough for her gait— sashayed forward. She pointed her muzzle at the moon, opened her mouth, and let loose with a howl that would have shamed James Brown. Earthy, plaintive, wild, it called to more than the hunter, it called to the lover, too.

The three wolves stood there immobile until the last peal was rung. Mutt shook herself and returned to Kate's side with an unmistakably smug look on her face.

The visitors, released from the spell, gave a few more yips and yowls, but clearly their hearts weren't in it. They put their muzzles together for a few moments, and then the big one came forward again and let loose with another call, shorter this time, one that seemed to end with a question mark.

Mutt looked up at Kate with imploring eyes.

"You aren't in heat, are you?" Kate said.

Mutt looked back at the wolves.

"Oh, go ahead," Kate said, and even before the words were all the way out of her mouth Mutt had exploded from her side, heading up the side of the canyon at the speed of light. The big wolf had enough time to take a half step back before Mutt cannoned into him. The two of them went into his pack mates with no perceptible diminution of speed and the resulting ball of fur and teeth resolved into a yipping, nipping mass that rollicked over the edge and spilled down the side of the canyon and nearly precipitated itself into the top pool of the hot springs.

Mutt executed a grand jeté that culminated in a neat and graceful four-point landing that Mikhail Baryshnikov would have wept to have seen. The big wolf screeched into a hairpin turn, while the smaller of his pack mates, a white female, couldn't stop herself and skidded over the side and into the water with a yip and a splash. There was a split second when Kate could have sworn that the other three stood there, laughing at her. She wasn't in the water for long and then the chase was on again, up and down the little canyon, over and around the seven pools, once in a circle around the cabin, through a clump of trees in which a great snowy owl was peacefully slumbering. He woke with an indignant squawk and launched himself into the air, his four-foot wingspan a vast and outraged sail against the half moon visible between the high walls of the canyon.

Kate, enchanted, sat down with her back to the door and lost all track of time, watching as the four of them hurtled in and out of the moonlight, playing tag and tug-of-war and capture the flag like a bunch of kids on a playground. An arctic hare whose black-lined ears had tips bent back by the velocity of his flight burst out of the undergrowth to take the first pond in a single panicked leap and vanished into a heap of snow-covered rocks, losing only a bit of his tail. A pure white ptarmigan exploded out of the other side of that same pile of rocks and beat frantically at the air to gain some desperately needed elevation, sharp teeth nipping at her all the way. She, too, escaped death by inches. But then Mutt and her new friends weren't trying that hard.

Kate herself was ignored as if she wasn't there. At some point she became aware of wetness on her cheek. Sitting on this ground, her back against this door, watching this scene play out over the homestead he had staked for whatever reason when he was younger than she was now, she felt more connected to Old Sam than she ever had before. The realization that she would never see him again, never talk to him again, never be yelled at by him again, never be tossed into Alaganik Bay by him again, never benefit from his wisdom and his counsel again, struck like a knife. Old Sam had been an irascible, mocking, unsympathetic son of a bitch as a general rule, but he'd been a giant of her childhood. The shadow he had cast was long, and its absence would be acutely felt for the rest of her life.

She bent her head and let the tears slide down her face and into the snow in his honor.

When she looked up again the moon and the moonlight had vanished, along with the wolves. Mutt was gone, too, but Kate wasn't alarmed. Mutt would escort them on their way to some boundary predetermined in her lupine brain and return.

Kate went back inside, added wood to the drum stove, and climbed back into her sleeping bag. She fell asleep as though felled by an ax.

Nineteen

SHE CAME AWAKE THE SECOND TIME that morning as she usually did, fully conscious and aware.

And knew that she wasn't alone.

She didn't move, but whoever it was must have sensed that she was no longer asleep. "Get up," they said.

She thought about it, considering and dismissing options.

There was an ungentle nudge in her back. "Get up," the same voice said. It was a male voice, not one she recognized, although the man would have to say more before she was sure.

She threw back the sleeping bag and rolled to her feet in one swift motion, balanced and ready. The man swore and jumped back.

He stood in the doorway clad in parka, bibs, and boots. He wore a dark blue balaclava pulled down over his face, and he had a bolt-action rifle in his hands, a Savage Model 110, easily recognizable even by non-gun nuts like Kate by its homeliness and by the barrel locknut. Hunters were willing to put up with its lack of aesthetics for its accuracy. A lot of Demetri's clients carried them, or the serious ones did.

The safety was off. She looked up. "What do you want?"

"Same thing you do. Where is it?"

She cocked her head, trying to memorize the tone and timbre of the voice so she would know it again. He kept himself very still, no betraying mannerisms or tics. His gear wasn't new. Neither was the rifle.

A lot of people made the mistake of thinking that a firearm was a great leveler. A lot of people were wrong. "I don't know what you're talking about," Kate said. "You're trespassing, you know."

"I want the map," he said.

"What map?" she said.

"Don't play cute with me. You've been following the same trail I have, a step behind all the way."

Arrogant. Kate noted it for future reference. "So you're the one who coldcocked me."

The hint of a shrug. "Hand it over."

"I don't have it," Kate said.

The Savage 110's barrel moved in a little wave. "On your knees," he said, "hands behind your head."

She looked past him out the open door. It was too early for the sun to have reached the bottom of the canyon, but it was light out. She saw no movement except for faint wisps of steam rising from the top of the first pond.

He raised the rifle and pointed it in a less general direction. She felt her belly contract in response, and she shivered in her long johns. She hoped it didn't show.

"On your knees," he said, "facing away from me."

She should have tackled him instead of talking. She got on her knees.

"Hands behind your head."

She put her hands behind her head and felt him approach, but she could feel that he was keeping what he thought was a safe distance, and he was taking his time, which allowed her to formulate a plan.

He took one of her wrists and she felt a loop slip over one hand. She spread her ankles, let her butt slide to the floor between them and pushed off with her knees into a backward somersault, rocking onto her back, bringing her knees together and her feet up in a single sharp kick. He was too tall for her feet to hit his jaw—she noted that for later—and instead both her feet hit him squarely in the sternum, just below his rib cage.

His breath whooshed out, but he didn't fall, only staggered back several steps. He'd had to tuck the rifle under one arm to deal with her hands, and her kick had knocked it loose.

The impact against the wall forced his lungs to expand and he caught his breath and the rifle before it hit the floor and was bringing it up when she completed the somersault. In the same smooth, continuous motions, she swiveled on both feet with knees bent and launched her right shoulder at his midsection in a tackle that would have earned her a starting position with the Seattle Seahawks. Or it would have if her fucking sleeping bag hadn't slipped beneath her feet. She lost traction and force and the tackle turned into more of an uncontrolled collision, during which she managed to push the barrel of the rifle to one side. It went off too close to her head and he fell backward with her on top of him.

Her ears ringing, she went for the rifle with both hands. He was bigger than she was and stronger than she was—also noted—but she was quick and slippery and he kept grabbing for her hands where they'd been a moment before and in the meantime she was kicking and biting and clawing and in general keeping him too occupied with protecting his groin to get to his feet.

"Fuck this," he said, and dropped the rifle for a hand in her hair and another on the seat of her long johns. He threw her across the cabin. As she felt herself sailing through the air, it felt like she had all the time in the world to think about where she was going to hit and how she would prefer to land. She gathered herself into a ball just in time for her butt to smash into the wall directly beneath one of the former loft supports. She bounced to her feet, only to find him there before her, rifle in hand and trained on her again.

"You'd better use that thing," she said, breathless, "because I won't get on my knees for you a second time."

The face beneath the balaclava moved in what might have been a snarl. The rifle came up to his shoulder and she dove for her own rifle tangled in the folds of her sleeping bag, and Mutt came through the door like a silent streak of vengeful lightning.

She hit the intruder in the torso with the full force of her one hundred and forty pounds and he hit the wall again, this time hard enough to shake dirt loose from the roof. He fell to the floor and she went for his gun arm with her teeth.

He let out a yell, his first unrehearsed speech of the morning, and dropped the rifle. There was the sound of tearing Gore-Tex. A cloud of goose down burst around Mutt's head, and when it had settled the arm of his parka was seen to be dangling from her teeth.

By then Kate had her rifle. "Hey! Hey, asshole, get your hands up! Mutt! Back off! Mutt!"

Mutt ignored her, dropped the sleeve, and attacked again, going for the arm now clad only in a red-and-black plaid shirtsleeve. He managed to roll over and tuck it beneath him. Undeterred, Mutt went for the seat of his bibs. She must have got her a mouthful because this time he screamed like Macaulay Culkin.

He rolled again and Kate realized he was rolling

toward the door at about the same time he managed to grab his rifle and scramble to his feet. There was a kind of *chunk* in the wall behind her a second before she heard the report of another rifle, this time from outside the cabin. She ducked instinctively, far too late if whoever it was had been any kind of a marksman.

The shot made Mutt hesitate for one second. It was all he needed to get out the door. Mutt took off after him. Kate went after her, bare feet and all, in time to see Mutt's tail vanish around the corner of the cabin.

From in back there was a bark and a thud and another yell and a creaking sound and a crash in quick succession. Kate rounded the second corner just in time to see the outhouse fall over again and the guy knocked either by accident or design into the hole.

Another yell and a curse and a bark from Mutt that sounded like savage joy personified. Amazingly, the guy scrambled up and out of the hole and took off again, covered in powdered lime and frozen shit, Mutt snapping at his heels. He, Mutt, and Kate rounded the corner of the cabin and the guy lit out down the canyon.

The shooter was either just around the corner of the dogleg or up on the little saddle above. A tiny fountain of water spurted up from the surface of the pond right in front of Mutt. Again, a second later, Kate heard the report, and the third shot kicked up snow in front of Kate. Shooter getting his range.

She dodged to the side and yelled. "Mutt! Mutt, no, come back!"

Mutt ignored her and made a leap that was poetry in motion to fasten her teeth one more time in the man's retreating behind. He screamed again, this time sounding like Daniel Stern.

Another shot, this one kicking up snow far too near Mutt's hind legs, and Kate put all her considerable force of will into the next shout. "Mutt! Come! Now!" She drew out the last word, the scar on her throat pulling at her vocal cords in a way it hadn't in years.

Mutt let him go, and in a gait that was half limp, half scuttle he made it around the dogleg and disappeared.

There was another shot. This one hit the gas tank of her snow machine.

Gas spurted out through the neat hole made in the blue tarp.

"You son of a bitch," Kate said, really pissed off now, and dove for her rifle in the cabin. She rolled outside again and up on her belly and elbows to pull the stock into her shoulder and sight down the barrel, bringing the little metal bead to bear about man-height on the edge of the dogleg. The downward slope of the canyon floor was on her side this time. She fired twice in quick succession, or as quickly as possible with a bolt action rifle, resighted on the top of the little saddle, and fired twice more.

Then something smacked her on the side of the head and she slammed into the wall of the cabin. She heard the report of the rifle just before she plummeted down into darkness.

Someone was sandpapering her face. Again.

"Ow," she said.

The sandpapering redoubled in speed, this time with the sander kicked up a notch. A background sound resolved itself into a frantic, high-pitched whine. She'd heard that same whine before, and not that long ago, either.

"Shut up," she said.

If anything, the whine doubled in volume and intensity. Somebody had to make it stop. She'd do it herself but she couldn't get her eyes open.

The sander went into overdrive and the whine achieved a decibel level reminiscent of the first few chords of any Metallica song. She had to do something or her ears would start to bleed.

With a tremendous effort she swung the boom over, attached the tackle to her eyelids, and hit the winch. The cable almost snapped under the strain, but slowly, one eyelash at a time, she got her eyelids open.

She was laying flat on her back in the middle of the cabin, although she couldn't see much of it because a frantic Mutt hovered over her, howling and whining and snapping and growling. It was all too familiar.

"God damn you, Uncle," she said, her voice sounding not at all like her own. "What the hell have you gotten me into?"

Mutt gave a joyful bark at Kate's return from the dead, and if she hadn't sprayed her with spit Kate might have been able to join in the celebration. Instead, she shoved Mutt to one side and levered herself into a sitting position. She reached up a shaky hand to discover a shallow, inch-long groove above her right eye. It was remarkably clean, as was the surrounding skin and her hairline. She looked at Mutt, yellow eyes filled with fury and dismay and, yes, shame. She also saw traces of her own blood on Mutt's muzzle.

Great. And she'd just been getting over the first set of shiners. Still, Mutt had cleaned her up pretty good. Not to mention saved her life. Again. "Thanks, girl," she said.

Mutt licked the side of her face one more time, and then looked around and growled, apparently giving the cabin notice not to make any sudden moves.

Kate blinked a little herself. The door was open. Hadn't she been outside?

Her shoulder felt sore, and she pulled at the neck of her top to look at it. Tooth marks, although none had broken the skin. "What, did you drag me inside?"

Mutt growled. She was still seriously unhappy.

The resemblance between the last cabin Kate had regained consciousness in and this one was just a little too close for comfort. The contents of her pack were scattered from corner to corner. Her bed was a tangled mess. The stack on the barrel stove was knocked askew but thankfully had not broken open or there would have been soot all over everything.

Nausea tickled uncomfortably at the back of her throat. She staggered outside, where four steps from the door she dropped to her knees and threw up. That, too, was all too familiar.

It made her feel a little better, although the wound in her head still throbbed. She washed her mouth and face with snow and stood up. There was no sign of the intruder. There was, however, a strong smell of gasoline. She moved on shaky legs to her snowgo and removed the tarp, although she had to stop every couple of seconds to make sure the lights were going to stay on.

The bullet had caught the tank dead center. The good news was that (a) the tank hadn't exploded, and (b) the flood of gas had eased as it sank beneath the hole. She ripped the tarp off the trailer and found the duct tape and taped off the hole so at least more wouldn't evaporate. After that, she tried to think past the throbbing in her temple. Numbers had never been her best thing.

Her Arctic Cat got between twenty and twenty-five miles to the gallon if she kept her speed reasonable, hard to do until she got out of the mountains. She'd spent the extra $400 to get the high-capacity fuel tank. If it was half empty it should hold a little over four and a half gallons. She had a five-gallon gas can in the trailer, and she'd topped off the tank yesterday to prevent condensation inside the tank from the cold temperature. So the gas can was probably two gallons down.

Be conservative, say four gallons in the tank and three gallons in the gas can, seven total. It was about sixty miles to Niniltna. Even taking into consideration the first fifteen miles, which would burn more gas in negotiating saddles and doglegs and hairpin turns and crevasses and dense stands of trees and boulder fields, she should be okay. Probably. Maybe.

But she did not have gas to burn indiscriminately, which precluded chasing whoever it was who'd attacked her. Which was no doubt why the shooter had holed the tank. Fucker. She thought of his cohort dripping limey shit all the way down the cabin, and hoped the ride back to civilization was an aromatic one for them both.

Suddenly, insanely, she started to laugh. She laughed so hard it rang off the rock walls of the canyon. She laughed so long all the energy drained out of her and she had to sit down hard on the trailer. "Goddamn son of a bitch," she said.

She had more and better curses but had no energy left to make the welkin ring as deafeningly as it deserved, so she sat there a while longer and thought them instead, loudly.

Mutt, anxious, trod over to her side, and Kate hung an arm around her neck and buried her face in Mutt's fur. "Sorry, girl. Gimme a minute here. I promise I'll get back up to speed."

Mutt looked unconvinced, and her anxiety pushed Kate to her feet again. She started looking around the clearing for signs of how the intruder had arrived. Before she got very far along in this endeavor she realized she was still in her longies and without her boots and that the temperature was in the mid-thirties. She gave out with another halfhearted curse and staggered back inside the cabin to disinter her clothes. She had a powerful urge to remake her bed and dive in but she was dimly aware that going to sleep with a head injury was a bad idea. So she kept moving.

She used socks for pot holders and straightened the smokestack and built up the fire in the stove. She stamped her feet into her boots and located the first aid kit in her pack. Antiseptic cream spread on a Band-Aid would have to do for her head wound until she could get back to Niniltna and the clinic. She was not looking forward to the commentary she would undoubtedly receive from the Grosdidier brothers. She bolted a couple of aspirin dry and followed them with a mouthful of snow. The cold shock on the tissues of her mouth and the trickle of moisture down her throat alleviated the worst of the nausea.

Shrugging into her parka, she abandoned the rest of the mess in the cabin to go back outside.

It was a gray day, with clouds that promised more snow. If her intruder had left anything of interest behind him, best to look for it now before it was covered up. Ignoring the little man with the hammer wasn't easy, it wasn't even possible, but by focusing grimly on the task at hand and taking it one minute at a time, and with an alert and vengeful Mutt at her side every step of the way, she kept herself upright and moving.

A set of tracks postholed through the snow past the steaming ponds and around the little saddle. There she found signs of a snow machine, from the track possibly one of the newer Polaris models, although she wasn't as up on her snowgo sign as she could have wished.

There was a second, separate set of human tracks. The second set of tracks was smaller, indicating either a smaller man or a woman. Or, she supposed, a teenager of either sex.

Mutt, always acute at sensing Kate's moods, growled, a deep, rumbling sound full of promising menace.

"You said it, girl," Kate said.

Either the aspirin were starting to work, the

little man's arm was getting tired, or being pissed off had its own healing properties. With the easing of the pain in her head her eyes cleared and she felt a little less like a sleepwalking bear. She studied the tracks some more.

Yes, just around the curve, against the wall of the saddle, there were the knee marks, and yes, there were the elbow marks where the shooter had leaned to take aim.

"Goddamn son of a bitch," Kate said again, only this time much more quietly and with infinitely more feeling.

The track of the Polaris led out of the canyon. She listened, but she couldn't hear anything. She squinted at the sky and figured the time, amazingly, at early morning, no later than ten. It felt like she'd been out for hours.

Had they traveled to the hot springs at night? If they had, they would have had to be local, or they never would have been able to find the way.

And then she remembered the moon. She could have read the fine print of the *Oxford English Dictionary* by the light of last night's moon. And it hadn't snowed between her arrival and this morning. All anyone would have needed to follow the track of her snow machine to Canyon Hot Springs last night was twenty-twenty vision.

The longer she stood here, the farther away they got. She wanted to get on the snowgo and head out after them. She spent several pleasurable moments imagining what she would do when she caught up to them.

The cold air eased the pain of her wound some, but not enough. She was hurt and tired and hungry and thirsty, and in no shape to go chasing after a couple of bushwhackers.

She went back to the cabin. No singing mice had cleaned up the mess in her absence, but the water was steaming on the stove. Her eyes were starting to feel puffy, too. She didn't get the mirror out of the survival kit because she didn't want to know. She looked down at Mutt, whose hair had yet to lay down on the back of her neck. The blood on her muzzle was still in evidence and Kate was sure that it contained cells from more than one donor. "Good girl," Kate said. "Well done."

Mutt gave her a look through narrowed yellow eyes. She was still pissed that Kate had called her off.

"They were shooting at you," Kate said. "Even you can't outrun a bullet, Mutt."

Mutt lifted her lip in what on a less august countenance might have been called a sneer. *I could have caught them.* She might as well have said it out loud.

"Yeah," Kate said, "I know, you're a working dog, and I'm supposed to let you do your job, which includes tearing the asses off assholes." Her eyes strayed to the most recent scar, by this time invisible in the gray fur to anyone who hadn't watched it heal day by day. Two years later, the image of Mutt unconscious on the vet's table in Ahtna was still vivid in Kate's mind.

She felt a sharp sting and looked down in mild surprise to see that Mutt had nipped her left ankle hard enough to draw blood. She looked up to meet a hard yellow stare and a hairy lip lifted to display a pair of sharp canines.

"Okay," she said, "that's fair. But you go any more psychic on me and I'm hiring an exorcist."

Mutt gave a high-pitched bark, one that Kate knew from experience denoted outrage and disillusionment. Kate almost shied away from meeting Mutt's eyes. Mutt barked again, and this time there was no mistaking the warning.

"I don't get in your way next time, is that it?" Kate said.

Another bark.

"Or what?"

Mutt barked a third time, turned her back, shouldered the door open, and marched outside.

"Mutt, don't," Kate said. "Come back here. Come on, girl."

But Mutt didn't, and Kate wondered miserably what she was supposed to do. Let Mutt go into harm's way, maybe wind up back on the vet's table in Ahtna?

She remembered Ruthe's look at Mutt when Kate had told her about the attack at the cabin.

Mutt's look of shame when Matt Grosdidier had looked at her, clearly wondering where Mutt had been when Kate had been under attack. Kenny Hazen not asking why she hadn't sent Mutt after Jane Silver's attacker, when they had actually heard him running out the back door. Johnny's care to say nothing at all.

Before Mutt got shot, the two of them had always gone into harm's way together, shoulder to shoulder, sharing the risk.

Now . . .

Moving slowly and with care, she reloaded her rifle and stood it against the wall next to the door. She poked up the fire and melted snow for coffee and biscuits and put bacon in a pan and set it on the stove. Grimly, she went outside to put up the outhouse again. This time it required some remedial work with hammer and nails, and this time she piled the snow so high against the walls it looked like it had flying buttresses. Although if she was going to keep this place she would have to come up with something a little more sturdy in the way of waste disposal.

She replaced the tools. The headache had receded to a dull throb, and her stomach growled. No sign of Mutt. She went back inside and shed her parka. The smell of frying bacon was beginning to perfume the air, and when she had made herself a cup of coffee the two smells combined were enough to raise the dead. She rolled biscuits and dropped them into the Dutch oven. They and the bacon were a delicious brown at the same time and she ate biscuit and bacon sandwiches sitting on the snow machine seat, leaning against the wall of the cabin, and tried not to think how lonely the cabin felt with Mutt gone.

She thought about the intruder that morning. Who the hell was he? Who the hell was his friend with the rifle? Why had they followed her all the way out here?

First things first, who had known she was coming to Canyon Hot Springs? She thought back. Johnny. Auntie Joy. Phyllis.

Oh. And Phyllis's aunt Virginia Anahonak, also known as the Niniltna town crier, who had been listening in on their conversation. That widened the field considerably.

She sat up with a jerk. "What map?" she said.

Kate poured herself another mug of coffee, doctored it with evaporated milk and a packet of sugar, and sat back again to study the interior of the cabin.

She'd tarped three of the four walls in an attempt to stem the cabin's natural air-conditioning, and on the admittedly lame theory that they might be covering something Old Sam had left her to find she pulled them down again. The fourth wall held the windows and the door, each its own wind tunnel. She'd duct-taped a trash bag over both windows. The door she'd left free for easy egress, as well as, as events transpired, ingress. She subjected each of the four walls to minute inspection, and found zero for her pains other than the remnants of first-rate craftsmanship.

The wood must have been very well seasoned before Old Sam had built the cabin. Kate wondered if he had felled the trees before the war and built the cabin afterward. She didn't know enough to know if that would have been good or bad, but she didn't think the temperature in this little canyon would have warmed up to the point that the logs, properly decked, wouldn't have lasted seven years. The logs had been hand hewn, the smooth, regular marks still evident through the graying of the wood. Old Sam had evened them up as much as possible, and would have filled the inevitable openings between the logs with a mixture of moss and mud. Kate didn't think Perma-Chink had been around then.

She thought about that dense thicket of spruce the snowy owl had been roosting in, and wondered if that was where Old Sam had harvested this timber. In the sixty-odd years since, even a copse in Alaska would have had time to recover. She thought she remembered a gravel foundation as well—he had one beneath the cabin in Niniltna—and wondered where he'd found gravel up here. Maybe in that little notch where the wolves had materialized the night before; it could have hosted a small hanging glacier at one time and on retreat left a gravel deposit behind. She wouldn't know until the following spring.

She'd been used to thinking of this cabin as on its knees, ready to fall down at the first mild breeze. She recognized now that its original construction had been so solid that with only a moderate amount of remedial care it would probably stand another fifty years.

"That's all very well, Kate," she said out loud, "but what about this map?"

Mutt wasn't there to answer. She banished the thought with another. Had Old Sam left a map behind to show her where he'd hidden the icon? If so, who else had he told about it? And why the hell would he?

She found herself getting annoyed with the old man all over again.

That, too, was a familiar feeling.

The cabin was high enough to accommodate a sleeping loft, as evidenced by the supports set two thirds of the way up the east and west walls of the cabin.

She was five feet tall. Old Sam had been a foot taller than she was.

She peered up, above the section of wall she'd smacked into with her butt that morning. Was one of the supports out a little farther than the others? A littler farther out of the wall than it had seemed to be last night?

She grabbed her mitts and went outside, where

she unhitched the trailer from the snowgo. It just fit through the door. She hauled it over to stand beneath the loft supports on the east wall. She put the snowgo seat on top of that. It wasn't the steadiest construction but it was what she had so it would have to do.

When she climbed on top of the seat her face was just below the supports.

They were log ends that had been notched into the walls at right angles to the wall logs. The second one out from the back wall extended a good half an inch beyond the ones on either side. Kate was sure that had not been the case the day before.

With a little coaxing, she managed to pull it from the wall. The edges of the cut were sharp and unsanded, and a shower of fresh sawdust sprinkled down on the snowgo seat. This hidey hole had been made very recently.

She wasn't quite tall enough to see back into the hole. She set down the notched piece of wood and reached as far back into the hole as she could stretch. Her hand closed over something. She pulled it out and looked at it. A package wrapped in newspaper, fastened with duct tape.

She put the notched wood back in its hole and used the hammer from the tool kit to tap it back into place, level with its fellow. No point in leaving behind any indication that something had been hidden, or that it had been found.

She spent a moment admiring the artistry of it. The cutout fit flush and seamless into the wall. You'd never have known it was there, not even looking straight at it.

If the force of her butt hitting the wall that morning hadn't knocked it loose in the first place, she might never have seen it at all.

One thing was for sure. Old Sam, pulling the puppet strings from beyond the grave, had not been interested in making things easy for her.

She climbed down and moved the seat back to the wall. She stared at the package for a full minute before she opened it.

It was another journal, the twin of the one she'd been reading in Old Sam's cabin when she'd been attacked. She opened it. Yes, here again was the flowing hand of U.S. Judge Albert Arthur Anglebrandt. This volume was dated 1939, two years after the volume that had been stolen.

She put down the journal and stuck her head outside. Small clouds that looked like torn cotton balls were scudding overhead, the sunlight winking in and out behind them, but in the protected little canyon it was still and calm. In the distance an eagle called, a wild, piercing cry that lasted seconds and faded. The sound was the wilderness itself on wings.

No sign of Mutt.

She tested the air against her cheek and found it crisp and cold and drier than it had been earlier in the day. She didn't think it was going to snow again for a day or two, if not more. If it did snow, she had enough supplies to see her through. Of course, if it did snow, she would have no tracks to follow in the morning.

Johnny was safe and snug at Annie's, nothing to worry about there. Jim was in California, everything to worry about there but nothing that going home today would cure. Best to take it easy and head back down tomorrow.

If it didn't snow, their tracks would still be there. If it did, she would live to fight another day.

Still no sign of Mutt.

Kate went back inside, poured herself another mug of coffee, and opened the journal to the first page. She read steadily through the rest of the day, marking names, setting the dates in context with what she already knew, and taking the occasional nap when her wound began to ache and her eyes began to blur.

By now, two years on, Judge Anglebrandt's court was a going concern, with a courthouse, a jail and a bailiff, and two territorial policemen assigned to Ahtna. He issued warrants, ruled charges reasonable or—rarely—unreasonable, appointed counsel for the indigent, set bail, heard pleas, and presided over trials both criminal and civil. There were some familiar names—Heiman in a civil trial involving embezzlement of funds, Katelnikof in a criminal trial involving burglary.

The apple hadn't fallen far from either tree. There were a few capital crimes, including two murders and one kidnapping that sounded pretty straightforward, all three of which resulted in conviction.

Life on the bench. Kate read on.

It wasn't until November of that year, November 17 to be exact, that she found what she was looking for.

The judge had received notification from a California court that Herbert Elmer McCullough, also known as Mac, also known as One-Bucket, had been released on parole from San Quentin. Since he had been imprisoned in part for crimes committed within Judge Anglebrandt's district, said judge would of course be notified. There had probably been notification of a parole hearing, for which his honor would have been solicited for recommendations, and probably to get into touch with Mac's victims to see how they felt about time off with good behavior.

In 1939, communications between Alaska and Outside would have been slow to nonexistent. By the time Judge Anglebrandt had received notification, Mac would have been on his way north, maybe even already back in the territory. Where he had been scooped up by General Simon Bolivar Buckner Jr. Kate did so love that name.

Why had Mac joined the Alaska Scouts? Okay, he'd tried to do as right by his son as a born con man knew how, but that didn't necessarily translate into a desire to serve one's country. She couldn't square patriotism with the man who had seduced Old Sam's mother, gotten her with child, and left her behind with barely a backward glance.

Kate had read Mac's protestations that he'd done everything for the sake of Elizaveta and his child with a disbelief verging on scorn. Mac was a thief. Thieves steal.

Still. She supposed a thief could be as patriotic as anyone else. For one thing, he had to know he was bound to prosper better in a free republic with ten constitutional amendments dedicated to giving him the benefit of the doubt.

Although. He had just gotten out of jail. She would have thought he'd taken enough orders to last him a lifetime. He'd been inside for nearly twenty years.

"Oh," she said out loud, and would have smacked her forehead if that morning's injury hadn't made that unwise.

Nobody spent twenty years inside without forming relationships. You had to talk to someone. Mac could have talked to someone about the icon, which story could have been handed down, one crook to another, possibly in written form, in a letter to a child, maybe, or to a friend on the outside.

She had another thought. Hammett, if Hammett's

hand it was that had shaped that very straightforward account of Herbert Elmer McCullough's life, had been a professional writer. Impossible to imagine him not making a copy of Mac's story. Impossible, too, to imagine he wasn't intrigued by a story of real-life stolen treasure. He could have set it aside after the war, meaning to go back to it, or even lost it in transition from the Aleutians to the South 48. It could have been found by someone else after he died.

So there were two explanations for her being attacked three times in eight days.

She wondered how much the icon was really worth. Her Google search had taught her that it could be valuable in itself. The stones embedded on the frame could be jewels of great price. It was valuable as an historical object to the state. It might be valuable as a cultural object to Kate's tribe. It would certainly be spiritually valuable to the tribal elders.

It wasn't likely that something that valuable had traveled in a trader's pack from Russia to Russian America, but it was possible. It wasn't likely that the trader had been killed in an attack on his stockade by the Kolosh and his pack rifled by warriors afterward, but it was possible. It wasn't likely that the warrior would recognize what he had and that it would become a family heirloom, but it was possible.

She wondered how it had gotten its reputation

for healing powers. Had some itinerant missionary seen it and used it to convert the heathen to the one true way?

She got up and opened the door, breathing deeply of the cold, invigorating air. What little sun the canyon walls allowed was long gone and the stars were lighting torches against the encroaching dark.

Still no sign of Mutt.

The pools stair-stepped in front of her down the center of the canyon, shallow and serene, the water rising from the floor of the first pool and disappearing down some subterranean passage after the seventh one. Old Sam had built with an eye to the hot springs. The first pond was within three long strides of the front door. She would have liked to have had a long soak in it but she was still too twitchy from that morning's mugging to take the chance of being caught outside the cabin, and naked in the bargain. She didn't think those particular two muggers were going to come back—for one thing, she didn't think one of them was going to be capable of riding a snowgo for a while—but at this point she had no idea who else Old Sam had told about some mythical map with buried treasure at the end of it, and she wasn't taking any more chances.

She made use of the facilities and went back inside to stoke the fire in the drum stove and light the lantern. She used more Bisquik, eggs, canned milk, a package of shredded cheese, and some canned green chilies to make a chile relleno pie, and washed it down with green tea, a new item in her pantry forced on her by Dinah Clark. It wasn't bad if you didn't mind grass-flavored water. Sweetened with honey it was almost tolerable.

She frowned down at her crossed ankles. Someone had known there was something to find at Old Sam's house, had known it before she did. Three days after he'd died they came to his house to find her reading one of Judge Anglebrandt's journals. They knocked her unconscious and took it.

It wasn't what you could have called a professional hit. It wasn't like they'd brought a sap with them. They'd used the first thing to hand, a piece of firewood. So, amateurs? But amateurs willing to commit assault, so either fairly earnest amateurs or ones unacquainted with Title 11, Chapter 41, Section 200 of the Alaska Statutes, and the penalties applied to the convicted thereof.

When they read the journal they had stolen from Old Sam's house and found, presumably, nothing relevant to their purpose, they would have known that the attack and the theft had alerted her, that she herself would now be looking for whatever it was, too. They must have followed her to Ahtna, to Jane Silver's office, from where they would have followed Jane Silver home. They'd waited to break into her house until Jane was gone, which argued some sense, and it was just Jane's bad luck that she had forgotten something and had come back home to get it, and their bad luck that Jane was a fragile old woman.

Afterward . . . of course. Of course the incident on the road was related to the whole mess. Either they thought Kate had found whatever it was that Jane had—this map the asshole had asked her about that morning?—or they'd wanted to stop her from finding it, and they'd run her off the road. They must have left Niniltna before she had and waited on the other side of the Deadman until they'd seen her headlights.

Which again argued in favor of locals. Strangers wouldn't know about the Deadman. The Deadman averaged about one Outsider a year, most of them fished alive and swearing out of either the ditch or the river.

And now this morning. They'd followed her all the way out from Niniltna, through the night. The one man's outerwear and 110 were not new, which also made them, if not Park rats, people who had time served in the Bush.

She went back in her mind over every detail of his appearance. Male, at a guess white or part white. Five ten accounting for the thick soles of his boots. A hundred and fifty pounds, although that was iffy given the added bulk of parka and bibs. There had been nothing familiar about his voice, but she had noticed that he took every care to speak as little as possible, single syllables spoken in a near monotone, as if he were afraid she might recognize it.

Which meant that she knew him. Or had met him. Or that he knew she would meet him in future.

She thought about Pete Wheeler.

And she thought about Ben Gunn.

She was certain that neither had been this morning's intruder, but Wheeler was in a position to be fully cognizant of Old Sam's affairs. Old Sam had not been what anyone would call loquacious, especially with strangers, but he might have let something slip in conversation with his attorney, some reference to something valuable in his possession. He might even have said something about sending his heir on a scavenger hunt, for which Kate could cheerfully kill him stone dead all over again.

And Pete Wheeler could have decided to find it first.

And then there was Ben Gunn. What with the loss of Old Sam and Jane Silver dying in her arms, her emotions had been far too close to the surface, and she had said too much to the newspaperman. He had said his grandfather had kept a journal (Had that been everyone's invariable habit back then?) of the life and times of the region, and when Kate had said she would like to read them one day he'd gone all vague. If he was really attempting a novel based on his grandfather's life, he would have had the journal ready to hand. Had George Washington Gunn written about the theft of the icon? Had he known who had taken it? And had that information passed to his son by way of his journal?

And had Ben Gunn, upon hearing of Old Sam's death, taken the first opportunity to come into the Park and look for it?

She remembered the monster truck parked in front of the *Adit*'s offices. It was white. She had been pretty sure the truck that had run her off the road had been dark. If Ben had run her off the road, that meant that he hadn't found anything in the journal he had stolen.

Had the intruder this morning been Ben Gunn? And if so, who was his buddy? She didn't know him well enough to know who he ran with. Kenny would.

She put down her mug to pick up the journal again, and leafed through it, pausing here and there to reread certain entries. Judge Anglebrandt had had a good sense of humor and a sly writing style. "Upon his incarceration in the Ahtna Jail, Mr. Selanoff was seized with such despair that he attempted to commit suicide by drowning himself in the toilet. He failed to succeed because he had to keep coming up for air."

Kate laughed and closed the journal again, examining the cover and the spine. Well, if Old

Sam had left the journal for her to find strictly for the entertainment value, he had been successful. For the life of her she couldn't see how the entry about McCullough was supposed to help her find the icon, or this alleged map.

She looked up at the wall. He hadn't made it easy for her to find, that was for sure. She had a dark suspicion that nothing else he'd left behind for her to find was going to be easy, either.

Had she mourned her loss a little less, she might have noticed the lift in her heart, the sharpening of her senses, the new intensity of the colors that came within her range of vision. She might have recognized the return of her curiosity, that most essential quality of the effective investigator, which had been dulled by recent cases without satisfactory resolutions, and blunted by the draining, enervating toil of being Everychair to every shareholder in the Niniltna Native Association.

Instead she just went to bed, and if she slept better that night on the hard floor of that derelict old cabin than she had since she'd been shanghaied onto the NNA board, even given the void left by Mutt's continued absence, she wasn't restless enough to notice.

Twenty

SHE ROSE WITH THE SUN THE NEXT morning and packed up after a breakfast of eggs and leftover chile relleno pie. The dishes washed with snowmelt, she lashed a tarp down over the trailer. The tarps she'd tacked to the walls of the cabin she left there for the next pilgrim. Who knew? It might even be herself.

She'd written a note on the inside of the wrapper of a Hershey bar, placed it inside a Ziploc bag, and duct-taped it to the door. The note read:

> Welcome, stranger!
> Feel free to use the cabin.
> Leave it as you found it.
> Thanks.
> —Kate Shugak, owner

She hoped that the invitation and the implied threat, combined with her signature, would rein in the more sober of the backwoods adventurers who made it this far. The kids and the drunks would probably ignore anything less than lights and a siren, but you do what you can.

She had given some thought to changing her mind about the hidden space behind the loft support. Maybe it would have been better to pull it out and leave it on the floor, so that if the people looking for the so-called map returned, they could assume she'd found it and would not tear the cabin down looking for it. In the end she had nixed the idea out of fear someone might use it for fuel in the woodstove.

That cut might be the last thing Old Sam had made with his own hands.

If they did come back, with any luck they would assume she had it, period, and would pick up her trail again in Niniltna.

She climbed onto the snow machine and started the engine. It kicked over without a hint of protest at being used for target practice the day before. She put on her goggles and pulled up her hood, fastening it at her throat, fixing the windshield with a steadfast gaze.

Nothing.

She revved the engine.

Nothing.

She revved it again.

Still nothing.

She swallowed hard and moved out slowly, following her incoming track down to the dogleg and around the saddle.

On the other side, Mutt was sitting in the snow, her front paws placed just so, a certain inflexibility about her jaw.

Kate stopped.

They exchanged a long look. Kate broke first.

"Okay," she said. "You're right. I've been scared you'd get hurt again. I've been holding you back from doing your job, the job I trained you to do, because of it." She swallowed hard, remembering that long, dark night spent laying on the steel examining table in the vet's office, one arm around Mutt so she could reassure herself that her dog was still breathing. It hurt to get the words out. "That stops now. You're back to being a full partner in the firm."

Angry at having her hand forced, she hit the gas and the snow mobile slid out.

Next to her, Mutt maintained a steady pace.

Downhill, the twists and turns and the steep little hills seemed more appropriate for a luge. She took them slowly and with care, Mutt trotting alternately before and behind, nose sniffing the air. They were out of the mountains before noon. She stopped on the same rise where they'd stopped for lunch on the way in to check the duct tape over the bullet hole and top off the tank. Lunch was leftover biscuits from breakfast and hot soup from the thermos.

She kept it at a steady forty miles an hour, stopping to refuel twice, which she admitted to herself was verging on paranoia, but just because you were paranoid didn't mean they weren't out to get you. Empirical evidence recently received indicated rather the opposite, and she kept a sharp eye out for attackers hiding behind every tree and rock they passed.

At the last foothill, the trail of the Polaris headed south for the river instead of west for Niniltna.

She stopped to consider.

The pain of her newest wound had receded to a dull ache, and she could see clearly with both eyes. She felt as well as someone shot in the head less than twenty-four hours before could expect.

The sky was partly cloudy, the horizon unthreatening. There was enough gas left in the spare can to see her to the river and back to Niniltna.

She grinned. Why the hell not?

"Hop on," she said to Mutt, and hit the gas.

It took a little over forty minutes, but when they got there Kate was presented with yet another mystery.

The Polaris tracks ran right over the edge of the river.

"What the hell," she said, and investigated.

She had to climb down the bank and she nearly got her boots wet before she figured it out. They'd taken the snowgo off on a boat. There was an indentation in the gravel where they'd nosed it in, and more indentations in the snow that showed where they'd laid planks to run the snowgo on board.

Well, shit. Depending on how fast the boat was

and which direction they'd headed, they were either at Ahtna or Alaganik by now.

Still, there wasn't much traffic on the river this late in the year. A lot of Park rats had cabins on the river and paid attention to who went by when. She turned around, feeling not entirely without hope. But the Arctic Cat finally took umbrage, first at being holed by a bullet, and then by being patched with duct tape, and it gave up the ghost five miles short of Niniltna. Naturally no one was traveling on their own snowgo or four-wheeler within a light-year of her when it did. Five feet was too far to walk in the Park without supplies at this time of year, let alone five miles, so she loaded her pack and set it to one side while she tarped up the snowgo and the trailer yet again.

The light was failing by the time she entered the village. She made directly for the Grosdidiers, shedding pack and snowshoes at the door. When she entered the clinic's waiting room everyone including the ill and injured backed up, as if the walls of the room weren't strong enough to contain both Kate's rage and them, too.

Matt appeared at this opportune moment and took in the situation at a glance. "Yeah," he said. "Come right on in here, Kate."

Mutt refused to be left behind, and in the exam room Matt gave her a wary glance. "Is she going to take a chunk out of me if I touch you?"

"She might," Kate said, and rejoiced at the

thought. Well, not about Mutt's taking a chunk out of Matt, specifically, but about Mutt's taking a chunk out of anyone on Kate's behalf.

She climbed up on the table, and wondered if she was going to have the strength to climb down again. Matt worked quickly and efficiently, removing the Band-Aid Kate had put on, cleaning and disinfecting the wound and applying a more professional dressing. He insisted on checking her pupils and reflexes and questioned her closely about her behavior between now and the time she'd been shot. He appeared satisfied with her answers, gave her some painkillers and some antibiotics, and shouted down the hall, "Hey, guys, come on in here and get a load of this!"

The other three Grosdidiers trooped in to radiate an incandescent and entirely unnecessary delight at Kate Shugak in their infirmary twice in one week, both times with shiners you could see from the moon.

"Yeah, yeah, very funny," Kate said. "Did any of you guys see a Polaris go through town, night before last? Two people on one machine, one large, one medium sized, dressed like they knew what they were doing, both armed, one of them with a Savage 110? Other one might have been a thirty-thirty. A hunting rifle, anyway." She hadn't been able to recover the bullet from the accidental shot the first intruder had fired, but she'd found the one that had ricocheted off her forehead embedded in the wall behind the green tarp.

An exchange of glances, a communal shaking of the head. "That who shot you?" Matt said.

"Yeah," she said.

The brothers gave a collective shrug. "With all those guys coming through on their way to and from the Suulutaq, you never notice a stranger anymore," Peter said.

"We could mount up, pick up their trail," Mark said eagerly.

Kate shook her head. "They left by the river."

They exchanged another glance over her head, this time one fraught with meaning. "Kate," Matt said, "let me take another look at your eyes."

She waved him off. "They took the snowgo off on a boat. I found the tracks."

There was a short silence. "Jesus," Matt said.

"Risky, this time of year," Mark said.

Luke cast an involuntary look over his shoulder, as if he could see the river through the walls. "That sucker can freeze solid overnight."

"You probably didn't see the boat go by yesterday, either," Kate said.

Nope.

"What the hell did they want?" Peter said.

They all looked at Kate with a marveling eye, incredulous that anyone in their right mind would take a shot at Kate Shugak.

"I don't suppose it's any use to say you should stay overnight for observation," Matt said.

"I need a ride out to where I left my snowgo," she said. "Can one of you give me a lift?"

Luke could and did. He towed her machine and trailer into town, at her request stopping briefly at the airstrip so she could talk to George Perry before heading for Herbie Topkok's garage. Herbie came out as Luke pulled away. "Kate." He looked at her eyes and at the bandage but he didn't say anything.

"Hey, Herbie," she said, and dismounted, groaning a little as she stretched out the kinks. "Ran into a little trouble. I was hoping you could help me out." She leaned forward and ripped the duct tape off the gas tank.

He stared at the neat hole that any Park rat except maybe Willard Shugak would instantly recognize as having been made by a bullet. He looked up at her again to contemplate the shiners, olds ones fading, new ones weighing in, bandage covering up something, probably bad. "Who'd you piss off this time?"

"I don't know," she said. "I'm just making this up as I go along."

Herbie's usually lugubrious expression lightened into what might have been almost a laugh.

"Can you fix it?"

Herbie was one of the newer members of the NNA's board of directors, but for his day job he ran what amounted to a garage for all makes and models of snowgo and four-wheeler in the Park, with a side dabble in boat engines. He shrugged. "Sure. I can patch the hole or I can replace the tank. Replacing it's quicker and more expensive. Patching it's cheaper and slower. Take your pick."

Kate took patching. Herbie ran up the garage door and they disconnected the trailer and pulled the snowgo inside. "Can I leave the trailer in the driveway until I can get Bobby over here to pick it up?"

Herbie shrugged, already mentally sparking his welding torch. What was it about men and fire? "Sure." He did look up for just a moment to say, "I was sorry to hear about Old Sam. I'll miss that cranky old bastard."

"So will we all."

"Heard he left you the whole shebang."

"He did."

"You want to sell that Honda FourTrax and that Polaris 800 of his, you come see me first. I'll make you a good offer."

She gave the Arctic Cat a rueful glance. "I might need a new snow machine myself, but I'll keep it in mind. Thanks, Herbie." She shouldered her rifle and she and Mutt hitched a ride with a couple of Park rats headed for the Roadhouse as far as Squaw Candy Creek. She snowshoed in from there, crossing the wooden bridge over the creek twenty minutes later.

The door to the A-frame opened and Dinah, an angelic blue-eyed blonde lacking only the wings and a harp, looked out with a welcoming smile. "Hey, Kate." Mercifully, she refrained from the obvious comment.

"Hey, Dinah."

Mutt eeled between Dinah and the door frame and disappeared into the house. There followed shortly thereafter a stentorian bellow. "God DAMN, Shugak! Fucking WOLVES in the fucking HOUSE again!"

Kate shed her snowshoes and entered the house to see Bobby sitting at a circular console loaded with electronic equipment, connected by a snake's nest of cables whose ends slithered up a pole through the roof, and by extension to the 112-foot metal tower out back. From here the word went forth to the Park from Park Air, the pirate radio station that featured music ("None of that shit recorded after CCR broke up"), a continuing swap-and-shop where Park rats bartered services for goods ("I'll cut your blowdown into firewood for smoke fish, one case per cord, straight trade"), and current events, including interviews with elected representatives like Pete Heiman that frequently ventured into the profane but were always entertaining and sometimes even informative.

Bobby had no license, of course, much less a dedicated bandwidth for broadcast, so he changed frequencies daily. So far he had eluded detection and arrest by the FCC. It probably helped that he broadcast from the back of beyond.

"Shugak!" he said, from beneath the enthusiastic tongue lashing he was receiving from Mutt, who was standing with her paws on his shoulders. "Shugak! Call OFF the fucking WOLF!"

Kate, grinning, did no such thing.

Bobby Clark had come into the Park many years ago by means that would not bear close scrutiny. Kate Shugak knew more about his past than most, and certainly more than she let on, but Kate wasn't talking. He was big and black and had lost both his legs below the knee to a land mine in one of America's many and apparently endless Asian wars. His head was shaved, his grin was broad, his shoulders and arms were roped with muscle, and he had a voice that sounded like a cross between those of James Earl Jones and Patrick Stewart, with a shivering timbre than made most women want to strip out of their clothes and fall flat on the nearest horizontal surface.

Kate Shugak knew more about that than she let on, too.

Mutt dropped back to the floor and laughed her lupine laugh up at him. "Fucking WOLVES in the house," Bobby said, but he was all bluff and bluster and she knew it. She sneezed, gave herself a vigorous shake, and trotted over to the wood box next to the big stone fireplace, where Bobby made a habit of keeping items that could be relied upon to keep the wolves at bay. Nor did this confidence betray her—she rooted around with such purpose that presently she emerged from the jumble of firewood with something that looked like the vertebrate of a finback whale. She settled happily in front of the fire and prepared to gnaw.

"Like woman, like dog, always thinking with her stomach." Bobby gave the wheels of his chair a quick, firm shove and then with a quick twist skidded to a hockey stop, as usual making Kate hop back so he wouldn't run over her toes. He inspected her face. "You look like you went three rounds with Muhammad Ali."

"Worse than I expected," Dinah said, looking her share.

"What's going on?" Bobby said.

"I got shot," Kate said, tactful as always, and then of course had to explain. Bobby got dangerously quiet, and Kate said, "Don't even think about it. Whoever it was is long gone."

"Might take a ride out there myself," Bobby said. "See what you missed."

"I didn't miss anything." Kate looked around the house, which seemed oddly empty. "Where is the child?"

Unconsciously, Dinah tracked her gaze, as if she wondered where Kate's four-year-old namesake was, too. "Auntie Balasha's granddaughter, the school nurse, what's her name?"

"Desiree."

"Yeah, Desiree. Anyway, Desiree, who has evidently decided that a life of administering oral vaccines and treating epidemics of the galloping crud is not enough for her, has pried funds loose from somewhere to create an after-preschool tumbling class. Katya, god help them all, is there."

"Really? She enjoys it?"

"Since she goes into a screaming fit every time I go to pick her up, my guess is yes." Dinah glanced up at the clock on the wall. "Another hour."

"Getting the feeling you're not going to be one of those parents who suffers from the empty nest syndrome when Katya goes to school full-time."

"Not hardly," Dinah said.

"Speak for yourself," Bobby said, glowering at his wife.

"Coffee," Kate said.

Caffeine accompanied by pound cake and stewed rhubarb did much to restore everyone's good mood.

"So what'd you do that pissed off someone so bad they felt they had to whack you between the eyes? Not that on occasion I haven't felt like doing the same thing myself." Bobby's grin was taunting.

Kate waggled her eyebrows. "Beats the hell out of me."

She looked at their expectant expressions. There was no one in the Park she trusted more to keep their mouths shut when she asked them to, and no one whose counsel could be more relied upon. Neither was a shareholder, and therefore they were not subject to the shifting allegiances of either shareholders or Park rats. Going into the beginning of an Alaskan winter was no time to start any rumors or fights. There were six long dark months ahead and they all needed each other to survive. "You don't tell anyone this," she said. "I don't care who comes asking, I didn't tell you anything, and you don't know anything."

Her voice dropped unconsciously and they leaned in. Kate told them everything, beginning with the first of Judge Anglebrandt's journals found on Old Sam's bookshelf ten days ago, and ending with the second, found secreted in the wall of his homestead cabin yesterday morning. The documents shown to her by Dan O'Brian, the talk with Jane Silver, followed by her death less than twenty-four hours later, the note Old Sam had left for her with his attorney, getting run off the road on the way home, Auntie Joy, Mac McCullough, and the manuscript, Demetri, Ruthe, the attack at the cabin yesterday morning, her suspicions of Pete Wheeler and Ben Gunn, all of it. When she was done she folded her arms and sat back, awaiting judgment and hoping for advice.

"Jesus fucking Christ," Bobby said, which was not unexpected. What followed was. "You're thinking it's the icon they're after."

"Well, yeah," she said. "Don't you?"

"Not necessarily." He pushed back from the table and rolled over to the console, pulling himself around to his computer, slapping the mouse to lighten up the screen. He had a satellite dish on the tower outside and he was never not online. Kate got up to peer over his shoulder, to see a Google for Dashiell Hammett give way to five hundred thousand hits. Five minutes' worth of clicking and Bobby sat back from the computer. "Get a load of this."

By this time Kate had been joined by Dinah and they read down the screen together. Dinah let loose with a long whistle. "A hundred and thirty-six thousand dollars is pretty steep. Even for a signed first edition of *The Maltese Falcon*."

"I had no idea," Kate said, and kicked herself. The problem was that she thought like a reader, not a collector, but even she had heard of Sotheby's. "So you think they're after the Hammett manuscript, not the icon?"

"No," Bobby said, "I think they're probably after both of them. Wouldn't you be? Double the treasure, double the score."

"Great," Kate said glumly. Of course he was right.

Bobby led the way back to the table, where Dinah refreshed their mugs and Bobby cut a second piece of cake to hide beneath the rest of the rhubarb. "About the icon," he said.

"Yeah?"

"You're not thinking big enough."

"How do you mean?"

"Yeah, it's a historical artifact. Yeah, it's a cultural artifact. Yeah, it might even have real value, if the description in the story is accurate and those stones are jewels and if nobody's prized them loose and sold them off individually since it was lost."

"Okay, and?"

Bobby's expression was uncharacteristically serious. "What you haven't taken into account is that it is also a political artifact."

Kate was silent for a long moment, and they let her be while she thought it through. "You mean . . . by tradition the chief held it in trust for the tribe."

"According to Ruthe's research, and to the ruckus Auntie Joy said the tribe raised when it was stolen. I bet Old Sam wasn't considered ineligible by Joy's parents only because he was part Filipino. I bet he was considered ineligible because his mother was the one who lost the icon."

"So it's like some holy grail for Park Natives," Kate said.

"Might be overstating it just a little, but yeah." He shook his head. "You've always been a little blind to symbolism, Kate. Symbols are important."

"You mean like the cross?"

He pointed a finger at her. "There it is, that knee-jerk assumption that symbolism has to be about religion. Well, people have been suborning religion to their own purposes since the first guy decided pouring a few drops on the ground from every bottle of wine they drank was an honor to Zeus."

"Zeus?"

"Whoever. You know what I mean."

"The thing I don't get," Kate said, "is why have I never heard of this icon before now? I am indisputably an Alaska Native, an Aleut and a Park rat. I've got more relatives than I ever wanted going back ten thousand years, and sometimes it feels like most of them are still alive and well and living within mug up distance of my house. Why, if this thing is this important to my people, to my tribe, has no one in my generation ever heard a peep about it?"

Bobby and Dinah exchanged glances. "Good question," Bobby said. "For which I do not have an answer."

Kate thought some more. "Okay," she said at

last. "So you're saying that someone is looking for the icon who wants the power it will give them, inherent or implied or imagined."

He shrugged. "I'm saying it's motive. You remember motive, don't you, Kate?"

"Smart-ass," Kate said without heat.

"It's what I do," Bobby said with modesty unbecoming. "And, you know, I'm good-looking." And he grinned.

Dinah rolled her eyes, and beneath the table rubbed her foot against her husband's thigh.

"And," Bobby said, serious again, "if that is the motive, then it's someone close to home, someone you know, someone we all know. Which would explain why he or she knew just where to wait to run you off the road, and had the mad skills to sneak up on you."

"The guy yesterday morning could have shot me in my sleep," she said. It still rankled that she hadn't heard anything, not even the door opening.

"And he didn't," Bobby said.

Kate stared at him. "No," she said slowly. "He didn't, did he."

Bobby meditated for a moment. "If Virginia did pass on your whereabouts to every Park rat she stumbled across that day—"

"As is her invariable wont," Dinah said.

"—then the field's wide open." He bent a sapient eye in Kate's direction. "Let's face it, it's

366

not like you're a member in good standing of the How to Win Friends and Influence People Club. By the way, when all of this was going on, where the hell was Mutt?"

In front of the fireplace Mutt looked up at the sound of her name, and then went back to her whale vertebrate. "Dancing with wolves," Kate said. "She showed up when it counted."

"Too bad she didn't go for his throat."

"He was pretty well-padded," Kate said. "She ripped the sleeve off his parka when she pulled him off me, and she did bite him in the ass, twice, once in the cabin, and again as she was chasing him out of the canyon. She had blood on her muzzle when she came back."

Bobby's look at Mutt this time was much more approving. "My kind of girl." Mutt's tail thumped the floor. "So now we're looking for a Park rat who has a parka with one arm and who can't sit down."

"Why didn't Old Sam just tell me?" Kate said, irritated all over again. "Why send me on a wild goose chase?"

"If that old fart sent you on a wild goose chase," Bobby said, "he must have thought you needed one."

Before Kate could formulate an answer to the unanswerable Dinah said, "I'd been taping him."

Kate looked at her, startled. "You're kidding."

Dinah shook her head. "No. I've got about three

hours' worth of uncut footage." She grinned. "He's hard to edit."

Dinah Clark had come to Alaska originally with the intent of honing her skills as a videographer. Life, in the shape of the Park, Bobby Clark, and a daughter, had only put that ambition into temporary abeyance. Dinah was seldom seen without a video camera in hand, fully half the center console of the A-frame was taken up with her editing equipment, and no one within a fifty-mile radius of Squaw Candy Creek had escaped the red on-air light.

Three hours of moving pictures of Old Sam in spate. Kate had only one still photo of him, taken unawares on the *Freya* the third summer she had deckhanded for him. He was standing on the starboardside gunnel, hanging off a guy wire with one hand to chew out a sheepish Ansel Totemoff, standing below on the deck of the *Tiffany T.*, for a rough docking. It was a sunny day, and Old Sam's face was outlined against a blue sky, the dark skin, the broad brow, the deep-set eyes, the beaky nose, the jutting chin, every fold and wrinkle faithfully recorded. And his mouth was open. She had been thinking that she should get the picture blown up and framed, and have copies made to give out at the potlatch along with the obituary.

But three whole hours of Old Sam off the chain, talking straight at a camera . . . it seemed that he was not done sending her messages from beyond the grave. Yet again, the old son of a bitch had her blinking back tears.

Dinah didn't notice, or pretended not to. "I've been trying to get as many of the old farts on tape as I can before they're gone. It's an incredible oral history, and since it's the only Park history there is, it will be invaluable in future."

"You going to make a documentary?" Kate said. Dinah was always going to make a documentary on this or that subject, before being sidetracked, usually by another topic uncovered in the investigation of the current one.

In response, as always, Dinah sounded as certain as she was enthusiastic. "Old Sam was like a—a prism for Alaskan history, Kate. He and his immediate family were part of or on the periphery of every big event in Alaska for the past eighty years. His grandparents died in the flu pandemic, he homesteaded, he fought in the Aleutians, he was in Juneau for the vote on the constitution—"

"What?"

"Yeah, he'd been herring fishing in Southeast and he delivered a load to a buyer in Juneau so his crew could vote. He was working on the Kenai Peninsula when the Swanson River oil field was discovered—"

"He was?" Kate said. "I didn't know that." It was a continuing shock to learn that Old Sam had had another life.

Possibly more than one.

"He was a supervoter," Dinah said. "He never missed an election, I checked the voting records. He was on a first-name basis with every governor we've ever had, and a couple of the territorial ones."

"I know he knew Ernest Gruening," Kate said.

"And boy was he pissed when Gruening failed reelection as senator," Dinah said, grinning. "He said—you want to see the footage for yourself?"

"Yeah," Kate said, and looked at the clock. "Can you make me a copy?"

"Sure, I can burn you a DVD. But you can watch it here right now if you want."

"I can't. I'm grabbing George's last flight to Anchorage this afternoon."

"Aha," Bobby said. "Kurt Pletnikof, PI?"

"Library?" Dinah said. "Museum? Archives?"

"My friends are smarter than the average bear," Kate said. "I don't know enough to figure out what the hell is going on here. I can sic Kurt on some of it, and I can look up some myself."

Bobby, watching Kate's face, said, "Yeah, bullshit, Shugak."

"What do you mean?" Dinah said.

Bobby with the finger again. He was as bad as Auntie Joy. "She's hoping they'll follow her to town."

"What?" Dinah said, looking from one to the other. "Kate, are you nuts? At least here you've got friends who'll watch your back. Anchorage . . ."

She shook her head. "Lots of dark alleys in Anchorage, and too many people who don't know you."

Kate remembered how easy it was to take down the guy in the cabin. "These people aren't professionals, whatever else they are."

"Even Dortmunder gets lucky once in a while," Bobby said.

"And they can always hire somebody for a pint of Windsor Canadian," Dinah said.

"Dinah," Kate said, getting to her feet, "welcome to my world."

Twenty-one

STILL PROTESTING, DINAH DROPPED Kate and Mutt at the airport, where George bundled them into the single Otter turbo and took off. Ninety minutes afterward they touched down at Merrill. A cab ride later, Kate was letting them into the town house on Westchester Lagoon, a three-story dwelling with a barn-shaped roof and common walls with identical homes on either side. It had belonged to Jack Morgan, Johnny's father, and was now part of Johnny's college fund. In the meantime they used it when they were in Anchorage, and the first thing Kate did was deliver half a dozen cans of last season's smoked salmon to the neighbors on either side. It was understood by both that they'd keep an eye on the place when it sat empty, as the mortgage was paid off and Kate didn't want the hassle of being an absentee landlord.

She let herself in the front door, turned up the heat, and turned on the refrigerator. The first floor was the garage, the second the living rooms, and the third the bedrooms. In the garage was a Subaru Forester. Kate made a quick run to City Market for essentials like coffee and half-and-half. An overheard conversation led her to the rebirth of Wings 'n Things on Arctic and Thirty-sixth, and while it lacked the ambiance of the converted wood-frame house of its original location, when you ordered your wings nuclear they still came in a dark, crisp golden brown, swimming in burnt orange grease and spicy enough to melt your esophagus. She missed all the religious tracts tacked to the walls, though, not to mention the life-size poster of the bleeding heart Jesus Christ.

Back at the condo she checked upstairs to see that she still had sufficient spare clothes in the dresser to keep her in clean underwear for at least a couple of days, since she hadn't allowed herself the time to go home and pack. Despite what she had told Bobby and Dinah, she didn't know quite what she was doing in Anchorage, other than responding to an instinctive feeling that the next piece of the puzzle Old Sam had left her as his main legacy was to be found there.

And of course Bobby was right. She hoped whoever else was chasing Old Sam's legacy would follow her here. She'd spent five and a half years in Anchorage, working sex crimes for the Anchorage DA, and there wasn't one seedy little corner of it she didn't know, whether said seediness was to be found on the top floor of a corporate office building on Eighth Avenue, or a dank little kitchenette off North Flower Street, or a five-thousand-square-foot home with six bedrooms and six bathrooms down Discovery Bay Drive. She could hold her own in Anchorage. If Bobby was right and her pursuers were Park rats themselves, they might not be able to.

If they weren't, if they were street-smart city dwellers, well, she'd deal with that when it happened.

She'd checked her cell phone before they landed and there were no messages waiting. She put the bags on the kitchen table and checked again. There still weren't any. She cursed herself for checking, she cussed out Jim for not calling, and she threw the phone in a drawer and slammed it shut so she wouldn't hear it if it went off.

She let Mutt into the backyard to use the facilities, loaded a plate with wings, blue cheese dip, and celery sticks, let Mutt back in, and moved operations to the living room, where she inserted Dinah's DVD of Old Sam into the player.

She turned on the television, put her feet on the coffee table and her plate in her lap, and pushed Play on the remote.

His cell phone rang. His heart, that heretofore reliable organ, gave an anticipatory thump. He fished it out and answered.

"Surf's up, board man," Sylvia said. "Want to catch a couple of waves?"

Well. Kate had told him to take his father's board out.

He'd almost forgotten the sting of salt water in his eyes and nose, the stretch down the board, the pull on his shoulders during the paddle, the quick push to his feet. He'd forgotten the triumph of achieving that perfect balance down the centerline. He'd forgotten the thrill of catching that line of white water at exactly the right moment, the sheer ecstasy of all three—man, board, water—moving as one toward the line of golden sand that was always too close too soon.

Sylvia, trim in a black one-piece, rode a board that showed steady use, and was ready with a laugh whenever he wiped out, which since he hadn't ridden a board in twenty years was often. It came back, though, slowly at first, and then fast in a rush of elation that he also remembered from those long-ago days. Surfing was probably the main reason he'd never bothered with drugs back in the day. He couldn't imagine, then or now, any high that would be comparable, let alone better, so why bother?

They watched the sun set that evening from their boards, sitting in the water beyond the surf, rising and falling with the gentle swell, legs touching occasionally and companionably beneath the water, and Jim felt more at peace in that moment than he had since he'd landed in LA.

Sylvia was easy to talk to, listening without comment to his account of the past week, of the reading of the will on Monday, the packing up of his father's clothes, the cleaning out of his father's office, the forced march of lunches and dinners and drinks at the club with his father's friends and colleagues.

The continued tension of living in an armed camp, although this he did not share with Sylvia.

"Why did your father want the will read aloud?" she said at one point.

"My question exactly," he said. "The lawyer said Dad specifically requested him to."

"But why?"

Jim thought it over. "I think," he said slowly, "it has something to do with the box."

"The antique writing box?"

"Yeah. She never sent me a copy of the revised will. I'm wondering if she was hoping I'd never know he wanted me to have the box."

"Which again begs the question. Why?"

He closed his eyes and let his head fall back.

His laugh was unamused. "I have never had the first idea why my mother does anything."

Sylvia was silent for a moment. "Maybe there's something in it she doesn't want you to see."

"I can't think what. And I've got it now."

"You haven't opened it yet?"

"No."

"Three, no, four days now, and you haven't opened it?"

"No."

She was silent for a moment. "It's the last message you'll ever get from your dad."

"Yes."

"I wouldn't be in a hurry to open it, either."

He turned his head to look at her, at the sun-kissed skin, the wet hair slicked back, the strong throat, the high, firm breasts. There were a lot of pleasant memories built into the package riding next to him, and even more promises, and he was fully alive to all of them.

He wondered how Kate Shugak would fill out that suit.

Sylvia turned her head to meet his eyes, and he knew she had known he was watching her. "Want to get something to eat?"

They went to a diner in Ventura he remembered from his high school days, where the burgers were thick and juicy, the fries salty and greasy, and the shakes too thick to drink through a straw. After that they went to a bar for a nightcap and talked for hours, playing catch-up and do-you-remember. They even danced.

It was after midnight when they went out to the parking lot. She leaned against her car and smiled up at him.

He bent his head to accept the invitation, with no thought but of paying homage with a perfect ending to the glorious day on the water, the good junk food, and time spent with the pretty girl. Inches away he stopped and said, "How did you get my cell number?"

Her eyes opened to blink up at him. "What?"

"How did you get my cell phone number?"

An interrogation was not how Sylvia had been expecting this evening to end, and she frowned. "Your mother gave it to me."

"Did she," he said, and took a step back.

He let himself into the darkened, quiet house and went upstairs to find that his room had been searched, probably right around his first wave.

It wasn't that easy to tell, given that the room bore no resemblance to the one he had left behind the day his father had driven him to the airport for his flight north. Beverly had probably been in here with a sledgehammer before the plane was off the ground. Or no, he wronged her, she would have been in here with a decorator and a contractor. Beverly would never have endangered her manicure with anything as plebian as tools.

The built-in bookcase that had covered one wall had been ripped out, the wall encased in a new layer of Sheetrock and hung with a painfully angular Picasso whose only saving grace was that it was the original and worth a fortune. His four-poster had been replaced by a severely modern platform bed, the reading lamps on either side replaced by a swirled glass pendant fixture that trained light everywhere except where someone attempting to read in bed might reasonably be expected to hold a book. There was an Eames chair made of uncushioned wood that was comfortable for just long enough to put on your socks and shoes, a floor lamp with a circular table on the pole that wasn't big enough for either a glass or a mug, and a low, six-drawer dresser planted squarely on the way to the bathroom with corners that felt as if they'd been sharpened on a whetstone. Jim's shins had the bruises to prove it.

But still. He knew. His room had definitely been searched.

Oh, it wasn't blatant, it wasn't as if his suitcase had been upended and everything in it dumped out, or the clothes hanging in the closet ripped from their hangers or drawers pulled out from the dresser or the bedclothes ripped free of the mattress and the mattress shoved to the floor. In other words, it hadn't been tossed.

No, this was a strictly amateur effort, an attempt to evaluate the contents of the room while leaving no trace behind. But the ditty bag he'd left on the right side of the sink was now on the left, the hangers in the closet were now neatly instead of irregularly aligned, and the book he'd left open and facedown on the nightstand was now faceup and closed, his place lost, a thing he never allowed to happen.

So. Not a professional job, then.

The next morning he went to the garage and found his mother fiddling with the trunk of his father's car.

He stood in the doorway until she looked up. Those cool cheeks went a pale pink.

He walked around to stand next to her. The trunk was still closed. "You have to use the key on this model," he said.

Her eyes narrowed, those electric blue eyes so disconcertingly like the ones that stared back from his mirror every morning.

"You gave Sylvia my cell phone number," he said.

She stared at him, eyes inimical, mouth a thin line.

"You wanted me out of the house so you could search my room."

"Where is your father's writing box?"

He had to admire her ability to cut right to it without shame or remorse. "What's in it that's so important that you'd risk chipping a nail to get at?"

"Nothing that concerns you."

"Which would be why he left it to me."

She looked at him with something that felt uncomfortably close to hatred. And perhaps a little, just a little, like fear. "It changes nothing."

"I don't know that." He got into the car and punched the button on the garage door opener. She watched as he backed out of the garage, a crease between her perfectly shaped eyebrows. She was still there when he pulled away down the street.

He drove at random, trying not to get either lost or T-boned by one of the Hummers that had become so ubiquitous on LA's streets while he figured out where to go. And then he remembered the local public library. Thankfully, it was still in the same place, although interior and exterior both had been remodeled. The librarian, a Ms. Millward, was new to him, too. There were three private reading rooms now, an unimaginable luxury that could only be justified by the Forbes ratings of the people who lived in its zip code. Two were in use. Ms. Millward let him into the third one, told him he had an hour, and left without question, for which incuriosity he was grateful.

The room was small, with enough space for a table, a chair, and a computer with Internet access. There was a sidelight next to the door, so his privacy was not complete, but it was infinitely better than the house, and after all, the librarians would need a way to check that he wasn't jerking off over www.blondbabesinbikinis.com. He locked the door and put the writing box on the table.

It really was beautifully made. The joints fit together seamlessly and the stain was a dark, rich brown. The brass fittings clung to each corner as if they'd been cast to it. It was an artifact of a life of privilege and leisure, redolent of the great divide between the noblessly obliged and the great unwashed.

He tore open the envelope and let the little brass key fall into his palm. It, too, was finely crafted, a skeleton key, heavy for its size, with a round shank and an oval bow. It was a good thing his mother hadn't managed to get her hands on the writing box, because a warded lock designed for a skeleton key could be as easily opened with a nail file.

He slid the bit gently into the lock. There was a muted click, and he raised the lid.

It was every bit the treasure chest he remembered.

The inkwells were crystal, with fitted ebony stoppers. The blotter had been recently replaced with something that felt very much like velvet. There were two fountain pens inside, both Montblancs. Each was a work of art in its own right, one made of rose gold and the other he was pretty sure made of platinum, both etched with flowers and leaves and embedded with tiny gemstones. The cost of either was probably equal to his salary for a year.

Both looked well-used and well-cared-for. His father had always preferred a fountain pen, and his penmanship, a graceful, flowing script with the letters and words evenly spaced, up and down loops equally sized, had done it justice. No blots, that went without saying. Jim remembered standing at his father's elbow, watching the nib of his pen move across the page, holding his breath until the dot of the period was placed exactly and precisely following the last word of the last line.

"What happens if you make a mistake?" he'd said once.

"I start over," his father had replied.

"No eraser?"

His father had looked down at him, one of his rare smiles lighting his face. "No eraser."

Jim's eyes were full of tears. He blinked them away, lifted up the green blotter, and set it to one side.

There was a hollow compartment beneath, containing an envelope bearing his name written in his father's hand, probably with one of the pens nestled into the tray between the inkwells above. He took it out and weighed it in his hand. The envelope was made of heavy paper that felt as if silk had somehow been woven into the mix.

He held it for a long time without opening it. James Chopin the elder had not been a demonstrative man. In that, he was well-matched with his wife. Jim had known little affection in his childhood, and he was self-aware enough to realize that it was probably why he had never married. Let him admit the truth now, at least, here within the four walls of this tiny room three thousand miles from what had become his home. Sylvia had been more an act of rebellion than of at long last love, proven by the alacrity with which he had decamped to Alaska when he'd been accepted to the trooper academy in Sitka. The string of women that had followed her had by design never lasted more than a year each, because after a year he found that a woman started to pick out china patterns, and because after a year he was bored.

Or maybe he was just afraid that after a year, he would start to bore them.

Kate Shugak had never bored him. Fascination, respect, yes. Terror, lust, rage, as much as it galled him to admit, even jealousy—he had felt all of those things in relation to Kate Shugak, but never boredom.

He pictured a meeting between Kate and his mother, and an involuntary grin spread across his face. He could sell tickets.

He pictured a meeting between Kate and his father, and the grin faded. What would his father have thought, presented with a five-foot package of Aleut dynamite? Would he have taken her down to the club and exhibited her as a curiosity?

He was immediately ashamed of himself. His father's friends and coworkers had been unrelentingly white, but he had never displayed any sign of being a bigot or a racist. True, he had allowed his wife to dictate the terms of his relationship with his son, but there was no honesty and less honor in ascribing more faults to him than he already had. If being a cop had taught Jim anything, it was to imagine no more than the evidence could prove.

He opened the envelope.

Only two wrong turns and one near collision with an iridescent Volkswagen Beetle whose driver had flipped him off and he was in West Hollywood. It was a bitch finding a parking space, and when he did find one in a lot that already had more cars than spaces he had to use his credit card in a machine that made him jump a foot in the air when it spoke. Oh, for the last-century ways of the Park.

The desk sergeant gave him the once-over and identified him as a fellow officer without any unseemly display of badge, which Jim displayed anyway as a gesture of solidarity. It got him in the door.

Sylvia met him on the other side. "What's up?"

He wasn't forgiven for the way their surf date had ended. He waited to reply until they were inside her office with the door closed. "I told you there was someone in Alaska."

"You didn't sound that convinced." Her lips tightened. "You didn't act like it, either."

"No, I didn't. I should have."

"So it's serious?"

He thought of Kate Shugak, and took a deep breath, held it for a couple of seconds, then blew it out again with an expressive sigh. "It's serious."

She raised an eyebrow. "Hey, that took some effort."

"Yes," he said grimly. "It did."

She'd painted the walls different colors—red, orange, yellow, green, all pastels, if anything red could be pastel. The ceiling was a pastel blue, and the walls were hung with Mexican folk art, a brightly colored serape, a mirror with a hand-painted tin frame, a sun plaque with eight arms embedded with milagros, tiny religious charms he remembered warded off the devil, or maybe they brought the rain. "Nice," he said.

"Why are you here?" she said, annoyed. "Certainly not to admire my office décor."

"I came to apologize," he said.

She looked at him, her face closed.

"I should have been up-front with you," he said, "and I wasn't. The thing is—"

Well, what was the thing about him and Kate

Shugak, anyway? Damned if he knew. "No excuse," he said. "I fucked up. I'm sorry."

"All you had to do was say," she said. "I don't poach."

"I know," he said. Jim Chopin, Diplomat.

"I knew you were going to Alaska," she said.

He looked up, startled.

One shoulder rose and fell again. "All those books about it. The walls of your room were papered with travel posters with totem poles on them, and how many times did you make me watch that horrible scratchy copy of *Nanook of the North* on VHS? And *Call of the Wild*, not to mention *North to Alaska*? And I hate John Wayne."

He laughed, and she relaxed into a reluctant smile. "I always knew you were not long for LA. So if you're thinking you broke my heart when you left and that I've been mooning around, waiting all this time for your return, think again." She fussed with some paperwork on her desk. "I was happy to see you again. We had some good times. I wouldn't have minded hooking up while you were here, but it's not like I expected a lifelong commitment out of it."

"I'm sorry," he said again.

"You sure are," she said, and laughed, her spurt of temper over. "Men," she said, to which he wisely returned no comment. "Okay. You in town for much longer? Dad would like to see you."

"Not much longer," he said. "I don't think."

She raised an eyebrow.

"Remember the writing box?"

"The one your dad left you? Sure."

"I opened it."

"Ah." She sat back in her chair. "What was in it?"

"An envelope with my name on it."

"Containing?"

"This." He handed it over.

It was a black-and-white photograph with a white border and scalloped edges. The image was of two girls in their early teens, slender, dressed in skirts and blouses and flats, arms wrapped around each other's waists, standing in what looked like a small yard with a lot of unkempt shrubbery in the background. They looked at the camera with shy, up-from-under expressions.

"Twins," Sylvia said.

"Looks like," he said.

She looked up at him and back at the photograph. "Boy, the gene for that jaw sure is a strong one. Can you tell which one is your mother?"

"The one on the left," he said.

"Really?" She fished a pair of cat's-eye reading glasses with rhinestone frames from the welter of debris on her desk and took a closer look. After a moment's study she took them off and handed the photograph back. "If you say so."

He looked down at the image again. "I think."

"Did you know your mother had a twin sister?"

He shook his head. "I don't remember Mom ever mentioning family, other than when I asked her who my grandparents were."

"And she said?"

"That they died young."

"Maybe the sister died, too."

He shrugged. "Why not say so?"

"And your father never said anything either?"

"Nope."

"But he left you a picture of the two of them together."

"Yep."

"And no explanation?"

"Nope."

"But if he left you the picture, he must have known."

"Yeah."

"And I think my family is dysfunctional." Her eyes narrowed. "What did you really come here for, Jim?"

He looked her straight in the eye and said firmly, "To apologize."

"Uh-huh," she said. "And?"

"And to ask you to run someone for me."

"Your mother?"

"Yes," he said.

Twenty-two

SHE ROSE EARLY THE NEXT MORNING and with Mutt walked up to City Market for a Kaladi Brothers venti americano and a canela, reason alone for the trip to Anchorage. There was a high, scattered overcast and the air had a bite, but there was no snow in Anchorage yet. Southcentral was the banana belt of Alaska.

She watched for tails and found none, although it didn't stop her from giving a hard look at every car that passed, most of them containing parents driving their kids to Inlet View Elementary School. Standing in the coffee line at the market, she checked out everyone before her and behind her to five places. They all looked guilty, in a half-asleep, early morning kind of way. The ones who weren't giving Mutt the nervous eye.

She had to pull herself up short when it was her turn to be served and the barista, a fresh-faced, cheerful young man with orange and purple hair and a Black Eyed Peas T-shirt took on a sinister air when he asked if she wanted room in her venti for half-and-half.

This was ridiculous. They hadn't killed her yet, they'd barely laid a glove on her. She repressed the memory of the dented roof of the pickup. What the hell, it was still running.

Back at the town house she got her cell phone

out of the kitchen drawer. A message. At last. She called. "Cell phones for seniors! Call 888—"

She gave in and called him. Voice mail. Naturally. "I'm in Anchorage, staying at the town house. I'm on my cell."

There. Nothing lovesick about that. She turned her mind to work.

First things first. If her own personal Maltese Falcon was a Russian icon, then it behooved her to learn a little more about them. She called the Anchorage Museum to find out what time they opened, and was at the doors when they unlocked them.

"That can't come in," the security guard said, looking at Mutt.

Kate gave the standard answer when faced by nitwits who refused to see the caliber of canine they were facing. "She's a service dog."

The guard looked at Kate, the picture of physical and mental health, and raised a skeptical eyebrow, but he stood back to let them both in.

At the information desk she was directed toward the resource center, and was shortly explaining what she wanted to a thin young man with an eager expression. He sported a wispy goatee that reminded her of the ones worn by the Old Believer fishermen who had delivered to the *Freya* in Alaganik Bay. His name was Lazary Kuznetsov and he admitted to being from Voznesenka on Kachemak Bay, and immediately endeared himself to Mutt by giving her half of the ham sandwich he was to have had for his own lunch.

Bona fides established all the way around, Kate explained that she wanted to learn something about Russian icons. Shortly thereafter she found herself seated at a table surrounded by books, articles, and photographs.

It was like being lost in the middle of a story by the Grimm Brothers, leavened with a lighthearted soupçon of medieval Christian fanaticism. The story of the icon began in Russia's immediate predecessor, Kievan Rus, which she learned to her great surprise had been founded by a Scandinavian warrior elite. She wondered how all the elders back in the Park, many if not most of whom were at least part Russian, would feel about that.

Kievan Rus had existed for about four hundred years, beginning in the late 800s. It was converted to Christianity a century afterward. With the Christians came the icon, a flat panel featuring an image from Christian mythology. This could be the cross or a person (usually Jesus), or both.

Or Mary, Kate thought.

Icons, she read, could be made from just about anything. They could be cast in metal, carved from stone, embroidered on cloth, painted on wood. True believers in the Russian Orthodox faith had for many years believed that three-dimensional sculpture was inhabited by demons, and to this very day Orthodox icons could never be more than three-quarter bas-relief. Three quarters of what? Kate wondered, and Lazary supplied the answer. No more than three quarters of any image could project from the panel. He showed her an illustration of a horse and rider connected to its original marble only by two legs and a tail, and she understood.

She thought about the alleged gemstones allegedly imbedded in the alleged frame of this alleged family treasure. They must not have counted.

Behave, she told herself. While a healthy skepticism was the cornerstone of any decent investigation, she was talking herself right out of believing in the existence of the icon at all. She laid the blame for this squarely at the door of one Dashiell Hammett, who had had the audacity to intrude on Old Sam's personal history. A man who wrote fiction, even good fiction, had no business straying into real life.

Someone had attacked her, she reminded herself, either the same people three times or three different sets of people on three different occasions. It argued a certain sincerity of purpose that lent the existence of the icon at least the ragged edge of credibility.

She paused in the act of turning a page.

Only Auntie Joy had ever mentioned the icon

and at that only after Old Sam's death. None of the other aunties, none of the elders, including her own grandmother Ekaterina Shugak, that living embodiment of tribal history, had ever breathed a word of it. Why not? Could losing it really have been such a disgrace?

Or . . . was it perhaps not lost at all? Did someone know where it was? Had they known all along, and had the tribal elders entered into a conspiracy of silence to protect it, to protect their possession of it?

Speculation was fine. Hard facts were better. She closed one book and opened another.

Icons were found on church altars and in private homes. Some icons were said to have "appeared" as opposed to having been made by human hands. The most famous of the icon makers had been canonized. Kate was introduced to the word *thaumaturgy,* and Lazary pointed her to a dictionary so she could look up its precise meaning. "The performance of miracles," said *Webster's*, also "magic."

So at least some icons were traditionally held to have mystical powers. Including perhaps the power to heal. To true believers, such an object would be valuable indeed. During the Middle Ages crusaders and pilgrims had brought back enough knucklebones of St. John the Baptist for altar reliquaries to reconstruct the man entire several times over. Nothing was too crazy for someone infected with the fatal virus of faith.

Again, Kate paused in the act of turning a page. Suppose she was looking at this from the wrong angle. Who had made the icon in the first place? For whom had it been commissioned? Who had brought it to Alaska from Russia? Had it been theirs to bring, or had it been stolen? Was someone's descendant fourteen generations removed, with the fall of the wall now able to travel freely in the West, hot on its trail?

Had they attempted to retrieve it with a piece of sixteen-inch firewood, and had her head gotten in the way?

"Enough," she said out loud, earning her a quizzical glance from Lazary and annoyed ones from several serious scholars who, judging by their elbow patches, were UAA professors on the lam from classrooms.

She thanked Lazary for his help and left the museum with more questions than she'd come in with, which had not been her object. Best to take a break from the past and attend to something in the present day.

From the pickup, she called her cousin Axenia. Axenia was, as usual, curt and unwelcoming, but she agreed to see Kate if Kate could get there in the next hour.

Axenia was Kate's younger cousin who while growing up in the Park had held the unfortunate reputation of being a screwup, although that was only because it was true. It was Emaa's wish for Axenia to follow Kate to college. She didn't, instead taking up with a series of boyfriends, each of which she had hoped would be her ticket out of the Park. On the heels of the murder of Axenia's last boyfriend, Kate, against her grandmother's express wishes, had spirited Axenia to Anchorage, set her up in an apartment with Native roommates so she wouldn't feel surrounded by aliens, and gotten her a job in the Anchorage district attorney's office.

Axenia had never forgiven her for it.

The job had lasted just long enough for Axenia to meet Lew Mathisen, a lawyer and lobbyist twenty years her senior. They had married, Lew had installed Axenia in a palatial home off 100th Avenue with satellite television, a dishwasher, and a housekeeper, and Axenia had rewarded him with an entrée into Alaska Native society and a measure of immortality with two children.

Kate pulled into the driveway and got out. The yard, free of leaves and fallen boughs, was as neat as the inside of the house. Axenia, short, trim, dark straight hair hanging to her waist, brown eyes unsmiling, led the way to the kitchen. "Have you had lunch?"

This was an unlooked-for courtesy. "No," Kate said, and wondered if Axenia would spit in her soup.

"I was about to make myself a salmon salad sandwich."

If the salad for both sandwiches came out of the same bowl, there was a good chance lunch would be spit-free. "Sounds good."

And it was good, made with onions and sweet pickles chopped fine and not too much mayonnaise, served on sourdough bread (store-bought) with chips on the side. They ate at the counter. "Where are the kids?" Kate said.

"Day care."

"Didn't know they were old enough," Kate said.

Axenia's eyes narrowed. "I didn't know you were an expert in child care, Kate."

"All I meant was they're growing so fast—" Kate gave it up as a lost cause.

"Why are you in town?" Axenia said, directing the conversation back to neutral topics with an iron hand. "Costco run?"

"I'm looking into something." Kate hesitated. Lew was now a registered lobbyist for Global Harvest Resources, Inc., the parent company of the Suulutaq Mine. She couldn't trust Axenia not to tell Lew everything. She couldn't for the moment imagine why GHRI would be interested in a lost tribal heirloom, but knowledge was power. On general principles it was simply none of their business. "You heard about Old Sam."

"Yes. I'm sorry."

Kate could feel the heat rise up the back of her neck. "Your sorrow overwhelms me."

"He barely noticed me. Especially not when you were in the same room."

"He was your elder." And your better. Although Kate did not speak that last out loud.

"My elder, maybe. My better, maybe not."

"What do you mean by that?"

"I've heard the stories. Grandma used to say he shouldn't have been a shareholder at all."

Auntie Edna was Axenia's grandmother. "What did she mean by that?"

"Some old scandal about his parents." Axenia shrugged again. "Besides, all you had to do was look at him. He was more gussuk than native."

Only last year Auntie Edna had been hectoring Kate about her choice of white boyfriends. "He was the grandson of a chief, Axenia."

"And the son of a thief," Axenia said coolly.

You can take the girl out of the Park, but you can't take the Park out of the girl. Again, Kate, hanging on to her temper by her fingernails, refrained from saying the words out loud. She would both praise and bury Caesar, she just wouldn't do it here. "So with Old Sam dead, you know there is a vacancy on the board."

"So?"

"So maybe you should think about running for it."

Axenia's eyes widened but she made no immediate response.

Kate, determined not to be sucked into the conversational vacuum, returned to her sandwich. After a moment, Axenia did, too.

It was quiet enough for a while that they could hear each other chewing. Finally Axenia, moistening a fingertip to chase an errant crumb around her plate, said in a tone that could almost be described as idle, "I thought you said I couldn't because I was married to the lobbyist for the mine. Conflict of interest."

"There aren't three hundred shareholders in the Association, Axenia." Kate pushed back her own plate. "There are barely seven hundred thousand people in the whole damn state. There aren't six degrees of separation in Alaska. I don't think there are three."

"What's your point?"

"After we talked last month, I looked up the ethics clauses in the Association bylaws. Emaa did a pretty good job on them. Maybe she was thinking ahead, recognizing that with so few shareholders the Association should make sure we didn't exclude our best and brightest from real power when we need them most. If you follow the rules she laid down and keep everything you do transparent, you should be fine."

Axenia's face was devoid of expression.

"And I will support you."

Axenia smirked. "Harvey and Ulanie running you that ragged?"

Kate closed her eyes and shook her head. "Okay, Axenia. You're pissed off at me because Emaa liked me better, I get that. You're pissed off at me because I rescued you, you didn't rescue yourself, I get that, too. The social obligation to display gratitude makes some people want to bite. Believe me, right there with you, babe. But really?" Kate slid to the floor and stood looking at Axenia over the counter. "In the context of the Niniltna Native Association, you, Axenia Shugak Mathisen? You don't matter one damn bit."

Axenia's face darkened.

"Don't get your back up," Kate said. "Neither do I. What matters is what we leave behind."

She left the kitchen with its au courant stainless-steel appliances and walked through the living room with its de rigueur leather furniture. At the door she raised her voice. "If you want to waste your time fighting with me instead of building something with a chance to last through your children's lives, be my guest. I won't be on the board that much longer anyway, and then you can run for chair."

She tried very hard not to slam the door behind her. It was how she usually felt leaving Axenia's house.

"Move over," she said to Mutt when she opened the door to the Forester.

Mutt moved over without a whimper and maintained a prudent silence all the way to Loussac.

• • •

At Loussac Library, Kate received the distressing information that Bruce, her favorite reference librarian, had retired. She spent an unnecessary amount of time mooching sullenly around the stacks. "Would you like some help?" the new librarian said for the third time.

No, Kate thought, I'd rather be miserable and pissed off. "Stuff about World War Two in the Aleutians?"

Soon she sat at another table surrounded by another welter of books, magazines, and journals, and a few academic dissertations with subtitles that went on forever, like "Unveiling the Secrets of the War in the Aleutians: The Failure of Japanese Strategy in the Central and North Pacific at Midway, Attu, and Kiska" and "The Aleut Diaspora: The Displacement of the Aleut People After the Bombing of Dutch Harbor and Its Effect on the Negotiations of the Alaska Native Claims Settlement Act." But there was also a copy of a government publication called *The Battle of the Aleutians*, published in 1944 and written by Corporals Robert Colodny and Dashiell Hammett. It was an elegant and well-written pamphlet, with black-and-white photographs. She looked for Old Sam's face under every helmet.

There were photographs in other publications of an Alaska Steam freighter burning in Dutch

Harbor after the Japanese attack, of the Japanese carriers that had launched the bombers, of before and after views of Aleut villages. Most of them had Russian Orthodox churches, each with its distinctive onion dome. She found photos of the USS *Delaroff* evacuating Aleuts from the war zone, most to old salmon canneries and defunct mines in Southeast, others to elsewhere in Alaska, including the Park. She looked for Shugaks leaning over every railing.

She found no record of Old Sam or of Mac McCullough or of the Sainted Mary in her cursory search, but the faces in the photographs stayed with her. The frightened and bewildered expressions of the Aleuts, who'd been allowed to take with them only what they could carry. Colonel Castner looking a little like Ike. The 807th Engineers in flat-brimmed World War I helmets, who built the landing strip on Adak in ten days. A shocking image of the Battle of Attu, showing a dotted string of GIs struggling across the almost vertical face of a snow-covered mountain.

It brought Old Sam's war home in a way Kate had never felt before. In front of Dinah's camera all he'd said was that the war had been cold, foggy, and bloody.

She understood a little better how Samuel Leviticus Dementieff and Herbert Elmer "Mac" McCullough could have forged a relationship that had nothing to do with patrimony and everything to do with survival.

Mac had given Old Sam life. Twice.

Find my father.

It didn't have quite the ring of "Follow the money," but it was pretty succinct nonetheless. Old Sam never had been one to babble.

Kate thanked the librarian and went out to the car and got in. Mutt sat up and looked at her, cocking her head a little.

She got out again and walked around the car, checking the lug nuts on every wheel. One time she hadn't, and in this very parking lot, too, with disastrous results.

All serene, and having recovered some sense of equanimity, she drove to Title Wave, where she bought new copies of *The Thousand-Mile War* and *Castner's Cutthroats*, and from there downtown, where she was further heartened by finding an empty parking space right in front of the DA's building.

"Kate!" The big man enveloped her in a comprehensive embrace that left her feet dangling in the air.

"Oof! Brendan, let me down!"

She found herself propelled into his office and seated in a chair he emptied of files by the simple expedient of tilting it forward to let them slide off into a jumbled heap on the floor.

Brendan McCord had been an assistant district

attorney for over fifteen years. During that time, he had resisted every attempt at transfer or promotion, steadfast through six different mayoral and four different gubernatorial administrations. He didn't care about money and he had no ambition to run for office. He was perfectly happy to beaver away where he was until retirement, putting bad guys away for as long as legally possible and even, on more rare and therefore more welcome occasions, seeing something like justice done. Large, as untidy as his office, ruddy-cheeked and red-haired, clad in a suit that came off the rack at Value Village and a tie sporting the remnants of his last three meals, he sat on the corner of his desk and beamed at her, his big-featured, good-natured face the first line of defense against the intelligence and curiosity in his sharp eyes. "Didn't expect to see you again so soon," he said, and leered. "Back to take me up on my offer of a life of unsanctified bliss?"

"Can you get me someone's prison record?"

"Sure." He made an expansive gesture. "Anything for you, my own, my black-eyed Kate. Give me a name."

"Guy named Herbert Elmer McCullough, alias Mac, alias One-Bucket."

One eyebrow went up. "One-Bucket?"

"Yeah."

He grinned. "Not One-Eye or Square One?"

"Nope. One-Bucket. I'll tell you why in a minute. Can you do it?"

"Uh-huh. Always interesting doing business with you, Shugak." He went around his desk and sat down in front of his computer. "Give me a date. Court conviction, incarceration."

"Uh, that's part of the problem. He went inside in 1921."

Brendan sat back in his chair. "Well. That makes it a little more difficult. But not impossible. The old records are being transferred into digital form as we speak. Of course the territory didn't have any prisons back then, but there will at least be a trial transcript, and I would guess records of transporting him out of the state. Whoever took him would certainly want to claim his expenses . . ." Brendan's voice trailed away when he saw Kate's expression.

"Yes, well, that's the other part of the problem. He wasn't convicted in Alaska of anything, so far as I know."

"Where did he stand trial?"

"California." If he hadn't been lying about it to Hammett. "He was arrested on the dock in Seattle."

"Ah." Brendan folded his hands over his substantial belly. "Also difficult. But again, not impossible." He leered again. "Especially if you're willing to put out for it."

Kate had to laugh. "Brendan," she said, drawing out the syllables of his name.

404

"Can't blame a guy for trying."

Her pocket gave out with the first six bars of Jimmy Buffett's "Volcano." Brendan's eyebrows went sky high. "Why, Kate, have you joined the real world at last?"

She fumbled it out. Of course it was Jim. "Hey," she said.

"Hey," he said. "Got your message. Never mind posting the love letters on the Internet. Wait till I get home and we can take some nude photographs."

"Let me have your cell number, Kate," Brendan said, raising his voice, "so I can talk dirty to you whenever I want."

"Who's that?" Jim said.

"Brendan," Kate said, getting up and going out into the hall. As she closed the door, Brendan sang, loudly and off-key, "When I'm calling you-ooo-ooo, will you answer too-ooo-ooo . . ."

She leaned against the wall in the corridor and ignored the glances of a couple of law clerks who passed within warbling range of the assistant district attorney with the most time served in the building.

Jim's voice cooled noticeably. "Brendan, huh?"

Kate smiled to herself. "Yeah. He's helping me with something."

"I'll bet. What? You've got a case?"

"Sort of. It has to do with Old Sam." She didn't want to get into it on the phone. "What's going on down there?"

"Buried him on Thursday. Read the will on Monday."

A week ago for the funeral, and four days ago for the will, and he was still there and not here. She wanted to ask him why he wasn't on a plane north already. "Anything unexpected?" she said.

"No. Well, not much. Something I need to clear up."

And then he'd be home? If Alaska still was home. "Touching base with old friends?"

"A few," he said. "There aren't that many left."

"Sylvia Hernandez one of them?" Kate said, and kicked herself for it.

"She came to the funeral," he said.

The quality of the following silence made her wait.

"And we went surfing yesterday."

"Surfer dude back on the board," Kate said, after a moment.

"Yeah."

Determined to at least act like the altruist she most emphatically was not, she said, "Feel good?"

"Felt great." She could hear the smile in his voice. "In Alaska the whole idea is to stay out of the water. It required some getting used to when I moved there."

Immersion in Alaskan waters generally resulted in hypothermia followed almost immediately by death. It was quick, you could say that for it. "I did hear that they've starting surfing on a beach near Yakutat," she said. "In dry suits."

"Yeah, I'd heard that, too." His voice lacked enthusiasm.

The door opened and Brendan stuck his head out. "When you hear my love call ringing clear . . ."

"Jesus," Jim said.

"Yeah," Kate said. "Later?"

"Later," he said.

She hung up and followed Brendan back into his office. "So?"

"So where's Jim that he's calling you on your cell phone?"

"California. His dad died."

Brendan's bushy eyebrows rose again. "Oh. Sorry to hear that." The eyebrows lowered and his grin was evil. "So you're here in my town all alone."

She had to laugh again. "Yes, I am, alone and at your mercy."

He looked at the clock on the wall. "Miracle of miracles, I get out of here on time today. May I take you to dinner, where I will wine you and dine you and attempt to take ruthless advantage of you in your abandoned state?"

"You may," she said.

"Orso's, seven o'clock, and for you I'll even put on a clean tie," he said, and handed her a printout that proved to be the prison record of Herbert Elmer "Mac" McCullough, convicted felon.

"Brendan," Kate said, "take me now."

1946

Seattle

Sam found the man Mac had sold his loot to only after months spent slogging through the Seattle rain. In the story Mac had referred to the man he'd sold the contents of his pack to as Pappy, but no one on the docks today had heard of anyone by that name, so Sam starting asking for anyone who had been in the trade in the 1920s, especially street dealers. One day, in a little store on Sixth Avenue that reeked of quaintness, the man behind the counter listened to his question with a fascinated gaze fixed on Sam's mouth and said, "Oh gosh, I don't know, I'm sure. I just moved up from the Bay Area myself."

He might have fluttered his eyelashes. He did invite Sam to dinner. His name was Kyle Blanchette. Sam was always hungry in those days, so he went. It was perhaps the civility of his refusal to Kyle's suggestion at the end of the evening that might have inspired further information. "Of course, there is old Pietro Pappardelle. Have you been to his place yet? No?" He grimaced. "Well, his shop is rather low end, but he is known to be the *ne plus ultra* authority whenever one of us is thinking of buying something of whose provenance we aren't quite sure." Kyle fluttered his lashes again. "I suppose there are those who could call him Pappy."

Tomorrow's Treasures was located on a dingy side street in the relatively new neighborhood of Fremont, a long streetcar ride and across a bridge from downtown. Like everywhere else in Seattle it was going through the postwar building boom, and the street-level shop in the sagging three-story building looked not much longer for this world. Inevitably, it would be leveled to make room for apartments for returning GIs and their brides.

A bell tinkled when Old Sam went in the door. It tinkled again when he had to step back before he knocked over a dusty porcelain bull with a gold ring through his nose. The bull was perched precariously on a tall table with a round, tiny top that did not look the least bit stable on its three long-stemmed legs.

The interior of the shop was dimly lit and crammed full of other such traps. Sam trod warily into this brittle knickknack jungle, and after a near collision with a mahogany armoire with a corniced top and lethal corners for a man of his height and a cautious sidle past a whatnot filled with china rebels in gray suits dancing the waltz with belles in hoop skirts, he achieved the relative safety of the counter that stood against the back wall. The wall was pierced by a doorway over which a dusty curtain made of flowered cotton hung from a dirty white piece of string wound around nails at either end.

"Hello?" he said. There was a tarnished brass bell on the counter. He raised it and gave a little jingle. "Hello?"

There was movement behind the curtain. It twitched back to reveal a short, stubby man with a bulbous nose, a red face, and eyes set so closely together that for a moment Sam thought he was cross-eyed. "Yes?"

"Mr. Pappardelle?"

"Yes?"

Old Sam would have thought of a more tactful way to approach the object of his Outside exile, but Samuel Leviticus Dementieff was a young man both in love and in a hurry. "Also known as Pappy?"

The near-together eyes narrowed. "I always appreciate at least an introduction to the person with whom I converse."

"My name's Sam Dementieff," Sam said. "You might have met my—my father down on the docks in 1920 when he got off a steamer from Alaska."

"Really. Young man, I have better things to do today than—"

"Mr. Pappardelle, he died in the war. He left a, uh, a letter for me, saying that he'd sold what he had in his pack that day in 1920 to a man on the Seattle docks named Pappy. I was hoping that was you."

"Whether it is or it isn't is none of—"

"If it is, he sold you something he shouldn't have. It was a family heirloom. He stole it."

Pappardelle's red face got redder. "If you are implying that I acted as a receiver of stolen goods—"

"No, sir," Sam said, although he'd seen enough shifty glances during the quest that led him to the door of Tomorrow's Treasures to have strong doubts about the entire profession of antiques dealing. "No, sir, nothing like that. Back then you couldn't have known, I understand that. I'm just trying to track it down, to find out who has it now, so I can get it back to the original owners."

Pappardelle eyed him for a long moment. Sam met his gaze without flinching, letting Pappardelle look him over. The threadbare state of his clothes, the gauntness of his countenance, the directness of his gaze—one or all of these things must have made an impression, because Pappardelle suddenly relaxed into a different man altogether, one much more like the man described by Sam's dinner date of the night before. "Please come through here, Mr. Demon—Demented—"

"Dementieff," Sam said, "but please just call me Sam," and ducked beneath the low door frame to follow Pappardelle into an apartment with a kitchenette, a sofa bed, and a tiny bathroom glimpsed through an open door. A back door led presumably to an alley. This back room was if possible even more crowded than the front room, with everything Pappardelle hadn't managed to wedge into the shop on the other side of the curtain crammed in here. A Victorian tea set with a cracked milk jug. A fake diamond necklace (at least Sam assumed it was fake or it would have been locked away in a safe, not left on a table between the butter and the sugar bowl). A pair of logger's lifting tongs. A brass ship's compass set on gimbals in a teak box that had seen infinitely better days.

He liked the look of the compass, but that wasn't why he was here. "Mr. Pappardelle—"

Pappardelle waved him to a seat. "I haven't had my coffee yet this morning, young man, and I refuse to talk business until I am fully awake." He busied himself with a percolator while Sam removed a stack of *Life* magazines, a lace tablecloth, a box of firecrackers, and a tabby cat from an aged wing chair. It had a high back and was upholstered in a revolting shade of dark red leather that looked like dried blood.

He seated himself nevertheless, and in due time and with due ceremony was served with the best cup of coffee he'd had since coming to Seattle, and then Pappardelle got to work on breakfast, ham and eggs and potatoes and thick slices of toast soaked in butter. Sam had been making good wages on the docks, but every penny he could spare was going into the bank for his return journey home and his stake once he got there, and he'd been skimping on meals. The second full spread in less than twenty-four hours required his complete attention.

When he sat back Pappardelle was regarding him with approval. "It is good to see a man enjoy his food," he said, and topped up Sam's mug with fresh coffee. "Now let's hear your story, young man. I have an ear for stories, and it tells me that yours will be a good one."

Pappardelle's near-together eyes were shrewd but kind, and Sam remembered what his date had said the night before. *The* ne plus ultra *authority whenever one of us is thinking of buying something of whose provenance we aren't quite sure.* His instincts told him that he would receive no honesty from this man unless he was prepared to share some of his own. "I told you the truth, Mr. Pappardelle. I'm trying to track down a family heirloom."

He told Pappardelle the story of the stolen

icon, beginning with the flu pandemic and its decimation of Kanuyaq and Niniltna, the funeral potlatch, the display of the tribal relic and its subsequent disappearance. He gave a detailed physical description of Mac, and the exact date of the sale.

"Hmm," Pappardelle said at the end. "And how did you come by that specific date, young man?"

"Like I told you, sir. My father left me a letter."

"He died, you said." The older man's face wore an expression that was hard to read.

"Yes, sir. In the war." It was close enough to the truth.

Pappardelle subjected him to a steady, narrow-eyed look. After some minutes he said, "Yes, well, perhaps you will tell me the truth of that one day, because it sounds like the most interesting part of your story." He sighed. "But then the parts left out are always the most interesting." He pushed himself out of a basket chair that creaked alarmingly under the pressure and moved nimbly through his overcrowded living quarters to a massive oak bookcase that took up all of one wall. He beckoned, and Sam edged cautiously through the accumulation to stand next to him.

"One of my proudest acquisitions," Pappardelle said. The bookcase's trim was carved with vines and leaves and flowers, the pulls were solid brass, and the glass in the doors was convex so that the titles of the books inside were magnified to the person reading them from the outside.

Sam had never seen such a thing and said so.

Pappardelle ran a caressing hand down the wood. "I could have sold this ten times over—in fact, there is a gentleman with a summer home on Lake Washington who has made three offers on it—but I can't bear to part with it. At least not yet." He sighed. "It is a great mistake in this business to fall in love with your stock. You end up dead in a room other people can't get into for the clutter."

Sam cast a glance around the room and refrained from the obvious reply.

Pappardelle opened the glass doors and ran a finger down the spines of a set of red ledgers that took up the middle shelf, each with a year in gilt letters on the spine. They ran all the way from the present year back to 1901. He smiled at Sam's expression. "What, you thought I did not keep records? Are you familiar with the word *provenance?*"

The first time he'd heard it said out loud was last night. Sam said, "No, sir."

"It is a fancy way of saying where the item you buy or sell comes from," Pappardelle said. "In the antiques trade, the history of the item is often even more valuable than the item itself. For example, if you have a letter from John Adams to Thomas Jefferson, one way to authenticate it is to have a record of how the letter got from Thomas Jefferson to you. Family members, heirs, dealers, collectors, names, and dates of acquisition—they can be listed in inventories, bequeathed in wills." Pappardelle's bulbous nose almost twitched. "Every item in my store, every item I've ever bought, has its own story."

"And how complete the story is directly affects how much you can charge for it," Sam said.

Pappardelle beamed at Sam as if he were a teacher and Sam were a particularly bright student. His formal style of speech and his deliberate diction bespoke a formal education, and he wasn't shy to display it, although never on this day or on any of the other days Sam spent in his company did he ever by word, look, or deed belittle Sam for his lack of same. Instructive, yes. Patronizing, never. "Exactly," he said.

He pulled out the volume for 1919 with something of a flourish and wove a path back to his basket chair. He set the heavy volume on his legs, moved his spectacles from the top of his head to the tip of his nose, and opened the ledger to peer nearsightedly at the pages.

This time Sam paused before sitting down, wondering for the first time what the history of the wing chair was, and if the color of the cracked leather had been accidental, deliberate, or simply a result of the chair's sitting too long in front of a sunny window. Who had put a cigar down on the right arm to cause that burn? Who had let the cat scratch at the left front leg? Who had worn the comfortable hollow in the seat? Was the hard lump in the back by accident or intent, part of a design determined to make an entire generation sit bolt upright?

He sat down. "What's the story on that compass?" he said.

Pappardelle raised his head to give the compass a fond look. "Ah yes," he said. "That particular piece is almost a hundred years old, according to a marine salvage expert I know. The man who sold it to me swore it was out of the CSS *Shenandoah*. Are you familiar with the vessel?"

Sam frowned. "The name sounds like I ought to be."

Pappardelle nodded. "And quite right, too, given your own provenance." He chuckled over his little joke. "The CSS *Shenandoah* was the ship purposed by the Confederate states to attack and sink Yankee whalers in the Pacific Ocean, with the stated object of doing harm to the Northern states' economy."

Sam sat up. "That's right," he said. "I served in the Aleutians during the war. There wasn't a lot to do, so every now and then to keep the enlisted out of trouble the brass would get the big idea to have educational talks by anyone they could sucker out of the ranks. Some of them actually were kind of interesting. One night this Signal Corps guy from Tacoma—what was his name? Morgan, that was it. Anyway, Morgan was some kind of writer or professor or something in real life and he gave us a talk about how the last shot fired in the American Civil War was fired in the Aleutians."

"By the CSS *Shenandoah*." Again, Pappardelle looked delighted at his star pupil's intelligence.

Sam put a tentative finger on the compass and gave it a gentle push. It swung on its gimbals and righted itself. According to it, he was facing north. "And this compass was off that ship?"

"Alas," Pappardelle said regretfully, "I am unable to trace it to the *Shenandoah* specifically, though my marine salvage expert does not rule out that possibility. He is certain it is of that era, and has provided me with documentation to that effect."

"Why isn't it out in the shop?"

"I like it," Pappardelle said. "I like looking at it and wondering how it came into the hands of the man who brought it in the door. I wonder how many ensigns—or is it bosuns?—stood their night watch before it. I wonder what happened to the ship it came out of, if she was delivered to the unmerciful hands of the ship breakers or if she survives, one day perhaps to sail into this very port." His smile was wry and self-deprecating.

"Like the bookcase," Sam said.

"I'm afraid so." Pappardelle sighed. "I would be a richer man by far if I could bear to part with some of my more treasured items."

"But maybe not a happier one?"

A slow smile spread across Pappardelle's face. "Perhaps not," he said. He gestured toward the ledger in his lap. "Are you ready to hear this now?"

Sam's stalling for time hadn't fooled Pappardelle for a minute. He braced himself. "I'm ready."

Pappardelle's glasses slipped down even further, so that they lodged just above the bulb on the end of his nose. It made him look like a de-bearded Father Christmas. "It is fortunate you have the month and year," he said. "July, July, July, here we are. Ah, yes. July 17." He showed Sam a closely scripted page in upright penmanship, the black ink now fading. "I met the Alaska Steam ship *Baranof* at the dock. At the time," he said, looking up, "it was the habit of many people to meet the ships when they docked from Alaska. Newspapermen. Wives and children of the men who had gone north. Creditors of same." He grimaced. "Various and sundry members of the law, hoping to close out a warrant of arrest on miscreants who had escaped their long arm in the North." He gave Old Sam a sharp look.

Old Sam kept his expression one of pleasant interest. Or he hoped he did.

"And of course people such as myself, people in the trade. Many, in fact most, of the people who sought their fortune in the north returned home with little more than the clothes on their backs. Usually, they were willing to trade the one keepsake they had managed to hold on to through the vicissitudes of the gold fields for a little cash so they could eat. I am not a pawnbroker, you understand, then or now, but I would guarantee that if the object did not sell in the meantime, when they had managed to save a little money, I would sell the item back to them for the same price for which I had bought it."

"One of the reasons you kept such good records," Sam said.

"Yes."

"Not a bad deal for a hungry man forced into a hard choice."

Pappardelle blushed at the compliment and cleared his throat. "Yes, well . . ."

"What kinds of keepsakes?"

"Small enough to fit in a pocket, most often jewelry. Portability would have been very desirable in objects of this kind, for reasons of both transportation and security. Pocket watches, signet rings, brooches, necklaces. The occasional tiara. I remember once a very fine engagement ring with the most enormous diamond in it. Rather vulgar, but undeniably valuable. The gentleman—he'd come south from Fairbanks, I believe—who sold it to me never wanted to see the ring again. I could not afford to pay him anything remotely close to its true value. He didn't care, he just wanted enough cash to get home to Minnesota." Pappardelle cleared his throat again. "I gathered that the lady in question had discovered the remunerative advantages of multiple partners, as opposed to just one."

It took Sam a minute to work this out. "Oh," he said. "She was working the Line."

His turn to explain, and Pappardelle said, "Ah. Yes. I believe it was something of that nature," and blushed again. "Well." He looked back down at the ledger and ran his finger down the page of July 17. "So. I met the Alaska Steam ship *Baranof* at the dock at three in the afternoon. It was the third steamer from Alaska that day. This one had debarked from the port of Seward." He squinted through his spectacles.

"I purchased items from three different passengers from the Baranof, it seems, and all with unique items for sale. The first was a five-by-eight floral sculpture, Chinese, Qing dynasty, sold by a young woman who, as I recall, it was obvious had seen better days, poor girl. The second item was a French telescope from the early 1800s, sold by a gentleman I took to have been a sailor at one time. I remember this item particularly because he was so loath to part with it, and I had hoped he would be able to redeem it before it was sold."

"Was he?"

"Unfortunately"—Pappardelle tapped a notation next to the price of purchase—"it sold the very next day to a collector of maritime memorabilia, who is still quite a good customer of mine today."

"Did the sailor come back for it?"

"He did, almost a year later, and I am happy to say looking much better fed. I believe he prospered in the timber industry. I introduced him to the gentleman who had bought it, and they came to some arrangement that restored the telescope to its original owner." He looked up and fixed Sam with a stare that was much at variance with the rambling style of his discourse. "And now we come to it. Young man, I have understood from the story you told me that you are searching for an item of great value, not so much to yourself as to your family. From the state of your physical condition and your attire, not to mention your appetite"— Pappardelle smiled faintly—"I believe you may even consider yourself cast off. It may be that you seek reinstatement in your family with the restoration of it to its rightful owners."

Sam could feel his spine stiffening. The old man saw too damn much.

Pappardelle acknowledged his resentment with an inclined head. "Nevertheless, I feel myself constrained to point out that no physical object can provide you with the redemption you may be seeking. These objects"—he waved a hand at the quarters crowded with the flotsam and jetsam of his trade—"are just that, objects. Things. The detritus of life. They can be lost, destroyed, stolen. The fullness of time can and will erase their very existence. The value they have is only and ever the value you are willing to assign to them."

Their eyes met and held, and Pappardelle nodded once for emphasis. "A wise man concentrates on the value he can accrue to himself through the practice of the golden rule. High ideals are much scoffed at these days, I know. It is the natural consequence of a long and hard-fought war. I saw such cynicism myself following the Great War, and in much of the literature written by its veterans. But your soul is what wants work, young man. Finding this object will advance you no farther down the road of its cultivation. Do you understand?"

Sam had gone red, then white, and then red again. "I have to find it." He swallowed hard. There were so many reasons why. He settled on the least painful of them. "If only to know the end of the story."

Pappardelle subjected him to another sharp scrutiny before a nod of acquiescence. "Very well. Decision is one trait in which you need no instruction or improvement." He bent over the ledger. "I also bought several items from a third passenger off the *Baranof*, a young man I would guess to be about your age now." Pappardelle's glance swept Sam from head to toe. "He was a little taller than you are, with much the same build and a certain similarity of countenance."

Sam felt the heat rise up the back of his neck. Again, he remembered Hammett's asking if he and Mac were brothers. Had everyone in the cutthroats seen the resemblance? And if so, why hadn't he?

Pappardelle continued in a meditative tone. "I remember particularly because of the variety of items he had for sale, and because of the haste which he exhibited."

"He was on the lam," Sam said shortly.

"Ah. 'On the lam.'" Pappardelle repeated the phrase as if it was the first time it had come his way. "Yes, well, that would explain it. At any rate, this Mr.—"

"McCullough."

Pappardelle didn't so much as raise an eyebrow. "No. No, the name he gave me was Mr. Smith."

"Original."

"There are in fact many Smiths in this world," Pappardelle said serenely. "There was no reason Mr. Herbert Smith could not have been one of them."

He'd kept his first name, Sam thought. Probably easier to remember when someone called it. "He sold you the icon?"

"He did."

"Can you remember what the icon looked like?"

"Certainly. It was one of very few examples of Russian iconography that has ever come my way. And of course I made notes." Pappardelle adjusted his spectacles and read out loud. " 'A Russian Marian icon, that is to say, an icon depicting the figure of the Virgin Mary. A triptych of three wooden panels hinged together, eight inches high and eighteen inches wide overall. The images themselves made of gold carved into bas-relief depicting first, mother and child, second, Mary at the foot of the cross, and third, Mary at the Ascension. The frame inlaid with rough-cut stones and gold filigree. The date on the back is September 1, 5508 BC, which is not the date of manufacture, but the date Eastern Orthodoxy regarded as the day the world was created by God.' An interesting fact but of little use in estimating the age of the icon itself."

Sam didn't care about the age of the icon. "How much did he shake you down for it?"

Pappardelle looked reproving. "He did not 'shake me down,' as you call it. I paid him two hundred dollars, and I was happy to get it at that price. It was a very rare piece. I have never seen anything like it since."

The reverential way Pappardelle spoke the words jolted Sam out of his bitter reflections. "If this icon was so very rare, and you say that you're not a fence, why did you buy it? You must have known Mac stole it."

Pappardelle sighed. "That day, may I be forgiven my arrogance, I considered myself the lesser of two evils."

"Say what?"

Pappardelle sighed again. "I was not the only curio dealer on the docks that day. A Mr. Armstrong was also there, a gentleman whose dealings I am afraid would not have borne close scrutiny. And, alas, did not for very much longer. One of his clients took umbrage at—"

Sam didn't care about Mr. Armstrong and

clients with or without umbrage, whatever the hell that was. "Did you sell it?"

"I did, eventually. It remained in the shop for many years." He smiled. "I confess, I was content to have it so." His brow wrinkled. "At the risk of sounding fanciful, young man, some objects carry with them their own sense of . . . let us say vitality. I remember once a pair of African harps that came into my possession, formed in the shapes of men, with elongated legs for the strings and tiny, laughing heads for the keys. They made me smile, just looking at them. One could imagine the artists carving them with the express view of making people dance when they were completed." He smiled in remembrance.

"And the icon?" Sam said.

"Ah, the icon. It presented an entirely different feeling, one of . . ." Pappardelle hesitated. "Spirituality, though I hasten to add, a spirituality not of a demanding or minatory nature. Rather, one of hope, and trust." His hand made a small, dismissive wave. "It may be that over time, such objects take on the hopes and fears of the people who treasure them. Who can say? It sounds far-fetched, I know. Yet I tell you such objects do exist."

Sam leaned forward. "Who bought it?"

Pappardelle closed the book and pushed his spectacles back up on his head. "I will give you his name so long as you guarantee me that you will approach him in a civilized manner." His smile took the sting out of the words. "I might have had my doubts about the provenance of the item, but I gave him no reason to believe he might be purchasing stolen goods. He bought it in good faith."

"Yeah, yeah, I promise not to beat it out of him," Sam said.

"There is no need for sarcasm, young man. The gentleman bought it in 1937." Pappardelle wrote down the name and handed it to Sam. He hesitated again, as one trying to make up his mind. "One more thing which you may find of interest."

"Yes?"

Pappardelle's look was solemn, and a little wary. "You are not the first person to inquire after this particular object."

Twenty-three

AT THE RESTAURANT THAT EVENING, Brendan got himself on the outside of a bottle of wine while they worked their way through caprese, insalata Orso, and petite filet mignon with Cambozola cheese. In between bites he caught Kate up on the doings of everyone she'd ever worked with in town, who'd been transferred, promoted, or fired, who'd been caught screwing whom on whose desk. She was cheered to hear that Steve Sayles had retired to a cabin on a trout creek in northern Idaho. "You know I never did hear that whole story," Brendan said.

"I gave a statement. There was an inquest."

"Kate."

She gave a slight shrug and looked into the cup that held her after-dinner coffee. "You know he was first on the scene."

Brendan maintained a hopeful silence, and Kate drained her cup and signaled for a refill. When the waiter had gone, she said, "I was working a child molestation case because the assistant DA prosecuting the case—Phillips? Rafferty? Klein, that was it—Klein was uncomfortable with some of the work the investigating officer had done. Jack wanted me to dot all the *i*'s and cross all the *t*'s before she took the case to court and the judge

431

bounced half the evidence as fruit of the poisonous tree."

Brendan made an encouraging noise.

Kate watched the traffic on Fifth Avenue pass by outside the windows, a lot of cars and trucks and semis moving very fast, rushing to catch the next light before it turned red. Someone had once said that Anchorage was a city best seen at thirty-five miles an hour, and Fifth Avenue was like a microcosm of Anchorage itself, two hundred and eighty thousand people in a hurry. Where the hell were they all going?

She'd lived among them for almost six years, doing the best job she could, until she couldn't do it anymore. "I spent some time on the phone with witnesses, checking their statements, talked to the lab about the physical evidence, and then I went out to the perp's house. The kids had been removed by then, of course, and I talked to them again, but Jack wanted me to evaluate the perp personally. He always liked my take on an interview." She met Brendan's eyes, from which all amusement had vanished. "The thing is, Brendan, the son of a bitch knew I was coming. I had called him. He must have gone out and grabbed the first kid he saw."

"Whoa," Brendan said. "You didn't make him grab that kid, Kate."

"Didn't I?" she said. "I could hear the kid begging from outside the door. 'Please don't. Please don't. Please.'"

She looked down into her mug again, stirring the contents so that the half-and-half formed a creamy spiral in the inky blankness. "I don't remember kicking the door in, but I saw the photographs of it hanging half off its hinges later, so I must have. He was doing the kid five feet from the door, facing it. He was holding a knife to the kid's throat, and he was grinning at me."

She was silent. "And then?" he said. He'd asked, he was by God going to hear it all.

Her hand came up to touch the white, roped scar on her throat. The husk on her voice had thickened when she spoke again. "I went for the knife. He got this in before I took it away from him and killed him with it." She raised the coffee cup halfway to her lips and paused. "It was a good knife, one of those fancy filet knives, razor-edge stainless-steel blade with a wooden handle, a pattern inset with dyed wood, veneered all shiny. I'll never forget how pretty it was."

The conversation seemed isolated in a pool of silence. The waiters going by with laden plates, other diners laughing and talking, the scrape of a spoon across the bottom of a bowl, none of it penetrated to this table.

"But you know what I remember most?" she said, still in that detached tone. "How easy the knife went in. Just slid right in, under his ribs and into his heart. I was watching his face. Have you ever seen someone die, Brendan? It's an exit, a departure,

I don't know, like their soul walks away."

"Not my part of the job," he said. "Thank god."

"It wasn't enough for me," she said to her coffee. "It was way too easy. I wanted to carve his heart out and feed it to Raven."

She met his eyes. "Then I looked up and saw the kid. Four years old. He'd jammed himself into a corner. He'd managed to pull his jeans back up, but he was too terrified to cry, too terrified to run. He'd been kidnapped and raped and then been an eyewitness to a murder committed within range of the blood spatter. My blood, the perp's, I still don't know. I stretched a hand out to him before I went horizontal, and he screamed." A brief pause. "I'll never forget that, either."

She drank coffee. "I woke up in the hospital the next day, to the news that Sayles had been first on the scene and that he was trying his damnedest to make it out to be a case of voluntary manslaughter. Said I'd gone there with intent."

"I remember that part," Brendan said.

"The charge went away after a while." Her smile was twisted. "And after not very much longer, so did I."

Beneath the table, Mutt's weight pressed comfortingly against her leg.

Brendan said, "The charge went away after Jack Morgan beat the crap out of him."

"What?" Kate, jerked out of her reverie, stared at him. "I didn't know that."

"It wasn't generally known. I wouldn't have known it myself if Jack hadn't been working a case of mine and I hadn't seen him the very next day. Sayles got in a couple shots. I backed Jack into a corner and weaseled it out of him. Sayles hung out at the Pioneer Bar. Jack waited three nights for him to come out alone and nailed him in the parking lot on the way to his car."

Kate put a hand on Mutt's head, scratching mechanically behind her ears. "I can't believe it. Jack wasn't a brawler."

"You'd never have known it," Brendan said cheerfully. "I visited Sayles in the hospital."

"He put Sayles in the hospital?" Kate's voice scaled up.

Brendan grinned. "He looked a lot worse than Jack did, believe me. Couple of cracked ribs and a fractured collarbone, as I remember. And shiners way worse than yours."

"You should have seen them a week ago," Kate said. "And Sayles didn't have him up on charges?"

Brendan tried to look modest and failed. "I had a word with his watch commander."

Kate's full lips indented at the corners.

"Go ahead, laugh," he said, "you know you want to."

She did, throwing back her head and letting loose with a husky rumble that raised the hair on the back of every male neck in the room. Beneath

435

the table Mutt's pressure eased. Kate looked at Brendan. "Thanks."

And Brendan McCord tried not to wriggle all over because Kate Shugak thought he'd done a smart thing.

Kate's cell phone rang at nine o'clock the next morning and she answered without looking at the screen. "Jim?"

"Um, is this Kate Shugak?"

Jim hadn't called her back yesterday, and when she'd tried to call him she'd gotten his voice mail again. "Yes," she said with a patience she felt it was a pity no one was there to witness. "Who is this?"

"Lazary. Lazary Kuznetsov."

It took her a moment to remember the Old Believer research assistant at the museum. "Yes, of course, Lazary." She walked into the kitchen and turned on the electric kettle. "How can I help you?"

"I didn't want to say anything yesterday in case it didn't work out, but my great-uncle is, well, he was a priest. A Russian Orthodox priest."

"Was? Is he dead?"

"No, just retired."

"And . . ." Kate put coffee in a filter and set the filter on a mug that said "Speed Limit 186,000 Miles per Second. It's Not Just a Good Idea. IT'S THE LAW!" Jack Morgan had been an astronomy nut, something he'd passed on to his son.

"And iconography is sort of a hobby of his."

"Is it." The kettle boiled and Kate poured hot water through the filter. "Does he live in Anchorage?"

"Yes."

"Would he talk to me?" Being that she was an unbeliever, and a woman to boot.

"He said he would." Lazary hesitated. "He's pretty old, Ms. Shugak, and a little wandery. I don't know if he can help you. But in his time, he knew icons chapter and verse."

He gave her the address and told her that Uncle Vladik was at his best in the morning. She looked at the clock and said, "You can tell him I'll be there in an hour. And Lazary? Thanks."

It was a group home for elderly gentlemen who wore their pants belted around their armpits. Their assisted living came in the shape of a formidable dragon with helmet hair rinsed a defiant and brassy blond who examined Kate's driver's license with minute attention before grudgingly allowing her and Mutt entry, admonishing them in stern accents not to tire the good father. Mutt looked as cowed as Kate felt.

The house was light and pleasant and excruciatingly clean, with an underlying smell of antiseptic. The dragon ushered them into a sunroom at the back of the house that was furnished with a rattan couch and chairs with cushions in a once colorful floral print. Tall windows overlooked a fenced yard with trees and shrubs surrounding a horseshoe pit and a croquet lawn. Next to the back fence was a section of hard-packed dirt suitable for bocce ball.

The dragon said in a tone that disapproved of any such thing, "Here are your visitors, Father Vladik," and went away again, although Kate harbored the strong suspicion that she was lurking right outside the door, ready to breathe fire all over Kate if Kate showed the least sign of harassing her charge.

Father Vladik gave Kate an impish smile. "She'll fry both our livers up for dinner if we don't behave."

Kate laughed, and he nodded at a chair.

"I'm Kate Shugak," Kate said.

He nodded, his eyes on Mutt. Kate made an unobtrusive gesture and Mutt paced forward to stand gravely while Father Vladik petted her with a spotted and fragile hand. "Lazary called to say you were coming. He says you want to know about icons."

Kate wasn't sure she'd ever met anyone this old, or at least anyone who had looked this old. His flesh clung to his bones like a layer of wet, washed-out cotton, and his eyes were sunken and enveloped in wrinkles. He was seated in a wheelchair, placed to catch the maximum amount of the day's sunlight, and he was dressed in a clean white button-down shirt and brown polyester slacks. A plaid blanket had been tucked over his legs, but he'd thrown it over one arm of his chair. His fingernails were clipped and filed, his wisp of remaining hair combed neatly back, and the thin, snow-white beard was allowed to flow into his lap only under the most strict restraints of cleanliness and neatness.

Still, Kate had the feeling that Father Vladik and his fellow inmates were very lucky. The twinkle in his eye told her he knew what she was thinking and shared the feeling. "What can I do for you, Ms. Shugak?"

He listened to her story without interruption. "A missing icon," he said thoughtfully when she came to the end. "A mystery, in fact."

"Yes," she said.

"Even a treasure hunt," he said, eyes twinkling.

He surprised a laugh out of her. "I guess you could call it that, too."

"Well, of course, icons have gone missing ever since icons appeared," he said, and Kate did not like to ask this venerable old gentleman if he meant "appeared" in the real or the religious sense. "You understand what an icon is?"

Kate, recognizing the signs of an enthusiast, settled down for the long haul with a dutiful expression of interest, interpolating the appropriate "Really" and "How interesting" at suitable intervals.

439

Father Vladik was definitely an authority, covering everything in Kate's research the day before and embellishing it with dogma as well as human interest. He asked questions as well, almost none of which could she answer. "Was the first image of your Virgin pointing at the Child?"

"I don't know," Kate said for the seventh or eighth time, although Father Vladik seemed never to tire of hearing it.

"Was perhaps the Virgin's hand on the right knee of Christ? You don't know?" Father Vladik seemed to sigh. "Unless I see it, I have no way to tell you if it was Greek or Russian. Greek icons were said to have been made from copies of a drawing Luke made of Mary."

"This icon was three panels hinged together," Kate said.

"A triptych," Father Vladik said. "Yes, I see."

"Do you know of any stories of a triptych brought to Alaska by the early Russians?" Kate said.

He frowned. "Of course there is the legend of the Lady of Kodiak."

Kate perked up. "The Lady of Kodiak?"

The Lady of Kodiak was an icon that, according to Father Vladik, had been revealed to Saint Juvenaly, who had been martyred while proselytizing to the unfaithful in 1796. "He came from Ekaterinburg," Father Vladik said, "and followed Archimandrite Joseph to Kodiak in

1794." He paused, and cleared his throat. "Conditions," he said, "were not what they had been led to expect." And then he added, "But then, when are they ever."

Kate appreciated this note of reality in the missionary experience and warmed even more to Father Vladik.

The Kodiak settlement was primitive and violent and there was no church, but in only two years the missionaries counted twelve thousand converts. Juvenaly took the work to mainland Alaska. "And there," Father Vladik said, "unfortunately, Father Juvenaly disappeared."

"What happened to him?"

"No one really knows. One Alaska Native oral history has it that he was killed by a fellow shaman." Father Vladik sighed. "Honest zeal is a requirement of the missionary vocation, but it is also the primary cause of mission failure. The greatest delicacy is called for when carrying the true faith to the heathen." He sank into a reverie, possibly induced by memories of missions of his own.

"And the triptych?" Kate said.

Father Vladik roused himself. "Juvenaly brought it with him to Alaska, of course. According to tradition, it served as the focus for the service, until a church was built. In Kodiak, miracles began to be reported in its presence, healing miracles, sight and hearing restored, a

441

barren woman made fertile, a paralyzed child made to walk again. The usual things. That was when she began to be called the Lady of Kodiak."

Kate was tempted to ask if the Lady of Kodiak had raised anyone from the dead, but forbore. Old Sam would not have approved of her poking even gentle fun at this good old man, and she was, in a manner of speaking, here in Old Sam's service. "What happened to it?"

One shoulder rose and fell in a slight shrug. He stared past her shoulder with eyes that had begun to dim. "Some say Baranov was jealous of the authority of the church and stole it, hoping to weaken our influence. Others say Saint Juvenaly took it with him into the north." He looked at her with disapproval. "Where is your head scarf, young woman?"

"I beg your pardon?"

"Your head scarf," he said impatiently. "How may I baptize your child if you will not show the proper respect to your church and your God?"

"I—"

The dragon materialized in the doorway. "It's almost time for lunch, Father. May I take you into the dining room?"

Kate became aware of a stir and other voices in another part of the house.

Father Vladik said, sounding querulous now, "I wish you people would quit bothering me about the Lady. She's gone. Gone with the saint into the wilderness. Prepare ye the way of the Lord, make his paths straight!"

Kate stopped halfway to her feet. "I'm not the first one to ask about the Lady of Kodiak?"

"O come let us worship and fall down before Christ, son of God," Father Vladik said.

"Father—"

"That will be all, Ms. Shugak," the dragon said.

Kate followed them out into the hallway and waited until the dragon had settled Father Vladik in at the table with his lunch in front of him. He was singing now, something that sounded Gregorian, the liturgy of the Russian Orthodox service, perhaps. "There, now," the dragon said, patting him on the shoulder. "Enjoy your lunch, Father."

She looked up and saw Kate in the doorway, and steamed toward her with magisterial impatience. "Yes?" she said, as if she expected sheer force of personality to be enough to send Kate scuttling for cover.

It nearly was, but Kate mustered up her courage and gave speech. "Has Father Vladik had other visitors recently?"

"None of the gentlemen receive visitors that often," the dragon said, "and such visitors would be their private business."

"Please," Kate said. "I'm not asking you to betray a confidence, but it would help me very much to know."

The dragon huffed out an impatient breath, and

condescended enough to say, "There was a gentleman here last week, who asked to speak with Father Vladik."

"When?"

"I believe it would have been Friday."

"What did they talk about?"

The dragon reared up. "I am not in the habit of eavesdropping on my gentlemen's conversations, Ms. Shugak."

"Of course not," Kate said, soothing, "but did you perhaps accidentally overhear something, anything, that would give some hint as to the topic of the conversation?" She saw the refusal in the dragon's eye and added hurriedly, "I wouldn't ask, but it is a matter of great moment to my tribe."

The dragon thawed a trifle. "Tribe?"

"The Niniltna Native Association. It concerns a, an artifact belonging to them, that was lost to them over eighty years ago."

"Ah." The dragon was silent for a moment. "I should have been a Chugachmiut shareholder."

"Ah," Kate said in turn, and realization dawned. "What's your blood quantum?"

"One eighth. My maternal grandmother was one-half Eyak."

"You're from Cordova," Kate said.

"My mother was," the dragon said, and turned to go back into the dining room.

The resentments spawned by those who had been and those who had not been included in the

Alaska Native Claims Settlement Act, Kate thought bitterly, had screwed yet another promising investigation.

She and Mutt were at the door when the dragon's voice sounded behind her, and she turned to see her standing in the hallway. "It might have been something about a lady."

"The Lady of Kodiak?"

"Perhaps. I can't be sure. As I say, I wasn't listening."

Kate walked forward to plant herself directly in front of the dragon. "My name is Ekaterina Ivana Shugak. What is your name?"

"Marilyn Barnes."

"Barnes," Kate said. "My paternal grand-mother's maiden name was Barnes, one of the Cordova Barneses. We're probably cousins." One cousin with shareholder status and a quarterly dividend and land, and one without. She didn't look Dragon Barnes in the eye; that would have been rude. Instead she inclined her head and said in a soft voice, "I see you, Marilyn Barnes."

The dragon hesitated. "I see you, Ekaterina Ivana Shugak."

They didn't exchange bows, but it was close.

Outside, Kate sat for a moment without starting the car.

Our Lady of Kodiak, a Russian icon reputed to work miracles, vanishes in 1796, possibly in the

Interior with the missionary priest who had brought it to Alaska. Also possibly not.

Alexander Baranov made Sitka the capital of Russian America when he became the head of the Russian-American Company in 1799. In 1802 the Tlingits booted the Russians back into the sea. In 1804 Baranov returned with a warship. Thus New Archangel, now known as Sitka, was born. If he had stolen the icon from Juvenaly, he would certainly have brought it to Sitka with him.

But in 1802, Baranov's settlement had been overrun with Tlingits, who had undoubtedly taken everything that wasn't nailed down as theirs by right, the spoils of war.

What if one of the things they took had been the icon?

More history flipped up in Kate's mental Rolodex. The Tlingits ran a regular trade route up the Chilkoot Pass, carrying in dentalium shells and cedar baskets and fish oil, and bringing moose and caribou hides and copper ore back out to the coast.

Tlingits, she thought, sitting up with a jerk that startled Mutt.

Tlingit tribes customarily married their sons to the daughters of powerful Athabascan chiefs, to cement ties between the tribes, to safeguard trade routes, to ensure peace.

Kookesh. A Southeast name, not an Interior name, not an Aleut name.

And what would be more natural than for a prospective husband to bring a miracle-bestowing artifact as a bride gift?

Look at it another way. Lev Kookesh hadn't been born to the title of Niniltna's chief. The icon could have been the price his tribe paid to have their son crowned with that laurel.

I wish you people would quit bothering me about the Lady.

Someone else had been asking questions about the Lady of Kodiak only last week.

Which meant someone was a week ahead of her.

She started the car and moved off down the street.

She didn't notice the tail for almost six minutes.

Twenty-four

It was a dark blue SUV with tinted windows and no front plate. "They could get a ticket for that," Kate said to Mutt, watching the rearview in what she hoped was unobtrusive fashion.

The SUV had pulled up behind her at the light at Lake Otis and Twentieth, also turning left. It had dropped back a few cars when she changed lanes after going through the light at Northern Lights, but it had moved up a car after the light at Thirty-sixth, and now, at Tudor, it was right behind her again.

"Not a pro," Kate said.

Mutt's ear twitched.

Kate was in the right-hand lane eight cars back from the light. When the electric pink Cadillac Seville next to her stalled out, she jumped on the opportunity to move into the right-turn-only lane and hit the gas. She made it around the corner just as the light turned red, sped down Tudor to the turnoff to the strip mall on the corner, negotiated the speed bumps in the strip mall's parking lot without sacrificing speed or launching them into orbit, and poked a cautious nose back into the exit onto Lake Otis.

The SUV was the second car back from the corner, behind the same electric pink Cadillac Seville that Kate had slipped in front of when it stalled out. It was driven by a woman with big hair who wore a sparkler on her right hand that gave out a series of blinding flashes as she tapped her hand on the steering wheel to Van Halen. She was still talking on her cell phone. The bass reverberated all the way back to the Subaru. The arrow was red but she was looking left at oncoming traffic, waiting for a gap to pull into.

Kate looked left and willed the driver of the white Bronco next to her to look her way before the light turned green. He, too, was talking on his cell phone. She rolled down her window. "Hey! Hey, mister!"

He looked up and then over at her. She gave him her most dazzling smile and goosed the Subaru ahead a couple of inches, nodding at the lane.

He responded with a scowl and pulled up to within a whisker of the chrome bumper of the ancient Buick Skylark in front of him.

The light turned green. The electric pink Cadillac Seville started to turn, the SUV snarling bad-temperedly right behind it.

She looked back at the man in the Bronco, who was watching her with a smirk on his face. He was still talking on his cell phone. Hell, every second person at this intersection was talking on their cell phone.

Kate grabbed the hem of her T-shirt and yanked it up to her neck and this time didn't bother with the smile.

The smirk vanished. His cell phone dropped from his hand and his foot slipped off the clutch. The Bronco lurched and stalled. An older man in a panel truck in the lane next to him had seen the whole thing and was laughing so hard he had tears streaming down his face. She threw him his very own spine-melter of a smile as she pulled her T-shirt back down and slipped in behind the Skylark, which was already put-putting up to the light. She made it onto Tudor just as the light changed back to red, six cars behind the SUV.

She stayed there, all the way down Tudor to Minnesota, where they turned right. They turned right again on Benson and drove east to a few streets short of C Street, where the SUV turned into the parking lot of a large office building whose sign proclaimed it to be the Last Frontier Bank of Alaska. It took up the whole block between Benson and Northern Lights.

Kate drove around the block and came into the parking lot from Northern Lights. The SUV was parked in front of the main entrance, in a handicapped spot, and so far as she could see through the tinted windows, it was now empty.

She pulled into a space in the row behind it and pulled out her cell phone and dialed. "Hello, Agrifina, it's Kate Shugak. Is Kurt in?"

"One moment please, Ms. Shugak."

Click, another click, and Kurt's voice came on. "Kate! You're back in town already?"

"Yeah. Kurt, can you have a vehicle towed for me? As in right now?"

A startled silence. "Uh—"

"I'll explain it all later, but it has to do with Old Sam." Translated: family.

"Let me make a call."

"I don't want this to look like enemy action," she said, "so I'm going to call the parking authority and tell them it's parked in a handicapped space so when the owner checks there will be an official complaint. They'll think the city towed it and it's lost in the system when the city can't find it for them."

"*Is* it parked in a handicapped space?"

"Two of them," Kate said, "and no sticker."

"I hate it when people do that."

"Have you got a place you can squirrel it away? I want to search it."

"Sure," Kurt said. "Give me fifteen minutes and then make your call."

"I just love having my own personal private dick," Kate told Mutt. She waited fifteen minutes. The SUV stayed where it was. She consulted the Anchorage phone book in the door pocket and dialed another number. "Hello, my name is Rita," she said, infusing her voice with just the right mixture of righteous indignation and citizen activism. "I'm at the bank and there is an SUV without a disability plate parked in the handicapped zone. It's taking up two spaces. Two spaces! Ordinarily I wouldn't waste your time, I know this happens too often, people are so inconsiderate"—her voice actually trembled— "but an elderly gentleman just dropped off his wife, who is making her way up the stairs with a walker because the SUV has blocked the ramp. I mean really. If ever anyone deserved to be towed, they are it."

She gave the address and the make, model, and tag number, avoided giving the rest of her name (Lovely Meter Maid), and hung up.

Five minutes after that, a tow truck showed up. It was driven by a couple of grizzled old farts in plaid shirts out at the elbows and bibbed Carharrts with serious miles on them. They hitched up the tow and were gone in five minutes. The cops never did show.

Kate had to wait another half an hour before the owner of the SUV came out.

He had a distinct limp.

He was three steps from the parking space before he realized his car was gone. He did what everyone does when they find their car gone. He looked around to see if he'd forgotten where he actually parked it. No. It was really gone. He swore, if the outraged expressions on the faces of the two older women who had followed him out were any indication, and got out his cell phone.

"Does he look like he might taste familiar?" Kate said to Mutt.

Mutt licked her chops.

It was the man in the balaclava, she was sure of it, not only because of the limp but because there was something instantly familiar about the way he moved. Hand-to-hand combat is an introduction that stays with you.

But there was something else familiar about him. Obligingly, he stood on the top step long enough for her to remember why.

"Holy shit," she said. "It's Bruce Abbott."

Bruce Abbott, generally up for sale to orchestrate political wet works for whoever could afford him. Last job known to her, gofer for the then governor. Abbott had offered her a bribe two years before to walk away from a case.

And now he was following her, first on a snow machine in the Park, and now in an SUV in Anchorage. But not for himself, because not for one moment did she believe he was acting on his own. Oily little weasels like Bruce Abbott were only rent boys for the rich and powerful.

And that would be why she'd gotten the drop on him in the cabin. Oily little weasels like Bruce Abbott always made sure they were one step removed from the dirty jobs. That way lay federal subpoenas, federal prosecutors, and time served in Club Fed.

Not to mention serious loss of income. Which begged the question. Why was Bruce Abbott, the original backdoor bag man slash rat fucker slash hatchet man being so hands-on this time?

He went back inside the bank, still talking on his phone.

Her phone rang. It was Kurt. "They got it."

"Yeah, I know, I watched them. Artists at work. Kurt, what do you hear about Bruce Abbott?"

"Abbott? The ex-governor's gofer?"

"Yeah."

He was silent for a moment, thinking. "Not much lately," he said at last. "Shall I inquire?"

"Please, but not so's anyone would notice."

He was hurt. "Does anyone ever?"

She hung up and started the Subaru. As she pulled out on Benson, a second tow truck pulled in.

She drove to an auto shop on the Old Seward Highway, a single cavernous building on a fenced lot barely big enough to hold it and a cramped eight-space parking lot. Alders sprung up wherever there was a grain of soil and dripped browning leaves over hoods, windshields, and pavement.

She squeezed the Subaru into the narrow lane between shop and fence and emerged into the backyard feeling like a cork being pulled from a bottle. The SUV had been unhitched and pushed to one side, and the two seedy-looking characters with the tow truck were standing around looking shifty, which was their second best thing. She parked next to it and got out. "Tom, Ray, how you doing."

"Hey, Kate," Tom said, and Ray mumbled something inarticulate.

"Any problems?"

"Nah," Tom said, and Ray looked like he didn't know what the words meant. Without further politesse they ambled into the shop, followed by Mutt. She'd been here before and she was well-acquainted with the assortment of snacks next to the coffeepot in the office.

Mutt was a world-class forager in town or Park.

What you couldn't learn about someone from their personal automobile wasn't worth knowing. Kate went to work.

Half an hour later she stood back and dusted her hands.

The SUV was three years old, with seventy thousand miles on it. Abbott had bought it from the dealer in Anchorage, according to the handbook in the glove compartment, and the registration form tucked into the back of the sun visor indicated no liens, which could mean he'd either paid it off early or bought it for cash.

However, it was fifty-two hundred miles past its next scheduled service per the sticker in the upper left hand corner of the windshield, and all four tires were bald. There was a crack on the windshield that started right in front of the steering wheel—windshield cracks invariably start right at driver's eye level—and crept all the way across the glass to dead-end in the molding on the passenger side.

The interior hadn't been detailed lately, either. A layer of dust covered the dash, there were coffee stains on the seats, and the floor was littered with wrappers from McDonald's and Taco Bell.

Abbott had been flush when he'd bought the car. He hadn't replaced it, and a new car every year was de rigueur for someone who wanted to be taken seriously by movers and shakers.

Resolved: he wasn't flush now.

Equally interesting was the file folder in the passenger seat marked "Shugak, Ekaterina Ivana" on the tab.

Most interesting of all was the scribbled note found in the driver's-side door pocket.

Kate skimmed her file. They'd misspelled her grandmother's name, they'd shortened her sojourn in Anchorage by a year, they didn't have Johnny listed as a dependent, and they'd missed half of the cases she'd worked after she went into private practice. The one case they knew chapter and verse was the Muravieff case two years back.

Kurt Pletnikoff would have sneered at this background check. She closed the file and replaced it on the front seat. The note she stuffed into a pocket.

She went to the shop and stuck her head in the door. Ray was under a venerable dark green International pickup, only his feet showing. Tom was under the hood of a silver Mercedes-Benz 450 SL, only his butt showing, a little too much of it. "Guys?"

Ray slid out from beneath the truck, Tom popped up from beneath the Mercedes' hood, and Mutt appeared in the doorway of the office.

Kate jerked her head back at the SUV. "Can you get that into the city's impound lot without anyone knowing? So it'll look like the municipality had it towed and they just lost the paperwork?"

Tom and Ray communed in silence for a moment or two. Ray nodded. Tom nodded back. "I reckon we could," Tom said.

"Excellent," Kate said. Money changed hands and adieus were said with good feeling all around.

Back on the road, Mutt smelling strongly of beef jerky in the passenger seat, Kate wondered when Abbott would find his missing vehicle, and what he'd think when he did. He had been illegally parked, after all, taking up not just one but two handicapped parking spots, a guaranteed producer of angry phone calls to the parking authorities. There was no reason for him to think she was onto him. It helped that he was white, male, and a boomer from Outside who would never make it past cheechako status no matter how long he stayed in Alaska, and that she was only five feet tall, a woman, and a Native to boot. Not to mention which, she'd turned down a state job that came with benefits a U.S. Senator would envy. There was no way Abbott would take Kate Shugak seriously as a threat.

He'd gone from gubernatorial gofer, yes-man, lobbyist, and flack to getting his hands dirty. It would explain why he wasn't very good at it. Shiners aside, the coldcock with the firewood hadn't been productive of anything more than common theft, and if the continued pursuit was any indication, the journal he'd stolen hadn't helped him. She wondered where he'd scored his gear, which had looked like the real deal. Borrowed, had to be, because it couldn't possibly be his. Perhaps from the second shooter?

Jane's death at his hands rang more true. He'd

broken into her house, she had come home and interrupted him, and he had shoved her aside in a panicked flight. His bad luck Jane had hit her head and died.

And Jane's.

He must have gone to Jane's house alone. A confederate would have kept watch and they would have been out the back door when Jane pulled into the driveway.

He'd known the exact place to wait to run Kate off the road, though. She tried to remember if she'd ever seen Abbott in the Park. With Pete Heiman, maybe, on a campaign swing? Had he been one of Anne Gordaoff's hangers on?

He had never convinced her he was going to actually shoot her in the cabin, and he'd been all too easy to take down. But by then he'd picked up a partner, someone with enough backwoods smarts, enough gear, and enough familiarity with the Park to be able to pick up Kate's trail and follow it. Or to know where she was going in the first place. Maybe he'd had the partner with him when he'd run her off the road, too.

"You know what?" she said to Mutt. "There is too damn much going on here."

Mutt cocked a sympathetic ear.

"Somebody got spooked when Old Sam died. Spooked and/or greedy. I've been attacked three times. Jane Silver is dead. What do we have in common? Old Sam."

The Subaru's tires squealed when she slammed on the brakes before she ran the red light at International and C. "Shit," she said, fear knifing through her. "Shit, shit, shit!"

She waited in a fever of impatience for the light to change, and when it did she stamped on the gas and crossed two lanes of traffic to get to the shoulder, where the Subaru squealed to a halt. There was honking, accompanied by digital commentary. She ignored it all, fumbling out her cell phone. She had to call the operator to figure out how to call the satellite phone at the Niniltna trooper post, and was warned that it was an international call that would be very expensive. She was not polite to the operator, who became very formal and much less helpful.

She waited, hand sweaty on her cell. Finally, Maggie answered. "Maggie, thank god, this is Kate Shugak."

"Kate? Where are you? What are you doing calling on the sat phone?"

"I'm in Anchorage. Listen to me, this is important, urgent. I need you to go down to Auntie Joy's and make sure she's all right. Tell her it's not safe for her to stay alone in her house. She needs to go stay with Auntie Vi or Auntie Edna for a while, and to take the story with her."

"What?" Maggie sounded mystified, as well she might.

Kate repeated her instructions. "If you've got

time, please wait and make sure she does it. Tell her it's very important."

"Is she in danger?" Maggie's voice was incredulous.

"She could be and I don't want to take any chances. It has to do with Old Sam."

"Okay." Maggie sounded bewildered but acquiescent. "I'll go right down to her house."

"Thank you," Kate said, making it heartfelt. "And could you do one other thing for me? Could you tell Johnny not to go out to our house alone? To stay at Annie Mike's until I get back?"

"What the hell is going on here, Kate?"

"I'm in Anchorage trying to figure that out. Will you tell Johnny?"

"I'll tell him. What was it Auntie Joy supposed to take with her?"

"The story. She'll know what I mean."

Kate hung up and sat there, the Subaru shuddering whenever a vehicle hurtled past, trying not to shake, cursing herself for not making sure Auntie Joy was safe before Kate left the Park.

If Old Sam was the contributory factor to all these assaults, then it followed that an ex-fiancée, were she known to exist, would be highly at risk. Wheeler, Gunn, and Abbott might all be amateurs, but as Bobby had rightly said, *Even Dortmunder gets lucky once in a while.*

When she stopped trembling, she started to get mad. She looked at Mutt. "If anyone lays a hand, if anyone lays so much as a finger, if they so much as look cross-eyed at my auntie, I will feed them to you. One. Piece. At. A. Time."

Kate pulled into the Last Frontier Bank parking lot and this time there was nothing surreptitious about her actions. She left Mutt in the Subaru with the windows rolled down and went inside.

The Last Frontier Bank had been founded back in the days of the gold rush by a missionary stampeder who had come north to do good and had stayed to do right well indeed. With Hermann Pilz and Isaiah Bannister, Lucius Bell had formed part of a commercial triumvirate that had been either primarily or peripherally involved in the construction of the state of Alaska from the Klondike on. Banking, transportation, consumer goods (a roaring business), natural resource extraction (gold, copper, coal, oil)—there was no Alaskan pie in which they didn't have a finger, if not their whole hand up to the wrist.

Bell had founded the first Alaskan bank in Circle, and when the gold played out moved operations to Fairbanks. In the 1950s his son, Marcellus, had upon the insistence of his wife moved the head office to Anchorage, where it was warmer and there was more light for longer and where there were more people and more things to do. It was also that much closer to a trip Outside, of which she took a great many.

Last Frontier Bank had built their new headquarters in downtown Anchorage, only to see the building destroyed during the 1964 earthquake. Marcellus and his son, Vitus, had been among the first to rebuild, making manifest their belief in the future of Alaska.

It was a handsome building, the first floor two stories high with pillars and marble flooring and original wood counters. Plush runners kept the noise from footsteps to a minimum. There were Art Deco wall sconces that gave the large room a retro feel. No Muzak profaned the air, and the security guard maintained an unobtrusive scrutiny from an alcove to one side of the door. Gray-haired, with a face that showed its age, he still looked more fit and much more alert than most bank security guards. Kate approached him. "Hi," she said. "Where's the museum?"

He showed her to the descending staircase and returned to his post.

Downstairs the ceiling was lower and the lights were fluorescent, but the shelving was solid and the display cases were made of plate glass. A receptionist sat at a desk that formed part of a railing. One did not just barge inside. All the better, Kate thought. "Hi," she said.

The receptionist, on the evidence about the same age as the security guard, was also conspicuous by her alert eyes and vigilant attitude. She gave Kate a quick once-over, was either smart enough or had enough time served in Alaska to discount the jacket, jeans, and tennis shoes as an indication of true worth, and said, "May I help you?" Her manner gave one to understand that only serious researchers were welcomed into the inner sanctum, and anyone on a mission to waste her time would not be tolerated.

Kate's instincts about people were generally good, and she decided to go with the truth, or at least some of it. "My name is Kate Shugak," she said. She pulled the crumpled piece of paper from the SUV and handed it over. "I lost my uncle recently, and I'm the executor of his estate. He left me a small mystery, and I'm hoping you can help me solve it."

The woman, whose name tag read Ms. S. Sherwood, smoothed out the piece of paper, which proved to be a call slip, with Bell's Legacy of Alaska Museum imprinted at the top. "That's my handwriting," Ms. Sherwood said.

"I thought it might be," Kate said. "Do you remember who asked for those materials, and when?"

Ms. Sherwood frowned. "A gentleman, I believe, on the Monday before last." She consulted her desk calendar. "The fourteenth."

The Monday after Old Sam died. "Might I look at those same materials?"

Ms. Sherwood considered. "Lucius Bell

collected many things of great value during his life in Alaska," she said. "Generally, we require references before we admit scholars to the collection. Are you a scholar?"

"No," Kate said.

"I see. Have you a reference?"

"No."

Ms. Sherwood nodded as if these brief and unequivocal answers had meant something more, and rose to her feet. She was a slim and elegant woman dressed in a slim and elegant gray knit dress with a white collar and cuffs, a thin white belt, and a hemline that hit her at mid-calf, over sheer stockings and elegant black pumps. She looked like Coco Chanel.

She walked through the swinging door in the railing and held it open. "Please come in."

Twenty-five

THE LEGACY OF ALASKA MUSEUM WAS the largest privately owned collection of Alaskana in the state. Lucius Bell had started collecting Native art and artifacts the moment he set foot in the territory. He had also been a pack rat of the first order, from the looks of it never having thrown away so much as a used-up book of matches.

The exhibit space took up almost the entire basement of the building, or a square block's worth of space. Every square foot of it was utilized to the maximum to present the entirety of Alaska history from the pre-Russian to the post-statehood days. There was an Alutiiq kayak suspended from the ceiling, and a P and H Lines stagecoach in one corner. A framed photograph was fastened to the door of the stagecoach. It recorded the ceremony at which Hermann Pilz, Peter Heiman Sr., and P and H's executive director donated the coach to the museum, presided over by a suitably grateful Marcellus Bell. The names listed on the caption at the bottom were interesting.

There was a copy of the state constitution signed by all fifty-five delegates to the constitutional convention. There were bears carved from ivory and soapstone; storyknives carved from ivory, wood, bone, and baleen; rye grass baskets from the size of an eggcup to a five-gallon bucket. The walls above the shelves were hung with paintings by Laurence and Ziegler, Anuktuvuk face masks, harpoons with enormous, elaborately carved ivory hooks. There was a case holding all the Fur Rendezvous buttons ever produced, right next to another filled with wooden drink tokens from every bar that had opened its doors north of the fifty-three. There was a metal cabinet with a dozen wide, shallow drawers that proved to hold maps of Alaska from the days of Captain Cook, when most of the coastline was only guessed at, to USGS maps that were still inaccurate today.

There was a display devoted to the oil industry from Katalla to Kenai to Prudhoe Bay, including a section of drill pipe attached to the tricone bit invented by Howard Hughes's dad. There was a display of artifacts from the salmon industry, including caviar jars nestled in their original wooden box with the bright blue-and-red Japanese lettering on the side, an egg basket stained from use, half-pound flats, and one-pound talls.

"I know someone who has a working salmon canning line set up in a shed in back of his house," Kate said.

"Really," Ms. Sherwood said. "Would he be interested in selling it?"

Kate looked around the room. "He might be interested in selling, but where would you put it?"

"We have off-site storage facilities."

A corner shelf played host to a miscellanea of gold mining relics, gold pans, gold leaf suspended in vials of water, what looked like the entire ton of supplies, including stove and fuel, required to get someone across the border into Canada during the Gold Rush. There were framed front pages from the *Dawson City Nugget*, the *Fairbanks Nugget*, and the *Nome Nugget*, all of which featured at least one murder resulting over a claim jumping. A dogsled held all the required gear of an Iditarod musher, parka, sleeping bag, ax, snowshoes, dog booties, food for musher and dog, plus mail and even a box marked "Serum" to commemorate the original 1925 run to a diphtheria-stricken Nome. It looked familiar. She paused for a closer look, and said, "Is this—"

Ms. Sherwood smiled. "Yes. It is the sled Ms. Baker was on when she won her first Iditarod. Along with all of the required items she carried during that race. The food is a representation, of course."

Mandy didn't give up on gear that worked for her. "When did she donate it?"

"In January," Ms. Swanson said. "It's one of our most recent acquisitions."

Just after she'd taken the job with Global Harvest, Kate thought. Mandy really had retired.

One wall was covered floor to ceiling with bookshelves, the books sorted by year, beginning on the left with Alaska Native studies, followed shelf by shelf in order by Russian America, the Alaska Purchase, the Gold Rush, World War II, the oil discoveries, and the Alaska Native Land Claims, much of it original documentation, some of it handwritten journals. She saw a lot of names she recognized—Wickersham, Mitchell, Gruening, Peratovich, Hensley.

Kate was enthralled, and she could have spent the rest of the day if not the rest of the year in this one room, but she was recalled to duty by a discreet cough. She looked up to see Ms. Sherwood standing nearby with her hands clasped lightly in front of her, head tilted to one side, the ghost of a smile on her lips.

"Sorry," Kate said, her voice hushed. "It's just—"

"I know," Ms. Sherwood said without being at all condescending. "It is a little overwhelming. Especially when you realize the bulk of it comes from the work of one man, during one lifetime."

Kate indicated a label on the shelf in front of a tin gold pan that had seen hard use, labeled "Gift of Mr. and Mrs. Hermann Pilz." There were other labels on other exhibits, all of them bearing names right out of the Alaskan history books. "He had help."

Ms. Sherwood's shoulders raised in a slight shrug. "Everyone wanted to be a part of Mr. Bell's museum."

Kate looked at the four wooden tables lined up behind Ms. Sherwood's desk. Three were occupied by two men and one woman consulting various tomes and scribbling notes. "You get a lot of people in here?"

Ms. Sherwood nodded. "Students from the university, scholars, writers doing research. There is nothing more valuable to a scholar than original source material." She smoothed an errant mote of dust from a shelf with a forefinger.

"It's impressive as hell," Kate said. "You've

packed an awful lot into a relatively small space."

Ms. Sherwood inclined her head, accepting her due. "Thank you."

"Well." With an effort, Kate pulled her head out of their collective past and back into the present. "What particular item does the slip refer to?"

And then it hit her.

Handwritten journals.

She rotated where she stood, running her eyes over the spines of the books.

She must have had a very peculiar expression on her face because Ms. Sherwood sounded worried. "Ms. Shugak? Are you all right?"

Kate turned to her. "Ms. Sherwood, have you ever heard of Judge Albert Arthur Anglebrandt?"

Ms. Sherwood looked surprised. "Why of course," she said. "We have the journals he kept while he presided over the court in Ahtna."

"Not all of them," Kate said.

"I beg your pardon?"

Kate held up the call slip. "Does this refer to one of them?"

"It refers to all of the Anglebrandt journals. The gentleman did not ask for a particular volume."

"Could you show me? Please?"

Ms. Sherwood navigated between various shoals of this historical and cultural sea to a bookcase halfway around the room and pointed at a shelf that was a good four feet over Kate's head. "One moment." She was back in short order with a wheeled ladder attached to a track that ran above all the bookcases. Very Henry Higgins. "Were you interested in a particular volume?"

"Nineteen thirty-seven and 1939," Kate said.

Ms. Sherwood climbed the ladder and sorted through a line of journals once, and then again. "How very odd," she said, and Kate could hear the steel threading through her voice.

"They aren't there," Kate said.

Ms. Sherwood descended the ladder. She looked angry, albeit in a repressed, upper-class Anglo-Saxon way. "No, they are not," she said. "Would you mind telling me how you knew that, Ms. Shugak?"

"When was the last time they were inventoried?" Kate said.

For the first time the curator looked nonplussed. She paused to collect herself, and then said, her voice returned to its muted lower register librarian tone, "During my tenure? Never."

She offered no apologies or explanations and Kate respected her for it. "Would there be a record?"

Ms. Sherwood led the way to a door hitherto partially concealed by a magnificent Tlingit button blanket, which led into a room with a bank of file cabinets behind a desk with a computer on it. Ms. Sherwood sat down at the computer and indicated a chair. "Please have a seat."

Kate did so and watched Ms. Sherwood start the

computer with a perfect composure that nonetheless gave the distinct impression that someone was for the high jump in the not too distant future. It took her only a few moments to access the needed data, whereupon Ms. Sherwood's spine if anything grew even more straight. "The judge left his journals behind for the judge who succeeded him when he left the state in 1945," she said.

The year Old Sam came home from the Aleutians, Kate thought. The year he proved up on his homestead. The year Auntie Joy turned him down for the second time. "How did they come here?" she said.

"They had been stored in the basement of the old courthouse in Ahtna," Ms. Sherwood said. "When they built the new courthouse five years ago, Judge Singh asked us if we would like to have them."

Five years ago, Kate thought. Old Sam had done some work for the new courthouse, hauling Kanuyaq River rocks to Ahtna for the façade. "Do your records show 1937 and 1939 as missing?"

Ms. Swanson shook her head. "I'm afraid they were not properly inventoried when they were accepted into the collection."

"So they could have been part of the collection," Kate said. "Which means they could have walked out of the building at any time."

Ms. Sherwood's nostrils flared slightly. "Not since I have been curator here, no."

"Why not?"

"Are you familiar with RFID technology?" She saw her answer on Kate's face. "Radio frequency identification. It was the second mission I undertook after I was appointed."

"What was the first?"

Ms. Sherwood nodded at the computer. "The digitization of all of our records."

"What does this RFID do?"

"A small electronic tag is placed on each item in the collection. It does two things. One, it trips an alarm if it is moved from its display. Two, it tracks the item."

A chill ran up Kate's spine. "How far?"

"Up to forty feet. It will be more eventually, as the technology advances, but at present, so long as staff is vigilant, it is enough to intercept the item before it gets to the parking lot outside. And presumably a getaway vehicle."

Kate breathed again. The 1939 journal was tucked safely away at the Westchester Lagoon town house a mile away. "Sounds expensive," she said.

"Not very, when you consider that the combined value of the collection is in the millions of dollars. Many of the items are priceless simply because they are irreplaceable." Ms. Sherwood hesitated. "Ms. Shugak. Am I correct in thinking you are related to Ekaterina Shugak?"

"She was my grandmother."

"I see." Ms. Sherwood rose to her feet. "There is something you might like to see."

She led the way back into the main room and to a glass-topped table planted directly in front of the Native studies bookcase. Inside was a Raven feast bowl, made of solid copper, eight inches wide, twelve inches long, and thirteen inches deep. The label read, "The gift of Ekaterina Shugak, 1972."

"Holy crap," Kate said. They had been speaking in hushed voices, but at this the three people seated at the tables raised their heads.

"Sorry," Kate said to them. "Sorry," she said to Ms. Sherwood. She looked back down at the bowl.

"Do you know anything about its history?" Ms. Sherwood said.

Kate shook her head. "It's the first time I've ever seen it," she said.

"Is there someone older you could ask? The story behind the artifact is as valuable, if not more so, than is the artifact itself."

Kate thought of the aunties, and looked back at the bowl. The original carving was blunted by long use, and there were dents on the interior and exterior surfaces and scratches in the patina. It looked Tlingit.

It looked, in fact, like something a Tlingit chief might bring as part of a bride price when he married into an Interior tribe. "I can ask," she said. "I can't promise you any answers. Is there a photograph?"

There was, and Kate tucked it carefully away.

Ms. Sherwood escorted her through the gate. Kate lingered while she reseated herself. "Ms. Sherwood?"

"Yes?"

"Would you mind very much telling me the name of the person who first came to look at the judge's journals?"

"He did not give me his name," Ms. Swanson said.

"But you let him in anyway," Kate said.

Ms. Sherwood forbore to point out that she had let Kate in, too. "He had a quite impeccable reference."

"Did he," Kate said. "Would you mind telling me who it was? And if he was in here again today?"

Ms. Sherwood had an uncharacteristic moment of hesitation.

"I wouldn't ask if it weren't important," Kate said. "I'm trying to track down another family artifact." She looked over her shoulder at the display case holding the feast bowl, and from the corner of her eye saw Ms. Sherwood follow her gaze.

She looked back to meet Ms. Sherwood's direct gaze. There were no flies on Coco Chanel. "And if I tell you, you'll try to find out about the history of the feast bowl?"

Kate didn't flinch. "Of course."

"Erland Bannister," Ms. Sherwood said.

Kate arrived back at the Subaru without any notion of how she'd gotten there. Mutt, snoozing in the sun with her chin on the passenger-side windowsill, woke up with a snort. "Tell me," Kate said to her, "explain to me how a guy I helped put away two years ago can be mixed up in this fucking scavenger hunt of Old Sam's?"

Mutt shook herself vigorously and let out with a large "Woof!" which startled a shriek out of a woman on the other side of the open window who was on her way into the bank to clean out the joint account she held with her husband, in preparation for filing for divorce that afternoon.

Kate fished out her cell phone and called Brendan. The deep rich tones rolled over her like a warm bath of caramel. "Babe! You're still in town! Dinner again tonight? I'm thinking sushi at Yamato Ya this time, and—"

"Brendan, where is Erland Bannister?"

A startled silence, then, "Right where we put him, last time I looked."

"You're sure?" Something in the quality of the silence that followed put her on alert. "Brendan? Is he getting out?"

"I'll call you back in ten minutes," he said.

She hung up and stared, unseeing, through the windshield.

Erland Bannister was an éminence grise of the Alaskan robber barons, every bit as eminent and successful as Lucius Bell and Peter Heiman the elder, and Hermann Pilz, his grandfather, and Isaiah Bannister, his other grandfather.

Erland Bannister had kidnapped Kate two years before because she had discovered a little too much about his family history. He'd had every intention of killing her shortly thereafter. She'd had other ideas.

Upon her escape he had been arrested, tried, convicted, and incarcerated for what almost everyone involved hoped would be the rest of his natural life.

She waited. The woman who had shrieked exited the bank and made a wide detour around the Subaru to get back to her own car. Seven minutes later Kate's phone rang and she snatched at it. "Brendan?"

"He's right where we left him, Kate. In Spring Creek." But she could hear the relief in his voice.

Spring Creek Correctional Center in Seward was the state's only maximum security prison, built for felony offenders. Seward was a hundred miles down the only road south from Anchorage, on a narrow fjord called Resurrection Bay. "For how much longer?" she said.

Again, he let the silence speak for him.

She swore, imaginatively and at length. "Can you get me in to see him?"

She could hear the surprise in Brendan's voice. "You want to see Erland Bannister?"

"Yes."

A short silence. "When?"

"As soon as I can get down there."

"Wait a minute." She heard the keys click on his keyboard. "He's in the general population. Tomorrow's Sunday, so either one P.M. to four P.M., or six thirty to nine."

"I can be there by one."

"I'll clear it with the superintendent." A pause. "He doesn't have to see you if he doesn't want to, Kate."

"He'll want to," she said.

Twenty-six

SHE PICKED UP A SLICED SMOKED HAM hock and a small cabbage on the way back to the town house. She put the ham hock into a pot of water with a bay leaf and a couple of cloves of peeled, smashed garlic, brought it to a boil, and reduced it to a simmer. "Come on," she said to Mutt, and they went out to join the throng of walkers, bikers, rollerbladers, and skateboarders on the Coastal Trail.

It was a clear, cool autumn afternoon during one of Alaska's rare Indian summers. The sky was pale blue, Knik Arm a pale gray, and the leaves of the deciduous trees every shade from pale yellow to golden brown, drifting delicately down to the ground one at a time to form crisp, colorful piles that begged to be scuffed into a cloud. Mutt romped through every one she came to, delighting a few commuters, alarming more. "You should keep your dog under control," one said.

"She is under control," Kate said.

"She should be on a leash."

Kate didn't raise her voice. "Mutt. Heel."

Mutt, sniffing at a promising hole in a way guaranteed to strike terror into the hearts of its inhabitants, streaked to Kate's side and took up station to starboard, her shoulder precisely even with Kate's hip, and cast a quizzical eye upon the volunteer trail warden.

They were allowed to continue on their way in peace. After Lyn Ary Park the traffic abated and Kate picked up the pace. It felt good to stretch her legs, and unless she went for a hike on one of the trails into the Chugachs, this was as close to a wilderness experience as she was going to get in Anchorage.

She had hiked those trails regularly when she lived in Anchorage, working for the DA. Flattop was too crowded for her taste, but the less-well-known Near Point was only three and a half hours trailhead to summit to trailhead, and in late June was awash in a sea of wildflowers, everything from chocolate lilies to western columbine. She'd climbed it two or three times a week in season, back in the day, and on visits to Anchorage after she'd moved back to the Park.

She hadn't hiked it since she had been kidnapped and brought unconscious to a cabin in the back range of those same Chugach Mountains.

Coincidence? Survey says not.

"Erland Bannister is in prison for murder and kidnapping," she had said to Ms. Sherwood after a moment of stunned silence.

Ms. Sherwood had waited a moment to reply. "That may be so, Ms. Shugak, but he is not forgotten by his friends."

Sherwood took her orders from the Bells, owners of the Last Frontier Bank. Which meant Bannister had asked for a favor, and one of Lucius Bell's descendants had granted it.

If Abbott was working for Bannister, then Bannister had ordered him after Kate. If it were simple revenge for locking him up for life, why would he have waited two years?

No, she'd been right the first time. Whatever was going on, it began with Old Sam.

So how did Old Sam know Erland? They weren't contemporaries, Old Sam must have had at least twenty years on the other man.

But the Bannisters had come north in the Gold Rush, if Kate remembered her Alaska history correctly. So Erland's father might have known Old Sam.

Mutt gave her an affectionate shoulder bump

that nearly knocked her off her feet. They had reached the bench below Earthquake Park. The light was fading and she wondered how long she had been standing there lost in thought.

She turned and headed for home. When she let them in the door, the aroma of dinner had flooded the entire house. Drool pooled in her mouth. She hadn't eaten since breakfast. Shoes kicked off, jacket tossed on a chair, she tuned in the radio to *All Things Considered* and cut half of the cabbage into one-inch squares. She removed the ham hock from the broth, cut up a potato, and added the cabbage and potato to the broth. She brought it back to a boil, reduced it to a simmer, and set the timer for twenty minutes. In the meantime she separated the meat from the bone and the fat. The meat went on a plate in a warm oven and the bone and the fat went into a bowl for Mutt, who settled down with it in the postage-stamp-sized backyard with an air of deep content.

The dinger went. She removed the plate of meat from the oven, ladled out potato and cabbage, buttered a slice of whole wheat bread from Europa Bakery, sat down, and tucked in. She didn't think about Old Sam or Bruce Abbott or Erland Bannister. Nothing ever came between Kate and food.

After cleaning up she let Mutt back in and moved operations to the living room, where she built a fire in the fireplace and put her feet up, watching the flames flicker over Mutt's prone form and sipping from a mug of steaming hot cocoa. Then and only then did she allow the case, for lack of a better word, to reinvade her consciousness.

Something had been tickling at the back of her mind since she'd found the second journal in the cabin.

Was Old Sam really leaving breadcrumbs for her? Had he known someone would come looking for something he had? Why would they wait until he died? She'd been attacked three times and Jane Silver once. The number argued in favor of someone looking for something valuable, and looking with considerable urgency, too. If they wanted it that badly, why not go after it when Old Sam was still living? He'd been a tough old bird, true, but no one was invulnerable. She thought about her pickup going ass over teakettle off the road.

But that was odd, too. The attacks in Old Sam's two cabins had robbery as a motive. The attack on the road, on the face of it, had only assault with intent as a motive. No one had come stumbling out into the snow after her to search her or her truck for the icon or a clue as to its whereabouts. Or to dispose of competition.

The person who had attacked her at the cabin in Niniltna didn't have to be the same person who had killed Jane Silver, and the person who had killed Jane Silver didn't have to be the same person who had run her off the road on the way home. And the two people at Canyon Hot Springs didn't have to be either of them. So it could be Wheeler and Gunn and Abbott all three, severally or together. And/or anyone within earshot of Virginia Anahonak.

She shook her head, frustrated. It was like playing Whack-A-Perp. It might be better to look at it from a different perspective. How many people could have known about the existence of the icon?

Other than what appeared to be an entire generation of Park rat elders, many of whom were still living.

Grandma used to say he shouldn't have been a shareholder at all.

And even if it had never percolated as far as Kate, at least one of those elders had told their children's children. Which widened the pool of suspects considerably.

Not a significantly better perspective, then. Her heart sank, but only for a moment. "Occam's razor, Kate," she said out loud.

Mutt cocked a warning ear without opening her eyes.

The simplest answer was the one most likely to be true. She wasn't going to complicate things until she had to. One set of antagonists with the one goal would do her just fine until she had hard evidence that there was more than one.

One thing was very clear. Old Sam was at the center of this, whatever it was.

What would Old Sam have done, confronted first with the knowledge of his true parentage, and then with the knowledge that that father had stolen a revered tribal artifact?

Well, he was young, and he was in love, and he was a guy. Maybe he thought given enough time Auntie Joy would change her mind. In the meantime he would go looking for the icon, because how could Auntie Joy possibly turn down the man who returned something that valuable to their common heritage?

On the face of it, in those pre-Google years, the task would have seemed almost impossible. According to Mac's story, the icon had been sold along with the contents of the rest of his pack on the docks of Seattle to the first person he'd met with cash in hand, whose name he said he couldn't remember.

One step ahead of the clap on his shoulder.

Old Sam had had two of the judge's journals, which he had probably acquired during the teardown of the old courthouse, very probably by means that would not bear close examination. One he had left in plain sight on the shelf in his cabin in Niniltna. The other he had secreted in a hiding place made specifically for that purpose in the old cabin at Canyon Hot Springs.

She got up and checked to see that the drapes were securely drawn, that no one standing in what was now the dark could see inside. From there she went to the book shelf that stood against one wall and pulled down a book whose bright jacket announced it to be an omnibus volume of *The Lord of the Rings*. Inside the jacket was the journal.

She took it back to the couch and spent the next hour paging through it, one part of her enjoying the judge's observations on his fellow man, the other impatient to discover why Old Sam had hidden it. She came to the last page with no further clue, and closed the book with more force that was owed a tome of its age and venerability.

Kate replaced the *Lord of the Rings* jacket, and noticed for the first time that the back cover of the journal was slightly thicker than the front cover.

Her heart skipped a beat. She pulled the lamp closer, so that it would shine directly on her lap, and opened the journal from the back. Substantial leather, marked with use and faded from age. The lining was of some paper so heavy it was almost fabric, trimmed to a finished edge and glued over the edges of the leather used to cover the book boards.

She compared the inside of the back of the book with the inside of the front of the book, and her excitement grew. The paper covering the inside of the back of the book was a different kind than had been used to cover the inside of the front of the book. And it was obviously newer.

She ran her fingers over it once, and again. Was there something hidden beneath it?

Still, she hesitated. Desecrating a book went against the Shugak grain. Maybe she could steam it open. But the steam might ruin whatever was beneath. She picked at an edge with a fingernail, and was rewarded when a tiny section of it separated from the leather.

Working steadily, so intent on what she was doing that she didn't notice the ache in her shoulders as she sat hunched over the task, she picked patiently at the paper lining the inside back cover of the journal of Judge Albert Arthur Anglebrandt, Ahtna Judicial District, Territory of Alaska, 1939. It was midnight before she had enough peeled away so she could see what lay beneath.

The board beneath the paper and the leather had been hollowed out, not much and very deliberately and carefully, so that what it contained fit into it so well one of Kate's fingernails could barely fit between it and the board. The small blade on her Leatherman did the job, though.

The piece of paper, folded twice, fell into her hand.

She unfolded it. It was a map.

She let out a breath she hadn't known she'd been holding, and took the map into the kitchen. She turned on the overhead light, which was of a wattage sufficient to illuminate Carnegie Hall, and spread the map on the kitchen table, smoothing out the creases and weighting down the corners with salt and pepper shakers, a bottle of malt vinegar, and an apple out of the refrigerator.

Unfolded, it was eighteen inches square, and it seemed to have been done by a professional cartographer, although it was hand drawn, not printed out of a computer program, and she was pretty sure it was the original, not a copy, but it was deteriorating. The folds and corners were frayed, the paper dry and brittle. Maybe this was what an as-built survey looked like circa 1920.

It was a faithful rendering of the Canyon Hot Springs homestead, all one hundred and sixty acres represented, contours drawn in. The cabin and the outhouse were there, along with a well, which Kate had never seen. Probably collapsed by now anyway. She couldn't conceive of the sweat equity that would go into drilling a well back then, or the backbreaking necessity of hauling the drilling equipment that far in country in the first place.

The homestead property included all of the little canyon from the switchback around the saddle to well above the switchback behind the springs. Kate's brow furrowed. She'd never thought to go back there. There there be glaciers, and what was the point, other than having a piece fall on you? She wasn't the suicidal type.

She looked more closely. The buildings of the homestead appeared to have been added to the topographical map much later. The ink of the topography was faded by comparison to the ink of the buildings.

She noticed something else, something she had thought at first were specks of ink or dirt or mildew, but no. They were small black dots—six, no, eight, no, nine of them—all located up around the corner of the higher switchback.

She straightened. Huh.

She bent over again, looking for a key. It was right on a crease, naturally, and the fold had frayed the key almost to the point of illegibility.

She went upstairs to the office and rummaged around in the desk until she found a magnifying glass, and brought it back to the kitchen.

Almost, but not quite. The magnifying glass, of a size and clarity that was worthy of Sherlock Holmes, caused the ragged edge of every minuscule fray and tear to spring into acute focus.

She looked at the black dots again. They weren't black dots at all; they were tiny little crossed picks and shovels.

The topographical symbol for a mine.

After a single, stunned moment, her first reaction was fury. Not for the first time that week, she could have reanimated Old Sam, she would have, for the pleasure of killing him and burying him all over again.

Just what the Park needed, another fucking gold mine.

And not just one more fucking gold mine.

Nine of them.

She sat there in stupefied silence for longer than she cared to remember, before tucking the map back inside the lining of the journal and placing the journal once more under cover of Tolkien and the journal back on the shelf.

That night she dreamed of Old Sam in the captain's chair on the bridge of the *Freya*, one hand on the spoke of the wheel, his head thrown back, laughing, and laughing, and laughing.

Twenty-seven

THE NEXT MORNING SHE GASSED UP the Subaru and hit the road that led east down Turnagain Arm, up through the red and gold autumnal glory of Turnagain Pass, and down again to Resurrection Bay. She stopped at the bakery in Girdwood for a cake donut to tide her over until breakfast in Moose Pass. There was little traffic on this Sunday morning in late September and it hadn't snowed yet enough to stick on the highway, so she was in Seward in less than three hours.

She spent those three hours thinking about Erland Bannister. She was not looking forward to the coming interview.

Other than at his trial—oh, and when he'd kidnapped her and tried to kill her—she'd only met him twice, once at a party at his palatial home in Turnagain and one evening for dinner at a restaurant. He was charming, intelligent, arrogant, manipulative, and absolutely ruthless. He also had, give the devil his due, immense courage, in that he had done his own kidnapping and attempted murdering instead of farming it out. Although, now that she thought about it, the decision to do so would have been more a matter of security. You do your own dirty work and then you only have to keep your own mouth shut, you never have to worry about anyone else's.

He had of course been able to afford the very best defense attorney, one imported from Texas, a colorful and eloquent man who had endeared himself to the jury with his cowboy boots and his cowboy hat. Alaskan juries, while notoriously determined to find someone guilty for every crime, were susceptible to someone who not only looked like a Texas Ranger, he sounded like Jimmy Stewart.

Fortunately for the state, they had Kate Shugak as their star witness, notorious for being impervious to any attempted seduction by the defense. Their case was also helped by the judge, whose grandfather had been a businessman who had come north during the gold rush, and whose attempts to join the coalition of the venal had been roundly snubbed by Pilz, Heiman, Bannister, et al. He eventually went bankrupt and killed himself in 1929, which event had been faithfully handed down to the next generation and the generation after that, sparing none of the gory details and taking no prisoners in naming names. We are what our parents make us.

Her sangfroid on the stand had not come without effort. Every moment she was in the courtroom, she could feel Erland's eyes on her. She met them from time to time, refusing to be intimidated. She saw no anger there, or resentment, only a cold calculation, a summing up of her every word and expression, filed away for future reference. She had thought little of it at the time, and less after his conviction, but alas, the enmity of the judge's family for the Bannister family had revealed itself in some of the judge's subsequent rulings at trial. According to Brendan's phone call that morning, the rulings provided a legitimate basis for an appeal. Which meant Erland could get out.

An Erland Bannister on the loose was not a pretty picture, especially an Erland Bannister with a grudge against Kate Shugak. This was a man with a lot of money and a lot of power, and he knew how to use them both. Kate had very little power and no money at all, and over the space of ten years she had somehow acquired a lot of hostages to fortune.

Auntie Joy being a case in point. She'd called the trooper post that morning to see if Maggie had talked to Auntie Joy, quite forgetting it was Sunday. No one had picked up, and only after a strenuous effort to convince herself that no news was good news did she manage to get herself on the road south instead of on a plane north.

Seward was a small town of three thousand people on a stunning fjord surrounded by jagged mountains capped with snow. She turned left on Nash Road and five miles later was pulling into the visitors' parking lot at Spring Creek Correctional Center. It was five minutes before one.

The prison was a large complex of half a dozen buildings on three hundred acres tucked into a valley surrounded by national park land. It could house five hundred prisoners, with two hundred staff, and it had a good reputation and a low incidence of violence, with so far only one escape attempt, cut short mostly because the two inmates involved had chosen to make a break for it in winter.

She went in, identified herself, emptied her pockets, and was shown into a large, airy room with not uncomfortable chairs and thick windows that looked out on the view. Kate couldn't make up her mind if the view was a good thing or a bad thing for the inmates. It was beautiful enough to feed the soul, but it was also emblematic of what very few inside these walls would ever be able to experience again.

She was one of many other visitors that afternoon, some mothers, no fathers, a lot of wives and girlfriends. She didn't spot any lawyers, but then she no longer testified in court on a regular basis. She recognized a couple of prisoners, and they recognized her right back, but she stared them both down. She even smiled at one of them, a murderous sadist who had kidnapped, raped, and killed two sisters a week apart. He would never get out of this place, and she was proud that she had helped make that happen.

Okay by her if the view through the windows tortured him with all he'd lost.

"Intimidating little thing, aren't you?" an amused voice said.

She felt her spine stiffen, and turned to face Erland Bannister.

"My goodness," he said, inspecting the fading bruises beneath her eyes and the healing scab on her forehead. "You aren't looking as beautiful as usual, Kate. What happened?"

"Like you don't know," she said.

He was a tall man, broad-shouldered, slim-hipped, long-legged, with a full head of thick hair and intent eyes so dark it took a while to realize they were blue. His nose and chin were strong, and he wore his prison fatigues with the same ease and style with which he had worn his tailor-made suits. He was in his sixties, but a privileged life with good food and all the quality medical care money could buy had left him looking much younger than his years.

His arrogance was still very much in evidence, and when he smiled, so was his charm. He smiled at her now, and nodded at a pair of chairs sitting in front of one of the row of windows. They were prime seats, a little apart from the rest and as close to being outside as you could get inside the wire. How he had reserved them for his own use was a mystery.

He waited until she was seated and then took the seat opposite. He was the kind of guy who made whatever chair he was sitting in look like a throne. "Nice to see you again, Kate," he said.

"I imagine you're happy to see anyone in here," she said.

He shook his head. "Not true. There is seldom a day when I don't receive visitors."

"Including Vitus Bell," she said, "or perhaps one of his brothers."

His eyes crinkled at the corners. "Perhaps."

"All I have to do is check the visitor log," she said.

He waved an airy hand. "By all means, check it."

"Does Victoria ever get down to see you?"

"I'm afraid my sister sends her accountant to speak with me these days." His expression darkened. "Or that antediluvian cop she hired."

"Morris Maxwell?" Kate was pleased.

He saw it and was displeased. "To what do I owe the honor?"

"You knew my grandmother," she said.

He inclined his head. "Ekaterina Shugak. A formidable woman."

"Did you know her cousin Samuel Dementieff?"

Something flickered in his eyes. "Probably. There aren't many people in Alaska I don't know. And she herself might have introduced us at some function." He sounded indifferent.

"He died two weeks ago."

"Did he. I'm sorry to hear it."

"I am his primary beneficiary."

"Congratulations."

The glint of amusement in his eye irritated her but she held on to her temper.

She wanted information, but Erland hadn't tripled the family holdings by giving anything away for free. What did she have to barter, beyond the negligible gift of her presence? Which could only offer him a respite from what had to be a mind-numbingly boring existence for a man of Erland Bannister's intellectual acumen. The only thing he could possibly want was his freedom.

What had men like Erland Bannister always

wanted? Power, all they could get, and more of it when they had that much. Erland would see it as a manifestation of his own power, her coming hotfoot down to Seward to see him.

Outside the window a cloud shifted, allowing a ray of weak fall sunlight to slant in through the windows. There was a simultaneous pause in the background murmur of conversation as every con in the room instinctively looked around to watch the bright gleam that lit up the dust motes in the air, that kissed the cheek with the most fleeting caress of warmth.

That same ray of sunlight fell upon Erland Bannister's face, reducing the prominent nose and the firm chin to the bone structure beneath. The bright eyes seemed even deeper set beneath more strongly marked brows, the cheekbones sharper beneath the skin.

For one fleeting, ephemeral moment, it was as if Old Sam himself were sitting across from her.

She realized that her eyes had been traveling over him in what must have been an expression of marveling astonishment. Erland mistook it for something else, and preened. She repressed a sudden urge to laugh out loud. It felt too close to hysteria to be allowed loose.

Old Sam must have known.

She wondered if Erland knew.

She wondered if Emaa had known. "Your father," she said.

His expression didn't change, but then a poker face was prized and cultivated among high rollers. "Emil Bannister. Yes?"

"He was involved in gold mining, wasn't he, back in the day?"

He stiffened involuntarily and relaxed again almost immediately, but she had her answer. "Of course," he said, and waved a dismissive hand. "Everyone was, to some extent, at least before oil came in. It's what Alaskans do, Kate. You should know that. You're involved in gold mining yourself these days."

"Isn't anything ever enough for you guys?" she said.

"I'm afraid I don't know what you mean."

"Enough," she said. "Enough things. Enough gold. Enough money." She shook her head. "Enough power."

He didn't answer, maintaining the amused smile at her flights of fancy without seeming effort.

The clock on the wall showed twenty past one. Time to cut to the chase. "Bruce Abbott," she said.

Erland preserved his calm. "How is Bruce?"

"He's fine," she said. "Other than having developed overtly criminal tendencies later in life."

"Old Bruce?" Erland loosed a guffaw that was almost too convincing.

"Yeah, I figured he learned from the best," Kate

496

said, impatient. That cut off the laughter. "What is Bruce looking for that you think I have?"

Erland maintained his bland expression. "I have no idea what you're talking about, Kate. How could I hire anyone to follow you from in here?"

"I didn't say he was following me," she said.

"He would have to be following you for you to discover his overtly criminal, er, tendencies." He raised an eyebrow, contriving to look a little bored. "Was there a question in there somewhere?"

"I'm wondering what Bruce Abbott can do for you, stuck in here," she said. "I seem to remember he has a law degree."

Erland's laugh seemed much more genuine this time. "My case is on appeal, Kate," he said. "I'll be out of here before the year is up. But Bruce Abbott is not my attorney."

"You might get out," she said. "And you might not." But she was afraid he was right. The mournful note in Brendan's voice had said it all.

"Oh, I will be out," he said, leaning forward, his voice silken. "So why would I bother hiring a second-rater like Bruce to do anything for me before I am?" His smile was a promise of menace yet to come. "I can wait."

Enough. She got to her feet to look down at him with amused contempt. "Who do you think you are, Erland, Lord Voldemort? If Bruce Abbott is the best you can do for a pet snake, I don't think so."

"You have adopted a son, I believe," he said.

Her laughter cut off like a switch. His eyes gleamed with satisfaction.

Kate told herself to take a deep breath. Kate told herself to count to ten. Kate told herself to step back.

Instead, she took a step forward, catching him in the act of rising from his chair, using one hand to push him back down. She stepped in close enough that he couldn't rise, one knee slightly advanced, just touching his crotch.

The smile vanished from his face. Some part of her was pleased to see it. She was further pleased to see that he couldn't stop himself from shrinking back a little bit, especially when she leaned down to place both hands on the armrests of his chair.

From the corner of her eye she could see the guard posted in the room look their way. She ignored the guard, and the sudden silence that had fallen over the visiting room. She bent forward until her nose was almost touching Erland's, until his eyes very nearly crossed trying to meet her gaze. When she spoke, her voice was even more silken than his had been, and infinitely more deadly. "The last time you fucked with me, Erland, you wound up in here. You mess with any of mine, next time you won't live to see the Seward Highway past McHugh Creek."

He might have paled, but he met her eyes

steadily. "Don't you want to know why I'm looking for the icon, Kate?"

She stared at him, arrested. Before she could formulate a reply he said, "My father bought it from an antiques dealer in Seattle on a trip Outside in 1945. It was one of the things that was stolen when a burglar broke into our house in 1959." He leaned forward, never breaking eye contact. They were close enough to kiss. "You might want to look up the case. It has certain, shall we say, family connections."

The guard was almost upon them, and she released the arms of Erland's chair and stepped back.

The light of malice in his eyes as she left the visitors' room stayed with her all the way back to Anchorage. She was furious with herself. She had let him get to her. She had lost her temper, and worst of all, she'd let him have the last word. Mirroring her inner tumult, a gusting wind that was the leading edge of a low blowing in from Prince William Sound battered the Subaru all the way through the Pass and down the Arm. She was grateful that the roads were still dry, and tired enough by the time she got past the sheltering outcropping of Beluga Point that she stopped at McHugh Creek and got out to stretch her legs and Mutt's.

The trees whipped back and forth, leaves falling in a dry rustle only to be swept into the air again to form miniature golden tornadoes. The shallow water of the Arm was choppy and grayer than usual with stirred-up glacial silt, moving fast on an incoming tide. The mountain wedges that succeeded one another from Portage west looked sharp and formidable, and the air had a distinct bite to it. Kate sniffed, considering. Snow? No, not yet, but rain, and soon. She grabbed her jacket and locked the Subaru.

The road up to the park was barred and padlocked. Mutt took the gate in an easy lope and Kate ducked under it and they followed the paved switchback together up to the top, which reduced the sound of the Girdwood going-home traffic to a minimum and improved the view. The eastern end of Turnagain looked dark and menacing.

Kate walked over to look at the creek, which tumbled headlong down the side of McHugh Peak in a mad and drunken dash that ricocheted from rockfall to boulder, a fast and deadly torrent. For many years back in the day, McHugh Creek had been the dumping ground of choice for the bodies of Anchorage murder victims. Now it was a handicapped-accessible park with a gate that was locked after the last tourist headed south.

Next time you won't live to see the Seward Highway past McHugh Creek.

She looked out at Turnagain Arm, so named because Captain Cook had sailed up it looking for the elusive Northwest Passage, the holy grail of eighteenth-century explorers. After the 1964 earthquake, which had caused the entire arm to rise five feet, a windsurf board was all the draft it could handle.

There weren't any out there this evening.

"Why didn't you tell me?" she said out loud.

Old Sam, of course, couldn't answer.

She kicked herself for not anticipating the possibility. Habits were hard to break, and the first thing a competent investigator noted. Mac McCullough had fathered one illegitmate son. Why not another?

She thought back to the first time she'd seen Erland Bannister, in his own home, surrounded by a crowd of suck-ups, sycophants, and stooges, in company with a wife, a mistress, a daughter, and a nephew. The wife's plastic surgeon. The daughter's lesbian lover. His home was palatial by any standards, his clothes, however casual, of the best quality and carefully tailored to a body that showed signs of moderation in food and drink and hours in the fully equipped gym undoubtedly in the basement. He cultivated an affable charm, but his air of privilege, his pride, and his sense of entitlement were manifest at first glance. He expected attention to be paid, and it was.

The last time she'd seen Old Sam he'd been wearing Carhartt bibs so stained with use you wouldn't have known they were Carhartt brown, over a plaid flannel shirt with a frayed collar and cuffs and aerated elbows that allowed his longies to show through. He looked like what he was, a fierce, predatory loner, a man with hands rough from making a living and knuckles scarred from fighting off whoever got in his way. He lived in a one-room log cabin and made his living on a seventy-five-foot fish tender older than he was. But he, too, expected attention to be paid, and it was.

A gust of wind tore at her clothes, her hair. At her confidence. How could she not have seen it?

One thing was certain. Mac McCullough hadn't died of the tuberculosis contracted in prison, exacerbated by wounds suffered in the Battle of Attu. Not immediately, he hadn't. No, Mac McCullough had lived to procreate another day.

Had Old Sam known? She thought of the map she had discovered the night before, which recorded the elevation and contour of each rise of ground, every boulder over five feet in diameter, every rivulet, brook, stream and creek. She knew now where Old Sam had gotten the gravel for the cabin's foundation, and as she'd guessed, it was from the moraine left behind by the retreat of the hanging glacier above it. She knew how deep the hole was beneath the outhouse. She knew there had been a cache, and where and how big it had been.

What she didn't know was why the map mattered as anything more than a faithful representation of a homestead proved up on sixty years before.

Erland wasn't going to tell her.

Who else would know?

The nephew, at his own request, was incarcerated in a facility Outside. The daughter was dead. The wife, now she might know something. If she hadn't hightailed it to Cabo with her plastic surgeon.

It has certain, shall we say, family connections.

Kate took a deep breath and let it out. There was another family member who might know something.

Mutt nudged her side about the same time the first drop of rain from the oncoming storm hit Kate's cheek. They returned to the car and headed for town.

1956

Juneau

The *Freya* went to Southeast that March for the herring season, and Sam took her into Juneau on April 24 so the crew could vote in the election to ratify the state constitution. He'd hired locally when he'd bought the *Freya* back in 1950, so they all had to vote absentee.

Being locals who worked in the fishing industry gave them an added incentive when it came to the third ordinance on the ballot. When Old Sam learned later that while citizens of the Territory voted only two to one for statehood as compared to five to one for outlawing fish traps, he was not at all surprised. The Outside fish processors and mine owners had fought a fierce battle against statehood in an attempt to protect their properties from federal taxation, and as a result not only lost the battle but pissed off a lot of Alaskans.

He escorted his crew up to the voting place to make sure they did their duty as citizens and then gave them the rest of the day off to celebrate in the local bars, with the warning that the *Freya* would be casting off at 8:00 a.m.

the following morning whether they were on board or not. He picked up a newspaper and adjourned to the Capital Café for a meal he didn't have to cook himself. Which reminded him, he was still looking for a cook. Not one of his four hands could fry an egg without setting the galley on fire. Which also reminded him, he should have all the fire extinguishers on board checked and refilled while he was in town.

He ordered half a pound of bacon crisp and four eggs over easy and a mess of fried potatoes and three slices of sourdough toast—"Sopping in butter, and I mean wet, and I mean real butter, Darigold butter right out of the can"—and settled in to read all about the seventy-five-day constitutional convention in Fairbanks, beginning last November and ending this February.

Seventy-five days in midwinter in Fairbanks. He shook his head. At a mean temperature of forty below, he would have thought it would have taken the fifty-five delegates a lot less time.

He ran his eye down the list of names, some familiar, some not. Pilz, Bell, Heiman, all the usual suspects and then some.

The list of names continued and he turned the page, reached for his mug, only to jump and spill hot coffee all over his leg.

"Honey, are you okay?" It was the waitress,

her round face a little too concerned, her hands a little too eager to help him mop up.

"I'm fine, sweetheart," he said. "A couple more napkins'll do the job." He turned her toward the counter, his hands on her waist, and gave her a gentle pat to send her on her way. He folded the newspaper open to the relevant page and stared down at the name.

Emil Bannister, Anchorage.

He reached for his wallet. Beneath the hidden flap was a piece of paper, crumpled, greasy, and coming apart along the folds. On it was the name Pete Pappardelle had written down for him nearly ten years before.

Emil Bannister.

Emil Bannister was the man to whom Pete had sold the icon.

The waitress brought him his food and was disappointed when it elicited nothing but an absent grunt. He'd looked pretty hungry when he came in, and sounded hungrier when he ordered, but now he sat staring at the laden plate as if it wasn't really there.

He had also given her ass an appreciative look when he came in. She twitched off, with a hopeful glance over her shoulder. Nothing.

It would not be fair to say that Sam had searched nonstop, unrelentingly, for Emil Bannister during the past decade. He had spent a year in Seattle, with Pappardelle's help trying to track down Bannister and the icon, but the postwar boom and the flood of returning veterans overwhelmed all other claims for attention. Public servants were run off their feet by new marriages, new births, new housing developments, new business start-ups. With the best will in the world, the few friendly bureaucrats Sam found were buried in paperwork and had no time to excavate dusty records for curiosity seekers.

The upside was that the docks had never been busier, exporting lumber and raw minerals, importing consumer goods. No cargo ship arrived without its allocation of diapers. The marine construction trade was booming right along with everything else, and Sam's employer had gone to a third shift.

Sam had never made so much money in his life. He banked almost all of it, staying in the shabby one-room studio apartment he'd found near Pioneer Square, and limiting his social life to dinners at Pete Pappardelle's, with the occasional Sunday spent in Wallingford, helping Kyle Blanchette restore the Craftsman home he'd bought before the war. Kyle turned out to be funny, smart, and good company, even if he did cast the occasional languishing look Sam's direction, which most times he turned into a wry joke and a laugh on himself.

It was Kyle who drew the obvious conclusion,

toward the end of that year, at a dinner at Lowell's in the Pike Place Market. They scored a table by the window and it was beer and clams all around as they watched the cargo ships, the ferries, and the passenger steamers move back and forth across Puget Sound. This time it was Sam's treat, a thank-you for all the hospitality he had been shown over the past year.

"You are really leaving then," Pete said.

Sam nodded. "I've got enough in the bank to make some kind of start back home. And my feet are itchy. It's time."

"What about the icon?" By now Kyle had been admitted to Sam's confidence.

Sam sighed. "I have tried everything—the DMV, the Bureau of Vital Statistics, even the 1930 census at the local branch of the U.S. Archives. None of the Bannisters I've found in Washington state is the right one."

"Well," Kyle said, considering, "he must be interested in Russian icons, which means he might also be interested in Alaska history. Did you ever think he might have gone to Alaska?"

Sam stared at Kyle for several seconds. "No," he said finally. "I did not."

Pete started to laugh, a deep, belly-shaking laugh that rumbled up out of the basement and rattled the glass bottles behind the bar.

Kyle shrugged and grinned. "Just a thought. Seattle is often the last port of call before Alaska for people who are traveling there. Suppose Mr. Bannister was doing a little shopping while waiting for his ship to debark north?"

"Suppose indeed," Pete said. He examined Sam's expression. "This not does appear to make you happy, Samuel."

"It doesn't," Sam said heavily. "It's still pretty much the wild west up there. There is no transportation, no communications, and the only record keeping is by the Department of Interior and those records are kept in Washington, D.C. How the hell am I supposed to find him?"

"You want the icon bad enough, you'll find a way." That came out a little sharper than Kyle had intended it to, and he smiled to take the sting away.

Sam, sitting in the Capital Café in Juneau ten years later, thought, Easier said than done.

He had returned to Alaska on the Alaska Steam ship Denali in the spring of 1947, and a long and tedious voyage it was, too. They stopped two days in Ketchikan, a day in Wrangell, a day in Petersburg, two days in Sitka, three days in Juneau, two days in Skagway, another day in Haines, and five days in Seward, before he finally got off in Cordova. He was one of two hundred passengers, a hundred and ninety-seven of whom were tourists, Alaska Steam having gone into tourism in a big way by then. The tourists on board seemed to find him colorful, or so they persisted in saying, delighted at this discovery of a real Alaskan among them. The attention drove Sam down into the engine room, where he lent a hand to the stokers until the indignant purser routed him out, scolding him for violating shop rules. After that he found a spot up top behind the stack where it was warm so long as he wore his parka. The purser, happy to be rid of him, found him a deck chair, and there he would retire with a book every morning after breakfast, not to be seen again until dinner that evening.

It was the longest period of time in his life up to then that he had ever spent both awake and at his leisure. It had the charm of novelty. He watched glaciers glow a ghostly blue beneath a low cloud cover, a pod of humpback whales form a bubble net for a banquet of krill, eagles swoop down for a salmon snack, drifters launch skiffs to pick fish from nets whose cork lines bobbed off the stern like a string of pearls. Now and then a totem pole could be glimpsed through the trees, Sitka spruce become art in the sure hands of Tlingit master carvers. On the Wrangell dock Boy Scouts were selling garnets from the Stikine River deposits. In Haines it was strips of smoked king salmon, and in Seward it was moose nugget jewelry.

He thought a lot.

He hadn't seen Joy in over eighteen months. He couldn't help resenting the fact that she had never written to him, although he had never written to her, either, mostly out of fear that some member of her family would intercept the letter. She could have asked his mother where he was, or even passed on a message.

Had she remarried? Single women were scarce in Alaska, especially in Bush Alaska, and Joy was still a young and attractive woman.

He allowed himself to dwell on just how attractive. He'd known she was the one the moment he had seen her in Mr. Kaufman's seventh-grade class. He had thought she had known it, too. He had been incredulous that she wouldn't go against her parents' wishes and marry him, and even allowing for the rough time Davy Moonin had given her during their short marriage, he thought her refusal to marry Sam the second time because she was barren was sheer folly.

He'd seen enough of the world that he didn't feel the need to rush out and personally repopulate it. They could have adopted ten kids if she'd wanted that many, and he would have fed them and clothed them and loved them all, but never so much as he loved her. He sure as hell wouldn't have beaten any of them, something she couldn't have said about the asshole who'd been her first husband. Her inability to understand that maddened him and—it was time to admit it—lessened his regard for her a little. This self-imposed banishment from the only place on earth worth living in had begun for her. He hadn't cared about the icon itself as anything other than a means of winning her hand. All he had wanted was her.

When he'd left Alaska, nothing had been more important than recovering the icon and returning it to his people. He'd fantasized about the potlatch that would be held to hail the conquering hero and the restoration of a piece of tribal history, an admiring Joy beaming at him from the sidelines, his mother wiping proud tears from her eyes, Joy's parents resigned to the inevitable with good grace, or at least enough grace that they could no longer actively oppose his suit.

The anguish of rejection and the remembered fury and frustration at her continued refusal to marry him was still there but no longer had the ability to hurl him into gloom and despair. His experiences in the Aleutians and in Seattle had seasoned him, matured him. He was a man full grown now, and full-grown men did not die for love.

He would not die for love. If there was a sense of gritted teeth about the declaration, it was nonetheless sincere.

Which left the question of the icon.

If marriage with Joy was no longer on his to-do list, should he still pursue the icon? For what purpose? The tribal elders had not supported his marriage to Joy, with the possible exception of his cousin, Ekaterina. Ekaterina was a daughter of one of the Niniltna Shugaks, who like Joy had been married off to a son of one of the Aleutian Shugaks to cement their emigration into the area, and who thus might know a thing or two about marriages dictated by one's parents.

No, with the sole exception of his mother, he owed his elders nothing, less even than they thought. He wondered how many of them had known about his true parentage.

He wasn't as angry at Mac McCullough as he had once been, either. Mac, who struck Sam as a guy with an eye always for the main chance, had nicked the icon and everything else within reach that wasn't nailed down, greatly helped by the fact that the local populace was laid out with the Spanish flu. Maybe he had loved Elizaveta, maybe he hadn't. Maybe he truly had meant to come back, maybe he hadn't. He'd told his story and made sure his son had seen it. Maybe it was even the truth.

And maybe it wasn't. Sam had thought about writing to Hammett, to see what he thought. By Seward he had discarded the notion. It didn't matter, or it wouldn't before much longer. Alaska was a place for starting over, whether you were new to the Territory or had been born there.

So he had turned his back on the vanished Mr. Emil Bannister, and on the lost icon, and on Joy Shugak. He reached Cordova to find his mother gravely ill. He stayed with her until she died the following year, taking on the harbormaster's job when the last one quit in a huff over a disagreement concerning back pay. The city council wanted him to take the job on permanently, but Sam wasn't ready for a life on shore. Besides, Niniltna was only a plane ride away, and he'd seen too many villagers in the Club Bar already. He wasn't going to wait around for Joy to show up.

When his mother died in the spring of 1948, he sold the house and everything in it. The following month he was talking to the skipper of a seventy-five-foot tender with a wooden hull, a high bow, a round stern, a deep draft, and a capacious hold. She'd been built in a shipyard in Ballard in 1912 and she'd been making her living in Alaska since 1914, fishing for herring and salmon mostly. She had started her life under sail, and had been converted to diesel in 1916.

There was a roomy fo'c'sle forward and a two-story house, wheelhouse, and chartroom above, a galley, three staterooms, and a head on the main deck. The engine room was below and aft of the hold. Her name was the *Freya*, which, the skipper told him with a wink and a nudge, was the Norse goddess of love.

Well, Sam had a history of falling in love at first sight. He haggled on the price and had enough money left over for repairs. When the papers were signed Sam took her to Seward and put her in dry dock. He installed a new engine, a new drive shaft and propeller, and a new boom and tackle. He remodeled the house so he didn't have to go out on deck to go to the head or climb to the wheelhouse, and he finished off the job with a new coat of paint, black hull with a white trim line and white house with black trim.

The last thing he did was write to Pete in Seattle, to ask him if he still had the brass ship's compass in the teak box Sam had seen in his shop the first time he'd gone there. Pete did, allowed as how he could only have parted with it to Sam, and insisted on its being a gift instead of a purchase. The compass was installed with due ceremony on the wheelhouse console.

Over the next twenty years there wasn't one of the thirty-six thousand miles of coastal Alaska the *Freya* didn't work, from Metlakatla to Kaktovik. The 1920 Jones Act had cleared Alaskan waters of foreign-owned competition, and Sam took full advantage of it. He took employers where he found them, the U.S. Navy in the Aleutians when they needed someone to run a load of supplies to those poor bastards manning the strategic intercept station on Amchitka, Alaska Steamship when they needed help delivering the goods to Barrow, Alaska Packers for picking up herring and salmon during the seasons when the price was right, the Forestry Service when they needed a tow for a log boom.

He had a good eye for crew and a keen nose for a buck, and he kept his eyes open on the job, learning the Gulf of Alaska and all its many moods by heart. There was always someone willing in every port, so he hadn't lacked for company, either. He hardly ever thought of Joy, unless it was with the indifferent curiosity of an old friend.

Or so he told himself.

It had been a pretty damn good decade, taken all in all, and the last thing he needed now was to go tarryhooting off on some silly quest after a piece of wormy wood and cheap gilt that could have at this point little meaning for his tribe, cultural, historical, or sentimental, and certainly had nothing at all to do with him.

So of course that was exactly what he did.

He did some snooping around the capitol and learned that Emil Bannister lived in Anchorage and was considered to be one of those behind-the-scenes political powerhouses, involved in everything from shipping to banking. He was a boon companion to the Bells, Pilzes, and Heimans and a charter member of the Spit and Argue Club, whose members had their fingers in every commercial pie north of the fifty-three. He had the ear of the territorial governor and was on the correct side of every issue from fish traps to statehood.

Sam made friends with an aide to one of the Anchorage representatives, from whom he learned that Bannister was partner in a consortium that was drilling exploratory wells on the Kenai Peninsula, hoping to strike oil. Sam remembered running supplies to a cannery in Tuxedni Bay and being beguiled for an evening by the old caretaker with tales of drilling for oil at Iniskin in the 1890s, but this was the first he'd heard about oil exploration on the Kenai.

He told his crew he was moving the *Freya* to Cook Inlet in hopes of scaring up some work running supplies for the exploration companies there. Five of his six hands were from Southeast and he paid them off in Juneau and left the next day. Cook Inlet was a dicey proposition, an ever-changing bottom caused by a constant flow of glacial silt pushed around by forty-two-foot tides. He put the *Freya* at Nikiski's rudimentary dock and went ashore. The next day he returned with a handshake contract to ferry supplies between Seattle and Nikiski for the Richfield Oil Company. He spent most of the following year in transit on the Gulf of Alaska.

Pete was dead by then, but Kyle was still at the old stand in Seattle, and Sam had a standing invitation to dinner whenever he was in town. The house in Wallingford was by now fully restored to sleek and gleaming health. Kyle had bought out Pete, opened a storefront in downtown Seattle, and opened a second store in Snohomish, which, he informed Sam, was rapidly becoming the antiquing capital of the Pacific Northwest. He had acquired a live-in friend that Sam didn't much like the look of. The friend returned the feeling with interest, and when Kyle sent him off on a spurious errand Sam cocked an eyebrow. Kyle sighed. "I know, but what can I do? I love him."

The conversation threatened to descend into melancholy, so Sam told him about finding Emil Bannister. Kyle positively glowed with excitement, even positing the possibility of traveling north with Sam on the *Freya* to meet the man in person. This caused Sam to choke on his after-dinner coffee, and they had a good laugh.

The following July he docked with a load of pinto beans and drill pipe when Richfield brought in the Swanson River discovery well, which tested out at nine hundred barrels a day. It was Alaska's first commercially viable oil discovery.

Sam was invited to the celebration, and ate ham hocks and beans washed down with large quantities of beer, surrounded by accents that ranged from Houston, Texas, to Dallas, Texas, with maybe a little Oklahoma thrown in there for seasoning. For sure he'd never seen so many cowboy boots outside of a Randolph Scott movie.

A couple of roughnecks got into an argument over who had been throwing the chain when the well came in, and Sam thanked the rig boss for his share of the celebration but said he had to get back to his boat now. The rig boss, a big man with a big belly and a big bald head named, originally, Tex, said, "Need you to run around to Seward, grab the latest shipment of freight off the docks, bring it right back here."

"Can do." Sam stood up, and Tex escorted him to the dock. En route a skinny little guy with a face like an orangutan named, originally, Okie, came rushing up in excitement to tell Tex than one of the partners had flown down from Anchorage with his son and wanted a tour.

Father and son appeared a few moments later, and Sam found himself shaking the hand of Emil Bannister, a fair man of medium height, in his mid-forties, with an incipient pot belly straining the vest of his three-piece suit. He had a shrewd eye and the indiscriminate and ingratiating smile of a politician. "Isn't this something?" he said, beaming. "First commercial discovery of oil in the territory. They can't say no the next time we come asking for statehood now, can they?"

Sam said no, they probably couldn't. Inevitably, Emil's next question was how long Sam had been in the state. His eyebrows went sky-high when he heard the answer. "Not many of your generation can say that," he said. "Most of the Alaskan-born are my son's age." Before Sam could point out that Alaska Natives pretty much had the drop on everyone else in that regard, Emil said sharply, "Erland! Get down off that thing."

The boy, who was up on a forklift being shown the controls by the operator, flushed and climbed down again.

"I didn't bring you down here to get covered in grease," Emil said. "Now shake hands with this good gentleman."

"Hello," Sam said, holding out his hand. "I'm Sam Dementieff."

And found himself staring into a face last seen in a hospital ward on Adak Island, fourteen years before.

Twenty-eight

IT WAS FULL DARK BY THE TIME SHE LET herself into the town house. She went into the living room and sorted through Jack's selection of music, settling on a compilation of live Jimmy Buffett performances and cranking up the volume so that it sounded like Jimmy was in the kitchen with her. She put the takeout pad thai in the microwave and sat down to the fresh spring rolls while it was heating. She was polishing off the last one when her phone rang. "This is Kate."

"Hey."

It was Jim. "Hey," she said indistinctly.

"Feeding your face?"

"It's what I do best."

"Don't I know it."

She swallowed. Mutt trotted in from the next room, ears cocked. "Your love slave says hi." She held the phone up so Jim could say, "Hey, Mutt!"

Mutt gave a happy yip in reply. Kate put the phone back to her ear. "I gather you're still in California?" A thousand miles from her.

"Not so much," he said.

She sat up. "Are you on your way home?" She was already making plans to pick him up at the airport. She looked at the kitchen clock. If he was about to get on a plane, flying in from LA would put him into Anchorage well after midnight. No problem, she could—

"I'm on the road," he said.

She was confused. "You're driving home? What, you bought a car?"

"Not exactly," he said.

Apparently, she would not be picking him up at the airport any time soon. She leaned back again, and tried not to sound as sulky as she felt. "What's going on?"

He sighed. "This'll take a while."

She crossed her feet on the table, ignoring the microwave dinger when it went off. "I'm all ears."

It didn't take that long after all, because he'd condensed the mini-drama into an incident report, referring to everyone involved in the third person, with the sole exception of himself. When he was done she let him listen to her breathe while she thought it over. "So you have an aunt you didn't know about," she said.

"Yes."

"Of whose existence your father ensured you would learn after he died."

"Yes."

"Can't wait to see that writing box, by the way."

"It's a work of art," he said. "Could we stick to the point?"

"So you had the girlfriend—"

"Ex-girlfriend," he said.

She smiled to herself and kept her voice very cool. "So the ex-girlfriend runs a make on your mother"—she closed her eyes and shook her head—"and turns up a birth certificate for twin girls."

"Yes."

"So you have the girlfriend—"

"Ex-girlfriend."

"So you have the ex-girlfriend run a make on the aunt."

"Yes."

"And she lives in Oregon."

"Yes."

"And you have an address."

"Yes."

"And you're driving up to see her."

"Not exactly."

"Meaning?"

"I'm already in Oregon, but she moved from the last address Sylvia could find for me."

"Which was?"

"In Portland. Found the house the first day, and the people in it now say they never heard of her. Took me a day to find a neighbor who said the sister moved three years ago, right after her husband died, and the house has changed hands twice since then."

"She didn't leave a forwarding address?"

"Yes, with the post office."

This was like pulling teeth. She reminded

herself it had to be that much worse for him. "And?"

"They finally gave it to me. It was for a condominium in Eugene. That's where I am now. According to the current owner, she remarried last year and moved in with her new husband."

"Jim," Kate said, and stopped, at a loss.

"What?"

Kate took a deep breath. "Why don't you just ask your mom?"

His turn to take a beat. "We don't have that kind of relationship."

"What, you don't talk to each other?"

"Not really, no. Well, she doesn't talk to me."

"I'm sorry?"

A faint sigh. "It's not a habit she ever got into."

Kate thought of her parents, whom she'd lost so long ago. Her smart, silent father, who had taken her hunting from before she was old enough to walk. Her kind and gentle mother, who had tried so gallantly and failed so miserably to stay off the booze.

What wouldn't she give to have them both back, drunk or sober. "You're an only child, Jim," she said. "You just lost your dad. You have no siblings, no other relatives so far as you know, this unknown aunt excepted. You mother is all you've got left."

"No," he said, immediately and distinctly, "she isn't."

Off-limits. Okay. "Where are you now?"

"I took I-5 up so I switched over to 101, the coastal highway, for back down. I stopped in Newport for dinner. You'd love it, Kate. If you look north you can practically see all the way home, and there are all these Art Deco bridges the WPA built back in—"

"Where are you going next?" she said.

He sighed. "Medford. The condo guy said she'd moved there with her new husband. I'll be there probably before midnight, check into a motel."

"And go looking for your aunt tomorrow."

"Yeah."

"And you've never met her."

"No."

"What if she doesn't want to meet you?"

"Why would it matter to her one way or another?"

Kate could think of a lot of reasons. Jim was on an unacknowledged quest for a family member he might actually like, and after passing her thousand and one relatives in quick review, she couldn't blame him all that much. But this meant he was that much longer Outside, that much longer away from the Park, that much longer away from her, and she missed him.

"Good," he said, and to her horror she realized she had said the last three words out loud.

"Yes, well," she said briskly, jumping to her feet, her chair going back with a loud screech,

"I've got to go, my dinner's getting cold on me. I'll be in Anchorage at least another day, so let me know what happens, okay? *The Case of the Missing Aunt*. Erle Stanley Chopin."

She was babbling now. Mutt, listening with all of her considerable ear power to the faint sound of Jim's voice, gave an admonitory yelp.

"Mutt says bye," she said brightly.

"I miss you, too," he said.

Later, dishes washed and put away, Kate shed her clothes for an old UAF sweatshirt washed to a smooth nap, flannel pajama bottoms, and a pair of thick wool socks, and came downstairs again to build a fire in the fireplace. The cord of wood Jack had laid in the last year of his life was by this time so well-seasoned that she could practically light a log with one match. She exchanged Jimmy Buffett for Bonnie Raitt, made herself a mug of strong hot cocoa, and curled up on the couch. She had detoured by Barnes and Noble on the way home to pick up the latest titles by Tanya Huff and Ariana Franklin. Both books sat forgotten on the coffee table while she tried to divine what came next in *The Tale of Old Sam* from the leaping flames.

Old Sam had put the map in the second of the judge's journals and hidden it in the cabin at the hot springs. He'd left the other book for Kate to find, and he must have left something in that first journal that would have pointed her to the second if the first one hadn't been stolen.

She looked up at the bookshelf. The spine of the omnibus volume of *The Lord of the Rings* stared back at her reassuringly.

She remembered the jumble on Jane Silver's floor, all the books pulled from their shelves. There was obviously some history between Jane and Old Sam that both had been reticent about, but assuming pillow talk for the moment, he might have told her about the map. And Jane might have, must have, told someone else. Pete Wheeler? Ben Gunn? She had to have had something in her possession relevant to Old Sam's past, or why the break-in?

Old Sam's death was the trigger to all subsequent events, and by then someone besides him had known about the icon. Kate still didn't know how he had found it again. Or even for that matter *if* he'd found it again. Everyone could be chasing around—and in the process committing injuries to Kate's person—after something that didn't even exist.

Still, there were the journals. And now there was the map. A map without a big red X on it, so she didn't know what use it was.

If Bruce Abbot was working for Erland, then Erland had to be after the icon, too. But why? How could possession of the icon be worth risking the possibility of an early release from prison?

She could hear Erland's smug drawl again. *It has certain, shall we say, family connections.*

She would go straight to Kurt's office in the morning. She had to explain the whole car tow thing, anyway, and she could ask him to do that record search wizardry for which he was becoming so well-known. A search on Mac McCullough, just to backstop Brendan, and a search on Erland, just to dot all the *i*'s and cross all the *t*'s.

She thought of Jim's running a make on his mom.

Maybe she should ask Kurt to run one on Old Sam.

And Bruce Abbott, so she could tell him he was blown and find out what he knew. Although if Erland was operating true to form, it wouldn't be much.

And then she could go home.

The flames wavered, and she imagined she could see Old Sam's face among them, those dark eyes with that customary expression of cynicism she now understood much better. She imagined that shit-eating, devil-worshipping grin spread across that narrow face. He'd been Puck and the Park his fairy land, although that comparison brought an involuntary grin of her own to her face. But he had certainly been a knavish sprite during the time she knew him, and he had lived his life believing what fools his fellows were.

Her grin faded. Old Sam had always been so attentive to the aunties. He had brought them the first kings of spring, filled their caches every fall with moose and caribou, made sure their woodpiles never shrank too low during the winter. She had thought he was being the good older brother, or surrogate brother. She saw now that it had all been a smoke screen, safety in numbers, that his real goal had been seeing to the needs of the object of his affections going back more than fifty years. Not that Auntie Vi and Auntie Balasha and Auntie Edna weren't worthy of devotion and tribute and sweat equity.

Well, maybe not Auntie Edna. But the other two, surely.

She thought again of the omnipresent platter of deviled eggs that Auntie Joy never failed to bring to Old Sam's end-of-summer blowout. None of the other aunties ever brought deviled eggs, which told Kate they knew. Maybe not everything, but something.

Kate shook her head. A love affair writ in deviled eggs. Go figure.

The four aunties were all about the same age, which made them contemporaries of Old Sam's. And Emaa's.

She went upstairs to Jack's office and rummaged around for a legal tablet and a couple of pencils and an eraser and brought them back to the couch. In her opinion, looking back was mostly a waste of time, but her family tree was beginning to feel like a mess of spaghetti, if not a nest of vipers. It might help disentangle Old Sam's story to try to disentangle it.

This story started with Chief Lev Kookesh, from the name a Southeasterner, imported to marry Alexandra, daughter of Clarence and Rose Shugak, from a family who had emigrated to the Park so many generations before that their only remaining link to their Aleutian forebears was their name.

Although it wouldn't have been called the Park then, Kate reminded herself.

Lev and Alexandra had a daughter named Elizaveta, who married Quinto Dementieff from Cordova, but had a son by Herbert Elmer "Mac" McCullough, itinerant scam artist. This son was Old Sam. So far so good. Or bad.

Alexandra, Elizaveta's mother, had a brother named Albert. Albert married Angelique Halvorsen from Fairbanks. They had one daughter (Kate had noticed before this propensity for Park rats to have either one child or nineteen), Ekaterina, and they adopted three more, Viola, Edna, and Balasha, who were all related by blood in some distant fashion that had never been fully explained by any of the elders to any of their children. Kate had asked, one time, and pointedly had not been answered. So, some mystery there, but nothing to do with the mystery at hand.

She didn't think.

Ekaterina married Feodor "Ted" Shugak of the Aleutian Shugaks. Like Auntie Joy's her marriage had been orchestrated by her parents to cement the relationship between residents and emigrant families. Ekaterina and grandpa Ted, who had died before Kate was born, had one son, Stephan, who married Zoya Shashnikof of Unalaska, a Shugak cousin he had met at Chemawa, the BIA school in Oregon. Kate was their daughter.

And now came Erland Bannister into the mix. It fair curdled her soul to imagine for one moment that they might be related, but if it was part of Old Sam's story then it was part of her story, too, and she would have to grit her teeth and bear it.

She looked at the digital clock on the DVD player and wondered if Jim had reached Medford yet. The gods had to be yukking it up somewhere, tossing Kate and Jim into the genealogical maelstrom at the deep end of two separate pools, and leaving them both to sink or swim on their own.

Erland was in his sixties. Old Sam had been nearly ninety. That left one hell of a gap in their ages. A gap just as long as a prison sentence, perhaps? Or a prison sentence and army service. Mac was inside for almost twenty years, after which he was scooped up by General Simon Bolivar Buckner Jr. (truly, one of the great names in American military history, Kate thought again, toes curling) and drafted into the Alaska Scouts. Colonel Castner had been concerned only with his recruits' survival skills in Bush Alaska. She doubted very much if anyone working for either delved too deeply into a Cutthroat's past history.

At any rate, he had joined, or been drafted, to serve from 1939 to 1943 in what had been dubbed by historians the thousand-mile war. Where he had saved his son's life.

Kate shook her head. She made another note to have Kurt find Mac McCullough's army records. She didn't expect to learn much, but the dates might be informative, and if as Hammett's message to Old Sam would have it he had died of his wounds, surely the record would say so. And if he hadn't, surely the record would say that as well.

If Mac McCullough hadn't died. If he had served his time first in San Quentin and then in the U.S. Army. He would probably have been demobilized about the same time as Old Sam, in 1945. If his wounds had been severe, he would have been shipped Outside to a veterans' hospital and demobbed there.

But Kate seemed to recall that Erland Bannister was a lifelong Alaskan, had been born in the Territory. Which seemed to indicate that if Mac McCullough had fathered him, then Mac McCullough had returned to Alaska.

Did tigers really breed true? Was Erland

Bannister's face a faithful representation of his parentage?

If it was, did Erland know it? Was that what all this was about, some ancient family scandal that Erland had hired Bruce Abbott to track down all traces of and destroy?

Had Old Sam known it?

She felt a cold chill.

If Mac McCullough had returned to Alaska, had he contacted Old Sam?

And if he had, what would Old Sam have done?

"No," she said, so violently that Mutt, snoozing peacefully before the fire, was startled awake. When no danger appeared imminent she gave Kate an indignant look and went through her pawing, circling, and flopping ritual, this time punctuating her displeasure with a loud and aromatic fart.

"Sorry," Kate said, and got up to open a window.

She picked up the family tree again, assembled with many slanting lines and erasures and crossings out. Ekaterina and Elizaveta were daughters of a sister and brother, Alexandra and Albert (again, Kate reveled in the names), so they were cousins. So Old Sam was Ekaterina's cousin's son.

And what did that make Old Sam to Kate?

Her uncle.

Good enough.

If Old Sam and Erland were, say, half brothers, what did that make Erland to Kate?

Still an asshole.

Shared blood changed some things, but not that.

Twenty-nine

WHAT?" SHE SAID INCREDULOUSLY. "When?"

"Nineteen fifty-nine." Kurt handed over the printout and pointed to the relevant passage. "Murdered. He caught someone robbing his house. There was a struggle, Emil was knocked down, and the robber escaped."

"And Emil Bannister died?" Kate still couldn't believe it.

"Evidently Bannister had this big collection of Alaska Native artifacts he'd been collecting since he came into the country."

"Like Bell?"

"All those old guys grabbed up everything they could back then. Sounds like it was kind of a contest between them. Anyway, crime scene evidence, such as it was in those days, indicates Bannister surprised the burglar in the act. There was a struggle and his desk got knocked over. He was under it at the time."

Kate winced.

"Yeah. Crunch. Must have been a heavy sucker. The family was asleep upstairs. The commotion woke them up, and the son came down in time to watch his father die."

Erland. "He see who it was?"

Kurt shook his head. "And they never caught the guy. It was a big deal, Kate. I think it's even in some of the history books. Bannister was a pretty prominent guy. He was a partner in the Swanson River oil leases and he was even a delegate to the constitutional convention."

Kate was sitting in Kurt's office, coffee forgotten in one hand, a hard knot in her gut. It was like being in Jane Silver's living room all over again, fifty years removed. "What was stolen?"

Kurt looked at her, concerned. "Are you okay, Kate? You look a little green around the gills." Like Erland, like everybody, Kurt took in her fading shiners and the scabbed-over crease on her forehead. "Not that anyone could tell. You want Agrifina to get you some aspirin or something?"

"I'm fine," Kate said. She remembered her coffee. It was hotter than hot, a little sweet, a lot creamy, and helped steady the world beneath her feet. "Does the police report have a list of what was stolen?"

He shook his head. "It just says some smaller antiques and Native artifacts." He closed the report and tossed it on the table. "This was Anchorage in 1959, Kate. Guys like Emil Bannister didn't get burgled. I bet he didn't even have insurance. Do you want me to track down the wife?"

"No," she said, after consideration. "Not yet, anyway. Let me see if I can get in to see Victoria."

The other eyebrow went up to join the first. "She kinda owes you."

"She kinda paid me," Kate said. "A lot. Services rendered, check cashed."

He was unconvinced. "Still . . . You got a way in?"

"Kate Shugak!" The wrinkled, shriveled giant beamed at her from behind an acre of desk.

"Hey, Max," she said.

"And Mutt, too, I see," he said when Mutt trotted around for her due. "This must be an official visit."

"I don't know what the hell it is, Max," Kate said ruefully.

"Sounds interesting, which is more than I can say for the rest of the crap that crosses my desk every day. Imogene! Imogene, goddammit!"

Imogene was a plump woman Kate guessed to be in her early sixties, with a face set in pleasant lines beneath a neat cap of soft gray curls. She materialized in the doorway and said in a tart but resigned voice, "Max, how many times do I have to tell you? You don't have to yell, all you have to do is press the intercom button."

Max, improbably, looked abashed. "I hate them

damn things," he said, which Kate correctly took to include anything run on electricity, with the possible exception of the ignition on a Piper Super Cub. "Could we have some coffee?"

"Certainly," Imogene said, and smiled at Kate. "How do you like yours, Ms. Shugak?"

"A lot of cream, a little sugar."

"Coming right up." She vanished, to reappear shortly with a laden tray. She set it down on Max's desk and vanished again.

Max's eyes followed her involuntarily out the door. "Nice woman," Kate said.

He looked instantly guilty, color climbing from his cheeks all the way up over his liver-spotted pate. "Too young for me," he said gruffly. "Now quit your yammering and pour me some goddamn coffee."

Kate did so and sat down again. "How the hell are you, Max? You're looking pretty good."

"You look like hell," he said. "Who's been using you for target practice?"

A member of the Territorial Police before Alaska became a state, then one of its first Alaska State Troopers, Morris Maxwell's boast was that he had flown into every town and village in state and territory during his time on the job, and that he had popped more perps than any ten state cops since, too. He was maybe a little younger than Old Sam but not much. The last time Kate had seen him he'd been living at the Pioneer Home and what little getting around he'd been doing had been by wheelchair.

There was no sign of the wheelchair today, just a handsome wooden cane carved from diamond willow, hooked over the edge of the desk within easy reach. He saw Kate's eyes linger on it and said, "Victoria gave it to me."

Kate raised her eyebrows. "She must be finding you good value."

"Yeah, well, whatever," Max said, unused to and clearly uncomfortable with praise of any kind.

He looked healthier, too, more color in his face, more weight on his body, and his clothes were less threadbare, although still casual, jeans, light blue shirt open at the neck under a tweed blazer. They fit, too, Kate thought. The last time he'd been swimming around inside garments that only emphasized his contraction from the world. Now, he looked expanded to fit, clothes and world both. Being needed had amazingly restorative powers. "You're looking good," she said again.

His face reddened even more. "Yeah, well, whatever," he said, this time glaring. "What the hell do you want, anyway?"

She looked wounded. "I can't drop by to see an old friend?"

He looked at her.

She laughed. "Okay," she said. "I'm hoping you can talk Victoria into giving me five minutes."

"Why?"

She met the fierce stare. Ruth, Demetri, the lawyer, Ben, even Johnny—to all these she had told only part of the story. Bobby and Dinah knew all of it up to the time she'd gotten on the plane for Anchorage.

To Max, she told it all, every bit of it: the assaults, the journals, the lawyer, Old Sam's last note, Mac McCullough, the Hammett manuscript, Jane, the trip to Canyon Hot Springs, the map, Bruce Abbott, the Russian Orthodox priest and the Lady of Kodiak, her interview with Erland, and the resemblance between Erland and Old Sam. "I asked Brendan to ask the warden to toss Erland's cell," she said, at the end.

Max grunted. "And?"

"And they found a copy of Old Sam's obit. Either someone had sent it to him or he'd clipped it out himself. I had it printed in a lot of the local newspapers."

Max grunted again. "Old bastard sure set something off. Be interesting to know if he meant to." He cocked a sapient eyebrow. "How do you think Victoria can help you?"

"I don't know that she can. She's his sister. Maybe she saw or heard something, maybe she picked up on something he said . . ." Her voice trailed away at his look. "Yeah, okay, I'm reaching. Max, did you know that their father was killed during a burglary at their house?"

"Emil? Sure." He shrugged. "Didn't have nothing to do with her case."

Kate knew enough to leave that where it lay. Good cops do their best on the job every day. Sometimes their best wasn't good enough, and it was always easier to agonize over the failures than it was to exult in the successes.

Reading her mind, something else good cops did well, he said, "I wasn't sure she'd take me on."

"I was," Kate said, and she wondered if by working for Victoria Max was doing a job or expiating a sin.

Victoria Pilz Bannister Muravieff looked thinner and her face had lost its prison pallor. Her hair was thinner, too, probably a result of the chemo. She didn't volunteer how treatment for her cancer was going and Kate respected her reticence. A firm, dry handshake and Victoria waved her to the chair opposite. There was no warmth in her greeting, and no gratitude in her expression. Kate felt neither surprise nor resentment. Victoria's daughter had died as a result of Kate's investigation into Victoria's thirty-year-old conviction. Her freedom had come at a very high price, and against her express wishes. Kate was a little surprised Victoria had consented to see her at all.

It was a corner office, on the top floor, on the southwest corner, with a commanding view from the Chugach Mountains in the east to Cook Inlet on the west. On a clear day, if you craned your neck a little, you might even be able to see Denali and Foraker. The Last Frontier Bank building was clearly visible, blocky and olive green and taking up as much of its square block as it could and still have a parking lot. "Do you by any chance know the Bells?" Kate said.

Ms. Muravieff followed her glance. "The Last Frontier Bells? Of course."

Of course. "Would they take a phone call?"

Ms. Muravieff raised an eyebrow. "Of course. What's this about, Ms. Shugak?" She glanced at her watch.

Here's your hat, what's your hurry. "I saw your brother yesterday."

Ms. Muravieff's eyes hardened. She looked a little like her brother, which meant that simply by association she also looked a little like Old Sam. It was disconcerting, to say the least, and again Kate wondered how she had not seen it before. It was a truism that most people saw what they expected to see, but she wasn't most people.

"You saw Erland?" Victoria said.

"My uncle died and left me a bit of a puzzle to solve in his will," Kate said. "It required a trip to the Last Frontier Bank's museum. You're familiar with it?"

Ms. Muravieff made an impatient gesture. "Of course. My family is a patron."

Naturally. "The curator told me that I was the

second person seeking that information this month. The first person was Bruce Abbott. As a patron, I'm sure you're aware that to use the museum's collection you must either be a credentialed scholar or be referred. Your brother was Abbott's reference." She nodded in the direction of the Last Frontier Bank building. "By way of Lucius Bell."

Ms. Muravieff's mouth thinned. "His case is on appeal."

"I know."

"My attorneys tell me he has a good chance of getting out."

"I know that, too."

"He'll want control of the company back." Ms. Muravieff met Kate's eyes. "Tell me everything so I can fight him."

Kate looked over at Max, who had been sitting to one side and keeping his mouth shut. "I don't know what he wants, but it has to do with my uncle's death," Kate said, and went on to tell Victoria most of the rest of the story. "I've just discovered that your father was killed when he interrupted a burglar," Kate said.

A shadow crossed Ms. Muravieff's face. "Yes."

"And that the burglar was never caught."

"No."

"And never identified."

Ms. Muravieff hesitated.

Kate waited. She could hear Max breathing.

"No," Ms. Muravieff said, "never identified."

Kate could feel herself tensing in her chair and forced herself to relax. "Will you tell me what happened?"

Ms. Muravieff shook her head. "Erland said a noise woke him up and he went downstairs. He was the one who found Dad, just as the intruder ran out the door. Erland said he didn't try to chase him because he could see Dad was badly hurt and he wanted to stay with him."

Kate thought about that for a while. "What happened then?"

"By then Mom and I were awake and downstairs. My father died. The police came."

There was something, some hint of reservation in that flat, unemotional voice. "What happened after that?" Kate said.

Victoria sighed. "Erland, young as he was, quit school and went to work in the company. The board of directors and Norman Edgars, the assistant director, pretty much raised him after that. My mother wasn't much use to either of us, especially after Erland was born. There was some trouble between my parents, I don't know what." Her brow creased. "There were times I thought . . ."

"Thought that Erland had good cause to be grateful to the burglar for killing his father?"

Ms. Muravieff met Kate's eyes, unflinching. "Yes."

"Ms. Muravieff," Kate said, and then stopped,

trying to figure out how to word it. But really the other woman had opened the door. "When I met with your brother yesterday, I was struck by the family resemblance."

"Between us?"

"No, Ms. Muravieff. Between Erland Bannister and my uncle, Old Sam Dementieff."

The other woman sat transfixed for a full minute, and then she shoved everything on her desk to one side. "You're going to have to explain that statement."

Kate did. At the end of it, Muravieff said slowly, "So you think my brother and I did not share the same father?"

"I don't know. But a DNA test would prove it one way or another."

She watched as slowly, one infinitesimal bit at a time, a smile spread across Muravieff's face. "Ms. Shugak, you interest me intensely."

"I'm glad," Kate said, and their eyes met in perfect understanding.

"What may I do for you in return?"

"As near as I can tell, my uncle left me something your brother wants, to the extent that he has hired someone to come after it." She raised a hand. "This is all circumstance and supposition, you understand. I have no proof. But do you have any idea what he might want?"

Muravieff gave a regretful shake of her head. "I do not."

"Could you call Vitus Bell and ask him if Erland contacted him to vouch for someone to get into the Bell museum?"

Victoria pressed a button on her phone. "Rhonda, could you get me Vitus Bell, please?"

A moment later the phone rang. "Hello, Vitus," Victoria said. "Thanks very much for returning my call. Where are you?" She listened, and laughed. "Put a hundred on black for me. Quick question. Has Erland contacted you lately to arrange credentials for someone for your museum? I see. Yes, thank you. No, I'm not upset. I understand; you were friends for a long time." Victoria's eyes narrowed, and Kate thought that Vitus Bell might want to keep a weather eye on his future, just in case. "Thanks again. Give Sally my love."

She hung up. "Erland wrote to him two weeks ago, asking for Vitus to give Bruce Abbott a visitor's pass to the museum."

Two weeks ago. After Old Sam had died, but before the obituary had come out. "Do you perhaps have a list of what was stolen from your house the night your father died?"

Muravieff looked surprised. "No, I—Well, I don't know. I'd have to look."

Max, silent until now, said, "If the items were insured and a claim was filed, there would be a record."

"Of course," Muravieff said, nodding. "I'll have someone look through the records."

"I'd appreciate it," Kate said, rising to her feet.

Max used his cane to lever himself to his feet. Kate said, "Max here appears to be doing a good job for you."

Max had been the investigating officer on Victoria's case, and the proximate cause of her imprisonment for a crime she did not commit.

"He has cause," Victoria said, not looking at Max.

Kate wondered again if getting the old man the job had been a blessing or a curse. She thanked Victoria and followed Max back to his office. "Get what you wanted?"

"Mostly," Kate said. "My credit still good?"

"Depends," he said. "What do you want now?"

Thirty

KATE AND MUTT FLEW HOME THE NEXT day, leaving a still snowless Anchorage behind, to find that it had snowed another foot in the Park. Everything was frosted like a cupcake, George's hangar, the post office, the Niniltna Native Association's headquarters driveway.

It was Tuesday, 10:00 A.M., and Kate went up to the school to tell Johnny she was home and that he could come home that evening, too. He looked glad to see her.

So did Maggie, who was looking a little frazzled. "Have you talked to him?"

No need to ask who "him" was. "A couple of

times," Kate said. She'd tried to call him this morning before she got on the plane. Voice mail.

"He say when he's coming back?"

"No." Kate thought of the odyssey Jim had told her about the last time they'd talked. "My guess is it'll be a few more days."

Maggie's groan was heartfelt.

"How's Auntie Joy?"

"Fine," Maggie said. "I've been checking on her every day, sometimes more than once."

"She move in with one of the other aunties?"

Maggie shook her head. "She refused to."

Big surprise. "But she's okay?"

"Yeah, like I said. I've been checking on her every day, and I've had everyone else checking on her, too. You frightened the living hell out of me with that phone call, Kate."

"I'm sorry, Maggie, I—"

"Never mind that. What's going on?"

"Family stuff," Kate said. "I haven't figured it out myself, yet."

It was as Maggie had said: Auntie Joy was alive and well, and she was adamant about remaining at the cabin. "My home, Katya," she said, thumping her breast and looking ruffled and indignant. "My things." She ran a loving hand over a china figure. "I don't leave."

Kate thought of Old Sam, two cabins up the river surrounded by books and ammunition. "Is the manuscript safe?"

Auntie Joy nodded at the armoire. Even though Kate now knew it was there, she could not distinguish the edge of the drawer from its corresponding hole. "Not moved since I show you."

"Good. Pretend like it isn't even there."

Auntie Joy gave an elaborate shrug. "What manuscript?"

At Herbie's, Kate's snowgo looked like it was in better shape than it had been when she bought it new, and when she took it out for a run it purred like a contented cougar. "You're a wizard, Herbie," she said.

Mutt pushed her head under his hand, her tail playing stick to his bibs' snare. Herbie hadn't been the object of this much female adoration in some time, and he kicked at the snow with the toe of his boot and knocked 10 percent off the bill. "Fella been asking around about you," he said, accepting the wad of cash, which even with the discount wasn't small.

"Really," Kate said. "Who?"

He shrugged. "Stranger. Bundled up to his eyeballs. My height, maybe my build, moved pretty good."

"When?"

"Two days ago."

"What was he driving?"

"Ski-Doo Rev XP," Herbie said.

Kate whistled. "The new model?"

"Lighter," he said. "More horsepower. No windshield, though. Might be okay for racing. Wouldn't like to drive it long distances, myself."

"Say who he was? What he wanted?"

"Didn't leave his name. Told him you didn't live in town. Wanted to know where you lived."

"Did you tell him?"

Herbie looked at her. There was a faint twinkle in his eye.

"Thanks, Herbie," Kate said.

There was a high overcast, and the Quilaks stood tall and proud and vicious against a thin line of blue, the edge of an incoming high. Clear weather on the way, but it would bring cold temperatures with it. Kate let the Arctic Cat take the fifty miles to the homestead in a fast chomp.

The homestead was drifted in, too. Mutt shot from behind Kate as if she'd been launched from Cape Kennedy and vanished into the undergrowth. Minding her manners in Anchorage was always a strain. She was as happy as Kate was to be home.

Johnny had been home to shovel the stairs, although he'd left the thermostat down. Kate cranked it back up, built a fire in the fireplace to hurry up the process, and unpacked, to the sound of one of Johnny's compilation CDs. Uncle Kracker rocked out of the speakers, followed by the Spin Doctors, Natalie Imbruglia, Michelle Branch, and Bon Jovi, with some Lynyrd Skynyrd and Eric Clapton thrown in for leavening. Johnny was as catholic in his music tastes as Bobby Clark, just a generation later, and had a real future in music piracy.

Kate threw together a batch of bread dough, a wet mix with a lot of yeast that rose in two to five hours and produced a crunchy crust and a chewy crumb. She got a package of caribou steaks out of the freezer and put it in the drainer to thaw. She'd miss Thai Orchid's fresh spring rolls and the Lucky Wishbone's Pop All Dark, but what she liked best to eat was food harvested, butchered, and/or cooked by someone she knew, preferably herself. She fiddled around after that, shelving the new books on her to-read shelf, putting a load of clothes in the washer, taking advantage of the cold, clear day to go outside and split some wood. Nesting.

Mutt reappeared, looking very pleased with herself, and followed Kate back inside to flop down on the crumpled quilt in front of the fireplace. Her quilt, her spot on the floor, her fireplace. Kate brewed a pot of coffee, appropriating a lavish portion of Jim's Tsunami Blend to the purpose. Hell with him. Absentee boyfriend.

She wondered where he was. She wondered if he'd found his aunt yet. She wondered when he'd be coming home.

She wondered if he'd be coming home.

She took her coffee over to the windows, and stood sipping it as she looked east and south, at the line of ragged, rugged mountains that formed the one wall of her world. She fetched the pocket compass clipped to her pack. Canyon Hot Springs was almost due east of the homestead. Ninety degrees and a hundred miles from where she was standing. Fifty from Old Sam's cabin.

How often had he been up there lately? Had the memories of that hopeful young man been so painful that he'd stayed away? The cabin had been abandoned. The outhouse had been supplied with toilet paper and lime when someone who came for a dip in the hot springs remembered to bring them. The cache and the well had vanished.

He had certainly never told anyone he owned it. He'd never warned anyone away from it. Even Dan O'Brian hadn't known it was privately owned.

She went back to the dining table and spread out the map. She was still poring over it when Johnny got home.

"Hey!" he said, kicking snow from his boots and slinging his backpack across the floor in the general direction of his room.

"Hey yourself," she said.

He inspected her face. "At least you're looking a little less like Alice Cooper these days."

"Good to know."

He looked at the map. "What's that?"

"A map of Old Sam's homestead," she said.

"No kidding? Cool." He bent over the table to peer at it. "Where'd you find it?"

"Where he left it for me. At least I hope it was me he wanted to find it."

He listened to her as she caught him up on events, a frown of concentration between his brows. "He's really running you all around the rosemary bush, isn't he."

"He sure is," Kate said with feeling.

"You know where the icon is yet?"

She pointed at the mine symbols on the map.

"I don't get it," he said. "Why nine? Do you really think he found nine gold mines up there?"

"He might have made nine tries," she said. "And it might not have been him, or only him."

"You think somebody else might have made this map? Maybe Mac McCullough?"

"It seems old enough."

"Why would Mac dig nine different mines?"

"So he could schnooker nine different saps, I expect."

"You think Old Sam hid the icon in one of them?"

"I sure hope so, because I don't know where the hell else it would be." She looked out the window. "I listened to the forecast this morning before I left town. This high is supposed to hang in for a while." She reached for her mug. The coffee had gone cold. She wrinkled her nose and went back into the kitchen to refill it. "I'm going back up there tomorrow."

"Back up to Canyon Hot Springs?"

"Yeah." She didn't mention Herbie's news, that someone had been looking for her.

He straightened. "You know, Kate, you've been beat up, run off the road, and shot. My guess is someone's trying to stop you finding the icon, or whatever it is that Old Sam wanted you to find."

She grinned. "Yeah, but they're not very good at it."

His head gave a disapproving shake. "You really shouldn't go back up there alone."

"You're volunteering?"

He brightened. "Can I?"

"Tomorrow is Wednesday. Been a long time since I've been in school, but I believe it's still in session on Wednesdays. And I'm overnighting up there, so that would be Thursday, too."

His face fell.

"Nice offer, though," she said. "I appreciate it."

He tried to sulk but it didn't come naturally to him, so he took himself off to his room in wounded silence, only to barrel back out again when the caribou steaks hit hot oil. The bread came out of the oven a little before the steaks came out of the pan. She made a Caesar salad with anchovies and lemons and romaine she'd brought back from town.

After dinner, he sat back from the table with a

satisfied burp. "I wonder what the poor folks are eating tonight." He stretched and shoved his plate away. "What are you going to do up there?"

"Find those mines. Find the icon."

He looked skeptical. "It snowed another foot while you were gone."

"I noticed."

"If it snowed a foot down here, it probably snowed five feet up there. Finding those mines won't be easy."

"If it was easy, everybody'd be doing it."

He gave her an appraising look. Even at seventeen there were no flies on Jack Morgan's son.

She sighed. "Someone's following me. Maybe, no, probably more than one. They have been since Old Sam died. It's starting to piss me off."

He was as quick as his father had been, too. "So, what, you're going to set yourself up as bait?"

"Anyone who's willing to travel fifty miles minimum across country on a snowgo at this time of year, chasing after a bit of wood and gilt with allegedly magical powers . . ." She shrugged. "I figure they're just crazy enough to do it again."

"I repeat," he said. "They got the drop on you three times already."

"Good-looking and smart, too," she said admiringly, and grinned when he blushed.

"You have to sleep sometime, Kate," he said.

"The difference this time is I know they're

coming," she said. "And it's long past time I met these yo-yos face-to-face."

He stacked the silverware on top of the plates. "Have you talked to Jim?"

"Yeah."

"When's he coming home?"

"He doesn't know."

He looked at the shining cap of black hair, all he could see when she was bent so intently over the map. "If you waited until the weekend, I could go with you."

She raised her head. Her smile looked a little forced. "I don't want to wait, Johnny. I've been chasing around after Old Sam for two weeks now, in a race with competitors I don't know for some lost treasure I've never heard of."

It has certain, shall we say, family connections.

"Maybe there is no treasure," Johnny said. "You don't even have a picture of it, Kate."

"Somebody thinks there is," she said. "If I do nothing, they'll just watch me until I start looking again. The guy who tried to jump me the last time I was up there was looking for a map. I'm guessing that map."

"Who told him about it?" he said.

"Exactly," she said.

She packed that night and rose early the next morning, her all! new! and Herbie-improved! Arctic Cat shining bravely in the early morning sun. The snow had hardened to a nice crust in the below-zero temperatures overnight and the road was trackless when they got out to it. Kate loved being the first down the road after a snowfall.

She escorted Johnny to school, next stop Annie Mike's. "What's going on, Kate?" Annie said.

There was no not answering a direct question from the most discreet person in the Park. Kate filled her in. At the end Annie said gravely, "Are you sure about this, Kate?"

"Yes," Kate said. "I'm sure."

From there she went to Bingley's and bought some stuff she didn't need just so she could tell everyone in line she was buying supplies for a trip up to Canyon Hot Springs, which, oh by the way, had been homesteaded by Old Sam back in the day and now belonged to her.

She continued to spread the awe and wonderment and some envy over breakfast at the Riverside Café. She lingered over her americano until she heard the mail plane overhead and adjourned to the post office along with the rest of the village. While they waited for Bonnie to sort the mail, she regaled everyone in line with the same story, too.

The Roadhouse was too far to get there and back again and still make the canyon before dark, so she did the next best thing, she went to Bobby's, where she hijacked the better portion of the morning edition of *Park Air*. She told everyone listening all about Old Sam's mysterious legacy and how she was going up to Canyon Hot Springs to take stock of the property.

She didn't mention Auntie Joy, or Erland Bannister, or the map. It was a long enough story as it was.

When he signed off, Bobby gave her the evil eye and spoke to her in an unaccustomedly stern voice. "You wanna be the worm, I got all kinda hooks for you to hang off of, Shugak."

She laughed, although it sounded a bit forced, and the concern from both Bobby and Dinah as she went out the door had her a little spooked. "They haven't killed me yet," she told Mutt staunchly as she threw a leg over her snowgo.

"Woof," Mutt said, hopping up behind her.

And with that, they left civilization, such as it was in the Park, behind them.

It took a little under three hours to make the hot springs, the second half of the journey undertaken up switchbacks and around ridges, but it was still light out when they emerged from behind the little saddle and made the run past the steaming ponds to stop in front of the cabin. By now it felt almost like coming home.

She killed the engine and listened. It took a moment for the intrusive noise of the snowgo's engine to stop echoing off the walls of the canyon. When it did, the only sound remaining was the scrape of spruce boughs against rock and the mocking caw of a raven.

"I think we're alone," she told Mutt, who yipped agreement but nonetheless stood guard as Kate unloaded the snowgo and the trailer. She'd brought spares of certain items this time—knives, weatherproof matches, fire starters, hand and foot warmers—and she cached a bundle of them in a weatherproof pack behind a rock near the cabin. She'd brought the shotgun, which she stood next to the door, loaded.

Her note was still on the door and the tarps were still up on the walls. The support behind which the second journal had been hidden was still flush with the wall. So far as she could tell, no one had been here since she left.

She brought in wood and started a fire in the stove and set up camp in the cabin. This time she put the bed behind the door. This was farther away from the stove, but whoever came in would have to step all the way inside to see her. By which time she'd have the business end of her shotgun in his face.

She emptied a Ziploc bag of moose stew into a pot and set it on the stove to thaw, and stood there, thinking for a moment. She hadn't noticed anyone following her, and for the first twenty-five miles it was a long, open stretch of snow. But you never knew. Smarter to be cautious.

"The hell with it," she said out loud and went

back outside, taking the shotgun with her. She stripped down to her skin, shivering in the cold and the approaching dark. She took a long, running jump, pulled herself into a ball in midair, and hit the first pool with a resounding splash. She surfaced again with a whoop, her feet on smooth stone. It was the only one of all the pools that had a gravel bottom. The rest of them were muddy. Had Old Sam lined it with the same gravel he'd used for the foundation of the cabin? She straightened her legs, pushing up to the surface, where she found Mutt jumping up and down on at the water's edge, barking hysterically. She slicked back her hair and grinned. "Scared you, didn't I?"

Mutt gave her a narrow-eyed look that promised retribution.

Kate hit the water with the side of her hand, sending a wave of water Mutt's way. There was a startled yelp, not unlike the sound Kate had once heard a woman in a bar give when her ass was pinched. Mutt's front half dropped to the ground, her tail wagging back and forth, her haunches gathering themselves for launch. And then she did launch, arcing over the pond and doing something on the order of a somersault with a half twist somewhere in the middle of it to nip Kate's shoulder in passing. She made a perfect four-point landing on the bank on the other side. Her great yellow eyes were dancing and her jaw dropped in a lupine belly laugh, tongue lolling out.

Kate nearly drowned in the rumpus that followed, but she was proud to see that they were both soaked when she came out of the water. They dried themselves in front of the stove, tired from the drive and the horseplay and replete with moose stew and snickerdoodles.

Kate did notice that Mutt's ears twitched with every sound that came from outside the cabin. Her ears were doing a little twitching of their own.

The next day she rose before first light, ate a hearty breakfast of sourdough pancakes, eggs, and bacon with hot maple syrup poured over the lot, and donned snowshoes. The first thing she did was take the empty Gerber baby food jars she had brought with her and, with the help of the map, locate the corners of the homestead closest to the springs. Into the tree nearest to each corner, she nailed the lid of one of the jars. She put a copy of her title deed into the jar and screwed it into the lid.

It was called taking possession. Kate had no illusions that she could keep people away from the hot springs or out of the cabin, not without mounting a twenty-four, three-sixty-five guard. But she could stake her claim. At least until she found the icon, she wanted everyone to be very clear who owned this homestead.

She returned the hammer to the toolbox, pocketed a candy bar and a Ziploc bag full of gorp, and set off on a slog up the valley.

Locating the mines on the map required every calorie she had ingested that morning and a whole lot more at lunch, and she was still ravenous by dinnertime. Some of the adits, or mine entrances, were low and accessible by snowshoe. Others were emphatically not.

Toward the end of the day, following a ripped mitten and skinned knuckles, a wrenched ankle and a short fall that knocked the breath out of her for what felt like several very long moments, Old Sam's character came under loud and pungent review. Indeed, some people might have been offended by her choice of words, and any law officer of her acquaintance might have been sufficiently concerned to consider the possibility of charging her under AS 12.60.040, had the threats to torture and dismember been made against someone living.

Matters were not helped when Mutt, whose memory of their last excursion to this canyon had not faded with time, and who had taken her reinstatement as full partner in the firm seriously to heart, sounded the alarm for everything from the raven who continued to caw at them from annoyingly well-placed branches just ever so slightly out of Mutt's reach, to a vole scuttling from beneath one bush to the shelter of another that fell dead from fright when Mutt pounced on her with a snarl that could have been heard in Canada. Mutt did look a little self-conscious after the vole incident, but she would not relax her excessive vigilance, not even at Kate's express command.

It made for a long day. Kate found six of the nine mapped mines in a string that led up and around the dogleg of the upper canyon. They were much of a muchness, upright rectangular holes in the rock face about the height of a tall man who didn't want to bump his head going in and coming out. They looked as if they'd been hacked out of the rock face with a pickaxe. Three of them didn't go back more than ten feet. One of them went back fifty. From the wear of weather and erosion on the tool marks, the closest mine was the oldest, with the mines decreasing in age the further one went up the canyon.

All of them had been concealed with slabs of rock cleverly stacked to look like they were part of the face of the cliff. The undirected eye slid right over them, especially beneath a thick layer of snow. Kate would never have been able to find them without the map, and she no longer wondered that she'd never heard anyone talking about stumbling into one.

She emerged from the eighth adit to find the sun low in the sky and alpenglow on distant peaks.

Any of its lingering warmth had long since vanished. Her breath steamed before her face, her nose felt numb to the touch, and her front teeth were frozen. If anything, it was even colder inside the adits than it was out here.

There had been so much climbing up and down and snowshoeing in between that she had very little feel for how far she was from the cabin. "Man, I am whipped," Kate said out loud. "And starving."

Ten feet below, pacing back and forth on the canyon floor, Mutt woofed her approval. It would be much easier to guard Kate's precious ass if she was at Mutt's elevation.

There had been nothing except the claw marks of the pickaxe in any of the mines, and Kate wasn't enough of an expert to see if Mac had ever found a legitimate claim or if Old Sam had struck it rich. But then, if he had, wouldn't he have said so? Wouldn't he have flashed it around? Bought a new truck? A new boat?

Well, maybe not a new boat. Old Sam and the *Freya* were a couple, an item, a long-term romance, even a religion. Thou shalt put no other boats before me.

Kate pulled the map from the inside pocket on her parka. The last mine was all the way around the next bend of the canyon and at a considerable increase in elevation. She could check it out tomorrow.

She climbed tiredly down the canyon wall, strapped herself unenthusiastically into her snowshoes, and slogged back to the cabin.

They had company.

Thirty-one

KATE THUMBED THE LATCH ON THE homemade door handle and pushed the door open as far as it would go. It hit the inside wall with a gentle thud.

Ben Gunn looked up from where he was crouched in front of the stove, into which he was poking wood. "Hey, Kate."

"Hey, Ben," she said.

"I thought you'd be surprised to see me," he said.

"No," she said. "I figured Old Sam talked to Jane, and she talked to you."

"I helped myself to some of your coffee," he said. "I hope you don't mind."

"Not a problem," she said.

He looked behind her. "Where's Mutt?"

"Around." She stepped inside and let the door swing closed, shedding her parka. She poured herself some coffee and sat down facing him, her back to the wall. "I gotta give you credit for coming here in broad daylight, Ben. Figured you'd wait until it was dark, see if you could take me out when I was sleeping."

He listened with a quizzical expression on his face. "You're pretty relaxed."

She blew at the surface of her coffee, and took a sip. "No reason not to be. You only beat up on old women."

His face reddened. "That was an accident."

Kate took another sip of coffee, cradling her mug in both hands. Outwardly she sat at her ease, but she was perched on the edge of the snowgo seat, her knees bent, her legs spread, leaning just that little bit forward with enough weight on her feet that she could move when she had to.

"So Jane told you about the manuscript," she said. "You weren't researching your grandfather's biography when I walked into the *Adit* office, you were establishing an alibi."

He was silent for a moment, debating the wisdom of telling her too much. "How do you know it was me? There's been a bunch of break-ins around town this fall."

"You had tears in your eyes when I told you she was dead," she said. "You were hoping she had lived."

He was silent.

"You saw me go into the courthouse," she said. "You heard me tell Judge Singh I was going to talk to Jane. You panicked, afraid Jane either had it herself or knew where it was, and I'd get to it first."

Still with the silent treatment.

"So," she said, "Jane told you about Old Sam's manuscript, that it had been written by Hammett. It's an unlikely story. What made you believe her?"

He made up his mind to talk, and Kate gave a silent cheer. So much of the mystery that Old Sam had left behind for her solve had involved too much guesswork.

"Like I told you, my dad was one of Castner's Cutthroats," he said. "He got wounded, and, like Old Sam, he met Hammett when he was in the hospital on Adak. Hammett mentioned that he was writing a story about one of the other men in the unit." He paused. "Hammett died without writing anything after *The Thin Man*."

"I didn't really suspect you of anything," Kate said, "until it was pointed out to me how much a new Hammett manuscript might get at auction."

"Are you kidding me? Sell it? Sell an original manuscript by Dashiell Hammett? I don't want to sell it. I just want to have it. To hold it in my hands." He sounded like Galahad talking about the Holy Grail. "To read it," he said in a hushed, reverent voice.

Kate snorted. "Which is why you killed Jane Silver when she caught you breaking into her house, looking for it. Just so you could hold it."

He reddened again. "That was an accident," he repeated.

"What happened?"

568

Again, he debated telling her the truth, and again, the eagerness to talk outweighed the need for self-preservation. Either that or he meant Kate never to leave Canyon Hot Springs.

"I was going through her bookshelves," he said. "She walked in." He leaned forward. "She rushed at me, Kate. She grabbed for the book I was holding. I tried to shake her off but she just wouldn't let go." His head dropped so that she couldn't see his expression. "She tripped. She lost her balance, and she just fell."

"Old people do that," she said.

He shook his head, his eyes shut. "Her head hit the corner of the table. It was the most awful sound. Then I heard someone coming up the steps. I ran."

"She didn't die right away," Kate said. "She managed to speak to me, a few words, only one of which I could understand. 'Paper.' I thought she meant some kind of document. Turns out she was trying to say newspaper, or newspaperman. That'd be you."

"I told you, it was an accident," he said.

"Involuntary manslaughter," she said.

"But not murder," he said.

"You figured I survived the same treatment, why shouldn't Jane?" Kate said.

He looked startled. "What?"

"When you clobbered me with the piece of firewood in Old Sam's cabin. Made me a nine-day

Technicolor wonder, I can't thank you enough. But hey"—she rapped her head with her knuckles—"takes a licking, keeps on ticking. The Grosdidier brothers regard me as a medical miracle."

He sat up. "I don't know what you're talking about. Old Sam was alive and well the last time I was in the Park, and I never went anywhere near his cabin that trip."

This, unfortunately, had the ring of truth, but then she'd been pretty sure he hadn't been the one wielding the firewood. "And then there's the little matter of you running me off the road."

He looked away. "I don't know what you're talking about. Did someone run you off the road?"

She shook her head. "Come on, Ben. I saw that big-ass truck parked in front of the *Adit*'s office. Looks about the same general size and shape as the one that ran me off the road."

"Everybody's got a big-ass truck in the Park," he said. "You've got a big-ass truck. That doesn't prove anything."

"You knew I was headed for home when I left your office. You didn't find the manuscript at Jane's that morning, so you figured Old Sam must have held on to it. You wanted to stall me, slow me down so you could search his cabin." She looked at him, and said softly, "Or you wanted to get me out of the way entirely."

"I don't know what you're talking about," he said again.

"Attempted murder, this time," she said. "At the very least assault with intent. You'll still do a healthy chunk of time."

"No," he said. "I won't."

"I will tell," she said mildly.

"No," he said. "You won't." He had let his hand slide down to rest on the butt of the pistol he wore in a holster at his belt. It looked very old, like something out of *Casablanca*. Another stellar Bogart performance, she thought irrelevantly. "It's a plan," she said to Ben, complimentary. "I can see only one flaw."

"What?"

"You don't have the manuscript."

"Not yet." He matched her look for look, hand still on his pistol.

"See, there's your problem."

"What?'

"I don't have it, either."

He looked disconcerted, then rallied. "But you know where it is."

"Doesn't mean I wouldn't let you shoot me before I told you," she said, and while he was still absorbing that cheerfully delivered statement she threw her coffee in his face. It wasn't that hot but he flinched, and she rocked forward to the balls of her feet and pushed off. A beat later he reacted, pulling the pistol free. It was one beat too long.

Sometimes it just didn't matter how many times they'd heard The Legend of Kate Shugak. When six-foot men faced a five-foot woman, they naturally assumed they had the advantage. It was Kate's very great pleasure to instruct them otherwise whenever she got the chance, and with all the considerable force and speed of one hundred twenty well-directed pounds of pissed-off woman behind it, Ben's hand slammed against the wall.

Bones cracked and he yelled. He was, in fact, bigger than she was, but he spent most of his time typing. She spent most of her time kicking ass. He heaved, trying to throw her off, but she clung like a limpet. He rolled, trying to push her into the hot stove, and she leaned forward and sank her teeth into his nose.

"Ahhh! 'Et 'oh, 'et 'oh!" She could feel his grip tighten on the pistol, which he had somehow managed to keep hold of. It fired a round at close quarters into the stove. Kate looked up to see the stack tremble, but the coffeepot was too close to the edge and it started to fall. She rolled out of the way just in time, before what was left inside the pot poured down his right thigh and his crotch.

Ben screamed like a little girl, and while his attention was diverted she pounced on the pistol and popped to her feet. He wasn't even looking at her as he frantically plucked the fabric of his jeans away from his crotch, shaking his leg, and giving out with what she considered to be pretty pedestrian language. "Ouch, shit, goddammit, shit, fuck, ow, ow, ow!" The blood gushing from his nose was a nice grace note, though.

It took a few moments for Ben's pants to cool off and for him to reacquire focus. By then Kate had some fourteen-inch zip ties she'd brought along specifically for the purpose out and ready, and before he could react she had his right hand bound to his left foot. It was an effective hobble she had used before. They were going to be here at least overnight and she didn't want to have to feed him or unzip his fly.

Mutt shouldered the door open and poked her head inside. Gunn froze in place. Kate wasn't sure he was even breathing, and given the speculative look in Mutt's yellow eyes she didn't blame him.

Satisfied, Mutt cocked an eyebrow at Kate. *Leave anything for me?*

"Back on watch," Kate said, and Mutt huffed out an indignant breath mostly for show and vanished again.

"You're not very good at this, are you?" Kate said to Ben, not unkindly but without much interest, either. "You should have read Mr. Hammett with more attention. Sam Spade would never have let me get the drop on him like that." She considered. "Well, Humphrey Bogart never would have, anyway."

She grabbed the collar of his jacket and the seat of his pants and hauled him to where he could lean up against the wall, sort of. She retrieved the pot, made a fresh batch of coffee, and poured them each a cup, taking care to set his down a little distance away, so she was safely out of reach by the time he could get to it.

"You broke my hand," he said, and in fact his right hand looked a little crushed. The flesh had begun to swell against the zip tie. He had a hard time picking up the mug, bound as he was, and finally rolled over on his right side so he could reach for the cup with his left hand. His nose was the size of a banana and his eyes were swollen half shut and beginning to blacken. Kate watched without sympathy as she unloaded his pistol and tucked it into her pack.

He sat up again, awkwardly. He kept his head down, unable to meet her eyes, and when he spoke his voice was barely above a mumble. "What happens now?"

"Now?" She gave him a sunny smile. "Now we wait."

"Wait?" he said. "What for?"

"Not what," she said, "who."

"I don't understand."

"This who would be the guy who clobbered me over the head in Old Sam's cabin in Niniltna, and ransacked it before you could. Why didn't you turn around and keep going to Niniltna that night, by the way? You'd already killed once that day, what the hell. You could have broken into the cabin and searched all night if you wanted to."

"My hand hurts," he said. "Haven't you got some aspirin or something you could give me?"

"Or I suppose you could have just lost your nerve," Kate said. "One killing that morning, another that night, both with no witnesses. You probably decided it was time to head for the barn."

He said nothing.

Night fell soon after. Kate fried moose liver with onions and apples and bacon and ate heartily. Ben, sadly not a liver fan, ate, too, although less heartily, and gulped down the 222s Kate offered as a side dish. "I need to use the, er," he said, and jerked his head at the door.

"Go right ahead," Kate said amiably.

He maneuvered himself to his feet, more or less, and looked at her, his face red from his hunched over position. "Aren't you afraid I'll run away?"

A long, low howl sounded from somewhere outside that wasn't far enough away, and his face lost some of its color. Kate smiled. "Not very."

Back inside, having lurched to his piece of the floor and clawed the spare sleeping bag around him, he said, "Can't I sleep closer to the stove? There's a draft coming through the walls under the tarp."

"No," Kate said.

The disarrangement of limbs caused by the zip-tied hobble frustrated his attempts to cover himself completely. Eventually he gave up and laid back. "Who's coming?"

She looked at him. "You don't know?"

He was silent.

"You ever hear of the Lady of Kodiak?"

"No."

He occupied himself again with grunting and yanking and thumping the sleeping bag in place. He got enough material over and under him to be satisfied, if not comfortable, finally, although he was breathing a little harder from the effort.

Kate wasn't feeling his pain. "I don't believe you, Ben," she said. "You're a newspaperman. So was your father, and so was your grandfather. Your grandfather had to have known the story. He was here, he was practically an eyewitness. He had to have told your father about it, and I don't for one moment believe that your father didn't tell you."

He tried and failed to zip up the bag. "The Lady?"

"The Lady of Kodiak. Or the Sainted Mary. It's the name of the icon."

He tried to shrug into the bag, but it just wasn't happening in his bent-over position. "Maybe I could remember something if you could zip up this goddamn bag."

She rose to her feet and stepped across the room. Before he could do or say anything she had her foot on his throat. Automatically his left hand came up to wrap loosely around her ankle. "Let go," she said, leaning her weight on her foot.

His eyes went wide. He wheezed. His hand tightened.

She leaned harder. "Let go," she said again.

His hand fell away. While he was gasping for breath she pulled up the zip on the bag and nipped back to the snowgo seat before he had a chance to recover.

When he got his breath back he scowled at her. "There was no need for that."

"No?" Kate said. "Then I apologize. Really I do. About the Lady?"

But he was sulky after the foot in the neck, so conversation lagged. After an hour of tossing and turning, he finally fell asleep. He snored, a deep, loud gurgle through his wounded nose that sounded like a clogged drain. Good thing Kate had no intention of sleeping.

Kate turned off the gas in the Coleman lantern, and the inside of the cabin was dark but for the light of the wood fire flickering through the cracks and the new bullet hole in the stove. If people kept shooting off weapons in here, a new outhouse was going to be the least of it to keep the place a going concern.

The hours crawled on, nine, ten, eleven, midnight, one. Kate had just reached the end of David McCullough's *John Adams*, and was trying, for the most part unsuccessfully, not to break into sobs over Abigail's death when she heard Mutt howl. It sounded a lot farther off than it should have.

Kate set the book down, turned off the book

light, and rose soundlessly to her feet. She was still fully dressed.

She looked over at Ben, whose snoring continued unabated. She stepped into her boots, shrugged into her parka, and slid outside and around the back of the cabin, pulling on hat and gloves as she went.

If she hadn't been listening for it she wouldn't have heard it: the faint buzz of an engine. Not a plane, not a four-wheeler. No, this was a snow machine. Kate couldn't tell if it was the Polaris that had followed her the last time she'd come to the canyon. The sound of the engine was muted, probably deliberately so. Without Mutt's warning she wouldn't have heard it until it was much closer.

It took another fifteen minutes for them to approach the saddle. Again, they stopped just before the canyon entrance. If it ain't broke, don't fix it.

Kate was leaning against the back wall and Ben's snoring was of such power and volume that she didn't hear the footsteps until they were almost at the door of the cabin. But she heard the latch click, and the creak of the door opening, and she stepped quickly and quietly around to the front, to reach the intruder still in the doorway. She pressed the muzzle of Ben's pistol into the small of his back. "Careful," she said. "There be dragons here."

The back froze in mid-step.

"Good plan," she said.

Something cold and hard pressed against her own back. "Better plan," a voice said.

"I don't think so," Kate said.

There was a corresponding growl so loud and so menacing that if it wasn't a grizzly it had to be a T. rex.

All three of them looked over their shoulders.

Mutt, a gray ghost scudding crablike and soundless across the snow, legs stiff, hackles raised, head lowered, lips drawn back. Luck was with Kate still and the moon chose that moment to crest the ridge. It lit Mutt's narrowed yellow eyes and sharp white teeth with an unearthly glow, just as she let forth with another rumbling growl that sounded like the promise of lightning striking.

The person standing behind Kate let out something between a scream and a squawk. "I'll shoot her! I will!"

"No, you won't," Kate said. "Mutt?"

The thunder filled the horizon.

"Take," Kate said.

1958

Anchorage

Emil had the true spirit of Alaskan hospitality. Sam, while marveling at the other man's evident inability to see the obvious resemblance between his son and his newfound friend, had to give him that. The hand of friendship might be oblivious but it wasn't insincere, and from the time they met in Nikiski, Emil treated Sam like any one of his two hundred best friends, grabbing the check for lunch at the Ace of Clubs, buying the first round at the Inlet Bar, holding out the promise of a room at his house in Anchorage should Sam make it to town. He wasn't too proud to visit Sam on the *Freya*, and ate enthusiastically of everything put before him, from moose tongue to seal liver.

He had a confiding nature that invited confidence in return. When he heard what part of Alaska Sam was from, Emil questioned him closely about the Kanuyaq Copper Mine and the possibility for other discoveries in the Quilaks. His enthusiasm was catching. At one point Sam found himself pulling out the map of his homestead, marked with all the mines Mac had dug into the granite walls. None of them had paid out, of course.

Erland, on the other hand, was the human equivalent of Switzerland, not quite unfriendly but distant, aloof, neutral. Sam understood, having suffered through his own discomforting doppelgänger recognition at that first meeting in the Nikiski oil field. And Erland was just a kid. It didn't help that Erland and Emil didn't get along, and again, Sam wondered if this was because at some level Emil knew Erland wasn't his son.

Sam had a half brother.

If nothing else, it proved that Mac had survived the wounds he'd received saving Sam's life, which made Sam feel less guilty.

And more pissed off. He thought again of writing to Hammett, but it seemed to him that most of his answers were right here. He developed a lively curiosity about Emil's wife and Erland's mother, and the year after their first meeting maneuvered a delivery to the embryonic port of Anchorage. After a hair-raising docking during which he nearly grounded the *Freya* twice, he almost forgot the purpose of his visit, expatiating in full and at length and with emphasis to Emil, who was by now one of the city fathers, on the dangers of building a port on a shallow and ever-shifting bottom of glacial silt, a situation unimproved by forty-two-foot tides. Emil replied soothingly, and tucked Sam into a two-tone Cadillac with foot-high fins and bug-eyed taillights. It was the first automatic shift Sam had ever seen.

Anchorage had grown from the military outpost from which Sam had transited to and from the Aleutians during the war to a bustling city of fifty thousand, with an air force base, an army base, a high-end residential district south of town, and farther south even a suburb. Spenard, Emil said with a wink, where all the action was. Sam made a noncommittal reply, eying the house in front of which the Cadillac was sliding ponderously to a halt. Two stories high, it had bow windows in both front corners connected by a large porch whose roof was held up by ornate wooden columns. Everything was painted white, reminiscent of Greek temples seen in schoolbooks.

Be hard to find the front door in a snowstorm, was Sam's first thought.

Erland opened the door as they came up the steps. Now that Sam was over the first shock, he saw that Erland was older than he'd thought from their first meeting, although that might have had something to do with the sullen expression Erland had worn then. No kid liked being scolded in public. This was not a boy, this was a young man near college age, and today his expression was carefully pleasant, his handshake brief but firm.

"And this is my daughter, Victoria," Emil said jovially.

The daughter looked nothing like her brother or her father. She was tall, with a chin too large for beauty, thick blond hair shoulder-length in a well-mannered pageboy, and steady blue eyes.

"Where's your mother?" Emil said. "Dorothy? Dorothy!"

"In here, Emil."

They followed the voice into what proved to be a dining room. It held the longest table lined with the most chairs Sam had ever seen. It was proving to be a day of firsts for him, and it wasn't over yet.

Dorothy, the genetic template from which her daughter had been constructed, was bent over the table, setting out china and flatware.

"Dorothy, this here's Sam Dementieff," Emil said.

Dorothy straightened up and turned, a practiced smile at the ready. Dressed in a yellow shirtdress and heels, diamonds sparkling in her ears and on her hands, Dorothy was the consummate society hostess, ready to welcome one extra guest or twenty for dinner at a moment's notice.

But the smile faded when her eyes met Sam's. Her face went paper white, and she reached blindly for the back of a chair. She recovered herself in an instant, and went on to serve a tasty dinner of meat loaf, canned green beans, and potatoes, with apple pie and ice cream for dessert. If her smile was more rigid, her gaze when she looked at Sam more set, then surely only he noticed.

But notice he did. After dinner the kids vanished upstairs and Emil took a phone call in his study. Sam got up to help when Dorothy started to clear the table. "No," she said quickly. "Really, there's no need."

He pursued her into the kitchen. "Mac McCullough," he said. "Was that his name?"

She was standing at the sink, her back to him, but he could see her shudder.

"He was my father, too," he said. "Is he still— Do you know how I could get in touch with him?"

She cast a quick look over her shoulder toward the door. "He's dead," she said.

He was silent for a moment, assimilating the news. He'd had plenty of time to mourn Mac's death, from the moment he'd received the package from Hammett until that morning in Seattle when Pete Pappardelle had told him Mac had come looking for the icon after the war. "When did he die?"

She cast another glance over her shoulder. "Not here."

"Where, then?"

Emil's cheerful bellow sounded. "Sam! Sam! Come on in here. Let's light up and set a spell!"

Sam looked at her. "The Fly By Night in Spenard, tomorrow morning," she said quickly. "I'll try to be there by nine."

"Sam!"

Sam joined Emil in his study, a square, dark-paneled room at the front of the house. There was a large mahogany desk and a leather chair in one corner, a slate fireplace in another, and a series of tall, glass-topped display cases spaced at intervals around the walls. Seeing Sam's interest, Emil said, "I've been collecting Alaskana since I came into the country. See this? It's a storyknife. Made of ivory. Brought that back from a trip to Bethel just last year. Even Marcellus Bell doesn't have one of them yet." Emil chuckled. "Little kids tell stories with it on the Y-K. And this of course is an oosik." Painful dig in the ribs. "Guessing I don't have to tell you what that's for."

Sam moved on to another case. "What's this?"

"That? Why, that's a Sydney Laurence. Got it off the bartender down at the 515. Laurence used to go in there and drink, and then he'd whip out a little painting to pay off his bar tab."

The subject was a blue and white church with a dome surmounted by a cross, standing high on a hill overlooking blue water, with the hint of a mountain or mountains in the background. The colors glowed like gemstones. "Where's the church?"

Emil shrugged. "Beats me. Kenai, Ninilchik, maybe Seldovia. It's a Laurence, is all I know. From what I hear he was all over the place. Say, if you're interested in Russian stuff, I got a shitload of that. Look here."

Sam joined Emil in front of another display case crowded with babushka dolls and amber. The amber was polished and set in rings and bracelets or carved into flowers and animals. There was one piece in its natural state, rough and lumpy, with a speck inside it that proved to be an imprisoned insect.

Next to the lump of amber sat a Russian icon. There were three panels, all featuring the Virgin. On the left she cradled the baby Jesus in her arms, in the center she was holding the adult Jesus at the foot of the cross, and on the right she was on her knees, arms upraised to a Jesus arrayed in sunbeams, ascending to heaven, a rolled stone in the background. The illustrations were impressed on sheets of soft metal that might be gold. The frame was wood covered with gilt and studded with dull, uncut stones set in more of that same soft metal.

"Nice, huh? Picked her up in a junk shop in Seattle a while back."

The Sainted Mary, the bride gift of Alexandra Kookesh, the purchase price of Lev Kookesh's chieftainship, and the long-lost heritage of the Niniltna Native tribe stared up at Sam, all three sets of her gilt eyes filled with foreseen pain.

The Fly By Night was a bar on the edge of Spenard Lake that was sufficiently dark inside for Dorothy not to be recognized. Still, she had tucked her hair beneath a brimmed hat pulled low over her eyes, had removed all of her jewelry including her wedding ring, and had wrapped herself in a nondescript black cloth coat. She wore dull oxford shoes with rubber soles that did not squeak.

It looked like a costume she had worn before. The bartender didn't give her a second glance, and she slid into the booth in the corner, her back to the door, her shoulder to the room.

"How's a lady like you know about a place like this?" Sam said.

"I used to work here," she said.

"Oh," he said. He rallied. "Coffee?"

She nodded, and he fetched two cups from the bar. Once he regained his seat, he didn't beat around the bush. "Mac McCullough is Erland's father."

She didn't, either. "Yes." A little bitterly, she added, "Anyone who looks at him can see that."

"Does Emil know?"

"I don't know how he can't." For a moment her face dropped its perfect housewife veil, and her eyes looked unutterably weary. "But he's never said a word."

"How did you meet Mac?"

It was the fall of 1939, before the war had reached Alaska, but the U.S. Army was moving into Anchorage in force and the town was booming. He was then traveling under the name of Marvin Mackenzie, retaining the nickname Mac, and had introduced himself as being an independent businessman with interests in natural resource extraction. Emil invited him to one of his mixer dinners, and there he had met Dorothy.

"Emil," she started to say, and stopped.

Sam wasn't interested in her relationship with her husband, good or bad, but he was aware that the price for the truth might be hearing Dorothy's confession, and he was prepared to listen. She was stronger than that, though, laying out the specifics in matter-of-fact terms. "We met for almost six months, long enough for Mac to tell me his real name, and why he was here."

"Why was he?" Sam said, although he thought he knew.

She shrugged. "Something out of my husband's Alaskana collection. He wasn't specific."

"Did he want you to help him steal it?"

She met his eyes. "Yes," she said, her voice bleak.

He was silent.

"It was over then, of course. I told him never to contact me again. A month later, I realized I was pregnant."

Mac McCullough made a habit of running out on women he'd left in the family way, Sam thought.

"I—I wanted help in getting rid of it. I tried to find Mac. And then I heard that he had joined the army."

"Did you ever see him again?"

She paled, and swallowed hard. "Once," she said, her voice very low. "After the war. It was the fall of 1945. He had been wounded in the war."

Saving my life, Sam thought.

"He'd been sent Outside to a veteran's hospital for treatment. He said that was why he hadn't been in touch."

Sam could tell she hadn't believed Mac, but Sam thought Mac might have been telling the truth this time. "He still wanted the icon," he said.

"Yes."

"And he was still hoping you would help him."

"Yes," she said. She took a deep breath and

let it out. "I might have," she said. "After Erland was born, after Emil . . ." She paused. "Life became . . . difficult," she said. "Mac promised he would take me away."

With great difficulty Sam repressed a snort of disbelief.

"I was so careful," she said, her voice the barest whisper of sound. "But Anchorage was such a small town then. Someone must have seen us, and told Emil."

"What happened?"

Her fingers shredded the cocktail napkin. In a dull voice she said, "There was an accident in Kenai, on one of the drilling rigs. Emil was taking a group of businessmen on a tour. Three of them were killed."

"And Mac was one of them."

"Yes."

Sam wondered what Emil had against the other two victims. Maybe nothing. Maybe he just considered them collateral damage, the regrettable but necessary price of removing a rival from the field of action.

It was a considerably different portrait of the man with the welcoming smile and the bottomless hospitality.

The bartender brought the coffeepot to refill their mugs. "Anything else?"

"No, thanks," Sam said, and the bartender went away again. "So, you think Emil knows about Mac, and about Erland?" About me? he thought.

"He has never said anything," she repeated, and aged ten years in the saying. She looked at her watch. "I must go, Mr. Dementieff, or I will be missed."

She moved across the floor, a walking shadow that vanished on the other side of the door.

The *Freya* was scheduled to pick up freight in Seattle, and Sam had no choice but to undock and head south. He wasn't too worried, as he didn't see Emil unloading the icon anytime soon. Emil was a collector, and Sam had spent enough time with Pete and Kyle to know that collectors were known and to a certain extent made by their acquisitiveness and their possessiveness. At long last, he knew where the icon was. It was safe enough there, for the moment.

In Seattle, he had a sudden inspiration and shared it with Kyle. "Certainly," said Kyle, adding, with a ravishing twinkle, "For a commission."

Sam left him with a genial curse on him and all his heirs. He was back in Seattle a month later, to be met at the dock by a very sober Kyle. "No dice," he told Sam. "Bannister says it isn't for sale, at any price."

Sam was silent for a moment. "Wait a couple

of months, let him get used to the idea," he said at last. "Then ask him again."

But a year later, the answer was still the same.

On impulse, Sam went home for the first time in fifteen years.

Everyone was older, married, parents. Some were divorced, widowed, dead. Most of them were living subsistence lives based on salmon fishing in the summer and hunting and trapping in the winter. Many others had moved, to Fairbanks, Anchorage, even Outside. "No money, no jobs," Ekaterina said when he went to see her. "In ten years, Niniltna will be a ghost town. There is nothing to keep us here." She looked grim. "And the ones who do stay are forgetting their culture. They see in the magazines what life is like in other places. They want pretty clothes and fast cars and television. They don't want to hunt moose or sew skins or learn to dance. They want to speak English, not Athabascan or Alutiiq or Eyak." She paused, and said softly, "We have nothing to offer them, Sam."

He let the news of his return percolate through the village before going to see Joyce. She received him with composure, and he fought his way through the lace ruffles and the china teacups to a seat as she made him coffee without asking. When he drank, he realized that she had remembered his preferred ratio of evaporated milk to sugar exactly. "I could have quit drinking coffee since the last time you saw me," he said.

She was older, thinner, quieter, but her smile had lost none of its radiance. "Not you," she said softly.

He looked at the armoire in the corner. "Glad to see Heiman's got it here from Valdez."

She turned her head to follow his eyes. "Yes. A wonderful thing, Samuel. I thank you. And for the tea set that came inside it." She touched her cup, smiling.

He shifted in his seat. "Yeah, well, I met a guy who sold old stuff," he said, "and I remembered you liked old stuff. And I've got a boat now, so I could bring it up myself."

"That *Freya*," she said, nodding.

He was unsurprised. There was no more efficient means of communication than the Bush telegraph. He doubted that there was very little he had done in the time since he'd been away that had not beaten him home. He told her about the *Freya*, about the work that he had done, was doing. "Where next you go?" she said.

He shifted again. "The money's good in the oil fields. But I do hear tell there might be better money in government contracts out on the Chain."

"Them islands like in the war?"

"Yeah."

Her brow puckered. "Bad weather."

He grinned. "But good money."

A faint shrug. "Money not everything."

He put the fragile teacup with its delicate rose tracery gently in its equally fragile saucer. "Are you asking me to come home, Joyce?"

She said nothing, regarding him steadily out of unblinking dark eyes.

"Because so far as I know, I got nothing to come home for," he said.

Remembered pain clouded her eyes, and he was ashamed of himself. "I'm sorry," he said. "I'm sorry, Joyce."

She did not hold out her hand, or her arms, when he took his leave.

He flung away from Niniltna that same night, hitching a ride on a Heiman freight truck to Valdez, where the *Freya* was waiting for him.

Emil was on the dock on his next trip to Nikiski, as jovial as ever, and took Sam to the Ace of Clubs for a beer and a burger. He let fall the information that he would be in Nikiski for the next three days, meeting with his partners in the Swanson River oil leases. He did his best to chivvy Sam into buying a piece of the pie— "Atlantic's going to buy us out. It's a sure bet, Sam"—but Sam laughed and refused to be drawn in.

That evening, Tex told him to pick up a load

of cement that had been landed in Seward and shipped by train to Anchorage. It was needed on Swanson River pronto.

The *Freya* undocked on the next tide.

He waited until three o'clock, sitting motionless beneath a spruce tree, the last one left standing on the block, thick branches creating a pocket of darkness around the trunk. The street was dead quiet this winter night, the sides of the streets high with berms of snow. The last light had gone out in the house four hours before.

It wasn't much different from stalking a moose.

Or one of the Japanese soldiers holding out on Attu.

He slid out from beneath the spruce, a slight wind setting the branches rustling and creaking, making the tree a friend to him, hiding the slightest sound of his passage. He drifted up the steps and used the darkness of the porch to jimmy the lock on the front door. It wasn't a neighborhood accustomed to illegal entry, and the door opened easily. He felt his way into the study, opening and closing the door behind him, and trod across the room to where memory told him the Sainted Mary waited for him.

A light clicked on. He whirled, crouching, one arm thrown up against the brightness.

Emil rose from the chair behind his desk. "Hello, Sam."

It took a moment for Sam's pupils to contract. When they did, he saw that Emil was smiling, satisfied with the successful springing of his trap. "I can't believe you came in the front door. A professional burglar would have used the back. But then I suppose you aren't a professional, are you? Unlike your father."

Sam straightened. He made no answer.

"Did you think I didn't see the expression on your face when I showed her to you? Did you think I didn't know you were the one who wanted to buy her? Did you think I didn't know what Mac was really after when he seduced my wife?" He saw the expression on Sam's face and gave a soundless laugh. "Oh yes, I know. I've always known."

He came out from behind the desk, and Sam saw the revolver in his hand. He straightened, falling back a step to balance his weight, to prepare to attack. He didn't think Emil was bluffing, but he had not come all this way to go down without a fight.

"And now here comes Mac's son." He laughed again at Sam's expression. "What is this attraction my little Russian lady holds for the men in your family, Sam?" His smile was taunting. "I knew the minute I saw you that you were another of Mac's get, half brother to the cuckoo in my own nest. Oh yes," he said, watching Sam's face, "Erland knows. I made sure of that. It's why he can't bear to look at you."

He looked at the glass case and back at Sam, raising an eyebrow. "Really, for a while there I thought I was going to have to give you an engraved invitation. It's been over a year."

"You told Tex to send me to Anchorage," Sam said.

Emil rolled his eyes. "Really, Sam." He held up the revolver. "Isn't that a little beside the point?"

"That icon belongs to my family," Sam said. "Give it to me and let me go. I give you my word you'll never see me again."

The smile hardened. "The icon is mine," Emil said softly. "As my wife is mine. As my son is mine." He gestured with the pistol. "Back up."

Sam backed up, all the while watching Emil, waiting for the moment that would surely come, because if every Japanese soldier in the Aleutians with an Arisaka 99 hadn't been able to take him down, this smug asshole in a three-piece suit didn't stand a chance.

"Open the case," Emil said.

Because he had to to get to the icon, Sam opened the case. The Lady stared up at him with her eternal, mournful gaze.

She looked suddenly familiar to him. She looked like Joyce.

"Take the icon out," Emil said.

"I'm going to be found shot dead with it in my hand, is that the idea?"

"Take it out," Emil said, no longer smiling.

Sam reached inside the case and brought out one of the babushka dolls instead and in the same continuous motion threw it directly at Emil's head.

Emil let out a startled cry and flung up both hands in instinctive reaction. Sam launched himself forward, hitting Emil in the gut with a hard shoulder. Emil staggered backward and his heel caught the edge of the rug. He tripped, and both men fell against the desk. There was a sickening thud, and then both men crashed to the floor.

"You son of a bitch," Sam said, gasping for breath. He levered himself up on his knees, pulling his arm back, curling his hand into a fist. "You son of a—"

But Emil wasn't fighting. Emil wasn't moving. Emil was unconscious, with a well of red blood sheeting down the side of his face from where the back of his head had hit the edge of the desk.

Sam was dimly aware of shouts and cries and the thud of feet from upstairs, and his one instinct was to get away. He blundered to his feet and staggered over to the display case to grab the Lady and stuff her inside his parka. He pulled his hood up and headed for the door.

Footsteps were thudding down the stairs behind him. "Dad? Dad!"

Sam recognized Erland's voice and kept going, through the front door, down the steps, and out into the dark, clutching the Sainted Mary to him as he ran.

Thirty-two

IT HAD BEEN A LONG DRIVE, BUT NOT an unpleasant one, especially when he was able to get off I-5 onto the state highways and back roads. Rolling hills thickly forested with pine and spruce and cottonwood and redwood—he had forgotten how tall trees could get, and how thick their trunks. Acres and acres of tilled land, hay and wheat and Christmas trees. He stopped at a roadside stand for tomatoes warm from the vine, bought salt and pepper from a general store, and found a pullout next to a little creek in which to have lunch.

It was a shallow creek, with a meandering current full of eddies and dim backwaters beneath low-hanging branches that dragged ripples in its surface. The water gave a low chuckle of sound as it passed. It had nothing of the verve and dash of Zoya Creek, which ran in back of Kate's house. And none of the salmon or the grayling or the trout, either.

The sting of the tomatoes on his taste buds brought literal tears to his eyes. All fresh produce in Alaska was picked green in Chile and New Zealand, and shipped green, and eaten green quick before it rotted. Unless you had a greenhouse, there was nothing like this to be found in Alaska.

Kate's greenhouse had burned in the fire. He wondered what Kate would say if he built her a new one. He imagined her curled in his lap on the edge of this lazy little creek. He imagined feeding her one of these tomatoes, one bite at a time. Hadn't he read somewhere that some cultures considered tomatoes an aphrodisiac? A tradition to be propagated, if so, in more ways that one.

Through the trees the low mounds of terraced landscapes dipped and swayed over a hazy horizon. Not a mountain worthy of the name in sight. Not a glacier. No grizzly was going to stumble over him in this quiet little backwater, no bull moose saunter out of the undergrowth. A bird chirped, a melodious, inquiring sound. It definitely wasn't an eagle.

He got his phone out and called her again. Voice mail. Crap. "Hi, it's me, still here, out among the flatlanders. Had car trouble, got delayed a day." He paused, and disconnected.

He rinsed his hands in the creek, got back in his dad's car, and drove on down the road.

He came to Medford at sunset and checked into a Motel 6 outside of town. The next morning, another sunny day in a place where it didn't seem like they had much else in the way of weather, he was up early. He found the visitors' center, where they gave him a map of the town, and with its help he navigated his way to a sleepy neighborhood consisting of old frame houses with wraparound porches. Every porch had a swing, and every roof had dormer windows. The streets were overshadowed by tall trees, oak and maple and larch and yew, the yards lined with flowering shrubs. The scent of roses was very strong through the open window.

He expected to see Wally and the Beav coming down the sidewalk at any moment.

He found Oak View without difficulty and stopped the car in front of the white-painted mailbox of 1120.

The door to the house opened before he got to the top of the stairs. A pleasant-looking man with a worn face and shrewd eyes warmed by a latent twinkle said, "Hi. May I help you?"

Jim halted. He realized that his heart was pounding, and he took a couple of deep breaths, trying to slow it down.

"Those stairs aren't that steep," the man said, and came out onto the porch to hold out his hand. "I'm Norman Beck," he said.

"Jim Chopin," Jim said.

Beck's handshake was warm and dry and still had plenty of strength in it. "How can I help you, Jim Chopin?" Beck said.

"Honey, who is it?" a voice said, and Jim looked over Beck's shoulder to meet a pair of blue eyes exactly like his mother's, and a jaw line exactly like his own.

"You're Shirley," he said.

Her voice caught in her throat.

"I'm James," he said. "Beverly's son. My father sent me to find you, and I'm hoping you'll tell me why."

Norman Beck supplied them with coffee and pastries and left them alone on the porch, sitting next to each other on the swing.

"Why did my father send me to you?" Jim said. It had taken so long, this unexpected and uncharted voyage of discovery into his own past. He was suddenly in a fever to have all the answers, now, immediately, before he drove another mile, another inch.

Next to him Shirley sighed, closing her eyes and leaning her head back. She nudged the swing into motion with her foot. It creaked a little as it drifted back and forth.

She was as like his mother to be her twin, long-limbed and square-jawed, but there were distinct differences that could be put down mostly to style. Her thick white blond hair was in a pixie cut, the fine wrinkles at eye and mouth and throat had never seen a scalpel or Botox, and she was dressed in chino capris and a cropped T-shirt in pale peach. She wore tiny gold hoops in her ears and a plain gold band on her left hand. Her nails were clipped short, filed smooth, and unvarnished.

She opened her eyes as if his gaze had weight,

and smiled at him. It was a smile with a lot of baggage, a lot of pain, and some plain ordinary everyday weariness.

Or maybe it just all came under the heading of history.

"We looked like twins, but I was actually a year older," she said. "That was the start of it all, really."

Beverly had been born barely a year after Shirley, who had preceded her sister in school in such a blaze of intellectual and social glory that Beverly had been outshone in everything she did. Honor student? Shirley got there first. Cheerleader? Beverly fell from a dismount during the tryouts, and Shirley was elected head cheerleader and dated the captain of the football team. Prom queen? Shirley wore the crown, Beverly made the court by one vote. National merit scholar, valedictorian? Shirley took all the awards, while Beverly's GPA never got over 2.9.

"She could have excelled. She was every bit as good a student as I was through junior high," Beverly said, "but by the time we got to high school I think she decided what was the point?"

UC Berkley? They were both accepted, but Shirley was premed, while Beverly majored in humanities. Shirley was a leading light on the collegiate social scene, while Beverly alternately amused and annoyed everyone with her tenacious efforts to work her way up the California social strata. She reached what she considered the zenith of her college career when she was admitted into the Kappa Alpha Theta sorority.

Her roommate was Eloise Locke Chopin.

Who was, of course, the sister of James Brant Chopin, older than Beverly but not unsusceptible to the adoration of a younger woman who made a point of hanging on his every word.

"Nephew, she married him," Shirley said.

"Was it his idea?" Jim said.

It surprised a laugh out of her.

Soon after they married, Jim's grandparents and sister were killed in the Kern County earthquake. "Beverly was all he had left," Shirley said. "He desperately wanted a child. They tried for years before finally going to a doctor, who told Beverly she was infertile." Shirley stopped then, as if she had run into a wall.

A woman walked down the sidewalk in front of the house, a terrier on a leash. She gave them a curious look. "Hi, Shirley!"

"Hi, Angie," Shirley said.

Lacking an invitation, Angie and her dog walked on.

Some inkling of the truth was beginning to dawn on Jim, but before he could say anything Shirley took up the tale. "If she disliked me before, imagine how she felt then. Here was something else I could do that she couldn't."

"You had children?"

"Two." Shirley smiled. "One is a pediatrician with Doctors Without Borders." She looked at him, a glint in her eye. "The other is a cop in San Diego."

"You're kidding."

She shook her head. "Are you sure you want to hear this, Jim?"

He ran suddenly sweaty palms down his jeans. "I'm sure."

"All right." She gave a faint sigh. "James would have adopted. Beverly, never. I was divorced by then, of course. It's a strong marriage that survives medical school, not to mention residency and a fellowship. She came to me and asked me if I would bear a child for them. James and I spent a weekend together at a lodge in Carmel. When it was over, I was pregnant."

"With me," he said, his voice hollow and a little echo-y. It was as if his known universe had receded somehow into a vast distance.

"With you," she said.

He had to get up and pace the length of the porch. "I get it now," he said. "I get it all."

"Get what?"

He stopped and looked at her, almost with hostility. "Why she has hated me every day of my life."

Shirley went very still. "Hated you?"

"Hated me." He flung the words at her like a weapon. "Distant, disapproving, unaffectionate. I

607

was ten years old at a sleepover at a friend's house before I knew parents hugged their children. And she wasn't only determined I would have no relationship with her. She actively interfered in the relationship I had with my father. She was always there, in between us. If Dad wanted us to take in so much as a baseball game, she was there before him with some goddamn society function they just couldn't miss. So-and-so was going to be there, Dad had to meet him, it meant business for the firm. It was all for the future of the family, she said. I'd understand when I was older. But I never did. Do you know why I live in Alaska?"

Another challenge. Her voice was calm when she answered it. "Why?"

"Because it was as far away from her as I could get and still be in the country. You know why I still live there?"

"Why?"

"Because the rudest thing you can do to a new Alaskan is ask them where they're from. Most cheechakoes leave their history at the Beaver Creek border crossing and never look back."

"And you're one of them?"

"Damn right."

"But you're here," she said.

"Dad died. Nothing less would have brought me back."

Her eyes were full of pity. She patted the seat of the swing. The strength went out of his legs and he slumped next to her. Mercifully, for the sake of his composure, she did not offer an embrace, or an apology. Instead she spoke calmly, rationally, almost clinically. She sounded, he thought, like a doctor. "There is something else you should know."

"Great," he said. "Can't wait. Serve it up."

She smiled a little, but she refused to let him off the hook. "That weekend I spent with your father? It turned out to be much more than the simple act of planting a seed. We had not spent a great deal of time together before then." She hesitated. "But it is possible to realize you care for someone in only forty-eight hours."

The image of Kate flashed before his eyes, the first time he'd seen her in the Roadhouse, when the scar on her throat was still red and angry, when her regard for him was little more than contempt laced with hostility, and spoke without thinking. "It's possible to realize you care for someone in five minutes."

"Then you will understand me when I say that by the time that weekend was over, your father and I both realized he'd married the wrong sister."

"Then why the hell didn't he divorce her?"

She shook her head. "Divorce simply wasn't in your father's vocabulary. There was a man who took his vows seriously. Forsaking all others. Everybody says it, but only your father meant it."

"Did you ever see him again?"

Her smile turned into a wince. "I never saw either one of them again. Beverly made sure of that, and for my own sanity, I moved away. Eventually I remarried, to a wonderful man with whom I was very happy."

"And Norm?"

"When Colin died, I was sure I'd never marry again. And then I went to a retirement seminar, where I met Norm." She smiled. "Never say never."

She started the swing moving again.

An errant breeze rustled the leaves of the maple in the yard. A hummingbird with emerald green feathers darted up to the feeder hanging in the opposite corner of the porch, his wings a blur. Norm came to the screen door, looked at them, and went away.

"She actually searched my room," Jim said. "She was looking for Dad's writing box, for whatever it was she knew he had left me that would lead me to you. Why didn't she want me to find you? It's not like she gave a damn about me one way or another, especially after I wouldn't fall in line with her plans."

"Which were?"

"What you might expect. Become a lawyer so I could go to work for Dad and in the fullness of time take over the firm." He shook his head. "To this day I don't know if I didn't do it because I didn't want to do it or because I just wanted to get back at her somehow for never loving me." He looked at Shirley. "So why would she care?"

This time her smile was a little sad. "Just one more thing her sister could do that she couldn't. She's had a lifetime of it, Jim."

He looked at her, and thought, Just one more thing.

Including inspiring love in her husband.

He stayed to lunch, and then to dinner, talking more to Shirley Beck in a day than he had to Beverly Chopin in a lifetime. That evening, as they stood on the porch saying good-bye, Shirley said, "Try not to be too hard on her. She may not have given you life, but she raised you to be who you are today. We are who our parents make us."

"Truer words were never spoken," he said, and kissed her good-bye. Norm hugged him, which was one more hug than he had ever received from his father.

He drove straight back to LA, all night and all day. Beverly heard the garage door go up and came out to meet him, her eyes wary.

"Beverly," he said, and walked past her into the house and up the stairs to his room. He tried Kate again on her cell, and when it went to voice mail he called Alaska Airlines and got a seat on the last flight north that evening. It meant an overnight layover in SeaTac, but he didn't care if he spent it stretched out on the floor of the D Concourse. He'd been too long from home.

He hung up and started to pack, aware of but unconcerned by Beverly's presence in the doorway.

"You found her then," Beverly said.

"I did," he said, almost lighthearted.

"I suppose she told you everything."

"Pretty much," he said, and closed his suitcase.

"I suppose you think I should have told you."

"Not necessarily." He put the suitcase on the floor. "Dad didn't tell me, either."

She had expected an attack, and this absence of recrimination disconcerted her.

"Could you have Maria call me a cab?" he said.

She gave him a baffled look and went downstairs. He tried Kate on her cell again, and this time when voice mail kicked in he said, "I'm on my way home, should be back by tomorrow night. I'm hoping you're not answering because you're already there."

He carried his suitcase downstairs. His mother was standing in the hallway, looking irresolute for the first time in his memory. "So you're leaving," she said.

"You don't usually make a habit of stating the obvious," he said.

Her lips tightened. "When will you be back?"

He looked around the hall, so exquisitely decorated and so expensively furnished. So utterly lacking in joy and life. He couldn't think of one good memory he'd had beneath this roof.

He thought of Kate's house, the jumble of books weighing down the shelves, the quilts and pillows scattered all over the floor, the plain wooden dining table heaped with bills and homework and that one lone glove of Johnny's whose mate could never be found. The Beatles and the Black Eyed Peas rocking out of the speakers, the dueling aromas of fresh-baked bread and moose stroganoff, the hum of an approaching snowgo announcing Chick and Mandy for dinner. The near view of shop and cache and spruce trees, the distant view of the Quilaks, that line of ragged giants against the eastern sky.

Kate.

"I'm thinking never," he said.

Her expression didn't change. She was a tough old bird.

"You used your sister to give your husband a son," he said. "And you haven't even asked how she is."

She said nothing, but he could see the hatred and, yes, the fear, too, in her eyes.

"She's retired," he said, "and remarried, and living in Medford, Oregon."

The cab honked out front. "Again, you don't ask, but she was an obstetrician. She earned a fellowship in reproductive endocrinology and infertility." He looked at her for what he knew would be the last time. "She's one of the people credited with inventing and perfecting the in vitro fertilization process." He hefted his bag. "I don't think I have to tell you what her motivation was."

He went to the door, knowing, too, that this would be the last time he passed through it, and feeling only a tremendous relief.

As he climbed into the cab, a copper Hummer with the sale sticker still on it drove up and pulled into the driveway as the cab pulled away from the curb. Through the cab's rear window he saw Methuselah from the reception climb out, dressed in his best come courting suit, with a gaily patterned ascot tied round his throat and a red rose pinned to his lapel.

Jim faced forward again. "Twenty bucks extra if you make LAX in thirty minutes."

"Fifty and I'll get you there in twenty."

"Done."

Jim was pressed back into his seat as the carefully manicured lawns accelerated into a blur of fast-fading memories and no regrets.

He was going home.

Thirty-two

BEN GUNN HAD HOBBLED FORWARD to crouch in the doorway, watching as Kate used more zip ties to immobilize her new visitors. Not very much to Kate's surprise, one turned out to be Sabine, the lady pilot George had hired last summer. "All for love, huh?" Kate said to her.

Sabine's reply was not very ladylike. She lashed out with a foot aimed at Kate's left knee, which Kate nimbly dodged. Before her leg was fully extended Mutt had both paws on Sabine's chest and her muzzle thrust in Sabine's face. Sabine froze, and Kate had her wrists and ankles in zip ties before she exhaled.

"Off," Kate said. Mutt gave a contemptuous bark two inches from Sabine's nose, and jumped to the side. "Guard," Kate said, pointing to Sabine's companion. Mutt trotted around to stand next to him.

Kate picked up the pilot's ankles by the zip tie and hauled her bodily into the cabin. Sabine's head hit the side of the door pretty hard on the way in, and she cursed Kate again.

"Do you kiss your mother with that mouth?" Kate said.

"Hey! Hey, goddammit, get her away from me!"

Kate went back outside to find Mutt squatting over their third uninvited guest, a stream of urine splashing on his face.

"Running water is such a cheerful sound," Kate said. "Don't you think so, Pete?"

Wolf urine being one of the rankest smelling substances in the known universe, Peter Pilz Wheeler, BA (University of Alaska Anchorage), MA (University of Washington), JD (University of Oregon), made no reply, as he was fully occupied with barfing up what had been a pretty substantial breakfast.

Mutt curled a lip at this display of unmanliness. "I know," Kate said, shaking her head. "We're just not up to our usual standard of villain on this case, are we?"

Kate dragged Pete into the cabin by zip tie with the same tender care she had demonstrated on his companion. Mutt padded in behind them and Kate shut the door. "So," she said, beaming around the room. "Welcome to Canyon Hot Springs, all. Generally my guests don't drop in uninvited, but since the springs have been public property for years, I'll let that slide this once. Let me just build up the fire and put the kettle on so we can all get comfortable."

She busied herself with poking up the coals in the stove and shoving in more wood. There was another curse from Sabine. There was a responding snarl. Sabine shut up. "Good girl," Kate said without looking around.

The coals were still hot. The wood caught and the fire began to crackle. Kate took the bucket outside to fill with snow, taking her time. When she came back inside Sabine was whimpering, crouched over a well of blood from one hand, that hand's mitten having been torn free and tossed in a corner.

"Yeah, she is kinda quick," Kate said, pausing to give Mutt a rough caress in passing.

Mutt raised a paw and began to clean the snow from between her toes.

By the time the snow melted the cabin was warm and filled with the aromatic scent of coffee, mixed unfortunately with the faint smell of Mutt's pee, which lingered about the head and shoulders of Lawyer Wheeler.

"Coffee all around?" Kate said. "I know, the sun won't be up for hours, but like they say, the early bird catches the worm." She smiled at Pete and Sabine. They didn't smile back, but they didn't turn down the coffee, either, holding their mugs clumsily in bound hands.

It had been a very early and an unusually active morning and a long time since dinner, and Kate was hungry. She put bacon on to cook and mixed up a batch of biscuit dough. "Here's what I think is going on," she said to the bacon as it began to sizzle.

It went very still in the room behind her.

"My uncle Sam died. He'd lived a long time, and not to quite everyone's surprise, it turns out he left a lot behind." She gave an airy wave with the fork. "Like this homestead." She looked over at Ben, who looked surprised, and nodded. "Oh yeah, he homesteaded Canyon Hot Springs back when he was barely out of school. He was thinking of getting married and settling down."

"Out here?" Ben said.

"Yeah, I know," she said. "But he was a good

son. He did what his mother told him, and she told him to stake up here."

"What's here besides the hot springs?" Ben said.

She bestowed an approving smile on him. "Good question." She spread a dish towel on the floor, dusted it liberally with flour, and patted the dough into a rough circle half an inch thick. She finished her coffee, rinsed out the mug, and used it to cut out the biscuits. She let the bacon drain on a paper towel and put the biscuits in the Dutch oven. She put the lid on and resumed her tale. "Without boring you with a lot of unnecessary detail, it turns out his father was a small-time scam artist and a part-time thief."

She opened the lid and peeked. The biscuits were puffing up nicely. She put the lid back on. "Some of the stuff he walked away with, turns out, was pretty valuable. Again, to make a long story short, he left it all to his son. My uncle Sam. Old Sam Dementieff."

She wiped her mug clean and refilled it with coffee. "My uncle was a pretty tough old bastard, and anyone who tried to take what was his was going to wind up bear bait."

"Your father served with Old Sam and Mac McCullough in Castner's Cutthroats," she said to Ben. "He brought back a lot of stories about Gore Vidal and Dashiell Hammett in the Aleutians. I'm guessing Old Sam wasn't the only buddy to have visited Mac McCullough in the hospital on Adak, or the only buddy he might have introduced to his other good buddy, Pop Hammett." She sat back on her heels, considering. "Meanwhile, back in Ahtna, Old Sam told Jane about the manuscript."

Ben met her eyes, a trace of defiance in his own, and didn't reply.

Kate nodded as if he'd confirmed it. "And Jane let something slip one of those times when you were interviewing her about the old days, something about Hammett writing a story about one of the Cutthroats. Somehow, maybe from something she said or maybe because you learned that Old Sam was one of Jane's regulars at Mrs. Beaton's, you figured out it was Old Sam. Now, Old Sam is too big a dog for you, but he can't live forever. You've got time. So you wait."

She meditated a little. "Shift to the present day. Old Sam dies, and before you can get to the Park, I show up in Ahtna. You panic. You're afraid I'll get to the manuscript before you do. So after she goes to work, you break into Jane's house. And she comes home and catches you at it."

She thought of that tough old Alaskan broad, the life leaching out of her on the floor of her own living room.

Ben said, as if the words were forced out of him, "Where is it? The manuscript?"

"Safe," Kate said.

"It's real, then?" he said in a wondering voice. "It exists?"

"It does," she said. "I've read it. Not a bad yarn."

"'Not a bad yarn'?" Ben said, his voice rising. "You've had an original manuscript by Dashiell Hammett in your hands, and you think it isn't a bad yarn? The guy invented one of the few original American literary genres!"

"I like to read, but I wouldn't set a life against a book, no matter who wrote it," Kate said, her voice deceptively mild.

Ben shut up.

"Backing up a little," Kate said, "a month ago, Old Sam wrote a will." She looked at Pete. "To do this, he went to the only attorney in Ahtna. And it was just the executor and chief heir's bad luck that this same attorney is a scion of the Pilz family."

"What?" Ben said.

She looked at him with amused contempt. "You really aren't much of a journalist, are you, Ben? You can't walk two feet in any direction in Ahtna without tripping over a great story, and you missed out on two of the biggest." She looked back at Pete. The coffee had revived him to the point that he could concentrate on her story, although he looked as if he wished he didn't have to. "Pete is a descendent of Alaskan royalty, on the white side, anyway. He's a grandnephew of

Herman Pilz, a Klondike stampeder who stayed on to found a shipping firm and stick a finger in the same Alaskan pies as Heiman and Bannister and all the rest of the members of the Spit and Argue Club."

"How did you find out?" Pete sounded tired, and no wonder. He'd had a long night, which hadn't ended as planned. And he smelled like wolf pee. Anybody'd be tired after all that.

"P and H donated one of their original coaches to the Bell Museum in Anchorage. There's a photograph of Herman Pilz, Pete Heiman Sr., and P and H's executive director at the ceremony on the coach. The executive director's name was Fritz Wheeler." Kate shrugged and glanced at Ben. "Not that hard to figure out. Every up-and-comer likes to marry into the boss's family. It facilitates promotion." She grinned. "Plus I saw your middle name on all those diplomas hanging on the wall in back of your desk."

The biscuits were a lovely golden brown. She used the spatula to remove them from the Dutch oven, added a little oil to the remaining bacon grease, and waited for it to heat before cracking four eggs into the bottom of the pan. They sizzled pleasantly.

"Pete, I'm guessing you've studied up a little on Park history. I'd even bet you've spent time with the *Ahtna Adit* archives." She looked at Ben, who hesitated, and then gave a reluctant nod.

"Thought so. At some point, you became aware of the theft of the Sainted Mary, and—"

"The what?" Pete said.

Kate rolled her eyes. "Come on, Pete, we're way past that. The Sainted Mary, also known as the Lady of Kodiak, an icon brought to Alaska by a Russian Orthodox missionary named Juvenaly back when Baranov was king."

"I don't know what you're talking about," Pete said.

"What's an icon?" Sabine said.

Kate looked from one to the other for so long she almost forgot the eggs. She moved the Dutch oven from the stove to an upturned pot on the floor. She split the biscuits, buttered them, and layered on the crisp bacon and the eggs, fried a little too hard. She shared them out. "Egg McShugak," she said. "I'd like you all to appreciate how hospitably I'm behaving, considering how hard each and every one of you has tried to kill me over the past two weeks."

Ben gave an inarticulate protest and Pete said, "I did no such thing."

Kate took a bite, and her time in replying. "You," she said to Pete. "I figure you for ambushing me the first time. Since Old Sam came to you to write his will, you were way ahead of the rest of us. The minute you heard he was dead, you were on your way to Niniltna to shake down his cabin.

"You stole the book I was reading, a journal written by the first presiding judge in Ahtna, back in the day. Old Sam stole two of them from the state, before the rest of them were donated to the Bell Museum."

"Two of them?" Pete said, unable to hide his dismay.

"The second was here, in this cabin. Old Sam hid it here for me to find, and I did." She did nothing to stop the grin from spreading across her face. "You know. The one with the map in it."

With one voice, Ben, Sabine, and Pete said, "What map?"

Wheeler dropped his breakfast. Mutt got up and trotted over to clean up his mess. Since most of it was in his lap, Pete sat very, very still until she had nosed out every scrap and returned to her prone position in front of the stove.

Wheeler let loose of the breath he had been holding. "You found a map?"

"Yes." Kate did not allow her eyes to stray to the hiding place Old Sam had so cunningly constructed not five feet above Pete's head. She might need it herself one day. "By the way, I figure there was something in the first journal I didn't get a chance to see. Something Old Sam put there that would have sent me here. What was it?"

"An old black-and-white picture of this cabin, sitting in front of the hot springs," Pete said. "I showed it around, and somebody told me what it was, and where."

Kate nodded. She remembered the collection of black-and-white photos in Old Sam's cabin, now residing in a box in her garage.

"Kate, come on," Pete said. "Did you find it?"

"Did I find the icon, you mean?" Kate shook her head. "Not yet, but I will today."

"What's an icon?" Sabine said again.

Pete kicked her with his bound feet, not gently. "Shut up."

Kate pretended not to notice. She wondered a lot, though.

After breakfast, she suited up.

"How do you expect to get all of us back to town?" Pete said.

"Shut up," Ben said. In spite of his alleged limitations as a journalist, he had written the story about Kate's bringing the Johanson brothers to justice for the front page of the *Ahtna Adit*. He thought he knew how she intended to get them back to town.

"She's going to have to turn us loose," Sabine said.

"Shut up," Ben said. "Really."

Kate opened the door. Mutt got to her feet. "Stay," Kate said. "Guard."

Nobody looked happy about that, especially Mutt, whose narrowed yellow eyes were the last thing Kate saw before the door closed.

The round plastic thermometer attached to the zipper tab of her parka read twenty-two degrees. She cast an anxious glance up at the sky, which was going a pale powder blue. The air on her cheek still felt dry. Reassured, she put on her snowshoes, shouldered the coil of rope and the crowbar, and followed her own trail back up the canyon behind the cabin.

The farther back it went, the higher and narrower it got, with unexpected twists behind outcroppings of bare, jagged rocks that felt like gauntlets thrown down by the Quilaks themselves. Birdsong and the rustling of hare and grouse through the undergrowth ended when the trail ascended above the tree line, and she was surrounded by walls of rock splotched with kinnikinnick. She felt alone, but not lonely.

A movement caught the corner of her eye and she looked around quickly to see a Dall sheep ewe bound over the top of the northern ridge, her white fleece thick as steel wool and her mammoth buttocks jiggling with all the fat she'd stored through the summer.

No, not lonely, and not that alone, either.

The map was not as specific about the location of the last mine as it had been about the first eight. Kate wondered if this was by accident or design. She decided it was probably design. "Just Old Sam's little joke," she said out loud, trying not to sound too bitter. Or maybe Mac McCullough's—

no way to know now. The snow was deeper here, and it was early season snow, newly fallen, not as well packed down as it would be a month or even a week later. Her snowshoes sank down a foot with each step. It made for very slow going. "Should have started at the top and worked my way back," she said out loud.

Kate stood still and took several deep, steadying breaths, and the uncomfortable thumping of her heart eased. She was beginning to wish she had an altimeter along with the thermometer on her zipper tab. The trail had turned steep, but it was still passable. How high up could she be? She was so hemmed in by the encroaching cliffs that she had no idea.

The trail back would be a lot easier. She cast another glance at the sky, still a deceptively innocent blue, the sun not yet high enough in the sky to shine down into the canyon. So long as the snow held off.

She plodded around yet another mini-saddle and stopped, astonished.

It was a level area almost like a mini-plateau. On the north was a sheared slab of solid granite whose weathered surface looked like it hadn't lost a single flake of quartz since before the first coming. On the south . . . she walked a few steps and peered over an edge that fell into an abyss so deep it would have given Wile E. Coyote pause. "Man," she said, and took a prudent step back.

"Where the hell am I?" Now she needed a GPS.

The peaks and glaciers of the southern half of the Quilak Mountains stretched out in front of her, a jumbled mass of rock and ice capped with a discreet line of termination dust that had now reached below the tree line. Somewhere out there, much farther than she could see, the mountains slowly decreased in height to melt reluctantly into rounded foothills. Those foothills subsided into the coastal plain formed by glacial silt and tidal action, occasionally broken here by a glacial erratic and there by a slip-faulted butte.

She turned and looked north, and laughed, more in disbelief than because she found the view funny. Around the corner of the cliff she could just make out the outline of Angqaq, Big Bump, the highest mountain of the Quilaks, slightly west and about twenty-five miles north of where she stood. If she wasn't quite at Big Bump's elevation, she was high enough to where the mountain did not overawe her with its usual arrogant, *noli me tangere* hauteur. "Besides, I've summitted you, and don't you forget it," she said.

She wondered if perhaps she was suffering just a little from high-altitude euphoria.

She continued east until the trail began, unbelievably, to descend. She didn't want to hike back up it, so she returned to the top to try to trace its path with her eyes as far down as she could.

"You're looking into Canada," she said out loud. "You know that, don't you."

It was as if this were some kind of unknown pass through the Quilaks, which simply wasn't possible. A passable trail would have been known to the people who lived in the area, known to her tribe. It would have been a part of song and story. It would have been a route for trade goods, perhaps even for war. One of the reasons Niniltna had been built where it was today was because the site had its back to a literally, impenetrable wall of rock. The old folks had known what they were doing. There was the river for water, salmon, and transportation, and the mountains for defense.

And if it had been known, if it had been used, it would inevitably have been learned by the earliest white explorers, because there just wasn't anywhere those long-nosed roundeyes didn't go. Some U.S. Navy lieutenant with a pack train of mules would have found it and plotted it on a map. Hell, FDR would have sent a CCC team up here to improve it and mark it. By now, it would have been on Dan O'Brian's map, and extreme hikers would have it on their bucket list of trails.

She consulted Old Sam's map, which gave her no clue. The trail simply ended at the ninth cave. "God damn you, old man," she said, exasperated.

Had he even known this trail, if that was what it was?

She dismissed that thought immediately. Old

Sam would have known. There wasn't one square foot of the Park he didn't know.

Was this the real reason his mother had told him to homestead here? Had she, a chief's daughter, known of this pass? Had she foreseen that it might be valuable one day?

Kate looked at the precipitous terrain that rose and fell on all sides, bisected only by this slender thread of a route that at its widest could not have accommodated Kate's pickup. Still, it was wide enough for a man with a pack. Or a mule. Maybe Old Sam was smuggling scotch into Alaska from Canada during prohibition. Although he'd only have been about twelve when the Noble Experiment had been repealed, Kate still wouldn't have put it past him.

She took a last look around before beginning her descent back toward the hot springs. There was no cave here. Maybe there was no ninth cave. Maybe it was only Old Sam's way of showing her the pass, of carrying the knowledge forward in the family. "Crazy old bastard."

She followed the trail she had broken down its switchbackian route, dodging around rocky outcroppings. She was almost to the tree line, about where she had seen the ewe, when a tumble of rock caught her eye. Even beneath its layer of snow it looked just a little too artful, a little too much like the concealing slabs in front of the first eight mine entrances.

It was above a ledge about twelve feet up the north face of the canyon, in a place where the wall below was especially smooth and free of outcroppings for hands and feet. She used her snowshoes to pack down the snow below it, and then sat down and pulled out an extra biscuit, held together with a thick layer of honey butter, and the small thermos of coffee. She forced herself to eat and drink slowly, leaning back against the rock wall.

She felt a lot better when she got back to her feet, and gave the wall beneath the tumble of rock a closer examination. She wasn't a technical climber by any means, but she had the line and a handful of eyebolts she'd found in her garage, and she could tie a slipknot with the best of them. And if she fell it wasn't that far, and there was enough snow to cushion a fall.

Best not to fall, though.

She used the flat end of the crowbar to hammer in the eyebolts one above the other, using each as a staging area to hammer in the next, and so made her way up the surface of the wall to the ledge. She got a knee up over it, saw that it was narrow but not too narrow, and used her arms to pull herself up the rest of the way.

By then she was so annoyed with Old Sam that she wasn't careful how she used the crowbar, jamming in the flat end and levering the slabs of rock away from what, yes, proved to be another entrance, letting them tumble over the side, where they raised smoke signals of snow when they hit.

This adit was smaller than the others, a short, narrow arch, the marks of the cold chisel and the pickaxe easily identifiable, not yet sanded to smoothness by decades of wind and rain and ice. The hood of her parka brushed the top of the arch. Old Sam would have had to stoop.

She pulled out her flashlight.

It wasn't much bigger inside than out. She could stand in the middle of the tunnel and flatten both hands on both sides. About a dozen steps in, though, it opened up into a larger space. Kate played the flashlight around and saw that it was a natural cave, from the lines of the strata probably formed when some softer layer of rock had fractured and fallen between two harder layers. She heard the drip of water, felt the moisture in the air on her cheek. Probably find a spring if she looked for it. She couldn't believe it wasn't frozen solid. She was.

There was nothing more corrosive than water. If Old Sam had left the icon in this cave for her to find, he had better by god have left it in something waterproof.

She spent half an hour covering every square inch of that damn cave, and came up empty.

She didn't believe it.

She couldn't believe it.

She wouldn't believe it.

She went over the cave again, more slowly this time, her face inches from the rock face, quartering the dome of the ceiling with the flashlight, too.

There was nothing there, not one damn thing, other than a few piles of rock left over from when the cave collapsed.

"I will dance on your grave, you old son of a bitch," Kate said, and she would have, too, if the beam from the flashlight hadn't come to rest on one of the piles of talus, hadn't lingered on one rock in particular. It was the same color as the others, an indeterminate gray, at least in this light, but it was larger, about the size of a small cantaloupe, and it had smoother edges than the rocks surrounding it. She crossed the cave floor, keeping the light on it, and bent to pick it up.

It was unexpectedly heavy.

She put the end of the flashlight in her mouth and used both hands. She needed to. It must have weighed twenty pounds.

She stood there, speechless, knowing instantly what it had to be. Mac McCullough's story, laid out in exquisite detail in even more exquisite prose on those frail, onionskin pages. The nuggets on Pete Wheeler's desk. *What's an icon?*

"Son of a bitch," she said. "Wheeler, you're nothing but another fucking gold bug."

She was so lost in thought that she didn't hear the scrabbling at the entrance of the cave until it was too late. She turned, and the beam from her flashlight caught Bruce Abbott's face, framed by the thrown-back hood of his parka. "Give it to me," he said. He was holding a pistol, and it was pointed right at her.

"I really have had it with all the guns people have been pointing at me lately," she said.

He waved the pistol at her. "Give it to me," he said again.

She was holding the rock at her side. He couldn't see it clearly. He couldn't see exactly what she held in her hands. She stuck her foot behind her and let the rock roll down her leg and turned as soon as it hit the ground, scuffing her feet in hopes of muffling the very loud thud it gave when it hit the ground. "Give what to you, Bruce?" she said, holding out empty hands.

"The icon," he said. "You found the map. It has to be here."

"I'm impressed," she said. "I thought you were a city guy. And yet you made it all the way out here, twice. Not bad."

"Give me the icon," he said.

"How did you know about the map?"

"I didn't," he said.

"Ah," Kate said. "Then it was Erland."

She couldn't see his face against the light coming from the cave entrance, but there was a distinct tremor in his voice. "I don't know what you're talking about."

"I wonder how he knew about it," Kate said. "His father, perhaps?"

He waved the pistol at her again. "Get back. You dropped something. I want to see what it is."

"Okay." She moved to the other side of the cave.

He edged around the perimeter of the cave toward the rockfall, pistol held on her at all times.

Amused, she said, "I'm not armed, Bruce."

He reached the pile of rock and kicked it apart with his boot. The smaller rocks scattered. The rock she had been holding stayed put. He didn't notice. "Where is it?" he said.

"The icon?" she said. "I don't know, Bruce. It isn't here, that's for damn sure."

The flat veracity of her answer stumped him. "It has to be here," he said at last. "Why else would you come back up here?"

"I think Old Sam was playing a little joke on all of us, Bruce," she said. "He left me a map. Here, look for yourself." She unzipped her parka and reached inside.

"Stop! Don't move!" He took a hasty step forward, raising the pistol.

She held up both hands, palms out. "I'm just reaching for the map, Bruce, that's all. I was telling you the truth. I'm not armed."

She could hear him breathing fast in the silence of the little cave. "Slowly," he said, "very, very slowly."

And so she very, very slowly extracted the map from the inside pocket of her parka. She held it out to him.

He stepped forward, reaching for it with his free hand. She watched the barrel of the pistol. His hand closed around the map and the barrel dropped, and in that same moment she took a step forward and grabbed the wrist of his gun hand in both of hers. She took another step, turning her back to him, and bent over, bending her legs, pulling him with her.

He was taken by surprise and lost his balance. He started to fall on her. As he did, she straightened her legs with a snap, still holding on to his wrist. His arm acted as a fulcrum and he made an almost perfect somersault, landing on his back with a thud that shook the cave.

Through all this he managed to hang onto the pistol. It went off, a big boom in a small room, followed by the sound of ricochets, two, three, it might have been four. Kate stood there, petrified, afraid that her impromptu plan was going to lead to an impromptu death.

Which it almost did, because the bullet's multiple impact caused mini-landslides all over the interior surface of the cave. Rock fell behind her, to her left, pieces fell from the side of the tunnel where it led into the cave. More rock fell from the roof, filling the air with dust and their hoods and hair with grit and sand and pebbles.

This was more than Erland was paying Bruce for and he let out a sound somewhere between a yelp and a squeal and was up and hobbling for the entrance.

Kate paused long enough to scoop up the heavy rock and stuff it in the pocket of her parka, where it knocked heavily against her knee as she ran down the tunnel. The rumbling falls of rock grew in size and strength and intensity behind her until it sounded as if the entire side of the mountain was caving in. Just short of the tunnel's mouth she was enveloped in a cloud of dust that stung her eyes and obscured her vision. She threw out her arms so that her fingers grazed the tunnel's walls and flung herself forward with such impetus she almost walked off the edge of the cliff face.

She stood there, coughing and blinking. When her vision cleared she saw that Bruce had regained the foot of the wall and was scrambling into snowshoes.

"Dumb fuck," she said. "Who shoots off a gun in a cave? You could have gotten us both killed."

He heard her voice and cast up one haunted glance before heading down the canyon at a spanking pace. Kate paused for a moment to admire his form. If Bruce Abbott could run on snowshoes, he was a lot more competent in the backwoods than she had previously supposed.

Kate removed the rock from her pocket, set it just inside the adit, and kicked some rockfall over it. Bruce had been in such a hurry he hadn't bothered to pull the eyebolts or untie the line. She took her time coming down. There was only one way out of the canyon, and if it came to that she could find him in Anchorage. She knew who he was working for, and what he wanted. Even if he went to ground, Max had baited him into a trap for her once, and she had no doubt that he could do it again. She strapped on her own snowshoes and followed at a more leisurely pace.

She made the cabin in good time and found Mutt in a considerable state of excitement but still on guard. "Good girl," Kate said. "Must have been torture for you when you heard him go by."

Mutt gave a half shake that was the equivalent of a shrug. It's what we professionals do. Kate surveyed her three prisoners. "What the hell am I going to do with the three of you while I go catch me another bad guy?"

They offered her no suggestions. In the end, she tossed everything that might be conceivably used for a sharp edge into a garbage bag and nailed the door of the cabin shut behind her. "Oh, stop whining," she said. "Ben's got one hand free, there's enough wood to see you through the night, and I left you the fire extinguisher in case you somehow set yourselves on fire. I'll try to be back to get you before then."

She dumped the garbage bag into the trailer, which she did not hitch to her snowgo. She'd topped off the fuel in the Arctic Cat when she arrived, and this time no one had put a bullet hole into the tank. More fool them. The engine started at a touch and Kate grinned at Mutt, who was quivering with eagerness to see some action. "Let's blow this pop stand, girlfriend!"

Mutt leaped up behind her and Kate hit the gas.

She took the first dogleg with caution, making sure Bruce wasn't waiting for her with a baseball bat, and found instead his tracks, and another snowgo, this one the Ski-Doo Rev XP Herbie had told her about, which undoubtedly belonged to one of the parties presently incarcerated in the Canyon Hot Springs Correctional. At a guess she'd say Pete. A lawyer could conceivably afford this sled, a journalist never. She almost missed the snowgo belonging to the second party, another Ski-Doo, although this one was so old it was nearly an antique. Had to be Ben's. It had been pushed into a clump of thick brush. If it had snowed a little between the time he had parked it and the time she had seen it, it would have been invisible.

She continued. Bruce was in headlong flight. There were some corners where he only left the track of one ski in the snow. "Moving at a pretty good clip," Kate said over her shoulder to Mutt. "I wonder if he knows how he's going to get out of the Park?"

She laughed and hit the throttle as they came

down into the last straight stretch before the last dogleg and leaned into the turn.

Not so dumb, after all, Bruce Abbott, because that's where he was waiting for her, not with a baseball bat in hand but a solid piece of deadfall about an inch in diameter. He timed it pretty well, too, so that she ran right into the swing he was bringing forward with both hands.

He was partially foiled when it caught the top of Kate's windshield, which deflected his stroke. It wasn't enough to miss her entirely, but it allowed her to take the brunt of the blow across her top of her head, which was covered with her parka hood, which further cushioned the blow.

Not, however, enough that she wasn't flung backward from her snowgo, carrying Mutt with her. She landed on Mutt, hard, the breath knocked out of both of them.

She lay on her back, still conscious, blinking up at the sky, and then was shoved to one side when Mutt scrabbled out from beneath her. She barked at Kate—*Get up! Get on your feet, soldier!*—and made an abortive leap toward their attacker. Kate could hear the engine of his machine roar to life and the machine head away at full throttle.

Mutt leapt back to her side and barked right in her face. *Get up! The bad guy's getting away! I could be tearing him a new asshole and here you are lazing around on your back! Get UP!*

Amazing the articulation and eloquence Mutt could achieve with one sound.

"You know what?" Kate said to the cold gray sky overhead. "I'm getting too old for this shit." Her head was starting to hurt. Again.

Mutt wasn't having any of it. She sank her teeth into the sleeve of Kate's parka, set her hindquarters, and began to pull. Kate slid willy-nilly across the snow in brief, powerful tugs.

"Mutt," she said.

Yank.

"Knock it off."

Yank.

"Just give me a minute. I'll be okay."

Yank.

"Mutt." She didn't even have the wherewithal to summon up a good bellow.

Mutt, with quicker recuperative powers, had no such problem. She dropped her mouthful of parka long enough to bark another command. *Shut up and breathe!*

This time she grabbed the leg of Kate's bibs and hauled.

This time Kate just went with it, watching the clouds sail by overhead, and the occasional alder limb revolve, bumping over hummocks covered with ice, sliding between overhanging bushes that dropped snow on her face, becoming a little too well-acquainted with the edges of rocks. "Ouch," she thought she said once.

640

The sky steadied and she realized that Mutt had hauled her to where her snow machine had stopped. Amazingly, the engine was still ticking over. With Mutt on his tail, Bruce hadn't had time to grab the key or disable the engine. Kate even found a moment to be grateful that his pistol had been buried in the cave-in.

Mutt let go of the leg of her bibs and pounced on her head, using her teeth to pull Kate's hood back, after which she gave Kate's face a thorough washing, in between minatory yelps and yips. Kate got tired of the yelping and yipping a lot sooner than she tired of the tongue bath, soon enough to discover that her arms still worked. She shoved Mutt off her. "It's okay, girl. I'll be okay."

Mutt wedged her snout under Kate's shoulder and shoved. She managed to sit upright. The earth took a revolution around the sun at a heretofore unheard-of pace.

Kate closed her eyes, which were starting to feel a little puffy. When she opened them a moment later, the world and she were both a little steadier, enough so that she could rummage in her pack, which was still on her back, for a bottle of water. She emptied it and felt the better for it, enough so that she could hoist a leg up over the seat of the snowgo.

There, she had handlebars to hold her up.

She felt her face. There was a lump coming up on her forehead, right at her hairline.

"Goddammit," she said, and felt a surge of rage, which filled her with a probably illusory energy. "I was just getting over the last set of black eyes."

Mutt barked.

"All right," Kate said, "get on."

This time she kept the throttle all the way down, and if anyone had been inclined to try to follow her tracks they would have seen that on this trip down the mountain her snowgo was more often airborne than it was earthbound. She took the straight path wherever and whatever it offered. If there was a ledge she jumped it, if there was a field of moguls she flew from top to top barely touching their crowns. She barreled through blueberry bushes and willow thickets alike, she frightened the life out of three peacefully browsing moose, and she saved an entire colony of shrews from the excavations of an arctic fox when she scooped him up with her front left ski and bore him a quarter of a mile before he finally regained enough sense to roll off. There must have been times, she thought later, that her speed had achieved something that could have launched her into low earth orbit. Certainly she had set some kind of land speed record that Arctic Cat would forever mourn they had not been present to record. Those parts of her face exposed to the wind felt frozen solid. She could hear nothing but the roar of the engine, and she could feel nothing but the pressure of Mutt against her back, teeth locked in a death grip on a mouthful of parka so she wouldn't fall off.

The edge of the high had moved far enough north that the setting sun was framed between horizon and the edge of the clouds the high was pushing northwest. Between its blinding rays, the new head wound, and the lingering cave dust, Kate's vision wasn't what it should have been, and she didn't acquire Bruce as a target until he was ten miles out of Niniltna. He had the faster vehicle but she was the better driver, and it took her only five more miles to close to within a hundred feet. He knew they were there and hunched down behind his handlebars, but he was getting all he could get out of his Polaris and he lost even more ground by panicking.

Kate drew up slowly, inexorably, level with his snowgo. "Go!" Kate said, and Mutt sprang, aiming straight for him.

He hauled on his handlebars and veered right. Mutt missed him by inches. She was going so fast her momentum sent her skidding for fifty feet before she managed to scramble up and give chase. In the meantime he'd straightened out and was back on course for Niniltna, the tiny houses of which were just now becoming visible against the snow. Kate didn't know what he thought he was going to do once he got there.

She pulled out the line she had taken from the cliff face and stuffed in the pocket of her parka.

There was one slip knot left in the end of it. She needed her right hand for the throttle. She tugged off her left mitten with her teeth, tossed it over her shoulder, and pulled the slipknot loose and large and let the loop dangle from her left hand.

She was coming up on Bruce's left now, pushing him off course, into the path of Mutt, who was coming up on his right, a flattened, elongated gray shape skimming over the snow. All his concentration was on Kate so he didn't see Mutt until the last minute, and when he did he pulled instinctively to his right to avoid crashing into her.

Kate, teeth bared in a grin savage with joy, dropped the loop around his shoulders. She whipped the loose end of the line quick around the handlebars and grabbed the handlebars in both hands and braced herself as her snow machine passed his.

Behind her there was a yell and her whole snowgo seemed to halt in midair, the engine revving to the decibel level of a 737 as the track revolved with nothing to push against. There was a loud thud when Bruce hit the ground, followed by another as the Arctic Cat hit the snow again in something approximating a controlled crash.

Kate ran at full throttle all the way to town and right down the main street, Bruce Abbott yelling and cursing at the end of the rope, dragging him past the Grosdidiers' clinic, past Auntie Edna's house, past the Riverside Café, past Bingley Mercantile, around the corner and up the hill past Auntie Joy's and Emaa's and Old Sam's.

All the way to the trooper post, where she slowed down and pulled in and finally, at last, let the Arctic Cat's engine die.

Mutt came trotting up to take Kate's temperature with her nose and give her a hearty Well done! lick, before taking up station next to Bruce, who was still cursing.

Kate dismounted and straightened her back, a little surprised that she could. She looked up at the porch, where an astonished Maggie stood staring down at her.

Kate pushed her hood back.

"Jesus," Maggie said, and actually took a step back.

Kate couldn't imagine what she looked like, but knew the grin she gave Maggie was lopsided in the extreme.

"I ride an old paint, I lead an old dan," she said, and laughed.

1965

Amchitka

Sam was in Kodiak for the Good Friday Earthquake, in the middle of delivering a load of king crab to Whitney-Fidalgo. He heard yells on the dock. When he looked out of the wheelhouse to see who'd fallen overboard, he saw instead the massive wooden dock rippling like waves, first in one direction and then in other. It looked like the piano keyboard in a Tom and Jerry cartoon.

When he broke free from his stupefaction he slammed out of the wheelhouse and slid down the ladder to the deck. The brailer was just coming out of the hold, the winch on the boom reeling it up to dump the crab into a tote on the dock.

"Attention on deck!" he yelled at the top of his voice. "You, let loose the bow line! You, get on the stern!"

A chorus of voices followed him back to the ladder. "What's up with the boss?" "What's going on, Sam?" "Hey, look at the dock!"

He jumped forward and yanked the pucker rope. The crab cascaded back into the hold.

"Earthquake, and it's a bad one! We're getting away from the dock!" He shoved a deckhand who was staring at the dock, stupefied. "Now, not this time tomorrow! Move your asses before I drop-kick the bunch of you over the side!"

The deck boss materialized next to him. "Sam, I live here. My wife and kids are here. I've got to go find them."

"Go ahead, if you think you can get up that ladder," Old Sam said.

The deck boss turned in time to see the last bolt pop out of the steel ladder and the ladder drop into the water a hand's breadth away from the *Freya*'s hull.

Sam slammed into the wheelhouse, slapped the engine into life, and had the bow pulling away from the piling as the bow line slid free. The deckhand on the stern line wasn't as quick and the rope burned his hands when Sam went all ahead full.

All around them boats, from thirty-foot seiners to hundred-foot crabbers, were pulling away from floats and docks and moorages and steaming north northeast. Sam didn't breathe again until Woody Island was on their stern. He kept the *Freya* offshore north of Spruce Island for the next twenty-four hours, the whole crew spending their off-watch hours huddled around the big marine radio bolted to the wall at the foot of the chartroom bunk.

There was no telephone service left in Southcentral Alaska. The Anchorage International Airport tower had fallen over. The Million Dollar Bridge fifty miles north of Cordova had collapsed. Twenty miles of the Seward Highway was below water. Later they would hear that nine people had been killed outright during the earthquake, a hundred and six in the tidal wave that struck nine hundred miles of Alaska coastline afterward. To the *Freya* and the other boats who had made it out of the Kodiak harbor, the tidal wave had been a long, hard, rolling swell that rocked their hulls and moved on, but some coastal villages and towns like Seward and Valdez were heavily damaged, and some villages, like Chenega in Prince William Sound and Afognak north of Kodiak had been completely destroyed. In some places the land had sunk five and a half feet, causing high tide floods. In others, the land had risen thirty feet, putting docks forever out of reach of high water.

By Sunday morning the deck boss was beside himself with worry over his family and they were getting close to the point of no return on fuel. The *Freya* headed back to port.

The first indication of what they would see when they got back to town was the house floating out to sea on the ebb tide. Two stories, for the most part intact, the tidal wave had simply lifted it off its foundations and carried it off. It was only the first. Sam, his jaw tight, stayed alert, picking his way through the detritus of totes, lengths of lumber, refrigerators, a red tricycle tangled in a fishing net. It was as if the entire town had been washed away.

Which was pretty much what it looked like when they got up close. The earthquake had reduced the town to a game of pickup sticks, and the tidal wave had washed half of them out to sea. There was no dock left. Sam hailed a drifter he knew to ferry the deck boss to the beach so he could go find his family.

The other three deckhands were from Seldovia, Valdez, and Seattle. The Seattle man opted off in Kodiak, going ashore with the deck boss. Sam got some fuel off a crabber who'd just finished topping off the tank when the quake hit. The *Freya* headed back out to sea, on a course for Seldovia, where he knew there was a fuel dock. Two days later they steamed into the bay. The town looked pretty much intact, except for the small boat harbor, which was being towed back in one float at a time by the fishing fleet. He refueled, emptied his hold of king crab for pennies on the dollar, dumped his Seldovia hand, and headed for Valdez.

The tidal wave had damaged Valdez so badly that three years later it was moved to a new location. He moored the *Freya* to an anchor buoy offshore, and allowed his Valdez deckhand to move his family on board since their house had been first destroyed by the earthquake and then washed away by the tsunami.

And then he headed up the Richardson Highway, hitching a series of rides until he got to Ahtna. The Interior town was shaken but mostly intact. He spent the evening with Jane Silver, who fed him a large meal of moose steaks and mashed potatoes, and at first light next morning he was on the road for Niniltna with a pair of snowshoes he borrowed from the local banker and a pillowcase full of smoke fish and fry bread over his shoulder. It was a slushy trip, but he was made welcome at homesteads along the way. Everyone was anxious for news, and the expression on Joyce's face when she opened the door of her cabin to see him standing there made the whole odyssey worthwhile. For the first time since before the war, she was moved to a spontaneous show of affection, throwing her arms around him and holding him close. God, it felt good.

He slept next door in Ekaterina's spare room and spent the next month chopping wood and hunting for Joy and Ekaterina and Edna and Viola and Balasha, although the few moose he found were thin and stringy. "No matter," Balasha said. "Anything tender you boil it long enough." By then all five women had lost their husbands through death, divorce, or abandonment. They worried more about the need to send the children away to school, and the subsequent decline of the village's population. Every other house was empty and beginning to deteriorate both from the depredations of scavengers and lack of care. He'd never seen the town looking so shabby.

Joyce had gone to the same school in Cordova as Sam had, and she spoke English better than he did, but he noticed that the other women's speech patterns were overtaking her own. She was misplacing modifiers and displacing clauses, and for the first time he heard someone refer to the women collectively as "the aunties."

It was also the first time he remembered anyone outside of the Cutthroats calling him Old Sam. Well, what the hell, he sure enough felt old enough that April.

Face it. He'd felt old ever since that night in Anchorage.

"You still have the manuscript?" he said one evening.

"Same place like always," she said.

Neither of them looked at the wooden armoire lurking in the corner, repository of one of the best-kept secrets in Niniltna.

What the hell, he thought again. What was one more?

He left in May to see to his boat, and got a job ferrying supplies for the U.S. Navy, back on the Aleutian Chain again but this time way the hell and gone to Amchitka, which was damn near all the way to Russia. He was there on October 29, 1965, when they detonated Long Shot, the first of three underground nuclear tests. He sat offshore on the *Freya*, wondering if a giant mushroom-shaped cloud was going to rise up over the island and roll out over the water and kill him dead where he sat. He didn't much care.

He'd hired his first woman deckhand this trip, a Norwegian Eyak from Cordova with a set net site on Alaganik Bay. Her name was Mary Balashoff. She laughed a lot, and after a while she was laughing in his bed. He told himself he didn't deserve her, but it didn't stop him from enjoying her. And slowly, steadily, that night in Anchorage let go of him, so that he didn't think about it more than once a day, then more than once a week. When a month had passed during which he realized he had not thought of the sight of Emil's smile, of Erland's voice yelling, "Dad! Dad!," he began to feel that life might be worth living after all.

He had found the map in the icon, where Mac had hidden it, probably one step ahead of the Pinkerton agents. Pete Pappardelle had not found it, and either Emil hadn't found it or, more likely, he had found it and, finding it, had taken a characteristic pleasure in retaining a reminder of the man whose life he had taken without shame or remorse. Old Sam put it back, hid the icon, and got on with it.

Mary was still with him three years later when he loaded most of a drill rig from Nikiski onto the *Freya*, lashing to the deck what he couldn't take apart and put into the hold. While he didn't see anyone he knew, he was relieved when they pulled out, even if the *Freya* was riding a little too close to her trim line.

They lucked out with the weather. It was almost flat calm all the way down to Unimak Pass, a thing Sam had never seen before in his life, after which they turned right and went past the Pribilofs and Nunivak and St. Matthew and St. Lawrence and Big and Little Diomede, all the way up through the Bering Strait to the Chukchi Sea and the Arctic Ocean, to land their cargo in Prudhoe Bay, on August 16, just a couple of miles from where the discovery well had been brought in the previous March. Sam was curious in spite of himself, and hitched a ride to the BP Base Camp, which high-sounding name resolved into a bunch of ATCO trailers and a couple of drill rigs, peopled with a bunch of men who hadn't shaved in a long time. He hadn't known such flat land existed in Alaska. There was only the barest hint of mountains on the southern horizon. He'd never seen so many birds, either, what seemed like seventeen different species of ducks and all the species of geese there were. He thought of the aunties' freezers, and his hands itched for a shotgun.

"Good fishing in the rivers, too," the redheaded radioman said, and offered him a beer and a ringside seat for *Tony's Nine O'Clock News at Ten*, a radio show comprised of news snippets read off a wire report, what music was available in the form of records played on a turntable with a scratchy needle, and a lot of bad and mostly unrepeatable jokes. It was an impressive example of what people would sit still for when they were that lonely, that bored, and that far from home.

Upon returning home safely, Old Sam took the *Freya* into Seward and put her into dry dock for some much-needed repairs. Mary wanted to go to Anchorage. He most emphatically did not, so she took the train up without him. He spent the interim perched on a stool in the Yukon Bar, drinking beer and thinking.

When Mary returned from Anchorage he said, "I'm going home."

In the last twenty-five years there wasn't much of Alaska's coastline he hadn't cruised, and he'd put away enough money that he wasn't nervous about his future even after he paid off the *Freya*'s repairs and maintenance. "Since they outlawed fish traps with the statehood," he said, "the fish are back in Alaganik Bay, and there's enough processors in Cordova to keep the price interesting. I'm going to refit the *Freya* for tendering, and spend the summers picking up fish and delivering them to Cordova, and winters in Niniltna."

"Yeah," she said. "Actually, I was going to tell you. I got a letter from my dad. He says none of the other kids want the family set net site on Alaganik Bay. I do."

"Uh-huh," he said. "Well, I'd be just offshore."

"Imagine that. You don't want to get married or anything, do you?"

"Hell, no," he said. "You?"

"I'd shoot myself first," she said, and laughed.

He did love that laugh.

So he'd sat out the pipeline years in what now, after ANCSA and the d2 lands bill, was coming to be called the Park. He bought an old cabin on the Kanuyaq River two houses up from Joyce's and wired it for electricity so he could read the books he was beginning to collect. Summers he spent on the *Freya*, delivering fish from Alaganik to Cordova for a penny a pound. When he wasn't hunting or splitting wood or completing honey-do lists for Ekaterina and the aunties, winters he spent exploring the Park that had been created around them, penetrating the fastness of the Quilak Mountains, following the creeks and rivers from their sources to their mouths, tracking the herds of caribou. He regained all the woodcraft he had put on hold when he had left the Park so long ago, and learned more, honing his carpentry and woodworking skills and slowly collecting a set of more and better tools. Long winters were made for that kind of thing.

He went to Canyon Hot Springs, and added the cabin and its outbuildings to Mac's map. After that, he mostly stayed away, the hope and love of the young man who had built that cabin still too strong, too immediate, for him to tolerate for long.

In the fullness of time Stephan Shugak married Zoya Shashnikof and their daughter Ekaterina Ivana was born. Old Sam took to her right off, and when her parents died so young, he stepped forward to share the privilege with Abel and the rest of the village of teaching her how to hunt and shoot and trap and fish. She was the child he had never had.

There were times he didn't think he deserved as much satisfaction as he had received in his life, a good boat, a good woman as independent as she was strong, a daughter so worthy of love and pride. There were times when he woke up from a dream of Emil Bannister laying on the floor of his study, his own blood drowning that gloating smile.

At those times he would force himself up out of his bed and down the ladder to brew himself a mug up, facing down his ghosts with a dose of caffeine and a taciturn front, the sweat of fear drying along his spine.

It seemed a small price to pay.

Thirty-four

BERNIE'S.

The belly dancers were out and in full regalia, castanets clicking, flirtatious glances beneath spangled veils tucked into knit caps, some of them wearing long underwear under sheer skirts. Pastor Bill's congregation, which these days just fit at the big round table, held hands and sent up a silent prayer for help in leading the heathens to the path of righteousness. It was the wrong time of year for Big Bumpers, more's the pity. Kate would have enjoyed watched Bernie force feed them Middle Fingers.

The four aunties sat at their usual table in the corner, the current quilt spread over their laps. Their number had been augmented by one this evening. Annie Mike was sitting between Auntie Vi and Auntie Joy, her needle flashing quickly and surely through some bright red scrap of fabric. She had smiled at Kate when she came in but had gone directly to take her place in the quilting circle.

An auntie in training.

Tall, mostly black men chased a basketball across the big television hanging from the ceiling. At the table beneath sat a group of old fart Park rats, talking trash on every pass and play. They looked diminished, somehow, without Old Sam in their midst.

On the other hand, Howie Katelnikof was nowhere in sight, which made for a good night in Kate's book. She wondered where Willard was, and decided not to borrow trouble.

The other big change was that the jukebox was gone, banished to that great old roadhouse in the sky, leaving a large rectangle of floor space much lighter than the surrounding wood. It had been replaced by a sound dock with an iPod, attached to a series of Bose speakers mounted on the walls, through which even Kate had to admit if only to herself Bon Jovi was presently keeping pretty good faith.

"I can't believe you got rid of the jukebox," she said.

"I heard you the first two times," Bernie said, squeezing a quarter of a lime into her Diet Sprite, her sinful second in half an hour. "Admit it, this sounds better. And it's a lot less temperamental, and it takes up one hell of a lot less room. Plus I get to make up my own playlists. There is no downside here."

Kate tried not to pout into her drink. Bernie ripped open another package of beef jerky and tossed it to Mutt, who had poked her head up over the counter in hopes of further largesse. She caught it neatly in her teeth and retired once more to the floor next to Kate's stool.

"You'll spoil her," Kate said.

Bernie smiled. "She's worth it." Tall, thin to the point of emaciation, with what hair he had left gathered in a ponytail at the nape of his neck, Bernie looked the same, and yet not. He was still suffering the loss of his wife and son. He was still coaching the high school basketball teams, Johnny had told Kate, with only a little less than Bernie's usual ferocity. Her eyes strayed over his head to the sign tacked to the wall. "Free Throws Win Ball Games."

His eyes followed hers. "They still do." He looked at her. "They always will."

The door opened and Petey Jeppsen came in, a wooden box beneath one arm. He spotted Kate and threaded his way through the tables. "Got something for you." He set the box on the bar next to her. Bon Jovi segued to Foreigner and urgent sax licks.

"That the compass?"

"Yeah. Hey, Bernie."

"Hey, Petey." Bernie eyed Petey with some caution. The last time Petey had been in the Roadhouse, he and his mother had been shooting up the place. He'd been banned from the Roadhouse ever since, over four years now.

Petey gave him a wry smile. "I come in peace. Can I have a beer?"

Bernie hesitated, and then made up his mind. No one could ever call him unwilling to give a guy another chance. Petey got his beer, and Bernie went off to tell the latest waitress everything she was doing wrong, which since it was her first night was most everything she was doing. A bleached blonde with a spiderweb tattoo on the back of her neck, she looked halfway intelligent, and the next time the group of Suulutaq miners at table number five took turns pinching her ass she would call Bernie over instead of slapping one and dumping a pitcher of beer on another.

Eric Clapton mourned the loss of Layla and was chased offstage under pressure by David Bowie and Queen. The dance floor, larger now by the size of one jukebox, was flooded with customers, about half of them single guys dancing, or a reasonable facsimile thereof, with themselves. Several of them were casting languishing glances Kate's way. Kate readied herself to repel boarders, another unwelcome change. In a place where everybody knows your name, they also ought to know you don't dance unless it's in a circle at a potlatch. Since Suulutaq started up, there just weren't enough Park rats of the female persuasion to go around. Not that there ever had been.

On the other hand, it meant Keith Gette and Oscar Jimenez could dance together without occasioning comment. Not that they ever did anyway.

"I heart the Park," Kate said.

Petey followed her eyes to Oscar and Keith, who were swaying together in a slow dance regardless of the music. Keith had his head tucked into Oscar's shoulder, and Oscar had his thumbs in Keith's back pockets. Petey gave a noncommittal grunt, which was better than calling them godless sexual deviants, which was what the old Petey Jeppsen would have done.

Kate raised the hinged lid of the box and peered inside at the brass compass. "I'll have to get some brass polish. Old Sam always made sure she shined." She looked at him. "You got something to replace her?"

"Hell, Kate, I got a GPS. Come to that, I got two."

He seemed taller somehow, and broader of shoulder and infinitely more mature. Owning property could do that for you. "Well, you need a compass," she said, and nodded at the box. "It's just going to sit around my house collecting dust."

For a moment he looked tempted, and then shook his head. "Old Sam wanted you to have her. He said so."

"He told you?"

"Yeah, last summer in Alaganik." A little awkwardly, he added, "He didn't tell me he was leaving me the *Freya* then. That's . . . I don't think I would have believed him, Kate." He looked at his bottle. "I'm not sure I believe it now."

"Better start," Kate said.

His smile was fleeting. "Anyway, he said he wanted you to have the compass. I couldn't take it. Old Sam's ghost would rise up and hang me from the boom by my testicles."

"Probably would," Kate said, and grinned. He grinned back, and they touched glass to bottle in salute to the old fart.

The door opened and Susie Kompkoff came in, her face glowing from the cold.

"Excuse me," Petey said, and slid from his stool to join her at a table.

"Something going on there?" Bernie said, but before she could answer, CCR started rolling down that river and there was a whoop fit to raise the roof and Bobby rolled out on the dance floor in his wheelchair with his wife in his lap. She hopped to her feet and he took her hands and they began some intricate dance that integrated rock steps with wheelie pops and underarm turns.

CCR melted into Three Dog Night exhorting all the girls to hide their hearts. Bobby and Dinah never missed a beat.

Dan O'Brian pulled up a stool and gave Mutt a good scratch between the ears.

"Dan," Kate said.

"Kate," Dan said. "I looked into the title of the Canyon Hot Springs homestead."

Kate's spine stiffened. "Yeah?"

"Yeah. And I'm going to look into it a little more, but I think it's yours."

Kate relaxed a little. "I think it is, too."

He looked serious, an expression she was not accustomed to seeing on his broad, freckled face. "I'd like the chance to talk you into selling it to the Parks Service," he said. "Let us incorporate it into the Park."

Kate thought of the narrow pass that threaded its way up through the mountains and crossed the border into Canada. "I'm sorry, Dan," she said. "It's part of my family history. It isn't for sale, at any price, not to the Parks Service." She looked at him. "And I can promise you, not to anyone else, either."

He looked a little wary. "What will you do with it?"

Kate smiled. "Nothing. Not one damn thing."

His face relaxed into a broad, relieved smile.

The spiderwebby barmaid returned to load up her tray and departed again.

Ruthe Bauman came in, stamping snow from her feet, and sat down next to Kate. "Beer and a bump," she said to Bernie, and to Kate, "How you doing?"

"Better," Kate said.

"Good." She tossed back the whiskey and followed it by a long pull of beer. "Old Sam told me you might come asking, and that if you did I was to tell you his father's name."

Kate, glass half raised, said, "What?"

Ruthe nodded. "So I did." She clinked her glass

to Kate's. "Here's one for the old fart. Won't be the last." She got up and pulled a chair next to the quilting circle. Not into the circle, not without invitation, but near enough to hear the conversation, contribute the occasional comment. Kate saw the aunties exchange a look.

Another auntie in training? Or Ruthe making peace because she was the one Dan had tapped to write down the Park's history? Both, maybe.

Coldplay drew a yellow line. Kate felt a cold draft of air. The noise in the bar fell to a muted level, then ceased entirely. She turned to see who had that effect on the Roadhouse besides herself.

He was out of uniform, dressed in jeans worn white at the seams and a bomber-style jacket in a blue that almost matched his eyes. Almost, because nothing was as blue as those eyes, which were looking straight at her, steady, questioning.

Mutt was on her feet, ready, willing, and able to render an appropriately besotted greeting, but something in Kate's attitude made her pause. She looked from Jim to Kate and back again, her tail upright but absent of motion.

Kate slid from the stool and walked toward him. The crowd parted before her.

He had a few seconds to gain a confused impression of Kate's eyes enhanced by a Technicolor rainbow of surrounding colors before, without breaking stride and in the same seamless motion that had begun at the bar, she made a single leap and landed with her legs wrapped around his waist. She looped her arms around his neck and swooped down for a kiss that took the breath of everyone watching.

For one startled moment he didn't move, and then he grabbed her ass and settled her firmly against him without breaking the kiss, and turned around and carried her outside.

It was the closest Mutt ever came to getting her tail caught in the door.

The next morning Kate woke up to find him grinning down at her. "You're glowing," he said.

"I am not," she said, trying to roll out of bed.

He wrestled her back into his arms. "Are too." He kissed her, which evolved into something else that went on long enough for Johnny to leave for school.

"Which was your plan all along," she said.

"You know my methods, Watson," he said, watching her very fine ass head into the bathroom without him. This was obviously a gross miscarriage of relationship justice, so he padded after her. He pulled back the shower curtain and was instantly jealous of the water coursing down her upturned face, her body. This was not to be borne. He stepped into the tub. She smiled without opening her eyes.

Breakfast was damp and interrupted often enough that the caribou sausage fried hard to the pan. Fortunately, there was bread for toast and butter and honey to go on it, and an unopened bag of Tsunami Blend for coffee. "Did you order this?" he said.

"No," she said, "it was the coffee fairy."

"Did you order it for me?"

"No," she said, "for the three other guys I took up with while you were gone."

They ate on the couch, leaning against opposite arms, legs entwined. Mutt had scraped the quilt into a pile and was sitting with her butt to the fireplace, yellow eyes fixed adoringly on Jim's face as he told Kate the story of his trip south. She made him bring out his father's writing case and show it to her.

"Why did he want you to know?" she said, her hands caressing the silken wood.

"I don't know," he said. "Probably wanted me to know why my mother disliked me so much."

She looked at him.

"She did, Kate," he said. "She does. And she was jealous as hell of my relationship with my father. She interfered in it whenever she could. Dad wasn't exactly affectionate, it wasn't his style, but I knew he cared. And I knew she didn't. I'd always figured it was because I ruined her figure. Now I know I didn't even do that."

"What's she like?" Kate said. "The sister? Uh, your birth mother?"

"I only spent a day with her, but okay. Very

much the doc. Smart, disciplined, analytical." He remember a warm embrace, the firm press of lips on his cheek. "She's got a heart, though."

"And she has kids of her own."

"One girl, one boy."

"So you have siblings."

He shrugged. "If I want to, yeah."

"Maybe they'll come visit."

"Haven't even met them, Kate."

"There are people in the world who share your DNA," she said. "That's not nothing."

"I don't know them," he said. "Be fine if they come. Be fine if they don't." He put his mug and saucer on the floor and reached forward to remove hers and set them on the floor, too, after which he picked her up and tucked her under his chin. She threw her leg over his and put her head on his chest. His heart beat strongly beneath her cheek. She'd missed that. "I missed you," she said.

"I missed the hell out of you," he said. "What were you up to while I was gone? The shiners and the scar on your forehead tell me it has to be good."

"Well," she said. "Funny you should ask."

The story took the better part of an hour. By the time she finished they were sitting up again, facing each other, Kate cross-legged in the circle formed by his legs. "And then Nick flew in and took the whole bunch of them off my hands," she said, "and I went down to the clinic and let the boys clean me up. For what I sincerely hope will be the last time."

His eyebrows puckered. "Who was it at the hot springs the first time again?"

"The first time? That was Bruce Abbott."

"Who was with him?"

"Some lowlife from Anchorage Abbott hired on because he could handle a rifle. Abbott says he was scared of bears."

"Scared of Kate Shugak, more like."

Kate grinned. "He is now."

"So, Abbot was looking for . . ."

"The icon."

"That Erland hired him to find."

"Abbott won't admit to it, but he can't explain how he knew about it otherwise."

"Which icon you still haven't found."

Kate's enjoyment in the telling of the tale dimmed a little. "No."

"Okay," Jim said, "Ben was looking for the Hammett manuscript. Erland, using Bruce, the tool, was looking for the icon. What were Pete and Sabine looking for?"

"That's almost the best part of the whole story," Kate said. "Come to find out, Pete's maternal grandfather was a stampeder, of the Pilz stampeders, no less, and Pete inherited the fever. He's got gold pans and pickaxes all over the walls of his office, along with a poster of all the largest gold nuggets in the world. Most of which come from Australia, by the way. The biggest one in Alaska is the Centennial Nugget, two hundred and ninety-four point one ounces." She looked at him expectantly.

He waved his hand in a come ahead motion.

"And he's got a shelf full of books about gold discoveries, stampeder accounts about Dawson and Circle and Livengood and Nome. He's a serious gold bug. I have no excuse for not noticing. I just took it all as Alaskana. Because the icon was the most valuable thing in Old Sam's past, I figured that's what everybody was looking for."

"So?" Jim said with what he felt was commendable patience.

"So, when most of the residents of Niniltna and Kanuyaq were laid out in the great flu pandemic of 1918–1919, Mac McCullough was free to waltz in and out of every building in both places, taking everything that wasn't bolted down. Hell, he had time enough to unbolt anything he wanted. Including the Cross of Gold Nugget."

"The what?"

"The Cross of Gold Nugget, found in 1917 by a miner who wouldn't say where. He sold it to the mine superintendent at Kanuyaq and left town, never to be seen again."

"Was this a large nugget?" Jim said.

"Smaller than a cantaloupe," Kate said, and

grinned. "But bigger than a grapefruit. Two hundred ninety-seven point seventy-four troy ounces."

"In English?"

"Twenty pounds six ounces," she said.

"That'd be pretty big," he said.

"The biggest one ever found in Alaska," she said. "Bigger even than the Centennial."

"You think Old Sam's dad took it? Same time as he took the icon?"

"He did take it."

He nodded, and then said, "Wait a minute. 'Bigger than a grapefruit, smaller than a cantaloupe'? You've seen a picture?"

She shook her head once, side to side.

"You've seen the nugget?"

She nodded once, up and down.

"That's what the map was to," he said, "the nugget. Not the icon, and not the manuscript."

"Yep."

"Where is it? The nugget?" He looked around the room. "I'd like to see a lump of gold bigger than a grapefruit."

"I left it there in the cave."

"You what!"

"Well," she said. "It was heavy, and I wanted to catch Bruce before he got away. And it's painted to blend in with the rocks. And everyone who knows anything about it besides me is in jail."

When he got his breath back, he said, "So we'll be headed back up to Canyon Hot Springs sooner rather than later. Jesus Christ, Kate, gold's over eleven hundred an ounce."

She looked at him, disappointed. "I didn't think you were a gold bug, too, Jim."

"Gold bug, hell, I'm a practicing policeman. Word gets out and people'll be killing each other to get their hands on it."

"Oh." She reflected. "I guess you're right."

"I know I'm right. We can give it to that museum in Anchorage you were talking about."

Kate thought of Ms. Sherwood's reaction, and smiled. "Okay."

"How did Old Sam wind up with the nugget?"

"I don't know that he did," Kate said.

Jim digested this. "You think Mac left it up there?"

"It's the only reason I can think of why Elizaveta insisted that Old Sam homestead up there. Mac wrote to her, remember. Old Sam might not have known about the nugget. I still can't believe I found it. I wouldn't have if I hadn't been looking so hard for the icon."

He shook his head. "I'm getting dizzy. So Auntie Joy has the manuscript."

"Yes."

"What are you going to do with it?"

"Nothing. It isn't mine, Jim. Old Sam gave it to Auntie Joy."

"Well." He almost squirmed. "Do you think she'd let me read it?"

She laughed at him. After a moment, he joined in.

"So, where the hell is the icon?" he said.

Kate's laughter died. "I don't know."

"Do you think Old Sam killed Emil Bannister to get it?"

Kate got up and went to the table. She brought back a sheet of paper.

"What's this?" He looked at it.

"It's the list of the items stolen from Emil Bannister's house the night he died. Victoria Muravieff sent it to me."

"So I see a Russian icon on it, along with some ivory carvings and, oh, look at that, another gold nugget, although this one's a lot smaller than yours."

"Erland probably padded the list to up the insurance payout," Kate said.

"You really think Old Sam stole the icon, Kate?" It just didn't square with Jim's memory of the old man.

It didn't square with Kate's, either. "I haven't found it," Kate said. "Until I do . . ." Her voice trailed off.

"If he did," Jim said, "it would explain why he couldn't give it back to the tribe. It would have been known to have been stolen, and given who Emil Bannister was, it would have been familiar to a lot of people. Someone would have recognized it." He thought it over. "Which is why he left it for you to do when you found it."

"But I haven't found it," she said again.

"Ah hell, honey," he said, tucking her under his arm again. "Don't sound so mournful. You haven't found it yet."

She sighed. "I've been running back and forth between Niniltna and Ahtna and Canyon Hot Springs and Anchorage and Niniltna and Canyon Hot Springs for damn near three weeks. He left clues for me, Jim. He told Jane about the map. He told Tony about meeting Hammett in the Aleutians. He told Ruthe Mac's name. I've pieced together most of the puzzle. I was sure the map was going to lead me to the icon."

"Why did he do it?" Jim said, rubbing the small of her back absently. "Why send you on a treasure hunt? Why not just tell you the whole story and hand everything over?"

Kate remembered that bright day in the clearing last spring, right before the bear charged them. *You're crankier than usual, girl. What's going on?*

It was one of the last real conversations they'd had, standing in a Park clearing taking a beat between collecting some human remains and creating some ursine ones. She had, in fact, been cranky, and Old Sam, as usual, had zeroed in on the cause. The Suulutaq Mine was changing the Park, changing it fast and not all for the better. She'd been feeling crowded, a fine thing in a place where there wasn't but one person for every sixteen hundred acres, and that included the towns.

She thought of the crazy adventure he'd sent her

on. He must have known, given what was at stake, that it could be dangerous, that it might even be deadly. And that it might be both those things but it sure as hell wouldn't be boring. He was right, it hadn't been. She'd been sandbagged, run off the road, ambushed, and shot at.

If the old fart sent you on a wild goose chase, he must have thought you needed one, Bobby had said.

"Up until I went to see Erland Bannister at Spring Creek," she said slowly, "it was like a scavenger hunt. Up until then . . ."

"Up until then," he said, "you'd been having fun."

"I guess," she said. "If you ignore the sequential shiners."

"Fortunes of war," he said. "You're still alive and kicking."

She raised her head again. "Aren't you supposed to come over all manly man and forbid the little lady from taking such risks with her fragile self?"

"I like my balls right where they are," he said, and she laughed and put her head back down on his chest.

It had been fun, if alarming, to see the expression on Ranger Dan's face when he realized who had title to Canyon Hot Springs, and to watch the gears ticking over as he thought how to rectify the situation.

It had been fun, and instructive, to talk to Jane

Silver, probably one of the last Alaska good-time girls around, a grand old dame. There weren't many of those left.

It had not been fun, admittedly, to witness Jane's last breath and to realize that she might have had something to do with hastening it.

It had been fun, delicious fun, to talk to the lawyer. She'd felt like Thorby Rudbek when he was returned to Earth. It had been fun to toy with the idea of suing the Parks Service, although it wasn't fun to contemplate Dan O'Brian's reaction, or the possible destruction of their friendship.

It hadn't been fun to be run off the road, but it had been fun to test her survival skills against the encroaching storm. She had survived, in spades and in style. Hell, she was near as dammit invulnerable at this point. Look at how she'd survived both attacks at Canyon Hot Springs, and hadn't she made it all the way home safely? More or less? Jim was right, fortunes of war. You pays your money and you takes your chances. You don't play, you can't win.

But that morning in Spring Creek, she had looked again into the eyes of a killer, a man who had covered up one murder for his own benefit, ordered a second, and been fully prepared to commit his own.

She thought about waking up in that hunting shack in the back range of the Chugach Mountains, how alone she had felt, how angry.

How frightened.

She still didn't think Erland Bannister would kill for a Russian icon, however historic, however storied, however culturally important, however connected to an unacknowledged side of his family, not even if the frame were studded with uncut diamonds the value of Cameroon's national debt. He had all the money in the world, enough, apparently, even to buy his way out of a well-earned prison sentence with hardly any time served.

So he was after something else.

What?

It had to be the truth of his parentage. He could buy his way out of everything but that. And it might be the only thing left to him that he was willing to risk everything for.

Kate found it difficult to credit as a motive for murder, but that didn't mean it wasn't true.

Someone knocked at the door. Kate, dressed only in Jim's shirt, scurried upstairs while Jim, dressed only in sweatpants, went to the door. He yanked it open and said, "What?"

Bernie was standing there with a big square wooden box in his hands. "Uh, Kate left this on the bar last night. Thought she'd want it."

"Thanks." Jim shut the door in Bernie's face. He was a guy. He'd understand. "It was just Bernie," he said, raising his voice. "He dropped off something for you."

"What?"

"A box. He said you left it on the bar." He heard a snowgo start and drive off. Good old Bernie.

It took her a moment. "It's the compass off the *Freya*. Old Sam left it to me."

"Oh yeah?" He sat down on the couch and unlatched the lid. "Wow. Nice." He touched a finger to the brass. It felt like gold to the touch, and it shone like it, too. "He took pretty good care of it."

She came pattering down the stairs, dressed to his sorrow in jeans and a sweatshirt, although, more promisingly, her feet were still bare. "He told me once he got it from some old antiques dealer he knew in Seattle."

"It looks pretty old, all right."

"He said it dated back to the American Civil War." She collected their mugs and plates and took them into the kitchen, returning with more coffee to see him fiddling with the bottom of the box. "What are you doing?"

"Doesn't the workmanship remind you of my dad's writing box?" He slipped his fingers down between the compass and the box. "I showed you, remember? There's a secret drawer," he said, "it looks just like—"

A drawer popped out of the bottom of the compass box.

Kate's mouth dropped open.

"There's something inside," Jim said, and drew

forth a package wrapped in a length of dusty black velvet tied with ordinary string.

Kate accepted it with hands that trembled. The string slipped free easily. She folded back the velvet.

Three wooden framed portraits of pressed metal, the same woman in all three portraits, the three frames hinged together.

The frames were studded with cabochon stones in inexpertly made bezels. Some of them were missing. Tarnish hid most of the gilt.

Kate slid from the couch and leaned forward to place the triptych gently on the floor, the sides bent in slightly so it would stand upright.

"The Lady of Kodiak," Jim said, awed in spite of himself.

"The Sainted Mary," Kate said. "Oh, Jim."

"What?"

"Don't you see?" Her voice broke and he looked up to see tears sliding down her cheeks. "He must have stolen it. Old Sam must have stolen her from Erland's house. He must have been the one who broke in the night Emil died."

Jaded law enforcement professional that he was, Jim still wanted to reject it. "Kate, no, I—"

She shook her head, her eyes closing. "He must have. He must have been the one who robbed the Bannister house."

She took a long, shaky breath.

"And if he stole the Sainted Mary, he must have killed Emil, too."

1959

Anchorage

Erland listened to the footsteps pound down the stairs and fade into the street without moving, watching his father's face.

He heard his mother cry out upstairs. "Emil! Emil? What was that noise?"

He heard the door of his sister's room open.

He invested as much power and authority in his voice as he could. "The two of you stay up there and lock your doors! There's an intruder in the house!"

Emil's breathing was labored and harsh in the stillness of the study. The blood flooded down the side of his head, soaking his white shirt collar, turning the shoulder of his suit jacket a darker blue.

Erland picked up a straight chair and threw it across the room. It hit one of the display cases, shattering glass and wood. "Stop that! Get out of our house!"

His father's eyes fluttered open and fixed on Erland's face. His lips parted.

Erland hooked an arm around a tabletop full

of ivory carvings and sent them crashing to the floor. "Mom! Call the police!"

His father was trying to say something, his chest heaving.

Erland smiled down at him, and walked around his father's heavy wooden desk. "Mom!" he shouted. "Call the cops!"

He put his hands beneath the edge of the desk, planted his feet, and with a mighty heave turned over the heavy mahogany desk.

The front edge landed diagonally across his father's chest. The sharp snapping of ribs was clearly audible. Erland watched, as the life faded from his father's eyes.

He reached for something, anything, and flung it across the room. Whatever it was made a very satisfying crash. "Mom! He's getting away! Call the cops!"

He went to one of the intact display cases, and with deliberate force smashed his head through the top of the glass.

He staggered back, sick and dizzy, something warm flooding into his eyes. "Mom! Vicky!"

He ran across the room to the door and down the hallway with exaggeratedly heavy steps. "He's getting away!" he shouted through the door his half brother had left open behind him. Lights were coming on up and down the street.

There was a distant sound of sirens. He

sagged against the door frame, and smiled drunkenly into the dark night.

He'd recognized Sam, even with his hood up, even from the back. It had been like watching himself run away.

In the few moments he had before the cops got there, he gave thought to whether he should say so. He decided he would not. Even with his own eyewitness testimony, even with his family's standing in the state, there was always the possibility that Sam could prove his innocence, and then the cops would have to look for another suspect. No, far better that Sam Dementieff disappear into the night, that his father's murder be the result of a simple burglary gone terribly wrong.

He went back into the study and sank to his knees next to his father's body, taking his father's hand between both of his own. He heard the footsteps behind him. "Erland? Emil! Oh my God!"

"Oh, Mom, Mom . . . I think he's dead." His shoulders heaved with sobs.

His sister, Victoria, stopped dead in the doorway, her hands clapping over her mouth to hold back a scream at the sight of her father's body beneath the desk. Her mother pushed past her and ran to her son, crouching next to him. "Are you hurt? Erland, tell me! Are you hurt?"

Before she pulled his head to her breast, he caught a glimpse of the expression on his sister's face, the tinge of suspicion in her eyes that underlay the undeniable horror there, and he had to work to repress a satisfied smile.

Erland Bannister was a born killer long before he met Kate Shugak.

Acknowledgments

I read some of these books for the first time during my childhood odyssey through the shelves of Susan Bloch English's Seldovia Public Library. This novel owes a lot to them but even more to her.

Hector Chevigny's *Lord of Alaska*
Pierre Berton's
Klondike: The Last Great Gold Rush
Judge James Wickersham's
Old Yukon: Tales, Trails, and Trials
Murray Morgan's
Confederate Raider in the North Pacific
Brian Garfield's *The Thousand-Mile War*
Ernest Gruening's *Many Battles*
Joe Rychetnik's *Bush Cop*
Victor Fischer's
Alaska's Constitutional Convention
Jean Potter's *The Flying North*
Naske and Slotnick's
Alaska: A History of the 49th State
Keith and Proenneke's *One Man's Wilderness*
Jim Rearden's *Castner's Cutthroats*
and pretty much anything ever published by the Alaska Geographic Society.

Other constant resources are the *Anchorage Daily News* online edition, rural Alaskan newspapers like the *Homer News* and the *Dutch Harbor Fisherman* (especially the police blotters) and more recently, AlaskaDispatch.com.

The story of Saint Juvenaly comes from several sources, including the Outreach Alaska page of the Russian Orthodox Diocese of Alaska Web site.

And once again, Don Ryan, aka Der Plotmeister, comes through. Thanks.

Center Point Publishing
600 Brooks Road ● PO Box 1
Thorndike ME 04986-0001 USA

(207) 568-3717

US & Canada:
1 800 929-9108
www.centerpointlargeprint.com

M
√/